Alternative Alices

Alternative Alices

Visions and Revisions
of
Lewis Carroll's *Alice* Books

An Anthology
Edited by Carolyn Sigler

THE UNIVERSITY PRESS OF KENTUCKY

Publication of this volume was made possible in part by a grant
from the National Endowment for the Humanities.

Editorial and Sales Offices: The University Press of Kentucky
663 South Limestone Street, Lexington, Kentucky 40508-4008

01 00 99 98 97   5 4 3 2 1

Library of Congress Cataloging-in-Publication Data

Alternative Alices : visions and revisions of Lewis Carroll's Alice
books : an anthology / edited by Carolyn Sigler.
      p.   cm.
Anthology of literary imitations, revisions, and parodies of Lewis
Carroll's Alice's adventures in Wonderland and Through the looking
-glass published between 1869 and 1930.
      Includes bibliographical references (p.   ).
      ISBN 0-8131-2028-4 (cloth : alk. paper). — ISBN 0-8131-0932-9
(paper : alk. paper)
      1. Carroll, Lewis, 1832-1898—Parodies, imitations, etc.
2. Carroll, Lewis, 1832-1898—Influence.   3. Fantastic literature,
English.   4. Satire, English.   I. Sigler, Carolyn, 1958-   .
II. Carroll, Lewis, 1832-1898. Alice's adventures in Wonderland.
III. Carroll, Lewis, 1832-1898. Through the looking-glass.
PR4612.A48   1997
823'.8—DC21   97-2205

This book is printed on acid-free recycled paper meeting
the requirements of the American National Standard
for Permanence of Paper for Printed Library Materials.

Manufactured in the United States of America

For Craig, who makes everything possible

Contents

Acknowledgments

I would like to express my gratitude to the interlibrary loan staff at Kansas State University's Farrell Library for four years of tireless assistance, and to the special collections staff at Florida State University for making the wonderful John Mackie Shaw collection available to me. I also deeply appreciate the support and assistance of the Kansas State University English Department and its former head, Dean Hall, and particularly want to thank my colleagues, friends, and best critics, Angela Hubler and Chris Cokinos.

Attempts to locate the author or illustrator of *Alice in the Delighted States* by Edward Hope (copyright © 1928 and 1955 by Edward Hope, illustrations by Rea Irvin, copyright © 1928 by Rea Irvin) or their heirs have been unsuccessful. The remaining selections in this anthology are in the public domain.

*I*ntroduction

It may be thought that in introducing a certain little lady **ALICE**nce
has been taken. But royal personages are public property.

—Jean Jambon, *Our Trip to Blundertown* (1876)

*A*lternative Alices brings together some of the most lively and original of
the almost two hundred literary imitations, revisions, and parodies of
Lewis Carroll's enduringly influential *Alice's Adventures in Wonderland* and
Through the Looking-Glass. Produced between 1869 and 1930, the works represented here do not passively imitate Carroll, but trace the extraordinarily
coherent, creative, and often critical responses to the *Alice* novels.

The *Alice* imitations of this period embody the golden age of Carroll's
influence on popular literature. They are associated in the ways they all adapt
the structures, motifs, and themes of the original *Alice* books and respond to
the issues they raise. These works are distinct from later, post-1930 imitations,
which tend simply to make references to the *Alice* mythos while commenting upon issues and concerns far from Alice's world.

The literary responses of this golden age range from Christina Rossetti's
angry subversion of Alice's adventures, *Speaking Likenesses* (1874), to G.E.
Farrow's witty fantasy adventure *The Wallypug of Why* (1895), to Edward
Hope's hilarious parody of social and political foibles in *Alice in the Delighted
States* (1928). Alternately enchanting, experimental, satiric, and subversive,
these *Alice*-inspired works reveal how variously Lewis Carroll's celebrated *Alice*
fantasies were read, reinscribed, and resisted in the late nineteenth and early
twentieth centuries.

Alice's Adventures in Wonderland and *Through the Looking-Glass* are the
most universally recognized and acclaimed Victorian works for children, having lost neither their appeal nor their mystique in the more than one hundred and twenty-five years since their publication. A few months after Carroll's
death, in an article entitled "What the Children Like," *The Pall Mall Gazette*
reported on a poll which asked children to list their favorite books. *Alice's
Adventures in Wonderland* was ranked a resounding first, with *Through the
Looking-Glass* following in eleventh place.[1] For children and adults alike, Lewis

Carroll's *Alice* books remain today both popular favorites and literary classics, sold by purveyors of fine editions, university presses, and shopping-mall bookstores, and available in a wide variety of editions ranging from picture books to annotated paperbacks to luxuriously illustrated hardbacks.[2] In high schools and universities the *Alice* books are regularly taught in English literature classes and appear on virtually every Victorian "great books" bibliography. They are the most widely quoted books after the Bible and Shakespeare's plays, and have been translated hundreds of times into languages which include Japanese, Croatian, Turkish, Danish, Maori, Bengali, Chinese, Gaelic, Russian, and Swahili.[3]

Though often cited as vanguards in the use of fantasy in children's literature, Carroll's *Alice* books actually reflect widespread shifts in nineteenth-century literary tastes. These changes were the subject of much discussion and debate in the years surrounding the publication of *Alice's Adventures in Wonderland,* as in an 1866 review-essay entitled "Children's Christmas Literature": "Fifty years ago . . . the literature of the young had a violent, bitter, and puritanical tone, calculated rather to harden and contract than to expand and vivify the minds of its readers. . . . All this has been amended for several years; but we may add that the improvement is progressive."[4] Like this review, which characterizes *Alice's Adventures in Wonderland* as "a charming tale," most Victorian reviewers praised the originality, humor, and lack of overt moralizing in the *Alice* novels. A critic for *The Spectator* (7 August 1869) declared *Alice's Adventures in Wonderland* "beyond question, supreme among modern books for children."[5] *The Publisher's Circular* (8 December 1865) deemed *Alice's Adventures* "the most original and most charming [of] the two hundred books for children which have been sent to us this year." The critical response was not, however, universally positive. One anonymous reviewer declared, "We fancy that any real child might be more puzzled than enchanted by this stiff, overwrought story,"[6] and *The Times* reviewer (13 August 1868) noted that while "we enjoy the walk with Alice through Wonderland . . . now and then, perhaps, something disturbing almost wakes us from our dream."

The popular and critical appeal of Carroll's *Alice* fantasies did, however, solidify a shift away from didacticism in children's literature and help to make fantasy a popular paradigm in children's and, a generation later, adult literature. Several children of the late nineteenth-century who were brought up reading the *Alice* books, including Virginia Woolf, T.S. Eliot, and James Joyce, went on to transform literature through their modernist rendering of psychological experience. As Juliet Dusinberre has shown, "Carroll's books ran in the bloodstream of that generation. . . . Radical experiments in the arts in the early modern period began in the books which Lewis Carroll and his successors wrote for children."[7] Anthony Burgess, who himself wrote an *Alice*-like fantasy called *A Long Trip to Teatime* (1976), has pointed out that James Joyce's linguistic experimentation in *Finnegans Wake* was influenced by Carroll's books, which Joyce had loved as a child: "What, with Carroll, began as a joke, ends, in Joyce, as the most serious attempt ever made to show how the dreaming mind operates."[8] After the 1920s, reviewers who had been fascinated by the *Alice* books as children—and who were of the same iconoclastic generation as Woolf and Joyce—began to study and critique them as more complex works, elevating their cultural status to that of innovative adult literature.

Despite the appropriation of the *Alice* books by academic literary culture, however, the *Alice* myth still informs popular culture in general. Both the *Wonderland* and *Looking-Glass* stories have been adapted for stage, ballet, opera, film, and television, and have served as the bases for many advertising campaigns, including the now-famous Guinness advertisements of the 1920s and '30s.[9] Numerous clubs and societies are devoted to *Alice* study and fandom, both in America and abroad. What Morton Cohen has labeled "the *Alice* industry" also continues to generate countless *Alice*-inspired commercial enterprises: collectibles from tee shirts to teapots, chess sets, postcards, thimbles, dolls, diaries, jewelry, clocks, figurines, music and music videos, comic books, puppet shows, cartoons, stage productions, and film adaptations ranging from musical comedies to soft-core pornography. This lucrative and popular "industry" responds to readers' desires, motivated originally by the marketing efforts of the author, to possess not only the books, but the mythos surrounding the books' heroine.[10]

Culturally diverse readers and collectors continue to be attracted to this rather conventional, albeit adventurous, staunchly middle-class Victorian seven-year-old. As Donald Rackin points out, "In spite of her class- and time-bound prejudices, her frightened fretting and childish, abject tears, her priggishness and self-assured ignorance, her sometimes blatant hypocrisy, her general powerlessness and confusion, and her rather cowardly readiness to abandon her struggles at the end of the two adventures—in spite of all these shortcomings, many readers look up to Alice as the mythic embodiment of self-control, perseverance, bravery, and mature good sense."[11] Yet the key to the enduring power of these two Victorian children's fantasy novels and their pinafored young heroine has both eluded and absorbed critics ever since the books' publications. "What is the key to their enchantment, why are they so entertaining and yet so enigmatic?" asks Morton Cohen in his recent biography of Carroll. "What charm enables them to transcend language as well as national and temporal differences and win their way into the hearts of young and old everywhere and always?"[12]

A possible answer may be found in the very number and variety of responses enabled by the form and content of the novels. Their loose, episodic dream structure and playful use of symbolic nonsense enable varied and even contradictory readings. The *Alice* books' enduring power and appeal may very well lie in the fact that, like dreams, they *can* mean whatever readers *need* them to mean. Indeed, Alice is herself a multifaceted and contradictory character whose identity even the Wonderland and Looking-Glass creatures attempt, and fail, to grasp. The White Rabbit in *Alice in Wonderland* believes her to be his housemaid, Mary Ann.[13] The Pigeon, in turn, declares that Alice is "a serpent . . . and there's no use denying it" (*Wonderland* 43). "'Mind the volcano!'" cries the tiny White Queen to the King, after Alice picks her up and sets her on a table in the Looking-Glass parlor (*Looking-Glass* 114). The flowers in the Looking-Glass garden believe Alice to be another blossom, albeit with rather untidy petals (*Looking-Glass* 123). The Unicorn perceives her as a "fabulous monster" (solemnly assuring her, "if you'll believe in me, I'll believe in you") (*Looking-Glass* 175). Even Alice questions her own identity, wondering after her plunge down the rabbit hole if she's become someone else: "It'll be no use their putting their heads down and saying 'Come up again, dear!' I shall only look up and say 'Who am I, then? Tell me that first, and then, if I like being that person, I'll come up: if not, I'll stay down here till I'm somebody else'" (*Wonderland* 16). Certainly, when the Caterpillar asks *Alice in Wonderland*'s central question, "Who are *you*?" Alice has difficulty answering: "I—I hardly know, Sir, just at present—at least I know who I *was* when I got up this morning, but I think I must have been changed several times since then" (35). Like the Caterpillar, she is mutable, in a constant process of becoming.

Along with many other interpretations, the *Alice* books have consistently been read as portrayals of the experience of growing up and the construction of agency and identity. A number of critics have pointed out how strongly readers identify with Alice, our surrogate and guide through this unpredictable, sometimes funny, often frightening and violent, process. Virginia Woolf observes that "the two *Alices* are not books for children; they are the only books in which we become children. . . . To become a child is very literal; to find everything so strange that nothing is surprising; to be heartless, to be ruthless, yet to be so passionate that a snub or a shadow drapes the world in gloom. It is so to be Alice in Wonderland."[14] Morton Cohen suggests that much of the books' power can be found in Alice's—and by extension the reader's—triumph over childlike confusion and fear. Together, he argues, they experience "a catharsis, an affirmation of life after Wonderland, and on this side of the Looking-Glass": "Once readers have associated with Alice and wandered with her through Wonderland, they are together on a survival course. They are thrown back upon their inner resources, determining whether their resources are strong enough to get them through."[15]

Yet, while the novels examine the triumphs and failures of growing up, they also address the deeply conflicted, complicated and, unfortunately, often violent feelings about children and childhood which Victorian and contemporary cultures share. James Kincaid has pointed out that Alice can be seen both as representative of "the joys and dangers of human innocence" as well as "the callous egotism and ruthless insensitivity that often pass for innocence," concluding that, through his heroine, Carroll "questions the value of human innocence altogether and sees the sophisticated and sad corruption of adults as preferable to the cruel selfishness of children."[16] Indeed, this coexistent ambivalence toward both childhood and maturity may provide contemporary adult readers of the *Alice* books with even more reasons to identify with the novels' heroine and her journeys. In a recent book about changes in the structure of life stages, Gail Sheehy argues that traditional expectations about age standards have been revolutionized by modern technological and medical advances, as well as recent social and economic changes:

> People today are leaving childhood sooner, but they are taking longer to grow up and much longer to grow old. Adolescence is now prolonged for the middle class until the end of the 20s, and for bluecollar men and women until the mid-20s, as more young adults live at home longer. True adulthood doesn't begin until 30. Most baby boomers . . . do not feel fully grown up until they are into their 40s, and even then they resist. . . . Middle age has already been pushed far into the 50s—if it is acknowledged at all today.[17]

Living in a world of changing technology, expectations, and beliefs about the future, modern readers have much in common with the original readers of the *Alice* books. Victorians of the 1860s and '70s also lived in an age of increasing mechanization and industrialization, of economic, social, and philosophic upheavals, of cultural redefinitions of "child" and "adult" identities, and of escalating apprehension and doubt about the future. The *Alice* books have continued to speak to the anxieties of succeeding generations and their ongoing desire to impose order and stability on a turbulent world. Readers have, as well, continued to identify with Alice herself, perhaps if only because—as Humpty Dumpty observes—she is "'so exactly like other people'" (*Looking-Glass* 168).

The range of interpretive possibilities presented by the *Alice* books has thus made them accessible to a wide variety of social, psychological, critical, theoretical, and aesthetic interests. The desire to "grasp" Alice (in both senses of understanding and possessing) has also been expressed through literary interpretations of her adventures. In the decades immediately following the publication of Carroll's work, hundreds of literary parodies, sequels, spin-offs and imitations began to appear. Significantly, these *Alice*-inspired works reveal the kinds of cultural work the *Alice* books performed at specific times among different kinds of readers, as authors either paid tribute to, reacted against, or attempted to revise their perceptions of the *Alice* books and their effects on child readers.[18]

The majority of these *Alice*-inspired works were produced in the fifty or so years following the books' publications and sharply decline after the 1920s when literary tastes and culture changed dramatically. The 1920s is also the period when Carroll's work was discovered and appropriated by high literary artists, critics, and theorists such as William Empson, Virginia Woolf, and Edmund Wilson. The decline of *Alice*-inspired literary efforts thus testifies to the very influence of Carroll and his successors on literary modernism. It was Wilson who in 1932 declared, "C.L. Dodgson was a most interesting man and deserves better of his admirers, who revel in his delightfulness and cuteness but do not give him any serious attention. . . . In literature, Lewis Carroll went deeper than his contemporaries realized and than he usually gets credit for even today."[19]

Since the early 1930s, critics have interpreted *Alice's Adventures in Wonderland* and *Through the Looking-Glass* as Freudian allegories of a desire to retreat back to the womb, as reflections of the nineteenthcentury ideology of imperialism, as archetypal journey myths, as metaphors for hallucinogenic drug experiences, as nostalgic visions of the comforting "secret garden" of childhood, as existential explorations of life as meaningless chaos, or conversely as meta-texts about the very "meaning of meaning": "'Is meaning necessarily contingent and relative?' 'How do we mean what we mean?' 'What does it mean to exist? to be human?' or 'What does it all mean?'"[20] Such interpretations may seem to suggest that the *Alice* books are, indeed, too complex for children.

Certainly, the *Alice* books' appropriation as high literary culture in the early 1930s marked a significant decline in their appropriation and interpretation by popular authors, particularly children's authors. Unlike the large and coherent body of works that comment upon the characters, themes, and structures of the originals, the few *Alice*-inspired works of the last sixty years usually refer minimally or obliquely to the *Alice* books and tend to be directed at a sophisticated adult audience. Recent works such as Maeve Kelly's *Alice in Thunderland* (1993), Rikki Ducornet's *The Jade Cabinet* (1993), Susan

Sontag's *Alice in Bed* (1993), and Alison Habens's *Dreamhouse* (1995) show the influence of feminist and poststructuralist theory, but not of specific, popular criticism of *Alice,* as do the earlier *Alice*-inspired works. These recent works use the *Alice* books as starting points from which to comment on questions unrelated to the books themselves and the issues they raise. This shift from imitating the *Alice* books to merely referring to details of the *Alice* mythos, of course, not only reflects changes in literary culture but larger social and cultural changes as well, such as the growth of the women's movement.

The works collected here date from the late 1860s to the 1920s, comment specifically upon the original novels and upon popular critical responses to them, and form a coherent body of *Alice* "imitations."[21] They thus share specific characteristics with Carroll's *Alice* books and with one another: an Alice-like protagonist or protagonists, male and/or female, who is typically polite, articulate, and assertive; a clear transition from the "real" waking world to a fantasy dream world through which the protagonist journeys; rapid shifts in identity, appearance, and location; an episodic structure often centering on encounters with nonhuman fantasy characters and/or characters based on nursery rhymes or other popular children's texts, including Alice herself; nonsense language and interpolated nonsense verse, verse-parodies, or songs; an awakening or return to the "real" world, which is generally portrayed as domestic (a literal return home); and, usually, a clear acknowledgment of indebtedness to Carroll through a dedication, apology, mock-denial of influence, or other textual or extratextual reference.

Attempts to imitate or revise his work alternately angered and flattered Carroll, whose diary entry for 11 September 1891 notes the acquisition of several *Alice*-inspired works for "the collection I intend making of the books of the *Alice* type."[22] Carroll's frustration may have stemmed from his own vain attempts to imitate his success, first with the more mechanical *Alice's Adventures in Wonderland* sequel, *Through the Looking-Glass,* and later with marketing schemes for authorized *Alice* merchandise such as a *Nursery Alice,* scaled down for very young readers, a Wonderland Postage-Stamp Case, and a biscuit tin decorated with characters from *Through the Looking-Glass.* He also produced several increasingly stiff and moralistic fantasies such as *The Hunting of the Snark* (1876) and *Sylvie and Bruno* (1889). In his somber preface to *Sylvie and Bruno,* and in the wake of Edward Salmon's unfounded suggestion that Carroll may have plagiarized Tom Hood's *Alice*-inspired *From Nowhere to the North Pole* (1874),[23] Carroll acknowledges that *Alice's Adventures in Wonderland* and *Through the Looking-Glass* were indeed part of larger historical developments in literary fairy tales:

Perhaps the hardest thing in all literature—at least *I* have found it so: by no voluntary effort can I accomplish it: I have to take it as it comes—is to write anything *original*. And perhaps the easiest is, when once an original line has been struck out, to follow it up, and to write any amount more to the same tune. I do not know if "Alice in Wonderland" was an *original* story—I was, at least, no *conscious* imitator in writing it—but I do know that, since it came out, something like a dozen story-books have appeared, on identically the same pattern.[24]

The range and variety of these books "on the same pattern" do offer fascinating insights into the cultural and literary situations in which the *Alice* books have been understood and appropriated by different audiences—female and male, Victorian and modern, British and American. They also illuminate how diversely the *Alice* narratives, as both literary and ideological commodities, were interpreted, expropriated, and converted in both critical and affirming ways to question those same situations and, in some cases, to question the representation of Alice herself. Victorian women writers, for example—such as Maggie Browne, Anna Matlack Richards, and particularly the evangelical Alice Corkran—clearly reconstructed an image of Alice more appropriate to their beliefs about women's cultural power and authority. Indeed, Nina Auerbach has argued that Victorian women writers use character studies, fictional biographies, and reinterpretations of classic texts to liberate female characters from "the single set of circumstances in which author and audience imagine [them]."[25] Though debate has been heated over whether Alice is or is not a feminist heroine, nineteenth- and early-twentieth-century women writers were able to appropriate and reinvent Alice to free her from the restrictions of Carroll's highly conservative narratives and, in so doing, to "reveal the conditions in which a particular ideology of femininity functions."[26] The invocation of the popular and widely disseminated images of both Alice and Lewis Carroll also provided one means for unknown female writers to authorize themselves in the growing literary marketplace of the late nineteenth century. In particular, these *Alice* revisions illustrate the transition—especially important in the emergence of women writers—from private to public discourse: the transformation of private occasional writing for a particular child to a public text for popular consumption.

Because these *Alice*-inspired works are as much a response to the myriad critical readings of the *Alice* novels as they are to the novels themselves, this collection has been organized according to the kinds of literary responses most common to interpretations and reviews of the *Alice* books and, indeed, to larger debates about the cultural role of children's literature. The subversive

Alice-revisions in part one respond critically to the original texts' conservative images of Victorian girlhood and domestic ideology and present Alice-like heroines who demonstrate power and authority over their fantasy adventures. Anna Matlack Richards's heroine Alice Lee tackles her adventures "not at all concerned as the other Alice had been . . . that she was too big."[27] Maggie Browne's dauntless heroine, Merle, defeats Endom's evil Grunter Grim by learning to "Defy, Deride, Desist, Deny, / Heed not a growl, or scowl, or sigh"—words of advice she often repeats and finds "very comforting."[28]

While authors such as Richards and Browne see Wonderland as too restrictive, the school of responses represented in part two questions whether it is restrictive enough. Their didactic revisions attempt to counter praise that focused on the novels' lack of moralizing: "Notwithstanding any remarks of the Duchess, *Alice* has no moral," declares a reviewer for *The Spectator*, agreeing with many earlier critics. The same reviewer also speculates about whether the books might be used didactically: "Will lessons become amusing by association with *Alice,* or will even *Alice* become hateful by being regarded as a lesson-book? The experiment is a hazardous one, and will demand no small skill and tact on the part of the operator."[29] *The Illustrated London News* (16 December 1865), however, praised *Alice in Wonderland* as suited for "the amusement and even instruction of children." Indeed, much of Carroll's post-*Alice* writings for children are quite didactic. As later critics have pointed out, "lessons and rules abound in Wonderland," and serve to educate Alice in the rituals and beliefs of middle-class ideology.[30] Alice Corkran transforms Wonderland into "Naughty Children Land," which echoes with the dismal howls of the "Sulkies." More ominous still, Corkran's heroine, Kitty, "fancied she heard the sound of smacking" above the sounds of screaming and shouting.[31] Corkran reasserts the very didacticism that Carroll satirizes in the Duchess's song:

> "Speak roughly to your little boy,
>   And beat him when he sneezes:
> He only does it to annoy,
>   Because he knows it teases." [*Wonderland* 48]

For evangelical women writers like Corkran, however, didacticism was an important means of asserting women's important social role as educators and, indeed, of extending the boundaries of the Victorian domestic sphere to include the literary marketplace.

In a 1927 essay entitled "Extensions of Reality," Anne Eaton suggests that the appeal of sentimental "escape" fantasies, like the *Alice* adaptations included in part three, lies in their exploration of what she calls "a third region, not to be definitely located in the real world or in fairyland." These fantasies "*join on* to real life and yet offer magical and mysterious spaces lying close at hand but hidden from view. There is more of a thrill in dwelling on the possibility of something unreal underneath the real, than in reading the conventional fairy tale."[32] Eaton cites the *Alice* books as such "betwixt and between" fantasies, also citing as "[a]mong her descendants who inherit something of the same joyous ability to play with words and ideas" Charles Carryl's *Davy and the Goblin*, E. F. Benson's *David Blaize and the Blue Door*, and Frances Hodgson Burnett's "Behind the White Brick."[33] Sentimental fantasies such as these read and reenvisioned the *Alice* novels as "pure sugar throughout,"[34] as reflections of "a child's simple and unreasoning imagination illustrated in a dream."[35] G.E. Farrow's *Wallypug* books respond to and expand both the playful and fantastic aspects of the *Alice* books, concocting elaborate and absurd fantasy creatures, puns, verse parodies, and adventures for the novels' heroes. In *The Wallypug of Why*, the Crocodile takes a weak cup of tea out for strengthening walks, "propped up with pillows, and carefully wrapped in a little woollen shawl," and Girlie attends a Fancy Dinner Party where guests are served empty plates and told to "fancy" they've been served real food.[36] These sentimental *Alice*-inspired fantasies are concerned more with escape and laughter than with lessons or criticism, and tend to be dedicated to real child acquaintances or readers, as in Charles Carryl's tender dedication to his son, Guy, and G.E. Farrow's long, affectionate prefaces to his child readers and correspondents.

As children's books, the *Alice* novels were accessible to all, including the parodist. Modernist critics, however, took Carroll's work out of the realm of childhood—by reinterpreting them as sophisticated literary classics which would even eclipse "the productions of the Carlyles and the Ruskins, the Spencers and the George Eliots"—thus, removing the *Alice* novels from the sphere of popular interpretation.[37] The pre-modernist political parodies in part four of this collection represent the first appropriations of the *Alice* books for adult audiences and concerns, and, though still closely paralleling the conventions outlined above, anticipate the gradual decline of the *Alice*-imitation phenomenon in the late 1920s, as the *Alice*-books were taken out of the literary public domain by virtue of their reclassification as serious objects of scholarship. These early-twentieth-century political parodies respond to yet another popular reading of the *Alice* novels: as containing veiled political references and satire, largely due to illustrator John Tenniel's popularity as a political cartoonist for *Punch* magazine. Martin Gardiner notes the wide belief among nineteenth-century readers "that Tenniel's lion and unicorn [in

Through the Looking-Glass] . . . were intended as caricatures of Gladstone and Disraeli respectively," adding that if Carroll—who was conservative politically and did not like Gladstone—intended the parody, then Alice's repetition of the line "The Lion beat the Unicorn all around the town" (172) becomes politically charged.[38] Michael Hancher has also pointed out Tweedledum and Tweedledee's strong resemblance to Tenniel's drawings of John Bull (a satirical embodiment of the British common man) in *Punch*.[39]

The literary enterprises represented here attempt not merely to follow, but to engage, to question, even to subvert the ideological assumptions behind Carroll's *Alice* books. They illustrate for us today some of the ways that Carroll's nineteenth- and early-twentieth-century readers responded to and resisted the *Alice* narratives' influential ideologies of gender, class, and childhood. These works are also full of new wonders to discover, dramatizing why children and adults alike continue to demand (echoing the title of A. L. Gibson's 1924 fantasy) *Another Alice book, Please!*

NOTES

1. *Pall Mall Gazette* (1 July 1898): 1-2.

2. In a 1990 article for *The New York Times Book Review* entitled "The Girl Is Everywhere," Vicki Weissman notes ninety-three *Alice*related entries in the then-current *Books in Print* (11 Nov. 1990): 55.

3. Warren Weaver, *Alice in Many Tongues: The Translations of Alice in Wonderland* (Madison: U Wisconsin P, 1964).

4. *The Daily News* (19 Dec. 1866). A large collection of early reviews of the *Alice* books are reprinted in *Jabberwocky: The Journal of the Lewis Carroll Society* 9 (winter 1979-80–autumn 1980).

5. This quote was used by Macmillan in early advertisements for *Alice in Wonderland*.

6. "Children's Books," *The Athenaeum* 1900 (16 Dec. 1865): 844.

7. Dusinberre, *Alice to the Lighthouse: Children's Books and Radical Experiments in Art* (New York: St. Martin's, 1987) 2, 5.

8. Burgess, "All About Alice," *Unesco Courier* (May-June 1986): 44.

9. Guinness produced a number of delightfully illustrated Christmas booklets as part of an extended *Alice*-themed advertising campaign. The booklets featured parodies of familiar verses and scenes from the *Alice* books, all, of course, emphasizing the characters' partiality for Guinness beer:

> The Walrus and the Carpenter
> Were walking down the Strand
> And all the little Oysters came
> And followed hand in hand,

"If we but had some Guinness now,"
They said, "it would be grand!"
"If seven men with seven tongues
Talked on till all was blue,
Could they give *all* the reasons why
Guinness is good for you?"—
"I doubt it," said the Carpenter,
"But that it's good is true."

From *The Guinness Alice* (Dublin: St. James's Gate, 1933). Other Guinness titles include *Jabberwocky Re-Versed and Other Guinness Versions* (1935), and *Alice Afore-thought, Guinness Carrolls for 1938* (1938).

10. The author's own desire for the child Alice may have played a part in engendering this appeal, though Carroll also worked on various commercial enterprises to market his literary creation.

11. Rackin, *"Alice's Adventures in Wonderland" and "Through the Looking-Glass": Nonsense, Sense, and Meaning.* Twayne's Masterwork Studies 81 (New York: Twayne, 1991) 14.

12. Cohen, *Lewis Carroll, A Biography* (New York: Knopf, 1995) 135.

13. Lewis Carroll, *Alice in Wonderland and Through the LookingGlass,* ed. Donald J. Gray, 2d ed. (New York: Norton, 1992) 27. Future references will be cited parenthetically in the text as *Wonderland* or *Looking-Glass*.

14. Woolf, "Lewis Carroll," 1929, *The Moment and Other Essays* (New York: Harcourt Brace, 1948) 82.

15. Cohen, *A Biography* 139.

16. "Alice's Invasion of Wonderland," *PMLA* 33 (Jan. 1973): 92, 93.

17. Sheehy, *New Passages: Mapping Your Life across Time* (New York: Random House, 1995) 4.

18. In *Sensational Designs: The Cultural Work of American Fiction, 1790-1860,* Jane Tompkins defines "cultural work" as "the way that literature has power in the world . . . [the ways that] it connects with the beliefs and attitudes of large masses of readers so as to impress or move them deeply" (Oxford: Oxford UP, 1985) xiv.

19. Wilson, "C.L. Dodgson: The Poet Logician," *Aspects of Alice: Lewis Carroll's Dreamchild as Seen through the Critics' Looking-Glasses,* ed. Robert Phillips (New York: Random House, 1971) 198, 200.

20. Rackin, *Nonsense, Sense, and Meaning* 16.

21. Definitions of what constitutes an "*Alice* imitation" vary. Sanjay Sircar describes a detailed list of elements that constitute what he calls the "*Alice* imitation mode" in "Other Alices and Alternative Wonderlands: An Exercise in Literary History," *Jabberwocky* 13.2 (spring 1984): 26-27. Sircar's article is also followed by a list of *Alice*-inspired works in the next (summer 1984) issue: 59-67. For additional lists of *Alice* imitations and parodies see R.B. Shaberman and Denis Crutch, "With Alice Aforethought: First Draft of an Annotated Handlist of Continuations and Imitations of *Alice,*" *Under the Quizzing Glass: A Lewis Carroll Miscellany* (London: Magpie P, 1972), and Charles C. Lovett and Stephanie B. Lovett, "Parodies, Spin-Offs, Imita-

tions," *Lewis Carroll's Alice: An Annotated Checklist of the Lovett Collection* (Westport: Meckler, 1990). A selected bibliography is also included at the end of this collection.

22. *The Diaries of Lewis Carroll,* ed. Roger Lancelyn Green, 2 vols. (London: Cassell, 1953) 2:486.

23. Salmon, "Literature for Little Ones," *The Nineteenth Century* 22 (Oct. 1887): 563-80.

24. Carroll, *Sylvie and Bruno* (1889; Mineola, N.Y.: Dover, 1988) xxxvi.

25. Auerbach, *Woman and the Demon: The Life of a Victorian Myth* (Cambridge: Harvard UP, 1982) 212.

26. Kathleen McLuskie, "The Patriarchal Bard: Feminist Criticism and Shake–speare," *Political Shakespeare: New Essay s in Cultural Materialism,* eds. Jonathan Dollimore and Alan Sinfield (Ithaca: Cornell UP, 1985) 106.

27. Richards, *A New Alice in the Old Wonderland* (Philadelphia: Lippincott, 1895) 31.

28. Browne, *Wanted—A King, or How Merle Set the Nursery Rhymes to Right* (London: Duckworth, 1890) 261, 262.

29. *The Spectator* (7 Aug. 1869).

30. Jan Susina, "Educating Alice: The Lessons of Wonderland," *Jabberwocky* 18 (winter-spring 1989): 3.

31. Corkran, *Down the Snow Stairs; or, From Good-Night to GoodMorning* (London: Blackie and Son, 1887) 48.

32. Eaton, *The Horn Book* 3.2 (May 1927): 17-18.

33. Eaton 18.

34. *The Sunderland Herald* (25 May 1866).

35. *The Times* (13 Aug. 1868).

36. Farrow, *The Wallypug of Why* (London: Hutchinson & Co., 1895) 43, 87.

37. Wilson, "C.L. Dodgson: The Poet Logician" 202.

38. *The Annotated Alice,* ed. Martin Gardiner (New York: Meridian, 1960) 288 n. 10, 283 n. 7.

39. "*Punch* and *Alice:* Through Tenniel's Looking-Glass," *Lewis Carroll: A Cele–bration,* ed. Edward Guiliano (New York: Clarkson Potter, 1982) 27.

PART ONE
Subverting Wonderland

Mopsa the Fairy

JEAN INGELOW
1869

JEAN INGELOW (1820-1897) was a well-known British novelist, children's writer, and poet, who was so highly regarded by such contemporaries as Tennyson, Ruskin, and Christina Rossetti that she was nominated for the post of poet laureate. A shy woman who never married (and who claimed, "If I had married, I should *not* have written books"), Ingelow was born in Lincolnshire but lived most of her life in London. She successfully supported herself and members of her family as a writer, noting: "I find it one of the great pleasures of writing, that it gives me more command of money for such purposes than falls to the lot of most women."[1] *Mopsa the Fairy*, Ingelow's best known work for children, is one of the earliest fantasy novels to respond to *Alice in Wonderland*. Though the book seems to begin similarly as Jack escapes from his nurse and baby sister and falls into a hollow tree, *Mopsa* is, however, a vivid and haunting fantasy of female power that subverts many of the familiar fairy-tale conventions invoked by Carroll in the *Alice* books. Contravening the idealization of passive femininity, Ingelow's Mopsa grows into her role as ruler of the fairies while Jack's role dwindles from protective hero to ordinary boy. Mopsa and Jack work together fearlessly to restore Mopsa's power and authority as queen of the fairies, but in the poignant final chapter, "Failure," Jack must accept that Mopsa has grown beyond needing his help. After Mopsa "gives back" his kiss—subverting another fairy-tale convention—Jack returns to his own world, just in time for bed.[2] In their travels through Fairyland, Mopsa and Jack encounter many creatures who offer satiric commentary on

1. Sarah K. Bolton, *Lives of Girls Who Became Famous* (New York: Thomas Crowell, 1886) 346.
2. Nina Auerbach and U.C. Knoepflmacher, *Forbidden Journeys: Fairy Tales and Fantasies by Victorian Women Writers* (Chicago: U of Chicago P, 1992) 208.

nineteenth-century Utilitarianism: a town full of clockwork people who must be wound up each day by their queen, and the Stone people, who are hardened by their lack of feeling. Powerful, complex, and among the most widely read and respected children's fantasies of the Victorian age, Ingelow's *Mopsa the Fairy* is long overdue for critical attention.

Mopsa the Fairy

CHAPTER 14. REEDS AND RUSHES

'Tis merry, 'tis merry in Fairyland,
When Fairy birds are singing;
When the court doth ride by their monarch's side,
With bit and bridle ringing.
—WALTER SCOTT.

THERE WERE MANY FRUIT-TREES on that slope of the mountain, and Jack and Mopsa, as they came down, gathered some fruit for breakfast, and did not feel very tired, for the long ride on the wing had rested them.

They could not see the plain, for a slight blue mist hung over it; but the sun was hot already, and as they came down they saw a beautiful bed of high reeds, and thought they would sit awhile and rest in it. A rill of clear water ran beside the bed, so when they had reached it they sat down, and began to consider what they should do next.

"Jack," said Mopsa, "did you see anything particular as you came down with the shooting stars?"

"No, I saw nothing so interesting as they were," answered Jack. "I was looking at them and watching how they squeaked to one another, and how they had little hooks in their wings, with which they held the large wing that we sat on."

"But I saw something," said Mopsa. "Just as the sun rose I looked down, and in the loveliest garden I ever saw, and all among trees and woods, I saw a most beautiful castle. Oh, Jack! I am sure that castle is the place I am to live in, and now we have nothing to do but to find it. I shall soon be a queen, and there I shall reign."

"Then I shall be king there," said Jack; "shall I?"

"Yes, if you can," answered Mopsa. "Of course, whatever you can do you may do. And, Jack, this is a much better fairy country than either the stony land or the other that we first came to, for this castle is a real place! It will not melt away. There the people can work, they know how to love each other: common fairies cannot do that, I know. They can laugh and cry, and I shall teach them several things that they do not know yet. Oh, do let us make haste and find the castle!"

So they arose; but they turned the wrong way, and by mistake walked farther and farther in among the reeds, whose feathery heads puffed into Mopsa's face, and Jack's coat was all covered with the fluffy seed.

5

"This is very odd," said Jack. "I thought this was only a small bed of reeds when we stepped into it; but really we must have walked a mile already."

But they walked on and on, till Mopsa grew quite faint, and her sweet face became very pale, for she knew that the beds of reeds were spreading faster than they walked, and then they shot up so high that it was impossible to see over their heads; so at last Jack and Mopsa were so tired that they sat down, and Mopsa began to cry.

However, Jack was the braver of the two this time, and he comforted Mopsa, and told her that she was nearly a queen, and would never reach her castle by sitting still. So she got up and took his hand, and he went on before, parting the reeds and pulling her after him, till all on a sudden they heard the sweetest sound in the world: it was like a bell, and it sounded again and again.

It was the castle clock, and it was striking twelve at noon.

As it finished striking they came out at the farther edge of the great bed of reeds, and there was the castle straight before them—a beautiful castle, standing on the slope of a hill. The grass all about it was covered with beautiful flowers; two of the taller turrets were overgrown with ivy, and a flag was flying on a staff; but everything was so silent and lonely that it made one sad to look on. As Jack and Mopsa drew near they trod as gently as they could, and did not say a word.

All the windows were shut, but there was a great door in the centre of the building, and they went towards it, hand in hand.

What a beautiful hall! The great door stood wide open, and they could see what a delightful place this must be to live in: it was paved with squares of blue and white marble, and here and there carpets were spread, with chairs and tables upon them. They looked and saw a great dome overhead, filled with windows of coloured glass, and they cast down blue and golden and rosy reflections.

"There is my home that I shall live in," said Mopsa; and she came close to the door, and they both looked in, till at last she let go of Jack's hand, and stepped over the threshold.

The bell in the tower sounded again more sweetly than ever, and the instant Mopsa was inside there came from behind the fluted columns, which rose up on every side, the brown doe, followed by troops of deer and fawns!

"Mopsa! Mopsa!" cried Jack. "Come away! come back!" But Mopsa was too much astonished to stir, and something seemed to hold Jack from following; but he looked and looked, till, as the brown doe advanced, the door of the castle closed—Mopsa was shut in, and Jack was left outside.

So Mopsa had come straight to the place she thought she had run away from.

"But I am determined to get her away from those creatures," thought Jack; "she does not want to reign over deer." And he began to look about him, hoping to get in. It was of no use: all the windows in the front of the castle were high, and when he tried to go round, he came to a high wall with battlements. Against some parts of this wall the ivy grew, and looked as if it might have grown there for ages; its stems were thicker than his waist, and its branches were spread over the surface like network; so by means of them he hoped to climb to the top.

He immediately began to try. Oh, how high the wall was! First he came to several sparrows' nests, and very much frightened the sparrows were; then he reached starlings' nests, and very angry the starlings were; but at last, just under the coping, he came to jackdaws' nests, and these birds were very friendly, and pointed out to him the best little holes for him to put his feet into. At last he reached the top, and found to his delight that the wall was three feet thick, and he could walk upon it quite comfortably, and look down into a lovely garden, where all the trees were in blossom, and creepers tossed their long tendrils from tree to tree, covered with puffs of yellow, or bells of white, or bunches and knots of blue or rosy bloom.

He could look down into the beautiful empty rooms of the castle, and he walked cautiously on the wall till he came to the west front, and reached a little casement window that had latticed panes. Jack peeped in; nobody was there. He took his knife and cut away a little bit of lead to let out the pane, and it fell with such a crash on the pavement below that he wondered it did not bring the deer over to look at what he was about. Nobody came.

He put in his hand and opened the latchet, and with very little trouble got down into the room. Still nobody was to be seen. He thought that the room, years ago, might have been a fairies' schoolroom, for it was strewn with books, slates and all sorts of copybooks. A fine soft dust had settled down over everything,—pens, papers and all. Jack opened a copybook: its pages were headed with maxims, just as ours are, which proved that these fairies must have been superior to such as he had hitherto come among. Jack read some of them:

> Turn your back on the light, and you'll follow a shadow.
> The deaf queen Fate has dumb courtiers.
> If the hound is your foe, don't sleep in his kennel.
> That that is, is.

And so on; but nobody came, and no sound was heard, so he opened the door, and found himself in a long and most splendid gallery, all hung with pictures, and spread with a most beautiful carpet, which was as soft and white as a piece of wool, and wrought with a beautiful device. This was the letter

M, with a crown and sceptre, and underneath a beautiful little boat, exactly like the one in which he had come up the river. Jack felt sure that this carpet had been made for Mopsa, and he went along the gallery upon it till he reached a grand staircase of oak that was almost black with age, and he stole gently down it, for he began to feel rather shy, more especially as he could now see the great hall under the dome, and that it had a beautiful lady in it, and many other people, but no deer at all.

These fairy people were something like the one-foot-one fairies, but much larger and more like children, and they had very gentle, happy faces, and seemed to be extremely glad and gay. But seated on a couch, where lovely painted windows threw down all sorts of rainbow colours on her, was a beautiful fairy lady, as large as a woman. She had Mopsa in her arms, and was looking down upon her with eyes full of love, while at her side stood a boy, who was exactly and precisely like Jack himself. He had rather long light hair and grey eyes, and a velvet jacket. That was all Jack could see at first, but as he drew nearer the boy turned, and then Jack felt as if he was looking at himself in the glass.

Mopsa had been very tired, and now she was fast asleep, with her head on that lady's shoulder. The boy kept looking at her, and he seemed very happy indeed; so did the lady, and she presently told him to bring Jack something to eat.

It was rather a curious speech that she made to him: it was this:

"Jack, bring Jack some breakfast."

"What!" thought Jack to himself. "Has he got a face like mine, and a name like mine too?"

So that other Jack went away, and presently came back with a golden plate full of nice things to eat.

"I know you don't like me," he said, as he came up to Jack with the plate.

"Not like him?" repeated the lady; "and pray, what reason have you for not liking my royal nephew?"

"Oh, dame!" exclaimed the boy, and laughed.

The lady, on hearing this, turned pale, for she perceived that she herself had mistaken the one for the other.

"I see you know how to laugh," said the real Jack. "You are wiser people than those whom I went to first; but the reason I don't like you is that you are so exactly like me."

"I am not!" exclaimed the boy. "Only hear him, dame! You mean, I suppose, that you are so exactly like me. I am sure I don't know what you mean by it."

"Nor I either," replied Jack, almost in a passion.

"It couldn't be helped, of course," said the other Jack.

"Hush! hush!" said the fairy woman. "Don't wake our dear little Queen. Was it you, my royal nephew, who spoke out last?"

"Yes, dame," answered the boy, and again he offered the plate; but Jack was swelling with indignation, and he gave the plate a push with his elbow, which scattered the fruit and bread on the ground.

"I won't eat it," he said; but when the other Jack went and picked it up again, and said: "Oh yes, do, old fellow; it's not my fault, you know," he began to consider that it was no use being cross in Fairyland; so he forgave his double, and had just finished his breakfast when Mopsa woke.

CHAPTER 15. THE QUEEN'S WAND

One, two, three, four; one, two, three, four;
   'Tis still one, two, three, four.
Mellow and silvery are the tones,
   But I wish the bells were more.
               —SOUTHEY.

Mopsa woke: she was rather too big to be nursed, for she was the size of Jack, and looked like a sweet little girl of ten years, but she did not always behave like one; sometimes she spoke as wisely as a grown-up woman, and sometimes she changed again and seemed like a child.

Mopsa lifted up her head and pushed back her long hair: her coronet had fallen off while she was in the bed of reeds; and she said to the beautiful dame:

"I am a queen now."

"Yes, my sweet Queen," answered the lady, "I know you are."

"And you promise that you will be kind to me till I grow up," said Mopsa, "and love me, and teach me how to reign?"

"Yes," repeated the lady; "and I will love you too, just as if you were a mortal and I your mother."

"For I am only ten years old yet," said Mopsa, "and the throne is too big for me to sit upon; but I am a queen." And then she paused, and said: "Is it three o'clock?"

As she spoke the sweet clear bell of the castle sounded three times, and then chimes began to play; they played such a joyous tune that it made everybody sing. The dame sang, the crowd of fairies sang, the boy who was Jack's double sang and Mopsa sang—only Jack was silent—and this was the song:

"The prince shall to the chase again,
The dame has got her face again,
The king shall have his place again
    Aneath the fairy dome.

"And all the knights shall woo again,
And all the doves shall coo again,
And all the dreams come true again,
    And Jack shall go home."

"We shall see about that!" thought Jack to himself. And Mopsa, while she sang those last words, burst into tears, which Jack did not like to see; but all the fairies were so very glad, so joyous and so delighted with her for having come to be their queen, that after a while she dried her eyes, and said to the wrong boy:

"Jack, when I pulled the lining out of your pocket-book there was a silver fourpence in it."

"Yes," said the real Jack, "and here it is."

"Is it real money?" asked Mopsa. "Are you sure you brought it with you all the way from your own country?"

"Yes," said Jack, "quite sure."

"Then, dear Jack," answered Mopsa, "will you give it to me?"

"I will," said Jack, "if you will send this boy away."

"How can I?" answered Mopsa, surprised. "Don't you know what happened when the door closed? Has nobody told you?"

"I did not see anyone after I got into the place," said Jack. "There was no one to tell anything—not even a fawn, nor the brown doe. I have only seen down here these fairy people, and this boy, and this lady."

"The lady is the brown doe," answered Mopsa; "and this boy and the fairies were the fawns." Jack was so astonished at this that he stared at the lady and the boy and the fairies with all his might.

"The sun came shining in as I stepped inside," said Mopsa, "and a long beam fell down from the fairy dome across my feet. Do you remember what the apple-woman told us—how it was reported that the brown doe and her nation had a queen whom they shut up, and never let the sun shine on her? That was not a kind or true report, and yet it came from something that really happened."

"Yes, I remember," said Jack; "and if the sun did shine they were all to be turned into deer."

"I dare not tell you all that story yet," said Mopsa; "but, Jack, as the brown doe and all the fawns came up to greet me, and passed by turns into the sunbeam, they took their own forms, every one of them, because the spell was broken. They were to remain in the disguise of deer till a queen of alien birth should come to them against her will. I am a queen of alien birth, and did not I come against my will?"

"Yes, to be sure," answered Jack. "We thought all the time that we were running away."

"If ever you come to Fairyland again," observed Mopsa, "you can save yourself the trouble of trying to run away from the old mother."

"I shall not 'come,'" answered Jack, "because I shall not go—not for a long while, at least. But the boy—I want to know why this boy turned into another ME?"

"Because he is the heir, of course," answered Mopsa.

"But I don't see that this is any reason at all," said Jack.

Mopsa laughed. "That's because you don't know how to argue," she replied. "Why, the thing is as plain as possible."

"It may be plain to you," persisted Jack, "but it's no reason."

"No reason!" repeated Mopsa. "No reason! when I like you the best of anything in the world, and when I am come here to be queen! Of course, when the spell was broken he took exactly your form on that account; and very right too."

"But why?" asked Jack.

Mopsa, however, was like other fairies in this respect—that she knew all about Old Mother Fate, but not about causes and reasons. She believed, as we do in this world, that

That that is, is,

but the fairies go further than this; they say:

That that is, is; and when it is, that is the reason that it is.

This sounds like nonsense to us, but it is all right to them.

So Mopsa, thinking she had explained everything, said again:

"And, dear Jack, will you give the silver fourpence to me?"

Jack took it out; and she got down from the dame's knee and took it in the palm of her hand, laying the other palm upon it.

"It will be very hot," observed the dame.

"But it will not burn me so as really to hurt, if I am a real queen," said Mopsa.

Presently she began to look as if something gave her pain.

"Oh, it's so hot!" she said to the other Jack; "so very hot!"

"Never mind, sweet Queen," he answered; "it will not hurt you long. Remember my poor uncle and all his knights."

Mopsa still held the little silver coin; but Jack saw that it hurt her, for two bright tears fell from her eyes; and in another moment he saw that it was actually melted, for it fell in glittering drops from Mopsa's hand to the marble floor, and there it lay as soft as quicksilver.

"Pick it up," said Mopsa to the other Jack; and he instantly did so, and laid it in her hand again; and she began gently to roll it backwards and forwards between her palms till she had rolled it into a very slender rod, two feet long, and not nearly so thick as a pin; but it did not bend, and it shone so brightly that you could hardly look at it.

Then she held it out towards the real Jack, and said: "Give this a name."

"I think it is a—" began the other Jack; but the dame suddenly stopped him. "Silence, sire! Don't you know that what it is first called that it will be?"

Jack hesitated; he thought if Mopsa was a queen the thing ought to be a sceptre; but it was certainly not at all like a sceptre.

"That thing is a wand," said he.

"You are a wand," said Mopsa, speaking to the silver stick, which was glittering now in a sunbeam almost as if it were a beam of light itself. Then she spoke again to Jack:

"Tell me, Jack, what can I do with a wand?"

Again the boy king began to speak, and the dame stopped him, and again Jack considered. He had heard a great deal in his own country about fairy wands, but he could not remember that the fairies had done anything particular with them, so he gave what he thought was true, but what seemed to him a very stupid answer:

"You can make it point to anything that you please."

The moment he said this, shouts of ecstasy filled the hall, and all the fairies clapped their hands with such hurrahs of delight that he blushed for joy.

The dame also looked truly glad, and as for the other Jack, he actually turned head over heels, just as Jack had often done himself on his father's lawn.

Jack had merely meant that Mopsa could point with the wand to anything that she saw; but he was presently told that what he had meant was nothing, and that his words were everything.

"I can make it point now," said Mopsa, "and it will point aright to anything I please, whether I know where the thing is or not."

Again the hall was filled with those cries of joy, and the sweet childlike fairies congratulated each other with "The Queen has got a wand—a wand! and she can make it point wherever she pleases!"

Then Mopsa rose and walked towards the beautiful staircase, the dame and all the fairies following. Jack was going too, but the other Jack held him.

"Where is Mopsa going? and why am I not to follow?" inquired Jack.

"They are going to put on her robes, of course," answered the other Jack.

"I am so tired of always hearing you say 'of course,'" answered Jack; "and I wonder how it is that you always seem to know what is going to be done without being told. However, I suppose you can't help being odd people."

The boy king did not make a direct answer; he only said: "I like you very much, though you don't like me."

"Why do you like me?" asked Jack.

The other opened his eyes wide with surprise. "Most boys say Sire to me," he observed; "at least they used to when there were any boys here. However, that does not signify. Why, of course I like you, because I am so tired of being always a fawn, and you brought Mopsa to break the spell. You cannot think how disagreeable it is to have no hands, and to be all covered with hair. Now look at my hands; I can move them and turn them everywhere, even over my head if I like. Hoofs are good for nothing in comparison: and we could not talk."

"Do tell me about it," said Jack. "How did you become fawns?"

"I dare not tell you," said the boy; "and listen—I hear Mopsa."

Jack looked, and certainly Mopsa was coming, but very strangely, he thought. Mopsa, like all other fairies, was afraid to whisper a spell with her eyes open; so a handkerchief was tied across them, and as she came on she felt her way, holding by the banisters with one hand, and with the other, between her finger and thumb, holding out the silver wand. She felt with her foot for the edge of the first stair; and Jack heard her say: "I am much older— ah! so much older, now I have got my wand. I can feel sorrow too, and *their* sorrow weighs down my heart."

Mopsa was dressed superbly in a white satin gown, with a long, long train of crimson velvet which was glittering with diamonds; it reached almost from one end of the great gallery to the other, and had hundreds of fairies to hold it and keep it in its place. But in her hair were no jewels, only a little crown made of daisies, and on her shoulders her robe was fastened with the little golden image of a boat. These things were to show the land she had come from and the vessel she had come in.

So she came slowly, slowly downstairs blindfold, and muttering to her wand all the time.

"Though the sun shine brightly,
Wand, wand, guide rightly."

So she felt her way down to the great hall. There the wand turned half round in the hall towards the great door, and she and Jack and the other Jack came out on to the lawn in front with all the followers and train-bearers; only the dame remained behind.

Jack noticed now for the first time that, with the one exception of the boy-king, all these fairies were lady-fairies; he also observed that Mopsa, after the manner of fairy queens, though she moved slowly and blindfold, was beginning to tell a story. This time it did not make him feel sleepy. It did not begin at the beginning: their stories never do.

These are the first words he heard, for she spoke softly and very low, while he walked at her right hand, and the other Jack on her left:

"And so now I have no wings. But my thoughts can go up (Jovinian and Roxaletta could not think). My thoughts are instead of wings; but they have dropped with me now, as a lark among the clods of the valley. Wand, do you bend? Yes, I am following, wand.

"And after that the bird said: 'I will come when you call me.' I have never seen her moving overhead; perhaps she is out of sight. Flocks of birds hover over the world, and watch it high up where the air is thin. There are zones, but those in the lowest zone are far out of sight.

"I have not been up there. I have no wings.

"Over the highest of the birds is the place where angels float and gather the children's souls as they are set free.

"And so that woman told me—(Wand, you bend again, and I will turn at your bending)—that woman told me how it was: for when the new king was born, a black fairy with a smiling face came and sat within the doorway. She had a spindle, and would always spin. She wanted to teach them how to spin, but they did not like her, and they loved to do nothing at all. So they turned her out.

"But after her came a brown fairy, with a grave face, and she sat on the black fairy's stool and gave them much counsel. They liked that still less; so they got spindles and spun, for they said: 'She will go now, and we shall have the black fairy again.' When she did not go they turned her out also, and after her came a white fairy, and sat in the same seat. She did nothing at all, and she said nothing at all; but she had a sorrowful face, and she looked up. So they were displeased. They turned her out also; and she went and sat by the edge of the lake with her two sisters.

"And everything prospered over all the land; till, after shearing-time, the shepherds, because the king was a child, came to his uncle, and said: 'Sir, what shall we do with the old wool, for the new fleeces are in the bales, and there is no storehouse to put them in?' So he said: 'Throw them into the lake.'

"And while they threw them in, a great flock of finches flew to them, and said: 'Give us some of the wool that you do not want; we should be glad of it to build our nests with.'

"They answered: 'Go and gather for yourselves; there is wool on every thorn.'

"Then the black fairy said: 'They shall be forgiven this time, because the birds should pick wool for themselves.'

"So the finches flew away.

"Then the harvest was over, and the reapers came and said to the child king's uncle: 'Sir, what shall we do with the new wheat, for the old is not half eaten yet, and there is no room in the granaries?'

"He said: 'Throw that into the lake also.'

"While they were throwing it in, there came a great flight of the wood fairies, fairies of passage from over the sea. They were in the form of pigeons, and they alighted and prayed them: 'O cousins! we are faint with our long flight; give us some of that corn which you do not want, that we may peck it and be refreshed.'

"But they said: 'You may rest on our land, but our corn is our own. Rest awhile, and go and get food in your own fields.'

"Then the brown fairy said: 'They may be forgiven this once, but yet it is a great unkindness.'

"And as they were going to pour in the last sackful, there passed a poor mortal beggar, who had strayed in from the men and women's world, and she said: 'Pray give me some of that wheat, O fairy people! for I am hungry, I have lost my way, and there is no money to be earned here. Give me some of that wheat, that I may bake cakes, lest I and my baby should starve.'

"And they said: 'What is starve? We never heard that word before, and we cannot wait while you explain it to us.'

"So they poured it all into the lake; and then the white fairy said: 'This cannot be forgiven them'; and she covered her face with her hands and wept. Then the black fairy rose and drove them all before her—the prince, with his chief shepherd and his reapers, his courtiers and his knights; she drove them into the great bed of reeds, and no one had ever set eyes on them since. Then the brown fairy went into the palace where the king's aunt sat, with all her ladies and her maids about her, and with the child king on her knee.

"It was a very gloomy day.

"She stood in the middle of the hall, and said: 'Oh, you cold-hearted and most unkind! my spell is upon you, and the first ray of sunshine shall bring it down. Lose your present forms, and be of a more gentle and innocent race, till a queen of alien birth shall come to reign over you against her will.'

"As she spoke they crept into corners, and covered the dame's head with a veil. And all that day it was dark and gloomy, and nothing happened, and all the next day it rained and rained; and they thrust the dame into a dark closet, and kept her there for a whole month, and still not a ray of sunshine came to do them any damage; but the dame faded and faded in the dark, and at last they said: 'She must come out, or she will die; and we do not believe the sun will ever shine in our country any more.' So they let the poor dame come out; and lo! as she crept slowly forth under the dome, a piercing ray of sunlight darted down upon her head, and in an instant they were all changed into deer, and the child king too.

"They are gentle now, and kind; but where is the prince? Where are the fairy knights and fairy men?

"Wand! why do you turn?"

Now while Mopsa told her story the wand continued to bend, and Mopsa, following, was slowly approaching the foot of a great precipice, which rose sheer up for more than a hundred feet. The crowd that followed looked dismayed at this: they thought the wand must be wrong; or even if it was right, they could not climb a precipice.

But still Mopsa walked on blindfold, and the wand pointed at the rock till it touched it, and she said: "Who is stopping me?"

They told her, and she called to some of her ladies to untie the handkerchief. Then Mopsa looked at the rock, and so did the two Jacks. There was nothing to be seen but a very tiny hole. The boy-king thought it led to a bees' nest, and Jack thought it was a keyhole, for he noticed in the rock a slight crack which took the shape of an arched door.

Mopsa looked earnestly at the hole. "It may be a keyhole," she said, "but there is no key."

CHAPTER 16. FAILURE

We are much bound to them that do succeed;
    But, in a more pathetic sense, are bound
    To such as fail. They all our loss expound;
They comfort us for work that will not speed,
And life—itself a failure. Ay, his deed,
    Sweetest in story, who the dusk profound
    Of Hades flooded with entrancing sound,

Music's own tears, was failure. Doth it read
Therefore the worse? Ah, no! So much to dare,
   He fronts the regnant Darkness on its throne.—
So much to do; impetuous even there,
   He pours out love's disconsolate sweet moan—
He wins; but few for that his deed recall:
Its power is in the look which costs him all.

At this moment Jack observed that a strange woman was standing among them, and that the train-bearing fairies fell back, as if they were afraid of her. As no one spoke, he did, and said: "Good morning!"

"Good afternoon!" she answered, correcting him. "I am the black fairy. Work is a fine thing. Most people in your country can work."

"Yes," said Jack.

"There are two spades," continued the fairy woman; "one for you, and one for your double."

Jack took one of the spades—it was small, and was made of silver; but the other Jack said with scorn:

"I shall be a king when I am old enough, and must I dig like a clown?"

"As you please," said the black fairy, and walked away.

Then they all observed that a brown woman was standing there; and she stepped up and whispered in the boy king's ear. As he listened his sullen face became good tempered, and at last he said, in a gentle tone: "Jack, I'm quite ready to begin if you are."

"But where are we to dig?" asked Jack.

"There," said a white fairy, stepping up and setting her foot on the grass just under the little hole. "Dig down as deep as you can."

So Mopsa and the crowd stood back, and the two boys began to dig; and greatly they enjoyed it, for people can dig so fast in Fairyland.

Very soon the hole was so deep that they had to jump into it, because they could not reach the bottom with their spades. "This is very jolly indeed," said Jack, when they had dug so much deeper that they could only see out of the hole by standing on tiptoe.

"Go on," said the white fairy; so they dug till they came to a flat stone, and then she said: "Now you can stamp. Stamp on the stone, and don't be afraid." So the two Jacks began to stamp, and in such a little time that she had only half turned her head round, the flat stone gave way, for there was a hollow underneath it, and down went the boys, and utterly disappeared.

Then, while Mopsa and the crowd silently looked on, the white fairy lightly pushed the clods of earth towards the hole with the side of her foot, and in a very few minutes the hole was filled in, and that so completely and so neatly that when she had spread the turf on it, and given it a pat with her foot, you could not have told where it had been. Mopsa said not a word, for no fairy ever interferes with a stronger fairy; but she looked on earnestly, and when the white stranger smiled she was satisfied.

Then the white stranger walked away, and Mopsa and the fairies sat down on a bank under some splendid cedar trees. The beautiful castle looked fairer than ever in the afternoon sunshine; a lovely waterfall tumbled with a tinkling noise near at hand, and the bank was covered with beautiful wild flowers.

They sat for a long while, and no one spoke: what they were thinking of is not known, but sweet Mopsa often sighed.

At last a noise—a very, very slight noise, as of footsteps of people running—was heard inside the rock, and then a little quivering was seen in the wand. It quivered more and more as the sound increased. At last that which had looked like a door began to shake as if someone was pushing it from within. Then a noise was distinctly heard as of a key turning in the hole, and out burst the two Jacks, shouting for joy, and a whole troop of knights and squires and serving-men came rushing wildly forth behind them.

Oh, the joy of that meeting! Who shall describe it? Fairies by dozens came up to kiss the boy king's hand, and Jack shook hands with everyone that could reach him. Then Mopsa proceeded to the castle between the two Jacks, and the king's aunt came out to meet them, and welcomed her husband with tears of joy; for these fairies could laugh and cry when they pleased, and they naturally considered this a great proof of superiority.

After this a splendid feast was served under the great dome. The other fairy feasts that Jack had seen were nothing to it. The prince and his dame sat at one board, but Mopsa sat at the head of the great table, with the two Jacks one on each side of her.

Mopsa was not happy, Jack was sure of that, for she often sighed; and he thought this strange. But he did not ask her any questions, and he, with the boy king, related their adventures to her: how, when the stone gave way, they tumbled in and rolled down a sloping bank till they found themselves at the entrance of a beautiful cave, which was all lighted up with torches, and glittering with stars and crystals of all the colours in the world. There was a table spread with what looked like a splendid luncheon in this great cave, and chairs were set round, but Jack and the boy-king felt no inclination to eat anything, though they were hungry, for a whole nation of ants were creeping up the honey-pots. There were snails walking about over the tablecloth, and toads peeping out of some of the dishes.

So they turned away and, looking for some other door to lead them farther in, they at last found a very small one—so small that only one of them could pass through at a time.

They did not tell Mopsa all that had occurred on this occasion. It was thus:

The boy-king said: "I shall go in first, of course, because of my rank."

"Very well," said Jack, "I don't mind. I shall say to myself that you've gone in first to find the way for me, because you're my double. Besides, now I think of it, our Queen always goes last in a procession; so it's grand to go last. Pass in, Jack."

"No," answered the other Jack; "now you have said that, I will not. You may go first."

So they began to quarrel and argue about this, and it is impossible to say how long they would have gone on if they had not begun to hear a terrible and mournful sort of moaning and groaning, which frightened them both and instantly made them friends. They took tight hold of one another's hand, and again there came a loud sighing, and a noise of all sorts of lamentation, and it seemed to reach them through the little door.

Each of the boys would now have been very glad to go back, but neither liked to speak. At last Jack thought anything would be less terrible than listening to those dismal moans, so he suddenly dashed through the door, and the other Jack followed.

There was nothing terrible to be seen. They found themselves in a place like an immensely long stable; but it was nearly dark, and when their eyes got used to the dimness they saw that it was strewn with quantities of fresh hay, from which curious things like sticks stuck up in all directions. What were they?

"They are dry branches of trees," said the boy-king.

"They are table legs turned upside down," said Jack; but then the other Jack suddenly perceived the real nature of the thing, and he shouted out: "No; they are antlers!"

The moment he said this the moaning ceased, hundreds of beautiful antlered heads were lifted up and the two boys stood before a splendid herd of stags; but they had had hardly time to be sure of this when the beautiful multitude rose and fled away into the darkness, leaving the two boys to follow as well as they could.

They were sure they ought to run after the herd, and they ran, but they soon lost sight of it, though they heard far on in front what seemed at first like a pattering of deers' feet, but the sound changed from time to time. It became heavier and louder, and then the clattering ceased, and it was evidently the tramping of a great crowd of men. At last they heard words, very glad and thankful words; people were crying to one another to make haste, lest the spell should come upon them again. Then the two Jacks, still running, came into a grand hall, which was quite full of knights and all sorts of fairy men, and there was the boy king's uncle, but he looked very pale. "Unlock the door!" they cried. "We shall not be safe till we see our new Queen. Unlock the door; we see light coming through the keyhole."

The two Jacks came on to the front, and felt and shook the door. At last the boy-king saw a little golden key glittering on the floor, just where the one narrow sunbeam fell that came through the keyhole; so he snatched it up. It fitted, and out they all came, as you have been told.

When they had done relating their adventures, the new Queen's health was drunk. And then they drank the health of the boy-king, who stood up to return thanks, and, as is the fashion there, he sang a song. Jack thought it the most ridiculous song he had ever heard; but as everybody else looked extremely grave, he tried to be grave too. It was about Cock Robin and Jenny Wren, how they made a wedding feast, and how the wren said she should wear her brown gown, and the old dog brought a bone to the feast.

> "'He had brought them,' he said, 'some meat on a bone:
> They were welcome to pick it or leave it alone.'"

The fairies were very attentive to this song; they seemed, if one may judge by their looks, to think it was rather a serious one. Then they drank Jack's health, and afterwards looked at him as if they expected him to sing too; but as he did not begin, he presently heard them whispering, and one asking another: "Do you think he knows manners?"

So he thought he had better try what he could do, and he stood up and sang a song that he had often heard his nurse sing in the nursery at home.

> "One morning, oh! so early, my belovèd, my belovèd,
> All the birds were singing blithely, as if never they would cease;
> 'Twas a thrush sang in my garden, 'Hear the story, hear the story!'
> And the lark sang, 'Give us glory!'
> And the dove said, 'Give us peace!'

> "Then I listened, Oh! so early, my belovèd, my belovèd,
> To that murmur from the woodland of the dove, my dear, the dove;
> When the nightingale came after, 'Give us fame to sweeten duty!'
> When the wren sang, 'Give us beauty!'
> She made answer, 'Give us love!'

"Sweet is spring, and sweet the morning, my belovèd, my belovèd;
Now for us doth spring, doth morning, wait upon the year's increase,
And my prayer goes up, 'Oh, give us, crowned in youth with marriage glory,
    Give for all our life's dear story
    Give us love, and give us peace!'"

"A very good song too," said the dame, at the other end of the table; "only you made a mistake in the first verse. What the dove really said was, no doubt, 'Give us peas.' All kinds of doves and pigeons are very fond of peas."

"It isn't peas, though," said Jack. However, the court historian was sent for to write down the song, and he came with a quill pen, and wrote it down as the dame said it ought to be.

Now all this time Mopsa sat between the two Jacks, and she looked very mournful—she said hardly a word.

When the feast was over, and everything had vanished, the musicians came in, for there was to be dancing; but while they were striking up the white fairy stepped in, and, coming up, whispered something in Jack's ear; but he could not hear what she said, so she repeated it more slowly, and still he could neither hear nor understand it.

Mopsa did not seem to like the white fairy: she leaned her face on her hand and sighed; but when she found that Jack could not hear the message, she said: "That is well. Cannot you let things alone for this one day?" The fairy then spoke to Mopsa, but she would not listen; she made a gesture of dislike and moved away. So then this strange fairy turned and went out again, but on the doorstep she looked round, and beckoned to Jack to come to her. So he did; and then, as they two stood together outside, she made him understand what she had said. It was this:

"Her name was Jenny, her name was Jenny."

When Jack understood what she said he felt so sorrowful; he wondered why she had told him, and he longed to stay in that great place with Queen Mopsa—his own little Mopsa, whom he had carried in his pocket, and taken care of, and loved.

He walked up and down, up and down, outside, and his heart swelled and his eyes filled with tears. The bells had said he was to go home, and the fairy had told him how to go. Mopsa did not need him, she had so many people to take care of her now; and then there was that boy, so exactly like himself that she would not miss him. Oh, how sorrowful it all was! Had he really come up the fairy river, and seen those strange countries, and run away with Mopsa over those dangerous mountains, only to bring her to the very place she wished to fly from, and there to leave her, knowing that she wanted him no more, and that she was quite content?

No; Jack felt that he could not do that. "I will stay," he said; "they cannot make me leave her. That would be too unkind."

As he spoke he drew near to the great yawning door, and looked in. The fairy folk were singing inside; he could hear their pretty chirping voices, and see their beautiful faces, but he could not bear it, and he turned away.

The sun began to get low, and all the west was dyed with crimson. Jack dried his eyes, and, not liking to go in, took one turn more.

"I will go in," he said; "there is nothing to prevent me." He set his foot on the step of the door, and while he hesitated Mopsa came out to meet him.

"Jack," she said, in a sweet mournful tone of voice. But he could not make any answer; he only looked at her earnestly, because her lovely eyes were not looking at him, but far away towards the west.

"He lives there," she said, as if speaking to herself. "He will play there again, in his father's garden."

Then she brought her eyes down slowly from the roseflush in the cloud, and looked at him and said: "Jack."

"Yes," said Jack; "I am here. What is it that you wish to say?"

She answered: "I am come to give you back your kiss."

So she stooped forward as she stood on the step, and kissed him, and her tears fell on his cheek.

"Farewell!" she said, and she turned and went up the steps and into the great hall; and while Jack gazed at her as she entered, and would fain have followed, but could not stir, the great doors closed together again, and he was left outside.

Then he knew, without having been told, that he should never enter them any more. He stood gazing at the castle; but it was still—no more fairy music sounded.

How beautiful it looked in the evening sunshine, and how Jack cried!

Suddenly he perceived that reeds were growing up between him and the great doors: the grass, which had all day grown about the steps, was getting taller; it had long spear-like leaves, it pushed up long pipes of green stem, and they whistled.

They were up to his ankles, they were presently up to his waist; soon they were as high as his head. He drew back that he might see over them; they sprang up faster as he retired, and again he went back. It seemed to him that the castle also receded; there was a long reach of these great reeds between it and him, and now they were growing behind also, and on all sides of him. He kept moving back and back: it was of no use, they sprang up and grew yet

more tall, till very shortly the last glimpse of the fairy castle was hidden from his sorrowful eyes.

The sun was just touching the tops of the purple mountains when Jack lost sight of Mopsa's home; but he remembered how he had penetrated the bed of reeds in the morning, and he hoped to have the same good fortune again. So on and on he walked, pressing his way among them as well as he could, till the sun went down behind the mountains, and the rosy sky turned gold colour, and the gold began to burn itself away, and then all on a sudden he came to the edge of the reed-bed, and walked out upon a rising ground.

Jack ran up it, looking for the castle. He could not see it, so he climbed a far higher hill; still he could not see it. At last, after a toilsome ascent to the very top of the green mountain, he saw the castle lying so far, so very far off, that its peaks and battlements were on the edge of the horizon, and the evening mist rose while he was gazing, so that all its outlines were lost, and very soon they seemed to mingle with the shapes of the hill and the forest, till they had utterly vanished away.

Then he threw himself down on the short grass. The words of the white fairy sounded in his ears: "Her name was Jenny"; and he burst into tears again, and decided to go home.

He looked up into the rosy sky, and held out his arms, and called: "Jenny! O Jenny! come."

In a minute or two he saw a little black mark overhead, a small speck, and it grew larger, and larger, and larger still, as it fell headlong down like a stone. In another instant he saw a red light and a green light, then he heard the winnowing noise of the bird's great wings, and she alighted at his feet, and said: "Here I am."

"I wish to go home," said Jack, hanging down his head and speaking in a low voice, for his heart was heavy because of his failure.

"That is well," answered the bird. She took Jack on her back, and in three minutes they were floating among the clouds.

As Jack's feet were lifted up from Fairyland he felt a little consoled. He began to have a curious feeling, as if this had all happened a good while ago, and then half the sorrow he had felt faded into wonder, and the feeling still grew upon him that these things had passed some great while since, so that he repeated to himself: "It was a long time ago."

Then he fell asleep, and did not dream at all, nor know anything more till the bird woke him.

"Wake up now, Jack," she said; "we are at home."

"So soon!" said Jack, rubbing his eyes. "But it is evening; I thought it would be morning."

"Fairy time is always six hours in advance of your time," said the bird. "I see glow-worms down in the hedge, and the moon is just rising."

They were falling so fast that Jack dared not look; but he saw the church, and the wood, and his father's house, which seemed to be starting up to meet him. In two seconds more the bird alighted, and he stepped down from her back into the deep grass of his father's meadow.

"Goodbye!" she said. "Make haste and run in, for the dews are falling"; and before he could ask her one question, or even thank her, she made a wide sweep over the grass, beat her magnificent wings, and soared away.

It was all very extraordinary, and Jack felt shy and ashamed; but he knew he must go home, so he opened the little gate that led into the garden, and stole through the shrubbery, hoping that his footsteps would not be heard.

Then he came out on the lawn, where the flower-beds were, and he observed that the drawing-room window was open, so he came softly towards it and peeped in.

His father and mother were sitting there. Jack was delighted to see them, but he did not say a word, and he wondered whether they would be surprised at his having stayed away so long. His mother sat with her back to the open window, a candle was burning, and she was reading aloud. Jack listened as she read, and knew that this was not in the least like anything that he had seen in Fairyland, nor the reading like anything that he had heard, and he began to forget the boy-king, and the apple-woman, and even his little Mopsa, more and more.

At last his father noticed him. He did not look at all surprised, but just beckoned to him with his finger to come in. So Jack did, and got upon his father's knee, where he curled himself up comfortably, laid his head on his father's waistcoat and wondered what he would think if he should be told about the fairies in somebody else's waistcoat pocket. He thought, besides, what a great thing a man was; he had never seen anything so large in Fairyland, nor so important; so, on the whole, he was glad he had come back, and felt very comfortable. Then his mother, turning over the leaf, lifted up her eyes and looked at Jack, but not as if she was in the least surprised, or more glad to see him than usual; but she smoothed the leaf with her hand, and began again to read, and this time it was about the Shepherd Lady:

I

"Who pipes upon the long green hill,
    Where meadow grass is deep?
The white lamb bleats but followeth on—
    Follow the clean white sheep.
The dear white lady in yon high tower,
    She hearkeneth in her sleep.

"All in long grass the piper stands,
    Goodly and grave is he;
Outside the tower, at dawn of day,
    The notes of his pipe ring free.
A thought from his heart doth reach to hers:
    'Come down, O lady! to me.'

"She lifts her head, she dons her gown:
    Ah! the lady is fair;
She ties the girdle on her waist,
    And binds her flaxen hair,
And down she stealeth, down and down,
    Down the turret stair.

"Behold him! With the flock he wons
    Along yon grassy lea.
'My shepherd lord, my shepherd love,
    What wilt thou, then, with me?
My heart is gone out of my breast,
    And followeth on to thee.'

II

"'The white lambs feed in tender grass:
    With them and thee to bide,
How good it were,' she saith at noon;
    'Albeit the meads are wide.
Oh! well is me,' she saith when day
    Draws on to eventide.

"Hark! hark! the shepherd's voice. Oh, sweet!
    Her tears drop down like rain.
'Take now this crook, my chosen, my fere,
    And tend the flock full fain:
Feed them, O lady, and lose not one,
    Till I shall come again.'

"Right soft her speech: 'My will is thine,
    And my reward thy grace!'
Gone are his footsteps over the hill,
    Withdrawn his goodly face;
The mournful dusk begins to gather,
    The daylight wanes apace.

III

"On sunny slopes, ah! long the lady
    Feedeth her flock at noon;
She leads them down to drink at eve
    Where the small rivulets croon.
All night her locks are wet with dew,
    Her eyes outwatch the moon.

"Over the hills her voice is heard,
    She sings when light doth wane:
'My longing heart is full of love.
    When shall my loss be gain?
My shepherd lord, I see him not,
    But he will come again.'"

When she had finished Jack lifted his face and said, "Mamma!" Then she came to him and kissed him, and his father said: "I think it must be time this man of ours was in bed."

So he looked earnestly at them both, and as they still asked him no questions, he kissed and wished them goodnight; and his mother said there were some strawberries on the sideboard in the dining-room, and he might have them for his supper.

So he ran out into the hall, and was delighted to find all the house just as usual, and after he had looked about him he went into his own room, and said his prayers. Then he got into his little white bed, and comfortably fell asleep.

That's all.

Amelia and the Dwarfs

JULIANA HORATIA EWING

Illustrations by George Cruikshank

1870

JULIANA HORATIA EWING (1841-85) was the daughter of Margaret Gatty, another well-known Victorian writer for children and the founder of *Aunt Judy's Magazine*, which Ewing later edited and where "Amelia and the Dwarfs" was first published. She was also a frequent contributor to Charlotte Yonge's *Monthly Packet*, where many of her longer works, such as *The Brownies*, were serialized. She wrote many fairy tales, as well as domestic stories such as *Jackanapes, Jan of the Windmill*, and *The Story of a Short Life*, and was an important influence on both Rudyard Kipling and E. Nesbit. Though her works address moral issues, Ewing does not moralize, and the vivid, realistic, often satirical energy of her writing enables her work to avoid sentimentality. Described as a "counter-fantasy to Carroll's *Alice's Adventures in Wonderland*,"[1] this vivid and wryly observed tale is most memorable for its early domestic scenes, which lampoon idealized feminine decorum. Unlike the anxiously polite Alice who, like a good Victorian child, attempts to please and placate adults, Amelia is powerful and aggressive. A satiric Victorian angel run amok, she terrorizes her mother's nervously genteel friends with her energy and curiosity while her ineffectual mother wrings her hands and pleads, "'My dear-r-r-r-Ramelia! YOU MUST NOT!'" (164). Chastened by her punishment in the dwarfs' world "under the haycocks," Amelia still triumphs through a quick-witted and daring escape and, though she is rendered "good and gentle" by her journey, the narrator reassures us that her experience has also made Amelia "unusually clever" (194).

---

1. U. C. Knoepflmacher, "Little Girls Without Their Curls: Female Aggression in Victorian Children's Literature," *Children's Literature* 11 (1983): 25.

Amelia and the Dwarfs

MY GODMOTHER'S GRANDMOTHER knew a good deal about the fairies. *Her* grandmother had seen a fairy rade on a Roodmas Eve, and she herself could remember a copper vessel of a queer shape which had been left by the elves on some occasion at an old farm-house among the hills. The following story came from her, and where she got it I do not know. She used to say it was a pleasant tale, with a good moral in the inside of it. My godmother often observed that a tale without a moral was like a nut without a kernel, not worth the cracking. (We called fireside stories "cracks" in our part of the country.) This is the tale.

AMELIA

A couple of gentlefolk once lived in a certain part of England. (My godmother never would tell me the name either of the place or the people, even if she knew it. She said one ought not to expose one's neighbors' failings more than there was due occasion for.) They had an only child, a daughter, whose name was Amelia. They were an easy-going, good-humored couple; "rather soft," my godmother said, but she was apt to think anybody "soft" who came from the southern shires, as these people did. Amelia, who had been born farther north, was by no means so. She had a strong, resolute will, and a clever head of her own, though she was but a child. She had a way of her own too, and had it very completely. Perhaps because she was an only child, or perhaps because they were so easy-going, her parents spoiled her. She was, beyond question, the most tiresome little girl in that or any other neighborhood. From her baby days her father and mother had taken every opportunity of showing her to their friends, and there was not a friend who did not dread the infliction. When the good lady visited her acquaintances, she always took Amelia with her, and if the acquaintances were fortunate enough to see from the windows who was coming, they used to snatch up any delicate knick-knacks, or brittle ornaments lying about, and put them away, crying, "What is to be done? Here comes Amelia!"

When Amelia came in, she would stand and survey the room, whilst her mother saluted her acquaintance; and if anything struck her fancy, she would interrupt the greetings to draw her mother's attention to it, with a twitch of her shawl, "Oh, look, mamma, at the funny bird in the glass case!" or perhaps, "Mamma, mamma! There's a new carpet since we were here last"; for, as her mother said, she was "a very observing child."

Then she would wander round the room, examining and fingering everything, and occasionally coming back with something in her hand to tread on her mother's dress, and break in upon the ladies' conversation with— "Mamma! mamma! What's the good of keeping this old basin? It's been broken and mended, and some of the pieces are quite loose now. I can feel them": or—addressing the lady of the house—"That's not a real ottoman in the corner. It's a box covered with chintz. I know, for I've looked."

Then her mamma would say, reprovingly, "My *dear* Amelia!"

And perhaps the lady of the house would beg, "Don't play with that old china, my love; for though it is mended, it is very valuable"; and her mother would add, "My dear Amelia, you must not."

Sometimes the good lady said, "You *must* not." Sometimes she tried— "You must *not.*" When both these failed, and Amelia was balancing the china bowl on her finger ends, her mamma would get flurried, and when Amelia flurried her, she always rolled her r's, and emphasized her words, so that it sounded thus:

"My dear-r-r-r-Ramelia! You MUST NOT."

At which Amelia would not so much as look round, till perhaps the bowl slipped from her fingers, and was smashed into unmendable fragments. Then her mamma would exclaim, "Oh, dear-r-r-r, oh dear-r-Ramelia!" and the lady of the house would try to look as if it did not matter, and when Amelia and her mother departed, would pick up the bits, and pour out her complaints to her lady friends, most of whom had suffered many such damages at the hands of this "very observing child."

When the good couple received their friends at home, there was no escaping from Amelia. If it was a dinner party, she came in with the dessert, or perhaps sooner. She would take up her position near some one, generally the person most deeply engaged in conversation, and either lean heavily against him or her, or climb on to his or her knee, without being invited. She would break in upon the most interesting discussion with her own little childish affairs, in the following style—

"I've been out to-day. I walked to the town. I jumped across three brooks. Can you jump? Papa gave me sixpence to-day. I am saving up my money to be rich. You may cut me an orange; no, I'll take it to Mr. Brown, he peels it with a spoon and turns the skin back. Mr. Brown! Mr. Brown! Don't talk to mamma, but peel me an orange, please. Mr. Brown! I'm playing with your finger-glass."

And when the finger-glass full of cold water had been upset on to Mr. Brown's shirt-front, Amelia's mamma would cry—"Oh dear, oh dear-r-Ramelia!" and carry her off with the ladies to the drawing-room.

Here she would scramble on to the ladies' knees, or trample out the gathers of their dresses, and fidget with their ornaments, startling some luck-less lady by the announcement "I've got your bracelet undone at last!" who would find one of the divisions broken open by force, Amelia not understand-ing the working of a clasp.

Or perhaps two young lady friends would get into a quiet corner for a chat. The observing child was sure to spy them, and run on to them, crush-ing their flowers and ribbons, and crying—"You two want to talk secrets, I know. I can hear what you say. I'm going to listen, I am. And I shall tell, too." When perhaps a knock at the door announced the nurse to take Miss Amelia to bed, and spread a general rapture of relief.

Then Amelia would run to trample and worry her mother, and after much teasing, and clinging, and complaining, the nurse would be dismissed, and the fond mamma would turn to the lady next to her, and say with a smile—"I suppose I must let her stay up a little. It is such a treat to her, poor child!"

But it was no treat to the visitors.

Besides tormenting her fellow-creatures, Amelia had a trick of teasing animals. She was really fond of dogs, but she was still fonder of doing what she was wanted not to do, and of worrying everything and everybody about her. So she used to tread on the tips of their tails, and pretend to give them biscuit, and then hit them on the nose, besides pulling at those few, long, sensitive hairs which thin-skinned dogs wear on the upper lip.

Now Amelia's mother's acquaintances were so very well-bred and ami-able, that they never spoke their minds to either the mother or the daughter about what they endured from the latter's rudeness, wilfulness, and powers of destruction. But this was not the case with the dogs, and they expressed their sentiments by many a growl and snap. At last one day Amelia was tor-menting a snow-white bull-dog (who was certainly as well-bred and as ami-able as any living creature in the kingdom), and she did not see that even his patience was becoming worn out. His pink nose became crimson with in-creased irritation, his upper lip twitched over his teeth, behind which he was rolling as many warning Rs as Amelia's mother herself. She finally held out a bun towards him, and just as he was about to take it, she snatched it away and kicked him instead. This fairly exasperated the bull-dog, and as Amelia would not let him bite the bun, he bit Amelia's leg.

Her mamma was so distressed that she fell into hysterics, and hardly knew what she was saying. She said the bull-dog must be shot for fear he should go mad, and Amelia's wound must be done with a red-hot poker for fear *she* should go mad (with hydrophobia). And as of course she couldn't bear the pain of this, she must have chloroform, and she would most probably die of that; for as one in several thousands dies annually under chloroform, it was evident that her chance of life was very small indeed. So, as the poor lady said, "Whether we shoot Amelia and burn the bull-dog—at least I mean shoot the bull-dog and burn Amelia with a red-hot poker—or leave it alone; and whether Amelia or the bull-dog has chloroform or bears it without—it seems to be death or madness everyway!"

And as the doctor did not come fast enough, she ran out without her bonnet to meet him, and Amelia's papa, who was very much distressed too, ran after her with her bonnet. Meanwhile the doctor came in by another way, found Amelia sitting on the dining-room floor with the bull-dog, and crying bitterly. She was telling him that they wanted to shoot him, but that they should not, for it was all her fault and not his. But she did not tell him that she was to be burnt with a red-hot poker, for she thought it might hurt his feelings. And then she wept afresh, and kissed the bull-dog, and the bull-dog kissed her with his red tongue, and rubbed his pink nose against her, and beat his own tail much harder on the floor than Amelia had ever hit it. She said the same things to the doctor, but she told him also that she was willing to be burnt without chloroform if it must be done, and if they would spare the bull-dog. And though she looked very white, she meant what she said.

But the doctor looked at her leg, and found it was only a snap, and not a deep wound; and then he looked at the bull-dog, and saw that so far from looking mad, he looked a great deal more sensible than anybody in the house. So he only washed Amelia's leg and bound it up, and she was not burnt with the poker, neither did she get hydrophobia; but she had got a good lesson on manners, and thenceforward she always behaved with the utmost propriety to animals, though she tormented her mother's friends as much as ever.

Now although Amelia's mamma's acquaintances were too polite to complain before her face, they made up for it by what they said behind her back. In allusion to the poor lady's ineffectual remonstrances, one gentleman said that the more mischief Amelia did, the dearer she seemed to grow to her mother. And somebody else replied that however dear she might be as a daughter, she was certainly a very *dear* friend, and proposed that they should send in a bill for all the damage she had done in the course of the year, as a round robin to her parents at Christmas. From which it may be seen that Amelia was not popular with her parents' friends, as (to do grown-up people justice) good children almost invariably are.

If she was not a favorite in the drawing-room, she was still less so in the nursery, where, besides all the hardships naturally belonging to attendance on a spoilt child, the poor nurse was kept, as she said, "on the continual go" by Amelia's reckless destruction of her clothes. It was not fair wear and tear, it was not an occasional fall in the mire, or an accidental rent or two during a game at "Hunt the Hare," but it was constant wilful destruction, which nurse had to repair as best she might. No entreaties would induce Amelia to "take care" of anything. She walked obstinately on the muddy side of the road when nurse pointed out the clean parts, kicking up the dirt with her feet; if she climbed a wall she never tried to free her dress if it had caught; on she rushed, and half a skirt might be left behind for any care she had in the matter. "They must be mended," or, "They must be washed," was all she thought about it.

"You seem to think things clean and mend themselves, Miss Amelia," said poor nurse one day.

"No, I don't," said Amelia, rudely. "I think you do them; what are you here for?"

But though she spoke in this insolent and unladylike fashion, Amelia really did not realize what the tasks were which her carelessness imposed on other people. When every hour of nurse's day had been spent in struggling to keep her wilful young lady regularly fed, decently dressed, and moderately well-behaved (except, indeed, those hours when her mother was fighting the same battle downstairs); and when at last, after the hardest struggle of all, she had been got to bed not more than two hours later than her appointed time, even then there was no rest for nurse. Amelia's mamma could at least lean back in her chair and have a quiet chat with her husband, which was not broken in upon every two minutes, and Amelia herself was asleep; but nurse must sit up for hours wearing out her eyes by the light of a tallow candle, in fine-darning great, jagged and most unnecessary holes in Amelia's muslin dresses. Or perhaps she had to wash and iron clothes for Amelia's wear next day. For sometimes she was so very destructive, that toward the end of the week she had used up all her clothes and had no clean ones to fall back upon.

Amelia's meals were another source of trouble. She would not wear a pinafore; if it had been put on, she would burst the strings, and perhaps in throwing it away knock her plate of mutton broth over the tablecloth and her own dress. Then she fancied first one thing and then another; she did not like this or that; she wanted a bit cut here and there. Her mamma used to begin by saying, "My dear-r-r-Ramelia, you must not be so wasteful," and she used to end by saying, "The dear child has positively no appetite"; which seemed to be a good reason for not wasting any more food upon her; but with Amelia's mamma it only meant that she might try a little cutlet and tomato sauce when she had half finished her roast beef, and that most of the cutlet and all the mashed potato might be exchanged for plum tart and custard; and that when she had spooned up the custard and played with the paste, and put the plum stones on the tablecloth, she might be tempted with a little

Stilton cheese and celery, and exchange that for anything that caught her fancy in the dessert dishes.

The nurse used to say, "Many a poor child would thank God for what you waste every meal time, Miss Amelia," and to quote a certain good old saying, "Waste not want not." But Amelia's mamma allowed her to send away on her plates what would have fed another child, day after day.

Under the Haycocks

It was summer, and haytime. Amelia had been constantly in the hayfield, and the haymakers had constantly wished that she had been anywhere else. She mislaid the rakes, nearly killed herself and several other persons with a fork, and overturned one haycock after another as fast as they were made. At tea time it was hoped that she would depart, but she teased her mamma to have tea brought into the field, and her mamma said, "The poor child must have a treat sometimes," and so it was brought out.

After this she fell off the haycart, and was a good deal shaken, but not hurt. So she was taken indoors, and the haymakers worked hard and cleared the field, all but a few cocks which were left till the morning.

The sun set, the dew fell, the moon rose. It was a lovely night. Amelia peeped from behind the blinds of the drawing-room windows, and saw four haycocks, each with a deep shadow reposing at its side. The rest of the field was swept clean, and looked pale in the moonshine. It was a lovely night.

"I want to go out," said Amelia. "They will take away those cocks before I can get at them in the morning, and there will be no more jumping and tumbling. I shall go out and have some fun now."

"My dear Amelia, you must not," said her mamma; and her papa added, "I won't hear of it." So Amelia went upstairs to grumble to nurse; but nurse only said, "Now, my dear Miss Amelia, do go quietly to bed, like a dear love. The field is all wet with dew. Besides, it's a moonlight night, and who knows what's abroad? You might see the fairies—bless us and sain us!—and what not. There's been a magpie hopping up and down near the house all day, and that's a sign of ill luck."

"I don't care for magpies," said Amelia; "I threw a stone at that one today."

And she left the nursery, and swung downstairs on the rail of the banisters. But she did not go into the drawing-room; she opened the front door and went out into the moonshine.

It was a lovely night. But there was something strange about it. Everything looked asleep, and yet seemed not only awake but watching. There was not a sound, and yet the air seemed full of half sounds. The child was quite alone, and yet at every step she fancied some one behind her, on one side of her, somewhere, and found it only a rustling leaf or a passing shadow. She was soon in the hayfield, where it was just the same; so that when she fancied that something green was moving near the first haycock she thought very little of it, till, coming closer, she plainly perceived by the moonlight a tiny man dressed in green, with a tall, pointed hat, and very, very long tips to his shoes, tying his shoestring with his foot on a stubble stalk. He had the most wizened of faces, and when he got angry with his shoe, he pulled so wry a grimace that it was quite laughable. At last he stood up, stepping carefully over the stubble, went up to the first haycock, and drawing out a hollow grass stalk blew upon it till his cheeks were puffed like footballs. And yet there was no sound, only a half-sound, as of a horn blown in the far distance, or in a dream. Presently the point of a tall hat, and finally just such another little weazened face poked out through the side of the haycock.

"Can we hold revel here to-night?" asked the little green man.

"That indeed you cannot," answered the other; "we have hardly room to turn round as it is, with all Amelia's dirty frocks."

"Ah, bah!" said the dwarf; and he walked on to the next haycock, Amelia cautiously following.

Here he blew again, and a head was put out as before; on which he said—

"Can we hold revel here to-night?"

"How is it possible?" was the reply, "when there is not a place where one can so much as set down an acorn cup, for Amelia's broken victuals."

"Fie! fie!" said the dwarf, and went on to the third, where all happened as before; and he asked the old question—

"Can we hold revel here to-night?"

"Can you dance on glass and crockery sherds?" inquired the other. "Amelia's broken gimcracks are everywhere."

"Pshaw!" snorted the dwarf, frowning terribly; and when he came to the fourth haycock he blew such an angry blast that the grass stalk split into seven pieces. But he met with no better success than before. Only the point of a hat came through the hay, and a feeble voice piped in tones of depression— "The broken threads would entangle our feet. It's all Amelia's fault. If we could only get hold of her!"

"If she's wise, she'll keep as far from these haycocks as she can," snarled the dwarf, angrily; and he shook his fist as much as to say, "If she did come, I should not receive her very pleasantly."

Now with Amelia, to hear that she had better not do something, was to make her wish at once to do it; and as she was not at all wanting in courage, she pulled the dwarf's little cloak, just as she would have twitched her mother's shawl, and said (with that sort of snarly whine in which spoilt children generally speak), "Why shouldn't I come to the haycocks if I want to? They belong to my papa, and I shall come if I like. But you have no business here."

"Nightshade and hemlock!" ejaculated the little man, "you are not lacking in impudence. Perhaps your Sauciness is not quite aware how things are distributed in this world?" saying which he lifted his pointed shoes and began to dance and sing—

"All under the sun belongs to men,
And all under the moon to the fairies,
So, so, so! Ho, ho, ho!
All under the moon to the fairies."

As he sang "Ho, ho, ho!" the little man turned head over heels; and though by this time Amelia would gladly have got away, she could not, for the dwarf seemed to dance and tumble round her, and always to cut off the chance of escape; whilst numberless voices from all around seemed to join in the chorus, with—

"So, so, so! Ho, ho, ho!
All under the moon to the fairies."

"And now," said the little man, "to work! And you have plenty of work before you, so trip on, to the first haycock."

"I shan't!" said Amelia.

"On with you!" repeated the dwarf.

"I won't!" said Amelia.

But the little man, who was behind her, pinched her funny-bone with his lean fingers, and, as everybody knows, that is agony; so Amelia ran on, and tried to get away. But when she went too fast, the dwarf trod on her heels with his long-pointed shoe, and if she did not go fast enough, he pinched her funny-bone. So for once in her life she was obliged to do as she was told. As they ran, tall hats and wizened faces were popped out on all sides of the haycocks, like blanched almonds on a tipsy cake; and whenever the dwarf pinched Amelia, or trod on her heels, they cried "Ho, ho, ho!" with such horrible contortions as they laughed, that it was hideous to behold.

"Here is Amelia!" shouted the dwarf when they reached the first haycock.

"Ho, ho, ho!" laughed all the others, as they poked out here and there from the hay.

"Bring a stock," said the dwarf; on which the hay was lifted, and out ran six or seven dwarfs, carrying what seemed to Amelia to be a little girl like herself. And when she looked closer, to her horror and surprise the figure was exactly like her—it was her own face, clothes, and everything.

"Shall we kick it into the house?" said the goblins.

"No," said the dwarf; "lay it down by the haycock. The father and mother are coming to seek her now."

When Amelia heard this she began to shriek for help; but she was pushed into the haycock, where her loudest cries sounded like the chirruping of a grasshopper.

It was really a fine sight to see the inside of the cock.

Farmers do not like to see flowers in a hayfield, but the fairies do. They had arranged all the buttercups, &c., in patterns on the haywalls; bunches of meadowsweet swung from the roof like censers, and perfumed the air; and the ox-eye daisies which formed the ceiling gave a light like stars. But Amelia cared for none of this. She only struggled to peep through the hay, and she did see her father and mother and nurse come down the lawn, followed by the other servants, looking for her. When they saw the stock they ran to raise it with exclamations of pity and surprise. The stock moaned faintly, and Amelia's mamma wept, and Amelia herself shouted with all her might.

"What's that?" said her mamma. (It is not easy to deceive a mother.)

"Only the grasshoppers, my dear," said papa. "Let us get the poor child home."

The stock moaned again, and the mother said, "Oh dear! Oh dear-r-Ramelia!" and followed in tears.

"Rub her eyes," said the dwarf; on which Amelia's eyes were rubbed with some ointment, and when she took a last peep, she could see that the stock was nothing but a hairy imp with a face like the oldest and most grotesque of apes.

"——and send her below"; said the dwarf. On which the field opened, and Amelia was pushed underground.

She found herself on a sort of open heath, where no houses were to be seen. Of course there was no moonshine, and yet it was neither daylight nor dark. There was as the light of early dawn, and every sound was at once clear and dreamy, like the first sounds of the day coming through the fresh air before sunrise. Beautiful flowers crept over the heath, whose tints were constantly changing in the subdued light; and as the hues changed and blended, the flowers gave forth different perfumes. All would have been charming but that at every few paces the paths were blocked by large clothes-baskets full of dirty frocks. And the frocks were Amelia's. Torn, draggled, wet, covered with sand, mud, and dirt of all kinds, Amelia recognized them.

"You've got to wash them all," said the dwarf, who was behind her as usual; "that's what you've come down for—not because your society is particularly pleasant. So the sooner you begin the better."

"I can't," said Amelia (she had already learnt that "I won't" is not an answer for every one); "send them up to nurse, and she'll do them. It is her business."

"What nurse can do she has done, and now it's time for you to begin," said the dwarf. "Sooner or later the mischief done by spoilt children's wilful disobedience comes back on their own hands. Up to a certain point we help them, for we love children, and we are wilful ourselves. But there are limits to everything. If you can't wash your dirty frocks, it is time you learnt to do so, if only that you may know what the trouble is you impose on other people. *She* will teach you."

The dwarf kicked out his foot in front of him, and pointed with his long toe to a woman who sat by a fire made upon the heath, where a pot was suspended from crossed poles. It was like a bit of a gipsy encampment, and the woman seemed to be a real woman, not a fairy—which was the case, as Amelia afterwards found. She had lived underground for many years, and was the dwarfs' servant.

And this was how it came about that Amelia had to wash her dirty frocks. Let any little girl try to wash one of her dresses; not to half wash it, not to leave it stained with dirty water, but to wash it quite clean. Let her then try to starch and iron it—in short, to make it look as if it had come from the laundress—and she will have some idea of what poor Amelia had to learn to do. There was no help for it. When she was working she very seldom saw the dwarfs; but if she were idle or stubborn, or had any hopes of getting away, one was sure to start up at her elbow and pinch her funny-bone, or poke her in the ribs, till she did her best. Her back ached with stooping over the wash-tub; her hands and arms grew wrinkled with soaking in hot soapsuds, and sore with rubbing. Whatever she did not know how to do, the woman of the heath taught her. At first, whilst Amelia was sulky, the woman of the heath was sharp and cross; but when Amelia became willing and obedient, she was good-natured, and even helped her.

The first time that Amelia felt hungry she asked for some food.

"By all means," said one of the dwarfs; "there is plenty down here which belongs to you"; and he led her away till they came to a place like the first, except that it was covered with plates of broken meats; all the bits of good meat, pie, pudding, bread and butter, &c., that Amelia had wasted beforetime.

"I can't eat cold scraps like these," said Amelia turning away.

"Then what did you ask for food for before you were hungry?" screamed the dwarf, and he pinched her and sent her about her business.

After a while she became so famished that she was glad to beg humbly to be allowed to go for food; and she ate a cold chop and the remains of a rice pudding with thankfulness. How delicious they tasted! She was surprised herself at the good things she had rejected. After a time she fancied she would like to warm up some of the cold meat in a pan, which the woman of the heath used to cook her own dinner in, and she asked for leave to do so.

"You may do anything you like to make yourself comfortable, if you do it yourself," said she; and Amelia, who had been watching her for many times, became quite expert in cooking up the scraps.

As there was no real daylight underground, so also there was no night. When the old woman was tired she lay down and had a nap, and when she thought that Amelia had earned a rest, she allowed her to do the same. It was never cold, and it never rained, so they slept on the heath among the flowers.

They say that "It's a long lane that has no turning," and the hardest tasks come to an end some time, and Amelia's dresses were clean at last; but then a more wearisome work was before her. They had to be mended. Amelia looked at the jagged rents made by the hedges; the great gaping holes in front where she had put her foot through; the torn tucks and gathers. First she wept, then she bitterly regretted that she had so often refused to do her sewing at home that she was very awkward with her needle. Whether she ever would have got through this task alone is doubtful, but she had by this time become so well-behaved and willing that the old woman was kind to her, and, pitying her blundering attempts, she helped her a great deal; whilst Amelia would cook the old woman's victuals, or repeat stories and pieces of poetry to amuse her.

"How glad I am that I ever learnt anything!" thought the poor child; "everything one learns seems to come in useful some time."

At last the dresses were finished.

"Do you think I shall be allowed to go home now?" Amelia asked of the woman of the heath.

"Not yet," said she; "you have got to mend the broken gimcracks next."

"But when I have done all my tasks," Amelia said; "will they let me go then?"

"That depends," said the woman, and she sat silent over the fire; but Amelia wept so bitterly, that she pitied her and said—"Only dry your eyes, for the fairies hate tears, and I will tell you all I know and do the best for you I can. You see, when you first came you were—excuse me!—such an unlicked cub; such a peevish, selfish, wilful, useless, and ill-mannered little miss, that neither the fairies nor anybody else were likely to keep you any longer than necessary. But now you are such a willing, handy, and civil little thing, and so pretty and graceful withal, that I think it is very likely that they will want to keep you altogether. I think you had better make up your mind to it. They are kindly little folk, and will make a pet of you in the end."

"Oh, no, no!" moaned poor Amelia; "I want to be with my mother, my poor dear mother! I want to make up for being a bad child so long. Besides, surely that 'stock,' as they called her, will want to come back to her own people."

"As to that," said the woman, "after a time the stock will affect mortal illness, and will then take possession of the first black cat she sees, and in that shape leave the house, and come home. But the figure that is like you will remain lifeless in the bed, and will be duly buried. Then your people, believing you to be dead, will never look for you, and you will always remain here. However, as this distresses you so, I will give you some advice. Can you dance?"

"Yes," said Amelia; "I did attend pretty well to my dancing lessons. I was considered rather clever about it."

"At any spare moments you find," continued the woman, "dance, dance all your dances, and as well as you can. The dwarfs love dancing."

"And then?" said Amelia.

"Then, perhaps some night they will take you up to dance with them in the meadows above ground."

"But I could not get away. They would tread on my heels—oh! I could never escape them."

"I know that," said the woman; "your only chance is this. If ever, when dancing in the meadows, you can find a four-leaved clover, hold it in your hand and wish to be at home. Then no one can stop you. Meanwhile I advise you to seem happy, that they may think you are content, and have forgotten the world. And dance, above all, dance!"

And Amelia, not to be behindhand, began then and there to dance some pretty figures on the heath. As she was dancing the dwarf came by.

"Ho, ho!" said he, "you can dance, can you?"

"When I am happy, I can," said Amelia, performing several graceful movements as she spoke.

"What are you pleased about now?" snapped the dwarf, suspiciously.

"Have I not reason?" said Amelia. "The dresses are washed and mended."

"Then up with them!" returned the dwarf. On which half a dozen elves popped the whole lot into a big basket and kicked them up into the world, where they found their way to the right wardrobes somehow.

As the woman of the heath had said, Amelia was soon set to a new task.

When she bade the old woman farewell, she asked if she could do nothing for her if ever she got at liberty herself.

"Can I do nothing to get you back to your old home?" Amelia cried, for she thought of others now as well as herself.

"No, thank you," returned the old woman; "I am used to this, and do not care to return. I have been here a long time—how long I do not know; for as there is neither daylight nor dark we have no measure of time—long, I am sure, very long. The light and noise up yonder would now be too much for me. But I wish you well, and, above all, remember to dance!"

The new scene of Amelia's labors was a more rocky part of the heath, where grey granite boulders served for seats and tables, and sometimes for workshops and anvils, as in one place, where a grotesque and grimy old dwarf sat forging rivets to mend china and glass. A fire in the hollow of the boulder served for a forge, and on the flatter part was his anvil. The rocks were covered in all directions with the knick-knacks, ornaments, &c., that Amelia had at various times destroyed.

"If you please, sir," she said to the dwarf, "I am Amelia."

The dwarf left off blowing at his forge and looked at her.

"Then I wonder you're not ashamed of yourself," said he.

"I am ashamed of myself," said poor Amelia, "very much ashamed. I should like to mend these things if I can."

"Well, you can't say more than that," said the dwarf, in a mollified tone, for he was a kindly little creature; "bring that china bowl here, and I'll show you how to set to work."

Poor Amelia did not get on very fast, but she tried her best. As to the dwarf, it was truly wonderful to see how he worked. Things seemed to mend themselves at his touch, and he was so proud of his skill, and so particular, that he generally did over again the things which Amelia had done after her fashion. The first time he gave her a few minutes in which to rest and amuse herself, she held out her little skirt, and began one of her prettiest dances.

"Rivets and trivets!" shrieked the little man, "How you dance! It is charming! I say it is charming! On with you! Fa, la fa! La, fa la! It gives me the fidgets in my shoe points to see you!" and forthwith down he jumped, and began capering about.

"I am a good dancer myself," said the little man. "Do you know the 'Hop, Skip, and a Jump' dance?"

"I do not think I do," said Amelia.

"It is much admired," said the dwarf, "when I dance it"; and he thereupon tucked up the little leathern apron in which he worked, and performed some curious antics on one leg.

"That is the Hop," he observed, pausing for a moment. "The Skip is thus. You throw out your left leg as high and as far as you can, and as you drop on the toe of your left foot you fling out the right leg in the same manner, and so on. This is the Jump," with which he turned a somersault and disappeared from view. When Amelia next saw him he was sitting cross legged on his boulder.

"Good, wasn't it?" he said.

"Wonderful!" Amelia replied.

"Now it's your turn again," said the dwarf.

But Amelia cunningly replied—"I'm afraid I must go on with my work."

"Pshaw!" said the little tinker. "Give me your work. I can do more in a minute than you in a month, and better to boot. Now dance again."

"Do you know this?" said Amelia, and she danced a few paces of a polka mazurka.

"Admirable!" cried the little man. "Stay"—and he drew an old violin from behind the rock; "now dance again, and mark the time well, so that I may catch the measure, and then I will accompany you."

Which accordingly he did, improvising a very spirited tune, which had, however, the peculiar subdued and weird effect of all the other sounds in this strange region.

"The fiddle came from up yonder," said the little man. "It was smashed to atoms in the world and thrown away. But ho, ho, ho! There is nothing that I cannot mend, and a mended fiddle is an amended fiddle. It improves the tone. Now teach me that dance, and I will patch up all the rest of the gimcracks. Is it a bargain?"

"By all means," said Amelia; and she began to explain the dance to the best of her ability.

"Charming! charming!" cried the dwarf. "We have no such dance ourselves. We only dance hand in hand, and round and round, when we dance together. Now I will learn the step, and then I will put my arm round your waist and dance with you."

Amelia looked at the dwarf. He was very smutty, and old, and weazened. Truly, a queer partner! But "handsome is that handsome does"; and he had done her a good turn. So when he had learnt the step, he put his arm round Amelia's waist and they danced together. His shoe points were very much in the way, but otherwise he danced very well.

Then he set to work on the broken ornaments, and they were all very soon "as good as new." But they were not kicked up into the world, for, as the dwarfs said, they would be sure to break on the road. So they kept them and used them; and I fear that no benefit came from the little tinker's skill to Amelia's mamma's acquaintance in this matter.

"Have I any other tasks?" Amelia inquired.

"One more," said the dwarfs; and she was led farther on to a smooth mossy green, thickly covered with what looked like bits of broken thread. One would think it had been a milliner's work-room from the first invention of needles and thread.

"What are these?" Amelia asked.

"They are the broken threads of all the conversations you have interrupted," was the reply; "and pretty dangerous work it is to dance here now, with threads getting round one's shoe points. Dance a hornpipe in a herring-net, and you'll know what it is!"

Amelia began to pick up the threads, but it was tedious work. She had cleared a yard or two, and her back was aching terribly, when she heard the fiddle and the mazurka behind her; and looking round she saw the old dwarf, who was playing away, and making the most hideous grimaces as his chin pressed the violin.

"Dance, my lady, dance!" he shouted.

"I do not think I can," said Amelia; "I am so weary with stooping over my work."

"Then rest a few minutes," he answered, "and I will play you a jig. A jig is a beautiful dance, such life, such spirit! So!"

And he played faster and faster, his arm, his face, his fiddle-bow all seemed working together; and as he played, the threads danced themselves into three heaps.

"That is not bad, is it?" said the dwarf; "and now for our own dance," and he played the mazurka. "Get the measure well into your head. "Lâ, la fǎ lâ! Lâ, la fǎ lâ! So!"

And throwing away his fiddle, he caught Amelia round the waist, and they danced as before. After which, she had no difficulty in putting the three heaps of thread into a basket.

"Where are these to be kicked to?" asked the young goblins.

"To the four winds of heaven," said the old dwarf. "There are very few drawing room conversations worth putting together a second time. They are not like old china bowls."

By Moonlight

Thus Amelia's tasks were ended; but not a word was said of her return home. The dwarfs were now very kind, and made so much of her that it was evident that they meant her to remain with them. Amelia often cooked for them, and she danced and played with them, and never showed a sign of discontent; but her heart ached for home, and when she was alone she would bury her face in the flowers and cry for her mother.

One day she overheard the dwarfs in consultation.

"The moon is full to-morrow," said one—("Then I have been a month down here," thought Amelia; "it was full moon that night")—"shall we dance in the Mary Meads?"

"By all means," said the old tinker dwarf; "and we will take Amelia, and dance my dance."

"Is it safe?" said another.

"Look how content she is," said the old dwarf, "and, oh! how she dances; my feet tickle at the bare thought."

"The ordinary run of mortals do not see us," continued the objector; "but she is visible to any one. And there are men and women who wander in the moonlight, and the Mary Meads are near her old home."

"I will make her a hat of touchwood," said the old dwarf, "so that even if she is seen it will look like a will-o'-the-wisp bobbing up and down. If she does not come, I will not. I must dance my dance. You do not know what it is! We two alone move together with a grace which even here is remarkable. But when I think that up yonder we shall have attendant shadows echoing our movements, I long for the moment to arrive."

"So be it," said the others; and Amelia wore the touchwood hat, and went up with them to the Mary Meads.

Amelia and the dwarf danced the mazurka, and their shadows, now as short as themselves, then long and gigantic, danced beside them. As the moon went down, and the shadows lengthened, the dwarf was in raptures.

"When one sees how colossal one's very shadow is," he remarked, "one knows one's true worth. You alsŏ have a goŏd shadow. We are partners in the dance, and I think we will be partners for life. But I have not full considered the matter, so this is not to be regarded as a formal proposal." And he continued to dance, singing, "Lâ, la fă, lâ, lâ, la, fă, lâ." It was highly admired.

The Mary Meads lay a little below the house where Amelia's parents lived, and once during the night her father, who was watching by the sick bed of the stock, looked out of the window.

"How lovely the moonlight is!" he murmured; "but, dear me! there is a will-o'-the-wisp yonder. I had no idea the Mary Meads were so damp." Then he pulled the blind down and went back into the room.

As for poor Amelia, she found no four-leaved clover, and at cockcrow they all went underground.

"We will dance on Hunch Hill to-morrow," said the dwarfs.

All went as before; not a clover plant of any kind did Amelia see, and at cockcrow the revel broke up.

On the following night they danced in the hayfield. The old stubble was now almost hidden by green clover. There was a grand fairy dance—a round dance, which does not mean, as with us, a dance for two partners, but a dance where all join hands and dance round and round in a circle with appropriate antics. Round they went, faster and faster, the pointed shoes now meeting in the centre like the spokes of a wheel, now kicked out behind like spikes, and then scamper, caper, hurry! They seemed to fly, when suddenly the ring broke at one corner, and nothing being stronger than its weakest point, the whole circle were sent flying over the field.

"Ho, ho, ho!" laughed the dwarfs, for they are good humored little folk, and do not mind a tumble.

"Ha, ha, ha!" laughed Amelia, for she had fallen with her fingers on a four-leaved clover.

She put it behind her back, for the old tinker dwarf was coming up to her, wiping the mud from his face with his leathern apron.

"Now for our dance!" he shrieked. "And I have made up my mind—partners now and partners always. You are incomparable. For three hundred years I have not met with your equal."

But Amelia held the four-leaved clover above her head, and cried from her very heart—"I want to go home!"

The dwarf gave a hideous yell of disappointment, and at this instant the stock came stumbling head over heels into the midst, crying—"Oh! the pills, the powders, and the draughts! oh, the lotions and embrocations! oh, the blisters, the poultices, and the plasters! men may well be so short-lived!"

And Amelia found herself in bed in her own home.

At Home Again

By the side of Amelia's bed stood a little table, on which were so many big bottles of medicine, that Amelia smiled to think of all the stock must have had to swallow during the month past. There was an open Bible on it too, in which Amelia's mother was reading, whilst tears trickled slowly down her pale cheeks. The poor lady looked so thin and ill, so worn with sorrow and watching, that Amelia's heart smote her, as if some one had given her a sharp blow.

"Mamma, mamma! Mother, my dear, dear mother!"

The tender, humble, loving tone of voice was so unlike Amelia's old imperious snarl, that her mother hardly recognized it; and when she saw Amelia's eyes full of intelligence instead of the delirium of fever, and that (though older and thinner and rather pale) she looked wonderfully well, the poor worn-out lady could hardly restrain herself from falling into hysterics for very joy.

"Dear mamma, I want to tell you all about it," said Amelia, kissing the kind hand that stroked her brow.

But it appeared that the doctor had forbidden conversation; and though Amelia knew it would do her no harm, she yielded to her mother's wish and lay still and silent.

"Now, my love, it is time to take your medicine."

But Amelia pleaded—"Oh, mamma, indeed I don't want any medicine. I am quite well, and would like to get up."

"Ah, my dear child!" cried her mother, "what I have suffered in inducing you to take your medicine, and yet see what good it has done you."

"I hope you will never suffer any more from my wilfulness," said Amelia; and she swallowed two tablespoonfuls of a mixture labelled, "To be well shaken before taken," without even a wry face.

Presently the doctor came.

"You're not so very angry at the sight of me to-day my little lady, eh?" he said.

"I have not seen you for a long time," said Amelia "but I know you have been here, attending a stock who looked like me. If your eyes had been touched with fairy ointment, however, you would have been aware that it was a fairy imp, and a very ugly one, covered with hair. I have been living in terror lest it should go back underground in the shape of a black cat. However, thanks to the four-leaved clover, and the old woman of the heath, I am at home again."

On hearing this rhodomontade, Amelia's mother burst into tears, for she thought the poor child was still raving with fever. But the doctor smiled pleasantly, and said—"Ay, ay, to be sure," with a little nod, as one should say, "We know all about it"; and laid two fingers in a casual manner on Amelia's wrist.

"But she is wonderfully better, madam," he said afterwards to her mamma; "the brain has been severely tried, but she is marvellously improved: in fact, it is an effort of nature, a most favorable effort, and we can but assist the rally; we will change the medicine." Which he did, and very wisely assisted nature with a bottle of pure water flavored with tincture of roses.

"And it was so very kind of him to give me his directions in poetry," said Amelia's mamma; "for I told him my memory, which is never good, seemed going completely, from anxiety, and if I had done anything wrong just now, I should never have forgiven myself. And I always found poetry easier to remember than prose,"—which puzzled everybody, the doctor included, till it appeared that she had ingeniously discovered a rhyme in his orders.

> "To be kept cool and quiet,
> With light nourishing diet."

Under which treatment Amelia was soon pronounced to be well.

She made another attempt to relate her adventures, but she found that not even the nurse would believe in them.

"Why you told me yourself I might meet with the fairies," said Amelia, reproachfully.

"So I did, my dear," nurse replied, "and they say that it's that put it into your head. And I'm sure what you say about the dwarfs and all is as good as a printed book, though you can't think that ever I would have let any dirty clothes store up like that, let alone your frocks, my dear. But for pity sake, Miss Amelia, don't go on about it to your mother, for she thinks you'll never get your senses right again, and she has fretted enough about you, poor lady; and nursed you night and day till she is nigh worn out. And anybody can see you've been ill, miss, you've grown so, and look paler and older like. Well, to be sure, as you say, if you'd been washing and working for a month in a place without a bit of sun, or a bed to lie on, and scraps to eat, it would be enough to do it; and many's the poor child that has to, and gets worn and old before her time. But, my dear, whatever you think, give in to your mother; you'll never repent giving in to your mother, my dear, the longest day you live."

So Amelia kept her own counsel. But she had one confidant.

When her parents brought the stock home on the night of Amelia's visit to the haycocks, the bull-dog's conduct had been most strange. His usual good-humor appeared to have been exchanged for incomprehensible fury, and he was with difficulty prevented from flying at the stock, who on her part showed an anger and dislike fully equal to his.

Finally the bull-dog had been confined in the stable where he remained the whole month, uttering from time to time such howls, with his snub nose in the air, that poor nurse quite gave up hope of Amelia's recovery.

"For indeed, my dear, they do say that a howling dog is a sign of death, and it was more than I could abear."

But the day after Amelia's return, as nurse was leaving the room with a tray which had carried some of the light nourishing diet ordered by the doctor, she was knocked down, tray and all, by the bull-dog, who came tearing into the room, dragging a chain and dirty rope after him, and nearly choked by the desperate efforts which had finally effected his escape from the stable. And he jumped straight on to the end of Amelia's bed, where he lay, *thudding* with his tail, and giving short whines of ecstasy. And as Amelia begged that he might be left, and as it was evident that he would bite any one who tried to take him away, he became established as chief nurse. When Amelia's meals were brought to the bedside on a tray, he kept a fixed eye on the plates, as if to see if her appetite were improving. And he would even take a snack himself, with an air of great affability.

And when Amelia told him her story, she could see by his eyes, and his nose, and his ears, and his tail, and the way he growled whenever the stock was mentioned, that he knew all about it. As, on the other hand, he had no difficulty in conveying to her by sympathetic whines the sentiment "Of course I would have helped you if I could; but they tied me up, and this disgusting old rope has taken me a month to worry through."

So, in spite of the past, Amelia grew up good and gentle, unselfish and considerate for others. She was unusually clever, as those who have been with the "Little People" are said always to be.

And she became so popular with her mother's acquaintances that they said—"We will no longer call her Amelia, for it was a name we learnt to dislike, but we will call her Amy, that is to say, 'Beloved.'"

* * * * * *

"And did my godmother's grandmother believe that Amelia had really been with the fairies, or did she think it was all fever ravings?"

"That, indeed, she never said, but she always observed that it was a pleasant tale with a good moral, which was surely enough for anybody."

Speaking Likenesses

CHRISTINA ROSSETTI

ILLUSTRATIONS BY ARTHUR HUGHES

1874

*B*RITISH WRITER AND POET Christina Georgina Rossetti (1830-1894) was a quiet, reclusive, and deeply spiritual woman. A close friend of Jean Ingelow, she was the author of several works for children, including *Goblin Market* (1862) and *Sing-Song* (1872). In a letter to her brother, Dante Gabriel Rossetti, the Pre-Raphaelite poet and painter, she describes *Speaking Likenesses*[1] as "merely a Christmas trifle, would-be in the *Alice* style, with an eye to the market."[2] Though it does share certain similarities with *Alice in Wonderland*—the dream-fantasy form, violent and threatening talking animals and animated objects, and abrupt changes in size and location—*Speaking Likenesses* is a highly original work that aggressively critiques and satirizes not only the conventions of the Victorian fairy tale and domestic fiction, but the gender conventions that inform them. *Speaking Likenesses* consists of three unrelated stories, the first of which is included here, which are told to a group of five girls by their aunt as they all sit and sew. The girls' constant interruptions to offer absurd questions and comments on the tales, as well as the stern aunt's equally absurd admonishments, ridicule sentimental Victorian idealization of young girls,[3] and the grotesque exaggerations of the aunt's tales poke fun at moralistic "improving" stories considered suitable for children. The first story describes eight-year-old Flora's disastrous birthday party, and her subsequent nightmare in which her bickering guests all become "speaking likenesses," distorted caricatures of their worst qualities.

---

1. The novel was originally titled *Nowhere,* though the title was later changed (possibly to avoid similarity to Tom Hood's *From Nowhere to the North Pole,* which was being released at about the same time). Lona Mosk Packer, ed., *The Rossetti-Macmillan Letters* (Berkeley: U of California P, 1963) 100, 101.
2. William Michael Rossetti, ed., *The Family Letters of Christina Rossetti* (New York: Scribner's, 1908) 44.
3. Rossetti indicates these interjections with brackets.

Speaking Likenesses

COME SIT ROUND ME, my dear little girls, and I will tell you a story. Each of you bring her sewing, and let Ella take pencils and colour-box, and try to finish some one drawing of the many she has begun. What Maude! pouting over that nice clean white stocking because it wants a darn? Put away your pout and pull out your needle, my dear; for pouts make a sad beginning to my story. And yet not an inappropriate beginning, as some of you may notice as I go on. Silence! Attention! All eyes on occupations, not on me lest I should feel shy! Now I start my knitting and my story together.

* * * * * *

51

Whoever saw Flora on her birthday morning, at half-past seven o'clock on that morning, saw a very pretty sight. Eight years old to a minute, and not awake yet. Her cheeks were plump and pink, her light hair was all tumbled, her little red lips were held together as if to kiss some one; her eyes also, if you could have seen them, were blue and merry, but for the moment they had gone fast asleep and out of sight under fat little eyelids. Wagga the dog was up and about, Muff the cat was up and about, chirping birds were up and about; or if they were mere nestlings and so could not go about (supposing, that is, that there were still a few nestlings so far on in summer), at least they sat together wide awake in the nest, with wide open eyes and most of them with wide open beaks, which was all they could do: only sleepy Flora slept on, and dreamed on, and never stirred.

Her mother stooping over the child's soft bed woke her with a kiss. "Good morning, my darling, I wish you many and many happy returns of the day," said the kind, dear mother: and Flora woke up to a sense of sunshine, and of pleasure full of hope. To be eight years old when last night one was merely seven, this is pleasure: to hope for birthday presents without any doubt of receiving some, this also is pleasure. And doubtless you now think so, my children, and it is quite right that so you should think: yet I tell you, from the sad knowledge of my older experience, that to every one of you a day will most likely come when sunshine, hope, presents and pleasure will be worth nothing to you in comparison with the unattainable gift of your mother's kiss.

On the breakfast table lay presents for Flora: a story-book full of pictures from her father, a writing-case from her mother, a gilt pincushion like a hedgehog from nurse, a box of sugar-plums and a doll from Alfred her brother and Susan her sister; the most tempting of sugar-plums, the most beautiful of curly-pated dolls, they appeared in her eyes.

A further treat was in store. "Flora," said her mother, when admiration was at last silent and breakfast over: "Flora, I have asked Richard, George, Anne and Emily to spend the day with you and with Susan and Alfred. You are to be queen of the feast, because it is your birthday; and I trust you will all be very good and happy together."

Flora loved her brother and sister, her friend Emily, and her cousins Richard, George and Anne: indeed I think that with all their faults these children did really love each other. They had often played together before; and now if ever, surely on this so special occasion they would play pleasantly together. Well, we shall see.

Anne with her brothers arrived first: and Emily having sent to ask permission, made her appearance soon after accompanied by a young friend, who was spending the holidays with her, and whom she introduced as Serena.

[What an odd name, Aunt!—Yes, Clara, it is not a common name, but I knew a Serena once; though she was not at all like this Serena, I am happy to say.]

Emily brought Flora a sweet-smelling nosegay; and Serena protested that Flora was the most charming girl she had ever met, except of course dearest Emily.

"Love me," said Serena, throwing her arms round her small hostess and giving her a clinging kiss: "I will love you so much if you will only let me love you."

The house was a most elegant house, the lawn was a perfect park, the elder brother and sister frightened her by their cleverness: so exclaimed Serena: and for the moment silly little Flora felt quite tall and superior, and allowed herself to be loved very graciously.

After the arrivals and the settling down, there remained half-an-hour before dinner, during which to cultivate acquaintance and exhibit presents. Flora displayed her doll and handed round her sugar-plum box. "You took more than I did and it isn't fair," grumbled George at Richard: but Richard retorted, "Why, I saw you picking out the big ones." "Oh," whined Anne, "I'm sure there were no big ones left when they came to me." And Emily put in with a smile of superiority: "Stuff, Anne: you got the box before Serena and I did, and *we* don't complain." "But there wasn't one," persisted Anne. "But there were dozens and dozens," mimicked George, "only you're such a greedy little baby." "Not one," whimpered Anne. Then Serena remarked soothingly: "The sugar-plums were most delicious, and now let us admire the lovely doll. Why, Flora, she must have cost pounds and pounds."

Flora, who had begun to look rueful, brightened up: "I don't know what she cost, but her name is Flora, and she has red boots with soles. Look at me opening and shutting her eyes, and I can make her say Mamma. Is she not a beauty?" "I never saw half such a beauty," replied smooth Serena. Then the party sat down to dinner.

Was it fact? Was it fancy? Each dish in turn was only fit to be found fault with. Meat underdone, potatoes overdone, beans splashy, jam tart not sweet enough, fruit all stone; covers clattering, glasses reeling, a fork or two dropping on the floor. Were these things really so? or would even finest strawberries and richest cream have been found fault with, thanks to the children's mood that day?

[Were the dishes all wrong, Aunt?—I fancy not, Ella; at least, not more so than things often are in this world without upsetting every one's patience. But hear what followed.]

Sad to say, what followed was a wrangle. An hour after dinner blindman's

buff in the garden began well and promised well: why could it not go on well? Ah, why indeed? for surely before now in that game toes have been trodden on, hair pulled, and small children overthrown. Flora fell down and accused Alfred of tripping her up, Richard bawled out that George broke away when fairly caught, Anne when held tight muttered that Susan could see in spite of bandaged eyes. Susan let go, Alfred picked up his little sister, George volunteered to play blindman in Susan's stead: but still pouting and grumbling showed their ugly faces, and tossed the apple of discord to and fro as if it had been a pretty plaything.

[What apple, Aunt?—The Apple of Discord, Clara, which is a famous apple your brothers would know all about, and you may ask them some day. Now I go on.]

Would you like, any of you, a game at hide-and-seek in a garden, where there are plenty of capital hiding-places and all sorts of gay flowers to glance at while one goes seeking? I should have liked such a game, I assure you, forty years ago. But these children on this particular day could not find it in their hearts to like it. Oh dear no. Serena affected to be afraid of searching along the dusky yew alley unless Alfred went with her; and at the very same moment Flora was bent on having him lift her up to look down into a hollow tree in which it was quite obvious Susan could not possibly have hidden. "It's my birthday," cried Flora; "it's my birthday." George and Richard pushed each other roughly about till one slipped on the gravel walk and grazed his hands, when both turned cross and left off playing. At last in sheer despair Susan stepped out of her hiding-place behind the summer-house: but even then she did her best to please everybody, for she brought in her hand a basket full of ripe mulberries which she had picked up off the grass as she stood in hiding.

Then they all set to running races across the smooth sloping lawn: till Anne tumbled down and cried, though she was not a bit hurt; and Flora, who was winning the race against Anne, thought herself ill-used and so sat and sulked. Then Emily smiled, but not good-naturedly, George and Richard thrust each a finger into one eye and made faces at the two cross girls, Serena fanned herself, and Alfred looked at Susan, and Susan at Alfred, fairly at their wits' end.

An hour yet before tea-time: would another hour ever be over? Two little girls looking sullen, two boys looking provoking: the sight was not at all an encouraging one. At last Susan took pouting Flora and tearful Anne by the hand, and set off with them for a walk perforce about the grounds; whilst Alfred fairly dragged Richard and George after the girls, and Emily arm-in-arm with Serena strolled beside them.

The afternoon was sunny, shady, breezy, warm, all at once. Bees were humming and harvesting as any bee of sense must have done amongst so many blossoms: leafy boughs danced with their dancing shadows; bell flowers rang without clappers:—

[Could they, Aunt?—Well, not exactly, Maude: but you're coming to much more wonderful matters!]

Now and then a pigeon cooed its soft water-bottle note; and a long way off sheep stood bleating.

Susan let go the little hot hands she held, and began as she walked telling a story to which all her companions soon paid attention—all except Flora.

Poor little Flora: was this the end of her birthday? was she eight years old at last only for this? Her sugar-plums almost all gone and not cared for, her chosen tart not a nice one, herself so cross and miserable: is it really worth while to be eight years old and have a birthday, if this is what comes of it?

"—So the frog did not know how to boil the kettle; but he only replied: I can't bear hot water," went on Susan telling her story. But Flora had no heart to listen, or to care about the frog. She lagged and dropped behind not noticed by any one, but creeping along slowly and sadly by herself.

Down the yew alley she turned, and it looked dark and very gloomy as she passed out of the sunshine into the shadow. There were twenty yew trees on each side of the path, as she had counted over and over again a great many years ago when she was learning to count; but now at her right hand there stood twenty-one: and if the last tree was really a yew tree at all, it was at least a very odd one, for a lamp grew on its topmost branch. Never before either had the yew walk led to a door: but now at its further end stood a door with bell and knocker, and "Ring also" printed in black letters on a brass plate; all as plain as possible in the lamplight.

Flora stretched up her hand, and knocked and rang also.

She was surprised to feel the knocker shake hands with her, and to see the bell handle twist round and open the door. "Dear me," thought she, "why could not the door open itself instead of troubling the bell?" But she only said, "Thank you," and walked in.

The door opened into a large and lofty apartment, very handsomely furnished. All the chairs were stuffed arm-chairs, and moved their arms and shifted their shoulders to accommodate sitters. All the sofas arranged and rearranged their pillows as convenience dictated. Footstools glided about, and rose or sank to meet every length of leg. Tables were no less obliging, but ran on noiseless castors here or there when wanted. Tea-trays ready set out, saucers of strawberries, jugs of cream, and plates of cake, floated in, settled down, and floated out again empty, with considerable tact and good taste: they came and went through a square hole high up in one wall, beyond which I presume lay the kitchen. Two harmoniums, an accordion, a pair of kettledrums and a peal of bells played concerted pieces behind a screen, but kept silence during conversation. Photographs and pictures made the tour of the apartment, standing still when glanced at and going on when done with. In case of need the furniture flattened itself against the wall, and cleared the floor for a game, or I dare say for a dance. Of these remarkable details some struck Flora in the first few minutes after her arrival, some came to light as time went on. The only uncomfortable point in the room, that is, as to furniture, was that both ceiling and walls were lined throughout with looking-glasses: but at first this did not strike Flora as any disadvantage; indeed she thought it quite delightful, and took a long look at her little self full length.

[Jane and Laura, don't *quite* forget the pocket-handkerchiefs you sat down to hem. See how hard Ella works at her fern leaves, and what pains she is taking to paint them nicely. Yes, Maude, that darn will do: now your task is ended, but if I were you I would help Clara with hers.]

The room was full of boys and girls, older and younger, big and little. They all sat drinking tea at a great number of different tables; here half a dozen children sitting together, here more or fewer; here one child would preside all alone at a table just the size for one comfortably. I should tell you that the tables were like telescope tables; only they expanded and contracted of themselves without extra pieces, and seemed to study everybody's convenience.

Every single boy and every single girl stared hard at Flora and went on staring: but not one of them offered her a chair, or a cup of tea, or anything else whatever. She grew very red and uncomfortable under so many staring pairs of eyes: when a chair did what it could to relieve her embarrassment by pressing gently against her till she sat down. It then bulged out its own back comfortably into hers, and drew in its arms to suit her small size. A footstool grew somewhat taller beneath her feet. A table ran up with tea for one; a cream-jug toppled over upon a saucerful of strawberries, and then righted itself again; the due quantity of sifted sugar sprinkled itself over the whole.

[How could it sprinkle itself?—Well, Jane, let us suppose it sprang up in its china basin like a fountain; and overflowed on one side only, but that of course the right side, whether it was right or left.]

Flora could not help thinking everyone very rude and ill-natured to go on staring without speaking, and she felt shy at having to eat with so many eyes upon her: still she was hot and thirsty, and the feast looked most tempting. She took up in a spoon one large, very large strawberry with plenty of cream; and was just putting it into her mouth when a voice called out crossly: "You shan't, they're mine." The spoon dropped from her startled hand, but without any clatter: and Flora looked round to see the speaker.

[Who was it? Was it a boy or a girl?—Listen, and you shall hear, Laura.]

The speaker was a girl enthroned in an extra high armchair; with a stool as high as an ottoman under her feet, and a table as high as a chest of drawers in front of her. I suppose as she had it so she liked it so, for I am sure all the furniture laid itself out to be obliging. Perched upon her hair she wore a coronet made of tinsel; her face was a red face with a scowl: sometimes perhaps she looked nice and pretty, this time she looked ugly. "You shan't, they're mine," she repeated in a cross grumbling voice: "it's my birthday, and everything is mine."

Flora was too honest a little girl to eat strawberries that were not given her: nor could she, after this, take even a cup of tea without leave. Not to tantalize her, I suppose, the table glided away with its delicious untasted load; whilst the armchair gave her a very gentle hug as if to console her.

If she could only have discovered the door Flora would have fled through it back into the gloomy yew-tree walk, and there have moped in solitude, rather than remain where she was not made welcome: but either the door was gone, or else it was shut to and lost amongst the multitude of mirrors. The birthday Queen, reflected over and over again in five hundred mirrors, looked frightful, I do assure you: and for one minute I am sorry to say that Flora's fifty million-fold face appeared flushed and angry too; but she soon tried to smile good-humouredly and succeeded, though she could not manage to feel very merry.

[But, Aunt, how came she to have fifty million faces? I don't understand.—Because in such a number of mirrors there were not merely simple reflections, but reflections of reflections, and reflections of reflections of reflections, and so on and on and on, over and over again, Maude: don't you see?]

The meal was ended at last: most of the children had eaten and stuffed quite greedily; poor Flora alone had not tasted a morsel. Then with a word and I think a kick from the Queen, her high footstool scudded away into a corner: and all the furniture taking the hint arranged itself as flat as possible round the room, close up against the walls.

[And across the door?—Why, yes, I suppose it may have done so, Jane: such active and willing furniture could never be in the way anywhere.—And was there a chimney corner?—No, I think not: that afternoon was warm we know, and there may have been a different apartment for winter. At any rate, as this is all make-believe, I say No. Attention!]

All the children now clustered together in the middle of the empty floor; elbowing and jostling each other, and disputing about what game should first be played at. Flora, elbowed and jostled in their midst, noticed points of appearance that quite surprised her. Was it themselves, or was it their clothes? (only who indeed would wear such clothes, so long as there was another suit in the world to put on?) One boy bristled with prickly quills like a porcupine, and raised or depressed them at pleasure; but he usually kept them pointed outwards. Another instead of being rounded like most people was facetted at very sharp angles. A third caught in everything he came near, for he was hung round with hooks like fishhooks. One girl exuded a sticky fluid and came off on the fingers; another, rather smaller, was slimy and slipped through the hands. Such exceptional features could not but prove inconvenient, yet patience and forbearance might still have done something towards keeping matters smooth: but these unhappy children seemed not to know what forbearance was; and as to patience, they might have answered me nearly in the words of a celebrated man—"Madam, I never saw patience."

[Who was the celebrated man, Aunt?—Oh, Clara, you an English girl and not know Lord Nelson! But I go on.]

"Tell us some new game," growled Hooks threateningly, catching in Flora's hair and tugging to get loose.

Flora did not at all like being spoken to in such a tone, and the hook hurt her very much. Still, though she could not think of anything new, she tried to do her best, and in a timid voice suggested "Les Grâces."

"That's a girl's game," said Hooks contemptuously.

"It's as good any day as a boy's game," retorted Sticky.

"I wouldn't give *that* for your girl's games," snarled Hooks, endeavouring to snap his fingers, but entangling two hooks and stamping.

"Poor dear fellow!" drawled Slime, affecting sympathy.

"It's quite as good," harped on Sticky: "It's as good or better."

Angles caught and would have shaken Slime, but she slipped through his fingers demurely.

"Think of something else, and let it be new," yawned Quills, with quills laid for a wonder.

"I really don't know anything new," answered Flora half crying: and she was going to add, "But I will play with you at any game you like, if you will teach me"; when they all burst forth into a yell of "Cry, baby, cry!—Cry, baby, cry!"—They shouted it, screamed it, sang it: they pointed fingers, made grimaces, nodded heads at her. The wonder was she did not cry outright.

At length the Queen interfered: "Let her alone;—who's she? It's *my* birthday, and we'll play at Hunt the Pincushion."

So Hunt the Pincushion it was. This game is simple and demands only a moderate amount of skill. Select the smallest and weakest player (if possible let her be fat: a hump is best of all), chase her round and round the room, overtaking her at short intervals, and sticking pins into her here or there as it happens: repeat, till you choose to catch and swing her; which concludes the game. Short cuts, yells, and sudden leaps give spirit to the hunt.

[Oh, Aunt, what a horrid game! surely there cannot be such a game?—Certainly not, Ella: yet I have seen before now very rough cruel play, if it can be termed play.—And did they get a poor little girl with a hump?—No, Laura, not this time: for]

The Pincushion was poor little Flora. How she strained and ducked and swerved to this side or that, in the vain effort to escape her tormentors! Quills with every quill erect tilted against her, and needed not a pin: but Angles whose corners almost cut her, Hooks who caught and slit her frock, Slime who slid against and passed her, Sticky who rubbed off on her neck and plump bare arms, the scowling Queen, and the whole laughing scolding pushing troop, all wielded longest sharpest pins, and all by turns overtook her. Finally the Queen caught her, swung her violently round, let go suddenly,—and Flora losing her balance dropped upon the floor. But at least that game was over.

Do you fancy the fall jarred her? Not at all: for the carpet grew to such a depth of velvet pile below her, that she fell quite lightly.

Indeed I am inclined to believe that even in that dreadful sport of Hunt the Pincushion, Flora was still better off than her stickers: who in the thick of the throng exasperated each other and fairly maddened themselves by a free use of cutting corners, pricking quills, catching hooks, glue, slime, and I know not what else. Slime, perhaps, would seem not so much amiss for its owner: but then if a slimy person cannot be held, neither can she hold fast. As to Hooks and Sticky they often in wrenching themselves loose got worse damage than they inflicted: Angles many times cut his own fingers with his edges:

and I don't envy the individual whose sharp quills are flexible enough to be bent point inwards in a crush or a scuffle. The Queen must perhaps be reckoned exempt from particular personal pangs: but then, you see, it was her birthday! And she must still have suffered a good deal from the eccentricities of her subjects.

The next game called for was Self Help. In this no adventitious aids were tolerated, but each boy depended exclusively on his own resources. Thus pins were forbidden: but every natural advantage, as a quill or fishhook, might be utilized to the utmost.

[Don't look shocked, dear Ella, at my choice of words; but remember that my birthday party is being held in the Land of Nowhere. Yet who knows whether something not altogether unlike it has not ere now taken place in the Land of Somewhere? Look at home, children.]

The boys were players, the girls were played (if I may be allowed such a phrase): all except the Queen who, being Queen, looked on, and merely administered a slap or box on the ear now and then to some one coming handy. Hooks, as a Heavy Porter, shone in this sport; and dragged about with him a load of attached captives, all vainly struggling to unhook themselves. Angles, as an Ironer, goffered or fluted several children by sustained pressure. Quills, an Engraver, could do little more than prick and scratch with some permanence of result. Flora falling to the share of Angles had her torn frock pressed and plaited after quite a novel fashion: but this was at any rate preferable to her experience as Pincushion, and she bore it like a philosopher.

Yet not to speak of the girls, even the boys did not as a body extract unmixed pleasure from Self Help; but much wrangling and some blows allayed their exuberant enjoyment. The Queen as befitted her lofty lot did, perhaps, taste of mirth unalloyed; but if so, she stood alone in satisfaction as in dignity. In any case, pleasure palls in the long run.

The Queen yawned a very wide loud yawn: and as everyone yawned in sympathy the game died out.

A supper table now advanced from the wall to the middle of the floor, and armchairs enough gathered round it to seat the whole party. Through the square hole,—not, alas! through the door of poor Flora's recollection,—floated in the requisite number of plates, glasses, knives, forks, and spoons; and so many dishes and decanters filled with nice things as I certainly never saw in all my lifetime, and I don't imagine any of you ever did.

[How many children were there at supper?—Well, I have not the least idea, Laura, but they made quite a large party: suppose we say a hundred thousand.]

This time Flora would not take so much as a fork without leave: where-

fore as the Queen paid not the slightest attention to her, she was reduced to look hungrily on while the rest of the company feasted, and while successive dainties placed themselves before her and retired untasted. Cold turkey, lobster salad, stewed mushrooms, raspberry tart, cream cheese, a bumper of champagne, a méringue, a strawberry ice, sugared pine apple, some greengages: it may have been quite as well for her that she did not feel at liberty to eat such a mixture: yet it was none the less tantalizing to watch so many good things come and go without taking even one taste, and to see all her companions stuffing without limit. Several of the boys seemed to think nothing of a whole turkey at a time: and the Queen consumed with her own mouth and of sweets alone one quart of strawberry ice, three pine apples, two melons, a score of méringues, and about four dozen sticks of angelica, as Flora counted.

After supper there was no need for the furniture to withdraw: for the whole birthday party trooped out through a door (but still not through Flora's door) into a spacious playground. What they may usually have played at I cannot tell you; but on this occasion a great number of bricks happened to be lying about on all sides mixed up with many neat piles of stones, so the children began building houses: only instead of building from without as most bricklayers do, they built from within, taking care to have at hand plenty of bricks as well as good heaps of stones, and inclosing both themselves and the heaps as they built; one child with one heap of stones inside each house.

[Had they window panes at hand as well?—No, Jane, and you will soon see why none were wanted.]

I called the building material bricks: but strictly speaking there were no bricks at all in the playground, only brick-shaped pieces of glass instead. Each of these had the sides brilliantly polished; whilst the edges, which were meant to touch and join, were ground, and thus appeared to acquire a certain tenacity. There were bricks (so to call them) of all colours and many different shapes and sizes. Some were fancy bricks wrought in open work, some were engraved in running patterns, others were cut into facets or blown into bubbles. A single house might have its blocks all uniform, or of twenty different fashions.

Yet, despite this amount of variety, every house built bore a marked resemblance to its neighbour: colours varied, architecture agreed. Four walls, no roof, no upper floor; such was each house: and it needed neither window nor staircase.

All this building occupied a long long time, and by little and little a very gay effect indeed was produced. Not merely were the glass blocks of beautiful tints; so that whilst some houses glowed like masses of ruby, and others shone like enormous chrysolites or sapphires, others again showed the milkiness and fiery spark of a hundred opals, or glimmered like moonstone: but the playground was lighted up, high, low, and on all sides, with coloured lamps. Picture to yourselves golden twinkling lamps like stars high overhead, bluish twinkling lamps like glowworms down almost on the ground; lamps like illuminated peaches, apples, apricots, plums, hung about with the profusion of a most fruitful orchard. Should we not all have liked to be there with Flora, even if supper was the forfeit?

Ah no, not with Flora: for to her utter dismay she found that she was being built in with the Queen. She was not called upon to build: but gradually the walls rose and rose around her, till they towered clear above her head; and being all slippery with smoothness, left no hope of her ever being able to clamber over them back into the road home, if indeed there was any longer such a road anywhere outside. Her heart sank within her, and she could scarcely hold up her head. To crown all, a glass house which contained no vestige even of a cupboard did clearly not contain a larder: and Flora began to feel sick with hunger and thirst, and to look forward in despair to no breakfast to-morrow.

Acoustics must have been most accurately studied,—

[But, Aunt, what are acoustics?—The science of sounds, Maude: pray now exercise your acoustical faculty.]

As I say, they must have been most accurately studied, and to practical purpose, in the laying out of this particular playground; if, that is, to hear distinctly everywhere whatever might be uttered anywhere within its limits, was the object aimed at. At any rate, such was the result.

Their residences at length erected, and their toils over, the youthful architects found leisure to gaze around them and bandy compliments.

First: "Look," cried Angles, pointing exultantly: "just look at Quills, as red as fire. Red doesn't become Quills. Quills's house would look a deal better without Quills."

"Talk of becomingness," laughed Quills, angrily, "you're just the colour of a sour gooseberry, Angles, and a greater fright than we've seen you yet. Look at him, Sticky, look whilst you have the chance": for Angles was turning his green back on the speaker.

But Sticky—no wonder, the blocks *she* had fingered stuck together!— Sticky was far too busy to glance around; she was engrossed in making faces at Slime, whilst Slime returned grimace for grimace. Sticky's house was blue, and turned her livid: Slime's house—a very shaky one, ready to fall into pieces at any moment, and without one moment's warning:—Slime's house, I say, was amber-hued, and gave her the jaundice. These advantages were not lost on the belligerents, who stood working each other up into a state of frenzy, and having got long past variety, now did nothing but screech over and over again: Slime: "You're a sweet beauty,"—and Sticky (incautious Sticky!): "You're another!"

Quarrels raged throughout the playground. The only silent tongue was Flora's.

Suddenly, Hooks, who had built an engraved house opposite the Queen's bubbled palace (both edifices were pale amethyst coloured, and trying to the complexion), caught sight of his fair neighbour, and, clapping his hands, burst out into an insulting laugh.

"You're another!" shrieked the Queen (the girls all alike seemed well-nigh destitute of invention). Her words were weak, but as she spoke she stooped: and clutched—shook—hurled—the first stone.

"Oh don't, don't, don't," sobbed Flora, clinging in a paroxysm of terror, and with all her weight, to the royal arm.

That first stone was, as it were, the first hailstone of the storm: and soon stones flew in every direction and at every elevation. The very atmosphere seemed petrified. Stones clattered, glass shivered, moans and groans resounded on every side. It was as a battle of giants: who would excel each emulous peer, and be champion among giants?

The Queen. All that had hitherto whistled through mid-air were mere pebbles and chips compared with one massive slab which she now heaved up—poised—prepared to launch—

"Oh don't, don't, don't," cried out Flora again, almost choking with sobs. But it was useless. The ponderous stone spun on, widening an outlet through the palace wall on its way to crush Hooks. Half mad with fear, Flora flung herself after it through the breach—

And in one moment the scene was changed. Silence from human voices and a pleasant coolness of approaching twilight surrounded her. High overhead a fleet of rosy grey clouds went sailing away from the west, and outstripping these, rooks on flapping black wings flew home to their nests in the lofty elm trees, and cawed as they flew. A few heat-drops pattered down on a laurel hedge hard by, and a sudden gust of wind ran rustling through the laurel leaves. Such dear familiar sights and sounds told Flora that she was sitting safe within the home precincts: yes, in the very yew-tree alley, with its forty trees in all, not one more, and with no mysterious door leading out of it into a hall of misery.

She hastened indoors. Her parents, with Alfred, Susan, and the five visitors, were just sitting down round the tea-table, and nurse was leaving the drawing-room in some apparent perturbation.

Wagga wagged his tail, Muff came forward purring, and a laugh greeted Flora. "Do you know," cried George, "that you have been fast asleep ever so long in the yew walk, for I found you there? And now nurse was on her way to fetch you in, if you hadn't turned up."

Flora said not a word in answer, but sat down just as she was, with tumbled frock and hair, and a conscious look in her little face that made it very sweet and winning. Before tea was over, she had nestled close up to Anne, and whispered how sorry she was to have been so cross.

And I think if she lives to be nine years old and give another birthday party, she is likely on that occasion to be even less like the birthday Queen of her troubled dream than was the Flora of eight years old: who, with dear friends and playmates and pretty presents, yet scarcely knew how to bear a few trifling disappointments, or how to be obliging and good-humoured under slight annoyances.

Behind the White Brick

FRANCES HODGSON BURNETT
1879

FRANCES HODGSON BURNETT (1849-1924) was born in England, where she grew up in Manchester. She later lived for a time with her family in Knoxville, Tennessee, and with her husband in Washington, D.C., and on Long Island, New York. Burnett was a prolific author of works for both adults and children, and such novels as *Little Lord Fauntleroy* (1886), *A Little Princess* (1905), and *The Secret Garden* (1911) are still popular with modern readers. Already known for her fiction for adults, Burnett was encouraged to publish some of the stories she had written for her own children after a meeting in 1879 with Louisa May Alcott, the author of *Little Women,* and Mary Mapes Dodge, the editor of *St. Nicholas* magazine. "Behind the White Brick" was one of the earliest of these, appearing in *St. Nicholas* later that year. Like Ewing's "Amelia and the Dwarfs," "Behind the White Brick" is a satirical fantasy of "female aggression in defiance of Victorian taboos."[1] In this tale, however, the protagonist Jem is a working-class rather than a conventionally middle-class Alice character, punished by a harsh aunt for resting and reading after a day of hard work. Like Alice's visits to the Wonderland and Looking-Glass worlds, Jem's journey up the chimney also demands a reconciliation of divided selves in that Jem must reject the dream manifestation of her own childish aggression, the surly baby "Tootsicums" with her sharp teeth and bald head. "Behind the White Brick" is, however, much more explicitly about Jem's self-mastery. Confronted in the Wish Room by her own fantasy image of Aunt Hetty with her mouth sewn shut, Jem "falls awake," having realized that dreams and wishes can, on a psychological level, have real consequences.

---

1. U.C. Knoepflmacher, "Little Girls without Their Curls: Female Aggression in Victorian Children's Literature," *Children's Literature* 11 (1983): 30.

Behind the White Brick

*I*T BEGAN WITH AUNT HETTY'S being out of temper, which, it must be confessed, was nothing new. At its best, Aunt Hetty's temper was none of the most charming, and this morning it was at its worst. She had awakened to the consciousness of having a hard day's work before her, and she had awakened late, and so everything had gone wrong from the first. There was a sharp ring in her voice when she came to Jem's bedroom door and called out, "Jemima, get up this minute!"

Jem knew what to expect when Aunt Hetty began a day by calling her "Jemima." It was one of the poor child's grievances that she had been given such an ugly name. In all the books she had read, and she had read a great many, Jem never had met a heroine who was called Jemima. But it had been her mother's favourite sister's name, and so it had fallen to her lot. Her mother always called her "Jem," or "Mimi," which was much prettier, and even Aunt Hetty only reserved Jemima for unpleasant state occasions.

It was a dreadful day to Jem. Her mother was not at home, and would not be until night. She had been called away unexpectedly, and had been obliged to leave Jem and the baby to Aunt Hetty's mercies.

So Jem found herself busy enough. Scarcely had she finished doing one thing, when Aunt Hetty told her to begin another. She wiped dishes and picked fruit and attended to the baby; and when baby had gone to sleep, and everything else seemed disposed of, for a time, at least, she was so tired that she was glad to sit down.

And then she thought of the book she had been reading the night before—a certain delightful story book, about a little girl whose name was Flora, and who was so happy and rich and pretty and good that Jem had likened her to the little princesses one reads about, to whose christening feast every fairy brings a gift.

"I shall have time to finish my chapter before dinner-time comes," said Jem, and she sat down snugly in one corner of the wide, old fashioned fireplace.

But she had not read more than two pages before something dreadful happened. Aunt Hetty came into the room in a great hurry—in such a hurry, indeed, that she caught her foot in the matting and fell, striking her elbow sharply against a chair, which so upset her temper that the moment she found herself on her feet she flew at Jem.

"What!" she said, snatching the book from her, "reading again, when I am running all over the house for you?" And she flung the pretty little blue covered volume into the fire.

Jem sprang to rescue it with a cry, but it was impossible to reach it; it had fallen into a great hollow of red coal, and the blaze caught it at once.

"You are a wicked woman!" cried Jem, in a dreadful passion, to Aunt Hetty. "You are a wicked woman."

Then matters reached a climax. Aunt Hetty boxed her ears, pushed her back on her little footstool, and walked out of the room.

Jem hid her face on her arms and cried as if her heart would break. She cried until her eyes were heavy, and she thought she should be obliged to go to sleep. But just as she was thinking of going to sleep, something fell down the chimney and made her look up. It was a piece of mortar, and it brought a good deal of soot with it. She bent forward and looked up to see where it had come from. The chimney was so very wide that this was easy enough. She could see where the mortar had fallen from the side and left a white patch.

"How white it looks against the black!" said Jem; "it is like a white brick among the black ones. What a queer place a chimney is! I can see a bit of the blue sky, I think."

And then a funny thought came into her fanciful little head. What a many things were burned in the big fireplace and vanished in smoke or tinder up the chimney! Where did everything go? There was Flora, for instance— Flora who was represented on the frontispiece—with lovely, soft, flowing hair, and a little fringe on her pretty round forehead, crowned with a circlet of daisies, and a laugh in her wide-awake round eyes. Where was she by this time? Certainly there was nothing left of her in the fire. Jem almost began to cry again at the thought.

"It was too bad," she said. "She was so pretty and funny, and I did like her so."

I daresay it scarcely will be credited by unbelieving people when I tell them what happened next, it was such a very singular thing, indeed.

Jem felt herself gradually lifted off her little footstool.

"Oh!" she said, timidly, "I feel very light." She did feel light, indeed. She felt so light that she was sure she was rising gently in the air.

"Oh," she said again, "how—how very light I feel! Oh, dear. I'm going up the chimney!"

It was rather strange that she never thought of calling for help, but she did not. She was not easily frightened; and now she was only wonderfully astonished, as she remembered afterwards. She shut her eyes tight and gave a little gasp.

"I've heard Aunt Hetty talk about the draught drawing things up the chimney, but I never knew it was as strong as this," she said.

She went up, up, up, quietly and steadily, and without any uncomfortable feeling at all; and then all at once she stopped, feeling that her feet rested against something solid. She opened her eyes and looked about her, and there she was, standing right opposite the white brick, her feet on a tiny ledge.

"Well," she said, "this is funny."

But the next thing that happened was funnier still. She found that, without thinking what she was doing, she was knocking on the white brick with her knuckles, as if it was a door and she expected somebody to open it. The next minute she heard footsteps, and then a sound, as if someone was drawing back a little bolt.

"It is a door," said Jem, "and somebody is going to open it."

The white brick moved a little, and some more mortar and soot fell; then the brick moved a little more, and then it slid aside and left an open space.

"It's a room!" cried Jem. "There's a room behind it!"

And so there was, and before the open space stood a pretty little girl, with long lovely hair and a fringe on her forehead. Jem clasped her hands in amazement. It was Flora herself, as she looked in the picture, and Flora stood laughing and nodding.

"Come in," she said. "I thought it was you."

"But how can I come in through such a little place?" asked Jem.

"Oh, that is easy enough," said Flora. "Here, give me your hand."

Jem did as she told her, and found that it was easy enough. In an instant she had passed through the opening, the white brick had gone back to its place, and she was standing by Flora's side in a large room—the nicest room she had ever seen. It was big and lofty and light, and there were all kinds of delightful things in it—books and flowers and playthings and pictures, and in one corner a great cage full of lovebirds.

"Have I ever seen it before?" asked Jem, glancing slowly round.

"Yes," said Flora; "you saw it last night—in your mind. Don't you remember it?"

Jem shook her head.

"I feel as if I did, but—"

"Why," said Flora, laughing, "it's my room, the one you read about last night."

"So it is," said Jem. "But how did you come here?"

"I can't tell you that; I myself don't know. But I am here, and so"—rather mysteriously—"are a great many other things."

"Are they?" said Jem, very much interested. "What things? Burned things? I was just wondering—"

"Not only burned things," said Flora, nodding. "Just come with me and I'll show you something."

She led the way out of the room and down a little passage with several doors in each side of it, and she opened one door and showed Jem what was on the other side of it. That was a room, too, and this time it was funny as well as pretty. Both floor and walls were padded with rose colour, and the floor was strewn with toys. There were big soft balls, rattles, horses, woolly dogs, and a doll or so; there was one low cushioned chair and a low table.

"You can come in," said a shrill little voice behind the door, "only mind you don't tread on things."

"What a funny little voice!" said Jem, but she had no sooner said it than she jumped back.

The owner of the voice, who had just come forward, was no other than Baby.

"Why," exclaimed Jem, beginning to feel frightened. "I left you fast asleep in your crib."

"Did you?" said Baby, somewhat scornfully. "That's just the way with you grown-up people. You think you know everything, and yet you haven't discretion enough to know when a pin is sticking into one. You'd know soon enough if you had one sticking into your own back."

"But I'm not grown up," stammered Jem; "and when you are at home you can neither walk nor talk. You're not six months old."

"Well, miss," retorted Baby, whose wrongs seemed to have soured her disposition somewhat, "you have no need to throw that in my teeth; you were not six months old, either, when you were my age."

Jem could not help laughing.

"You haven't got any teeth," she said.

"Haven't I?" said Baby, and she displayed two beautiful rows with some haughtiness of manner. "When I am up here," she said, "I am supplied with the modern conveniences, and that's why I never complain. Do I ever cry when I am asleep? It's not falling asleep I object to, it's falling awake."

"Wait a minute," said Jem. "Are you asleep now?"

"I'm what you call asleep. I can only come here when I'm what you call asleep. Asleep, indeed! It's no wonder we always cry when we have to fall awake."

"But we don't mean to be unkind to you," protested Jem, meekly.

She could not help thinking baby was very severe.

"Don't mean!" said Baby. "Well, why don't you think more, then? How would you like to have all the nice things snatched away from you, and all the old rubbish packed off on you, as if you hadn't any sense? How would you like to have to sit and stare at things you wanted, and not to be able to reach them, or, if you did reach them, have them fall out of your hand, and roll away in the most unfeeling manner? And then be scolded and called 'cross!' It's no wonder we are bald. You'd be bald yourself. It's trouble and worry that keep us bald until we can begin to take care of ourselves; I had more hair than this at first, but it fell off, as well it might. No philosopher ever thought of that, I suppose!"

"Well," said Jem, in despair, "I hope you enjoy yourself when you are here?"

"Yes, I do," answered Baby. "That's one comfort. There is nothing to knock my head against, and things have patent stoppers on them, so that they can't roll away, and everything is soft and easy to pick up."

There was a slight pause after this, and Baby seemed to cool down.

"I suppose you would like me to show you round?" she said.

"Not if you have any objection," replied Jem, who was rather subdued.

"I would as soon do it as not," said Baby. "You are not as bad as some people, though you do get my clothes twisted when you hold me."

Upon the whole, she seemed rather proud of her position. It was evident she quite regarded herself as hostess. She held her small bald head very high indeed, as she trotted on before them. She stopped at the first door she came to, and knocked three times. She was obliged to stand upon tiptoe to reach the knocker.

"He's sure to be at home at this time of year," she remarked. "This is the busy season."

"Who's 'he'?" inquired Jem.

But Flora only laughed at Miss Baby's consequential air.

"S. C., to be sure," was the answer, as the young lady pointed to the door-plate, upon which Jem noticed, for the first time, "S. C." in very large letters.

The door opened, apparently without assistance, and they entered the apartment.

"Good gracious!" exclaimed Jem, the next minute "Good*ness* gracious!"

She might well be astonished. It was such a long room that she could not see to the end of it, and it was piled up from floor to ceiling with toys of every description, and there was such bustle and buzzing in it that it was quite confusing. The bustle and buzzing arose from a very curious cause, too,—it was the bustle and buzz of hundreds of tiny men and women who were working at little tables no higher than mushrooms,—the pretty tiny women cutting out and sewing, the pretty tiny men sawing and hammering, and all talking at once. The principal person in the place escaped Jem's notice at first;

but it was not long before she saw him,—a little old gentleman, with a rosy face and sparkling eyes, sitting at a desk, and writing in a book almost as big as himself. He was so busy that he was quite excited, and had been obliged to throw his white fur coat and cap aside, and he was at work in his red waistcoat.

"Look here, if you please," piped Baby. "I have brought someone to see you."

When he turned round, Jem recognized him at once.

"Eh! Eh!" he said. "What! What! Who's this, Tootsicums?"

Baby's manner became very acid indeed.

"I shouldn't have thought you would have said that, Mr. Claus," she remarked. "I can't help myself down below, but I generally have my rights respected up here. I should like to know what sane godfather or godmother would give one the name of 'Tootsicums' in one's baptism. They are bad enough, I must say; but I never heard of any of them calling a person 'Tootsicums.'"

"Come, come!" said S. C., chuckling comfortably and rubbing his hands. "Don't be too dignified,—it's a bad thing. And don't be too fond of flourishing your rights in people's faces,—that's the worst of all, Miss Midget. Folks who make such a fuss about their rights turn them into wrongs sometimes."

Then he turned suddenly to Jem.

"You are the little girl from down below," he said.

"Yes, sir," answered Jem. "I'm Jem, and this is my friend Flora,—out of the blue book."

"I'm happy to make her acquaintance," said S. C., "and I'm happy to make yours. You are a nice child, though a trifle peppery. I'm very glad to see you."

"I'm very glad indeed to see you, sir," said Jem. "I wasn't quite sure—"

But there she stopped, feeling that it would be scarcely polite to tell him that she had begun of late years to lose faith in him.

But S. C. only chuckled more comfortably than ever and rubbed his hands again.

"Ho, ho!" he said. "You know who I am, then?"

Jem hesitated a moment, wondering whether it would not be taking a liberty to mention his name without putting "Mr." before it; then she remembered what Baby had called him.

"Baby called you 'Mr. Claus,' sir," she replied; "and I have seen pictures of you."

"To be sure," said S. C. "S. Claus, Esquire, of Chimneyland. How do you like me?"

"Very much," answered Jem; "very much, indeed, sir."

"Glad of it! Glad of it! But what was it you were going to say you were not quite sure of?"

Jem blushed a little.

"I was not quite sure that—that you were true, sir. At least I have not been quite sure since I have been older."

S. C. rubbed the bald part of his head and gave a little sigh.

"I hope I have not hurt your feelings, sir," faltered Jem, who was a very kind hearted little soul.

"Well, no," said S. C. "Not exactly. And it is not your fault either. It is natural, I suppose; at any rate, it is the way of the world. People lose their belief in a great many things as they grow older; but that does not make the things not true, thank goodness! and their faith often comes back after a while. But, bless me!" he added, briskly, "I'm moralizing, and who thanks a man for doing that? Suppose—"

"Black eyes or blue, sir?" said a tiny voice close to them.

Jem and Flora turned round, and saw it was one of the small workers who was asking the question.

"Whom for?" inquired S. C.

"Little girl in the red brick house at the corner," said the workwoman; "name of Birdie."

"Excuse me a moment," said S. C. to the children, and he turned to the big book and began to run his fingers down the pages in a business-like manner. "Ah! here she is!" he exclaimed at last. "Blue eyes, if you please, Thistle, and golden hair. And let it be a big one. She takes good care of them."

"Yes, sir," said Thistle; "I am personally acquainted with several dolls in her family. I go to parties in her dolls' house sometimes when she is fast asleep at night, and they all speak very highly of her. She is most attentive to them when they are ill. In fact, her pet doll is a cripple, with a stiff leg."

She ran back to her work and S. C. finished his sentence.

"Suppose I show you my establishment," he said. "Come with me."

It really would be quite impossible to describe the wonderful things he showed them. Jem's head was quite in a whirl before she had seen one-half of them, and even Baby condescended to become excited.

"There must be a great many children in the world, Mr. Claus," ventured Jem.

"Yes, yes, millions of 'em; bless 'em," said S. C., growing rosier with delight at the very thought. "We never run out of them, that's one comfort. There's a large and varied assortment always on hand. Fresh ones every year, too, so that when one grows too old there is a new one ready. I have a place like this in every twelfth chimney. Now it's boys, now it's girls, always one or t'other; and there's no end of playthings for them, too, I'm glad to say. For girls, the great thing seems to be dolls. Blitzen! what comfort they *do* take in dolls! but the boys are for horses and racket."

They were standing near a table where a worker was just putting the finishing touch to the dress of a large wax doll, and just at that moment, to Jem's surprise, she set it on the floor, upon its feet, quite coolly.

"Thank you," said the doll, politely.

Jem quite jumped.

"You can join the rest now and introduce yourself," said the worker.

The doll looked over her shoulder at her train.

"It hangs very nicely," she said. "I hope it's the latest fashion."

"Mine never talked like that," said Flora. "My best one could only say 'Mamma,' and it said it very badly, too."

"She was foolish for saying it at all," remarked the doll, haughtily. "We don't talk and walk before ordinary people; we keep our accomplishments for our own amusement, and for the amusement of our friends. If you should chance to get up in the middle of the night, some time, or should run into the room suddenly some day, after you have left it, you might hear—but what is the use of talking to human beings?"

"You know a great deal, considering you are only just finished," snapped Baby, who really was a Tartar.

"I was FINISHED," retorted the doll. "I did not begin life as a baby!" very scornfully.

"Pooh!" said Baby. "We improve as we get older."

"I hope, so, indeed," answered the doll. "There is plenty of room for improvement." And she walked away in great state.

S. C. looked at Baby and then shook his head. "I shall not have to take very much care of you," he said, absent-mindedly. "You are able to take pretty good care of yourself."

"I hope I am," said Baby, tossing her head.

S. C. gave his head another shake.

"Don't take too good care of yourself," he said. "That's a bad thing, too."

He showed them the rest of his wonders, and then went with them to the door to bid them good-bye.

"I am sure we are very much obliged to you, Mr. Claus," said Jem, gratefully. "I shall never again think you are not true, sir."

S. C. patted her shoulder quite affectionately.

"That's right," he said. "Believe in things just as long as you can, my dear. Good-bye until Christmas Eve. I shall see you then, if you don't see me."

He must have taken quite a fancy to Jem, for he stood looking at her, and seemed very reluctant to close the door, and even after he had closed it, and they had turned away, he opened it a little again to call to her.

"Believe in things as long as you can, my dear."

"How kind he is!" exclaimed Jem, full of pleasure.

Baby shrugged her shoulders.

"Well enough in his way," she said, "but rather inclined to prose and be old-fashioned."

Jem looked at her, feeling rather frightened, but she said nothing.

Baby showed very little interest in the next room she took them to.

"I don't care about this place," she said, as she threw open the door. "It has nothing but old things in it. It is the Nobody-knows-where room."

She had scarcely finished speaking before Jem made a little spring and picked something up.

"Here's my old strawberry pincushion!" she cried out. And then, with another jump and another dash at two or three other things, "And here's my old fairy-book! And here's my little locket I lost last summer! How did they come here?"

"They went Nobody-knows-where," said Baby.

"And this is it."

"But cannot I have them again?" asked Jem.

"No," answered Baby. "Things that go to Nobody-knows-where stay there."

"Oh!" sighed Jem, "I am so sorry."

"They are only old things," said Baby.

"But I like my old things," said Jem. "I love them. And there is mother's needle case. I wish I might take that. Her dead little sister gave it to her, and she was so sorry when she lost it."

"People ought to take better care of their things," remarked Baby.

Jem would have liked to stay in this room and wander about among her old favourites for a long time, but Baby was in a hurry.

"You'd better come away," she said. "Suppose I was to have to fall awake and leave you?"

The next place they went into was the most wonderful of all.

"This is the Wish room," said Baby. "Your wishes come here—yours and mother's and Aunt Hetty's and father's and mine. When did you wish that?"

Each article was placed under a glass shade, and labeled with the words and name of the wishes. Some of them were beautiful, indeed; but the tall shade Baby nodded at when she asked her question was truly alarming, and caused Jem a dreadful pang of remorse. Underneath it sat Aunt Hetty, with her mouth stitched up so that she could not speak a word, and beneath the stand was a label bearing these words, in large black letters—

"I wish Aunt Hetty's mouth was sewed up. Jem."

"Oh, dear!" cried Jem, in great distress. "How it must have hurt her! How unkind of me to say it! I wish I hadn't wished it. I wish it would come undone."

She had no sooner said it than her wish was gratified. The old label disappeared and a new one showed itself, and there sat Aunt Hetty, looking herself again, and even smiling.

Jem was grateful beyond measure, but Baby seemed to consider her weak minded.

"It served her right," she said.

But when, after looking at the wishes at that end of the room, they went to the other end, her turn came. In one corner stood a shade with a baby under it, and the baby was Miss Baby herself, but looking as she very rarely looked; in fact, it was the brightest, best tempered baby one could imagine.

"I wish I had a better tempered baby. Mother," was written on the label.

Baby became quite red in the face with anger and confusion.

"That wasn't here the last time I came," she said. "And it is right down mean in mother!"

This was more than Jem could bear.

"It wasn't mean," she said. "She couldn't help it. You know you are a cross baby—everybody says so."

Baby turned two shades redder.

"Mind your own business," she retorted. "It was mean; and as to that silly little thing being better than I am," turning up her small nose, which was quite turned up enough by Nature—"I must say I don't see anything so very grand about her. So, there!"

She scarcely condescended to speak to them while they remained in the Wish room, and when they left it, and went to the last door in the passage, she quite scowled at it.

"I don't know whether I shall open it at all," she said.

"Why not?" asked Flora. "You might as well."

"It is the Lost Pin room," she said. "I hate pins."

She threw the door open with a bang, and then stood and shook her little fist viciously. The room was full of pins, stacked solidly together. There were hundreds of them—thousands—millions, it seemed.

"I'm glad they *are* lost!" she said. "I wish there were more of them there."

"I didn't know there were so many pins in the world," said Jem.

"Pooh!" said Baby. "Those are only the lost ones that have belonged to our family."

After this they went back to Flora's room and sat down, while Flora told Jem the rest of her story.

"Oh!" sighed Jem, when she came to the end. "How delightful it is to be here! Can I never come again?"

"In one way you can," said Flora. "When you want to come, just sit down and be as quiet as possible, and shut your eyes and think very hard about it. You can see everything you have seen to-day, if you try."

"Then I shall be sure to try," Jem answered. She was going to ask some other question but Baby stopped her.

"Oh! I'm falling awake," she whimpered, crossly, rubbing her eyes. "I'm falling awake again."

And then, suddenly, a very strange feeling came over Jem. Flora and the pretty room seemed to fade away, and, without being able to account for it at all, she found herself sitting on her little stool again, with a beautiful scarlet and gold book on her knee, and her mother standing by laughing at her amazed face. As to Miss Baby, she was crying as hard as she could in her crib.

"Mother!" Jem cried out, "have you really come home so early as this, and—and," rubbing her eyes in great amazement, "how did I come down?"

"Don't I look as if I was real?" said her mother, laughing and kissing her. "And doesn't your present look real? I don't know how you came down, I'm sure. Where have you been?"

Jem shook her head very mysteriously. She saw that her mother fancied she had been asleep, but she herself knew better.

"I know you wouldn't believe it was true if I told you," she said; "I have been

BEHIND THE WHITE BRICK."

Wanted — A King

Or, How Merle Set the Nursery Rhymes to Right

MAGGIE BROWNE

ILLUSTRATIONS BY HARRY FURNISS

1890

MAGGIE BROWNE was the pseudonym of Margaret Hamer Andrewes, a British author of poetry, travel books, and fantasies for children. Both her *Wanted—A King* and *The Book of Betty Barber* (1900) show the influence of the *Alice* books. Indeed, Carroll owned a copy of *Wanted—A King* as part of his collection "of books of the *Alice* type."[1] Browne's heroine, Merle, however, is an original and engaging character, courageous and defiant in her determination to vanquish the autocratic Grunter Grim. Unlike Carroll's Alice, who attempts to survive in the Wonderland and Looking-Glass worlds by adapting and acquiescing, Merle is encouraged to "Defy, Deride, Desist, Deny, / Heed not a growl, or scowl, or sigh." The constantly shifting identities of Endom's characters enable Browne playfully to explore and challenge social and gender roles, as Merle's successes reveal the ways that nonsense and imagination can oppose socially imposed expectations and constraints.

---

1. Roger Lancelyn Green, ed., *The Diaries of Lewis Carroll,* 2 vols. (London: Cassell, 1953) 2:486.

Wanted—A King

THE BEGINNING OF IT ALL

*I*T CERTAINLY WAS A beautiful screen. Merle always said that she liked the pictures on it better than all her story-books put together.

It was a screen covered with brightly-coloured pictures of all the Nursery Rhymes. On one side were Jack and Jill rolling down a hill, Bo-peep and Boy Blue, to say nothing of the Man in the Moon and the Old Woman who lived in a Shoe; and on the other side were illustrations of all the Fairy Tales.

The screen always stood by the side of Merle's bed, between the bed and the door; so that when Merle was in bed she could look at the pictures and say the rhymes over to send herself to sleep.

She had needed something to send her to sleep, too, since the day she tumbled. Merle dated everything from that tumble. Two months had passed since then, but Merle was still in bed. It had been a bad fall, so bad that at first every one thought that Merle would never again be able to run about and play like other children; but after a time the doctors said that if only Merle would lie still and wait patiently, some day she would be able to romp as much as she used to do.

Merle thought it was very easy to say "lie still and wait patiently," but she knew it was very difficult to do it when her head was so hot, and her body seemed full of aches and pains.

This afternoon, too, the pain was bad, and would not let Merle get any sleep.

She was staring at the screen, and gently singing to herself—

> *"Jack and Jill went up a hill*
> *To fetch a pail of water,"*

when there was a tap at the door, and an old gentleman came into the room.

"Uncle Crossiter," said Merle—for this old gentleman was Merle's uncle —"Uncle Crossiter, I cannot get to sleep. What shall I do?"

"Well, my dear," said the old gentleman, "I should say you had better let me move the screen away; you are not likely to go to sleep staring at those silly nursery rhymes. Such nonsense! Filling children's heads with such rubbish!"

"It is not rubbish, Uncle," said Merle, indignantly. "Please don't move the screen; I love to look at it."

But Uncle Crossiter took no notice of Merle, and only continued to grumble to himself.

"I should like to burn all the silly nursery rhyme books," he growled.

"That would do no good, Uncle," said Merle, quietly—"the rhymes are in the children's heads, and they will never be forgotten. I wonder what hill it was that Jack went up. It always says 'a hill,' you know, Uncle."

Uncle Crossiter started up. "Oh dear! oh dear!" he said to himself, "the child is wandering. There, keep quiet, my dear," he said to Merle; "I will send your mother to you."

"I am all right, Uncle," said Merle. "I won't talk about the nursery rhymes if you don't like them; but why don't you like them, Uncle?"

"Such silly nonsense, my dear!"

"Not nonsense, Uncle—they are beautiful. I do wish I had known Boy Blue and Bo-peep. It would have been such fun playing with Bo-peep's sheep," said Merle, quite forgetting that she had promised not to mention the rhymes.

But it did not matter, for Uncle Crossiter had disappeared. He was a matter-of-fact old gentleman, with no sentiment in him, and with rather a short temper. He was very fond of his little niece, and was very sorry for her; but he did not know in the least how to show his affection, for he did not understand children at all, his one idea about them being that they ought not to read nursery rhymes.

Merle, however, did not notice that he had left the room. She kept on talking to herself, saying, "Bo-peep's sheep—Sheep's Bo-peep—Bo-sheep's peep," and so on. How long she would have gone on with this silly nonsense I do not know, if she had not been startled by a voice behind her, saying quickly,

"IF YOU WANT TO COME IN,
YOU MUST LEAVE YOUR BODY OUTSIDE."

OVER THE TURNSTILE WITH TOPLEAF

"If you want to come in you must leave your body outside," said the voice again. "You need not be alarmed; I shall give you a ticket for it, and it will be quite right under my care."

Merle turned round astonished. The bed, bedroom, and screen had all disappeared, and she herself was no longer lying down, but standing—actually standing—in front of a turnstile.

Behind it was a little man, and he was evidently waiting for an answer to his question. Merle looked at him when she had recovered from her surprise. He was an ugly fellow—so short, really, that he only came up to Merle's shoulder, but as he wore a very tall pointed black hat he looked much bigger than Merle.

He was dressed all in black, for a long black cloak covered him from head to foot. In front of his hat were two red letters—two G's.

"G. G.," said Merle to herself; "what can that mean?"

"Children are so rude," grumbled the little man, who was still waiting for an answer, "they cannot even reply to a question. I suppose this child does not *want* to come in."

He turned round as he spoke, and was just going back into his little ticket-office, when Merle at last found her voice, and ventured to ask how she should get on without her body.

"Children ask so many questions," said the little man; "this child shall *not* come in."

This time he walked straight into his office and slammed the door.

Merle felt very much disappointed, and rather inclined to cry. She had no idea what she was going in to; but, nevertheless, it was very annoying to be shut out.

Just then she saw a big, thin, yellowish-brown thing—a thing rather like a very large stiff piece of paper being blown towards her. It was curled round, and bent at the top.

To her astonishment, the thing stopped in front of her, and bending a little more, as if making a bow, said—

"Can I do anything for you, Merle? You don't know me, of course, but I know you very well. My name is Topleaf. I am—or perhaps I ought to say I was—the leaf that was on top of the highest branch of the lime-tree in your garden. I have often peeped in at your window and nodded to you."

"I saw you this morning," said Merle, "and I know I said to mother that I should think you must be very lonely up there all by yourself. The other leaves have fallen long ago."

"It was lonely," said Topleaf; "but I could see a very long way, so that comforted me. At last I got my friend Mr. E. Wind to help me down, and here I am."

"But how is it you are so very big?" asked Merle. "You were not that size this morning."

"Ah, my dear! That shows how little you know. Have you never yet heard that every leaf tries as soon as ever summer is over to make its way up to Endom?"

"Endom?" said Merle, "where is Endom?"

"There," said the leaf, and he pointed over the turnstile. "I thought you were going there, perhaps, and I was glad, for a fresh child is badly wanted."

Merle did not know what Topleaf meant by the last part of his remark, so took no notice of it, but said again, "But how did you grow so tall?"

"Ah, dear!" sighed Topleaf, "I forgot all about your question, and as usual, my dear, wandered from the subject. Have you not noticed how leaves never go anywhere straight, and never keep to one purpose? They run off in a most flighty manner with the first breeze that takes any notice of them."

As the leaf was speaking the little man appeared at the gate once more.

"Hullo, Topleaf!" he said, "so you've arrived at last. I cannot say I am glad to see you. Are you coming in?"

Then he caught sight of Merle.

"That child still here?" he growled. "Disgraceful, I call it! Children are so obstinate," and without waiting to say another word to Topleaf, he shook his fist at Merle, and went back into his ticket-office.

"Who is that?" whispered Merle.

"That, my dear, is the evil spirit of Endom. He it is who has done all the harm to Mistress Crispin and her family. He it is who is the curse of all leaves," said Topleaf, and he rustled with rage. "If he could help it, we should never reach Endom. He puts every difficulty in our way. I had a brother"—here Topleaf lowered his voice—"but it is too sad a story to relate here. I only say that now he is a skeleton leaf." Topleaf was so overcome with his anger and sorrow that he curled up tightly.

Merle did not quite know what to do or say. She was anxious to hear the rest of Topleaf's story, but did not like to disturb him. At last, to her great relief, he uncurled, and once more began to speak.

"I got here in spite of him," he said. "I conquered every difficulty, and so, of course, I grew. You know, my dear, that every time a leaf conquers a difficulty he increases in size. But we are wasting precious time. Come, let us go together into Endom."

Topleaf stood in front of the turnstile and shook himself vigorously.

Once more the little man appeared.

"So you've made up your mind to leave your body outside at last, have you?" he said, turning to Merle.

"Indeed I have not. I shall do nothing of the kind," said Merle quietly.

"But you *must!* you *must!* " said the little man angrily, stamping his foot. Merle noticed that the red letters on his cap grew brighter and brighter.

"All children must leave their bodies in my care. You mortals can only enter Endom in this way. Now then, if you are coming, come. Very well, I am not going to wait any longer," and he locked up his office and disappeared. Merle could not make out where he had gone to this time.

"Now what is to be done?" said she. "I did so want to go in—what a perfect little wretch he is!"

"My dear," said Topleaf, "you don't know what you have done. You have offended the mighty, the powerful

"Grunter Grim!!!"

"Grunter Grim?" said Merle.

"Yes, Grunter Grim," said Topleaf. "I can't understand why he's acting as porter to-day: for no good purpose, I am quite sure."

"Well, it is done now, and cannot be helped," said Merle. "All the same, I must get in. Can't you help me?"

"I might, perhaps, if one of the Mr. Winds would give a helping blow. The worst of it is, you are so heavy. You don't happen to know anything about the Wind Family, I suppose?"

"I am afraid I don't," said Merle.

"Very well, then; I will do the best I can. Get inside me," said Topleaf. He carefully uncurled himself, and then getting behind Merle, slowly curled himself up again round her, so that she was completely hidden from sight.

"Now hold on tight!" shouted Topleaf. "Here comes Mr. East Wind."

Then Merle heard someone whistle loudly, and she supposed that must be Mr. Wind; next she heard Topleaf slowly chanting these words:—

> *"Blow, blow, blow,*
> *Wind of the ice and snow;*
> *Just one gentle puff*
> *Will be quite enough,*
> *And over the fence we'll go;"*

and then she felt herself lifted from the ground, and carried into the air.

It was all over in a moment, for it was a very short journey—only over the turnstile—and Merle soon found her feet touching the ground once more. Topleaf slowly uncurled, and Merle stepped out.

She began to thank Topleaf, but he did not take any notice of her. He

just waited to see that she was uninjured by the journey, and then whirled away with his friend Mr. East Wind.

WHAT MERLE FOUND IN THE BOX

For a minute or two after Topleaf had left her, Merle stood perfectly still. Although the journey through the air had been short, it had also been quick, and had quite taken Merle's breath away.

"Well," she said at last, "here I am in Endom, I suppose. I wonder what kind of a place it is, and what sort of people live here? This is a funny kind of ticket-office."

As Merle spoke she was staring about her, and yet did not notice a long box on the ground. As she was leaning forward to peep in through the office window, her foot knocked against the box, and immediately a deep groan was heard.

Merle started back frightened, expecting to see the horrid little man once more, but he was not there.

"It must have been my fancy," said Merle.

But it was not, for by accident she knocked against the box again, and again came the groan; and this time it was louder than before.

"Why, it comes from the box, I do believe," said Merle, when she had looked in the ticket-office and could see no one. "It comes from the box! I do wonder if there can be anything or anybody inside?"

"Anybody inside? Of course there is. I'm inside," said a voice. "Who ever you are, let me out, oh do let me out!" The groans grew louder than ever.

"It is all very well saying that," said Merle, "but the box is fastened, and I don't know how to open it."

"Get the key, of course. It is in the office," said the voice, impatiently.

Merle ran quickly to the little door, and tried to open it, but it was fastened. Peeping in through the window to see if she could catch sight of any keys, Merle was astonished to see rows of paper-covered books standing on shelves round the walls, and she wondered what they were. However, there were no keys, so once more she returned to the unhappy creature in the box, who by this time seemed too tired to groan, and was only sighing faintly.

"I cannot get into the office," said Merle, sorrowfully; "and if I could, I don't see any keys hanging up."

"Hanging up? Whoever heard of keys hanging up? How would you hang them up?" asked the voice, angrily. "Didn't you see them standing on the shelves?"

"I saw some books on the shelves, but——"

"And what else would you have?" interrupted the angry voice. "If you want to open this box, you must find the right book, and read the proper rhyme, of course. You don't seem to know what a key is. What is the key to your arithmetic book like?"

Merle felt there was something wrong somewhere, but she didn't quite know where. She felt, however, that arguing wouldn't release the poor creature from his sufferings, so she hastened to say—

"But the office door is fastened."

"Then there is nothing else for it—you must sit on me—I will do my best not to hurt you," said the voice; "but if I don't get out somehow, I shall certainly die."

"You won't hurt me," said Merle, "but if I sit on you I am afraid I shall hurt you. However, I will do as you wish."

She sat down on the box, and the groaning grew louder than ever. Presently, however, it altogether ceased. There was a very loud noise, as of something bursting, and then Merle felt herself shot up high into the air.

The box-lid seemed to have tossed her as if she had been sitting on the

horns of a bull. It was startling, and she did not recover from her astonishment for some time. When she did, she found herself sitting on the ground. Staring at her, standing upright in the box, was a very tall boy, dressed in a very old-fashioned coat, with large round buttons. Round his neck was a big, wide, stiffly-starched frill, which Merle thought must be decidedly uncomfortable.

"Thank you very much," he said, bowing politely. *"What a good boy am I!"* he continued.

Merle looked somewhat astonished.

"My name is Jack Horner," he said, bowing again, "and I——"

"Sit in a corner," interrupted Merle, eagerly, "eating a Christmas pie; and you put in your thumb——"

The boy frowned and looked very cross, but Merle did not notice it, and went on talking——

"And pulled out a plum, and said——"

But the boy could bear it no longer, and began shouting at the top of his voice, "To be a good boy I will try——"

"That's quite wrong," said Merle, indignantly. "You made a very conceited remark—you said, 'What a good boy am I!'"

"But I didn't, I didn't!" said Jack Horner. "It was Grunter Grim who told the fairy who makes the Rhymes that I said so, and now I have to keep on saying—'What a good boy am I.'"

As he said this he got very excited, waved his arms about, and sat down suddenly in the box. At once the lid closed down, and he was a prisoner again.

Merle released him as quickly as she could, but begged him not to do it any more, as she did not enjoy being shot up into the air.

"I hope you are not hurt," said Jack.

"Not a bit, thank you," said Merle—"I only feel rather giddy. Would you mind telling me why you got into that box at all? It surely isn't very comfortable?"

"What a good boy am I!" said Jack, angrily. "Comfortable!—Got in!—Do you suppose I got in? It was Grunter Grim who shut me up, and even now I can't get right out."

"Why, you are a regular Jack-in-the-box," said Merle, beginning to laugh.

"There," said Jack, indignantly, "that is another thing Grunter Grim has done. He not only puts me in the box, but he tells the fairy who makes the Toys about it, and then the children hear of my disgraceful situation. He is horrible! I suppose you thought I did nothing all day but sit in a corner and say, 'What a good boy am I?'"

"Why, do you do anything else?" asked Merle.

"Do anything else!" screamed Jack. "Why, I am the porter of Endom, and Grunter Grim shut me up to-day, so that I couldn't let you in. He is nothing less than a monster!"

"He does seem to have treated you badly," said Merle, sympathisingly. "I must say I am very glad to know that you are not really so conceited as I always thought you were."

"What a good boy am I!" said Jack, very dolefully. "Yes, I know that sounds conceited, but you understand now, don't you, that I only said, 'To be a good boy I'll try?' It is all Grunter Grim's fault."

"He must be dreadful!" said Merle.

"But you will save us all, I hope," said Jack. "Go up the hill and talk to mother: she will show you what to do——"

He was about to tell Merle more about his mother, when it suddenly began to grow dark, as though a black cloud were coming down from the sky to the earth.

"Run, run!" shouted Jack. "Grunter Grim is coming!" and he quickly sank down into his box.

Merle did not wait to be told twice, but ran quickly away from the office. She never stopped, and never once looked behind her until she found herself in front of a large black house.

Mistress Crispin's Story

"It is a queer house," said Merle, aloud: "a very queer house. It's such a funny shape."

Merle was quite right: it was a queer house, and a very peculiar shape. To begin with, the house was certainly not built of bricks; then it was very long and low, and what Merle called "uppy-downy." The windows were in such funny places—and as for the front door, why, there was none. The only way to get into this house seemed to be to climb up a rope ladder which hung down from the middle of it. Part of it, too, was entirely without a roof, and another part was so narrow that Merle felt quite sure she would never be able to get into it. She noticed that there was a bright shining piece of brass fastened on to the narrow part, and when she looked at this more closely, she found that it was evidently used as a door-plate, for on it was written, in very plain letters,

> MISTRESS CRISPIN.

"I suppose that it is the name of the person who lives in the house?" said Merle; "but what a funny door-plate: why, it has a big hole in the middle! And what a very, very, very funny house!" Merle walked right round it twice. "It is not a house at all," she said, and she walked round it again. Then a bright idea came into her head—"Why, why, why," she cried, "it's nothing but a big shoe!"

And so it was—a great big shoe. The rope ladder was the shoe-lace, and the brass door-plate the shoe-buckle!

"Now," said Merle, in a satisfied tone, "the next thing, of course, is to find the old woman and the children.

"*There was an old woman who lived in a shoe.* Of course, this is the shoe, and I suppose the old woman's name is Mistress Crispin."

By standing on tiptoe, she managed to peep through one of the little windows that was let into the side of the shoe. She could see what looked like a very comfortable little room inside. There was a fine big fire burning brightly, and on the fire were two huge pots, which were evidently bubbling and boiling with all their might and main, for the smoke was coming from them in big clouds.

There was no one in the room, but there was evidently some one in the house, for Merle heard a very great noise of beating and banging.

"Oh dear!" said Merle, greatly distressed, "she must be at the '*whipped them all soundly*' part, I should think, by the noise. I must go and stop her."

She ran quickly round the house to the rope ladder, and, after some little trouble, managed to climb right up it and get inside the shoe.

She found herself in a tidy little room, evidently a sleeping room, for there were a number of little beds, as many as could be got into the room, against the wall. Merle thought she heard a noise in the next room, so she hurried on.

Directly afterwards she found herself in the room she had seen from outside; but now there was some one in it.

By the side of the fire was a tiny little old lady. She was stirring something in the pot with one hand, and with the other was wildly waving a big birch-rod, nearly as big as herself. As she waved she kept knocking the chairs and tables that were within her reach, so that she made a good deal of noise.

"What I expected," said Merle; "this, of course, is Mistress Crispin."

The old lady turned as Merle pronounced her name, and said, in the very crossest of cross voices,

"So delighted to see you, my dear!"

Merle was most astonished.

"Do keep out of my way, darling," said the old lady, angrily, "or I shall be obliged to beat you."

Merle quickly got outside the door, and only popped her head in to talk to the old lady. The voice and tones were so very cross, and yet the words were so kind, what could it mean?

"Where are the children?" asked Merle, at last summoning up all her courage.

Poor Mistress Crispin looked crosser than ever, though the tears rolled down her cheeks as she said,

"Gone, my dear, gone! They simply could not stand the beating and the broth."

"Why, how wicked of you!" said Merle. "How cruel of you to drive all your children away from you!"

"Oh, my dear! you don't understand, or you would never talk like that. Come and stir this broth whilst I fetch something soft to beat, so that I shan't make such a noise, and then I will tell you all about it."

Merle ran at once, and took the spoon from the old lady's hand. Mistress Crispin turned away directly, so as not to be able to beat Merle; but although she tried her hardest, she could not help hitting her twice.

Merle looked rather angry, but before she could say anything the old lady kissed her, and ran to fetch a pillow from the bedroom.

Then when Merle was comfortably settled in a chair, and Mistress Crispin had once more taken the spoon to stir up the broth, she began her story.

"A long time ago I lived happily with my family in this comfortable roomy house, I had so many children——"

"That you did not know what to do," interrupted Merle.

"On the contrary, my dear, I always knew what to do. I never had a minute to spare, I was so busy; but I did not mind that, for I loved my children, and they loved me."

"But if you loved them so much, why did you whip them all soundly and send them to bed?" asked Merle.

"If you will wait a minute, I will come to that," said Mistress Crispin. "Well, as I was saying, we were once all very happy, but troublous times came to the country, and discontent seized the land. Grunter Grim deceived us, and by deceiving us got power over us."

"All the same, I don't see why you gave those poor children broth," said Merle. "I don't like broth myself, especially without any bread."

"Oh, my dear!" said Mistress Crispin, in the crossest of cross voices, whilst the tears rolled down her cheek, "I didn't give them broth. I cooked the dinner as usual, and a very good dinner it was—roast beef and plum pudding. Well, I cooked the dinner, and put it all on the table, and told the children to begin, while I went out just to wash my hands. When I came back—I hadn't been a-way more than a minute—I found all the children fighting and quarrelling——"

"Oh, how dreadful!" said Merle.

"Indeed it was. When I asked them what was the matter, they said they wanted to know why I had given them such a dreadful dinner."

"What peculiar children! How funny of them not to like beef and plum pudding!" said Merle.

"That was what made me angry; and without stopping to think," said the old woman, beginning to cry again, "I fetched out the birch-rod and began beating them."

"And they quite deserved it," said Merle, very decidedly.

"No, they didn't: it was all a mistake. Let me finish my story," said poor Mistress Crispin. "In the middle of the bother, when they were crying, and I was beating, it grew dark, and in came Grunter Grim. He laughed a horrid laugh. 'I am glad you like my broth,' he said; 'you shall always have it; and since you are so fond of beating, you shall always beat,' and then with another laugh he went away."

"What did he mean by talking about broth?" asked Merle.

"Why, don't you see," said Mistress Crispin, "it was he who had changed the beef and plum pudding into broth."

"Oh, how wicked of him!" cried Merle.

"Next day," continued the old lady, "I was still obliged to speak angrily and beat the children, and every day after, until at last they ran away and left me. And now, although I am all alone, I can do nothing but beat the children that are not there, and make this horrible broth."

"What a shame!" said Merle. "I wish I could punish Grunter Grim."

"You can," said Mistress Crispin.

Just then a girl popped her head in at the window.

"Good morning, mother," said she. "May I come in?"

"Don't, dear, don't," said the old lady, angrily. "You know I must beat you if you do. Have you found the tails?"

"No, mother, not yet," said the girl. "I dream of them every night, but in the morning I find my poor sheep still without them."

"Are you Bo-peep?" said Merle, eagerly. "I have long wanted to know you. I have heard of you so often," and she began to sing—

"Little Bo-peep has lost her sheep,
And doesn't know——"

But she stopped suddenly, for she saw the girl look very angry, and then run away from the window.

"There, of course, she is offended," said Mistress Crispin; "it was very rude to remind her of that insulting story. But perhaps you do not know who stole the sheeps' tails. You must get her to tell you some day."

"Is she your daughter?" said Merle, hoping to change the subject.

"Of course she is my own dear daughter Bo-peep. You have much to learn yet about my family, and I want you to do it quickly, for then you will help us. Can you not see that it is Grunter Grim who is our great enemy? He has done all the harm, and worked all the mischief."

In her eagerness and excitement, the old lady had gradually spoken louder and louder, and had drawn nearer and nearer to Merle.

At last she was so close that her birch-rod actually touched Merle, and at once, though poor Mistress Crispin tried to stop herself, she began to beat Merle. Each time she apologised most humbly in the angriest tone of voice.

"I beg your pardon," she said, stamping her foot. "I am so sorry. I hope I don't in any way hurt." Thwack, thwack, went the birch-rod, and Merle began to make her way to the door. "I don't want to hurt you," continued the old lady, "but I feel one of my bad attacks coming on. Please, oh, please, do get out of the house!"

She followed Merle, beating her all the time with the birch-rod, and begging her pardon, until Merle once more reached the ladder and got out of her way.

A——Hill

As soon as she reached the bottom of the ladder, Merle stopped to think. The question was, what ought she to do next?

She was very anxious to find out all about the Rhymes and Grunter Grim, but she certainly could not go back to Mistress Crispin, it was too dangerous. She shut her eyes tightly. When she opened them again, to her surprise, Mistress Crispin's house and the road to the turnstile had entirely disappeared, and in front of her rose a high hill. At the foot of the hill was a sign-post, and on it was written "A——Hill."

"That's the name, I suppose," said Merle; "but why don't they put it in full. What is the use of giving only the first letter of a name?"

"That shows you don't know anything about it," said a voice quite close to her ear. Merle turned round quickly, and was surprised to see a girl and boy, carrying an empty pail between them, walking beside her.

The boy and girl did not seem at all astonished to see her, however.

"Well, you've come at last!" said the boy, crossly. "It was time you did, though I don't suppose you'll be any better than all the others."

The girl took no notice of his remark.

"The name is put like that," she said to Merle, "so that other children shall not have to waste their time as we do, fetching and spilling water."

"Excuse me," said Merle, very politely; "but are you Jack and Jill?"

"Of course," said the boy, "and we are going up Argument Hill to fetch a pail of water."

"Oh, Jack," interrupted Jill, "you shouldn't have told her the name. Now every child will find out where the hill is, and will follow our example, and try to carry pails up it. You know what a bother it was to me to persuade the Rhyme Fairy to leave the real name out of the story-books."

"I can't help it," said Jack, "I forgot."

All this time they were gradually climbing the hill—indeed, they had almost reached the top.

"You're always forgetting," said Jill.

"'Tis your fault," said Jack.

"It's yours," retorted Jill.

"Oh dear, please don't quarrel," said Merle, stepping between them. But she was too late, for just then the hill seemed somehow to rise up, and in a minute Jack fell, and began rolling down the hill. As for Jill, she didn't even wait to fall, but at once lay down, and rolled after Jack.

"Just what I expected," said Merle. "I only hope Jack's crown is not quite broken."

When the two reached the bottom, they picked themselves up, and Jack immediately pulled some plaster out of his pocket, which Jill fastened on his head, and then shaking hands, they once more started to carry the pail up the hill.

They seemed to be friends again, and to be talking quite kindly to one another. Merle sat down on the ground, and determined to wait until they arrived.

"Don't quarrel again," she shouted.

Jack nodded and smiled, and Jill put her finger over her mouth to show that she was not going to talk at all.

It was no good, however, for, just as they reached Merle, Jack kicked a stone. At once Jill turned round, took her finger from her lips, and said angrily,

"Do be careful."

"It was your fault," said Jack.

The words were scarcely out of his mouth before down he tumbled, down sat Jill, and away the two went rolling to the bottom of the hill.

"This is all very well," said Merle, "but if they are going to do that for ever, of course I can't stop here."

She only waited to see that neither the brother nor sister was badly hurt, and then picking herself up, walked on over the top of the hill and down the other side.

She had not walked very far before she came to a narrow, straight lane, with a high hedge on each side. It looked dismal and lonely, and Merle was just coming to the conclusion that she would not go any further, when she caught sight of a bit of blue petticoat and a black shoe peeping out from underneath the hedge, half-way down the lane. She walked quickly to the place, and there found a girl lying fast asleep under the hedge, and she at once recognised her as the one who had come to see Mistress Crispin.

"*Little Bo-peep fell fast asleep,*" said Merle, gently, for she did not want the girl to be offended again.

As she said the words, however, Bo-peep sat up and rubbed her eyes.

"Come, my pretty lambs," she said, sleepily. "I am glad indeed to see you again."

Merle stared at her, and wondered whatever she was talking about. She was just going to ask a question, when Bo-peep suddenly stood up and burst out crying.

"They are not there," she sobbed, "and I dreamt so plainly that I heard them bleating."

"Never mind," said Merle, kindly. "I'll help you find them. Who stole your sheep, dear, was it Grunter Grim?"

"Of course it was," said Bo-peep; "but come, let us hasten," and she quickly wiped her eyes and stopped crying. "If we are sharp, we shall be in time for the meeting."

"What meeting?" asked Merle.

"The meeting of the Family," said Bo-peep. "Every night at twelve o'clock we are all free for one hour. Until one, Grunter Grim has no power over us, and we are able to leave our work. Then we meet together and discuss our plans for overcoming the tyrant."

"But can I come?" said Merle. "Won't he be angry if he knows I am there?"

"He won't know," said Bo-peep. "I will get you in, it is a secret meeting."

She took hold of Merle's hand, and at once everything became dark. Then she heard a clock begin to strike twelve, and then another, and then another, until all round her the air seemed full of the sound of striking clocks. Some had deep notes, some silvery ones, but the noise was so great that Merle put her hands over her head to keep out the sound. When she took them away again, she was no longer in the narrow lane, but in a large room.

FROM TWELVE O'CLOCK TO ONE O'CLOCK

It was a very large hall indeed, and quite unlike any hall that Merle had ever seen before. Instead of having a raised platform at one end for the speakers, and rows of chairs in front of it for the listeners, nearly the whole room was taken up by an enormous platform, and there was only one row of chairs in front of it. Even this, as Bo-peep told Merle, was not really necessary, for every one always wanted to talk, and no one to sit down and listen.

"Well," said Merle, "there will be some one to listen to-day, so I will sit on one of the chairs."

But Bo-peep would not hear of it, because she said if Merle sat by herself Grunter Grim would notice that a child was present.

There were several people already on the platform when Merle and Bo-peep took their seats. The clocks were still striking; but whenever any clock struck for the twelfth time, some new visitor arrived.

Merle soon recognised her friend Mistress Crispin sitting quietly in a chair, and not even trying to beat any one. Jack and Jill were sitting side by side, laughing and talking happily together, although Jack's head was tied up in a big red handkerchief, and Jill's arm was in a sling.

Merle soon found out, too, who all the others were, for each one wore a small ticket, on which a name was written.

There was little Boy Blue, as wide-awake as could be, and next to him the Man in the Moon. In the front row of chairs Goosey Goosey Gander and Miss Muffet, sitting side by side, were talking away to Pollie Flinders and Tom, Tom, the Piper's Son, and making a great deal of noise. Miss Muffet looked such a dashing young lady, that Merle wondered how it could have happened that she should have been frightened by a spider.

Just as the last clock finished striking, Mother Hubbard came hurrying into the hall, followed by a dog and quite a number of people, a cobbler, a baker, a tailor, and many others. Merle was just going to ask Bo-peep who these people were, when Mistress Crispin stepped forward and began to speak.

"My children," she said, "it must be fully twelve by the earthly clocks; what is the time by the nursery clock?"

Directly she asked the question, each one present produced a dandelion clock, and began solemnly and seriously to blow upon it. Mistress Crispin counted aloud "One—two"—and so on, up to twelve, and by that time the seeds were scattered in every direction, and she and the others held dandelion stalks only in their hands. At the same time, the hall, which Merle had thought very badly lighted before, became brilliantly bright. It seemed as though the stars had come down from the sky, and had fastened themselves upon the walls, but really there were no stars. Each dandelion seed had turned into a bright shining lamp.

Then once more Mistress Crispin began to speak.

"Merle," she said, "listen to our wrongs, and help us to make them rights. You can do it if you will. You know my story, now listen to some of the others."

She quickly sat down, without wasting more time, and at once Bo-peep, Humpty Dumpty, the Man in the Moon, and Boy Blue all rose together, and began talking very quickly.

Merle could not in the least understand what they were saying. She only heard one name, which they each used several times, and that name was Grunter Grim. After they had been speaking a minute, Mistress Crispin held up her hand, and they all stopped and sat down.

"There, Merle," she said, "you know now how wrongly and wickedly Grunter Grim has treated us all. It saves so much time if four of the children speak at once, and it does not matter if you do not hear each word, for you can judge of the tyrant by his deeds. You have seen the result of his actions, and after that, words make no difference."

"But how can I send him away?" asked Merle.

"Choose us a king," said Humpty Dumpty.

"Have faith in yourself, and defy him," said Boy Blue.

"Do anything you like, only do it quickly," said Mother Hubbard.

"Yes, indeed," said the cobbler, the baker, the tailor, and all the other people who had come with Mother Hubbard, "do it quickly."

Merle stared at them all. She did not in the least understand what they were talking about.

"A king?" she said at last; "what do you want a king for?"

"Oh dear! oh dear!" said Mistress Crispin, "we must go back to the beginning of all things, and explain matters to her. Well, Merle, we had a king who was able to keep Grunter Grim in order. At that time Grunter Grim had no power over us, he could only growl and grumble to himself."

"Then the time came," said the Man in the Moon, taking up the story when Mistress Crispin paused to take breath—"then came the time when our king finished his reign, and because Grunter Grim deceived us, we had not chosen a new one. We could not agree which of the claimants was the right one, and so we quarrelled."

"That's the whole point," interrupted Boy Blue, "we quarrelled. You see, Merle, as long as we were all contented Grunter Grim had no power over us; but as soon as we quarrelled he just took the power into his own hands, and since then he has treated us shamefully."

"But how very silly of you to quarrel!" said Merle.

"It is easy enough to say that now," said a girl who had not spoken before.

Merle did not have to ask who she was, for she saw at once by the ticket fastened on her dress that she was "Mary, Mary, quite contrary."

"Hush, hush, Mary!" said Bo-peep, "please don't be rude to Merle."

"But why don't you stop quarrelling?" asked Merle.

"Because as long as Grunter Grim has power over us, we can't help it," said Mistress Crispin.

"If we only once got up that Hill without disagreeing," said Jack, "we shouldn't tumble down, of course, but it isn't all our fault. Grunter Grim makes us fall out, and fall down too," he added, rubbing his head.

"If this goes on much longer my arms will be too much bruised ever to get well again," said Jill, dolefully.

"It isn't all temper that makes us quarrel, Merle, don't you see that?" said Mistress Crispin.

"Besides," put in Bo-peep, "if you spent your whole day looking for sheeps' tails, I don't think you would be sweet-tempered."

"Now, Bo-peep! don't get cross," said Mistress Crispin, "that is no good. Our time is nearly up, it is a quarter to one. Cannot some one tell this child what she is to do to help us?"

"I will," said Goosey Goosey Gander, drawing herself up, and stretching out her feathers. "Merle, listen. The next time you see our common foe, you must stand up and defy him, and banish him from the land. You *can* do it, if you *will.* Then, when he has gone you must choose a king for us."

"I will do my best," said Merle, "but I'm afraid I am not much good."

"I never expected you would be," said Mary, Mary, quite contrary.

"Do be quiet, Mary!" shouted Boy Blue.

"She can give her opinion if she likes," said Jill.

"Yes, of course," said Mother Hubbard.

"Of course, of course," called out the cobbler, the baker, the tailor, and the others.

"Oh, please don't begin quarrelling now," said Mistress Crispin. "It is only five minutes to one, and then——"

But the hall was beginning to grow dark, although the dandelion-seed lamps were shining as brightly as ever. Merle took hold of Bo-peep's hand, for she felt rather frightened. But Bo-peep did not take any notice, for she seemed to be gradually dropping off to sleep. Then Merle looked at Mistress Crispin, and she was no longer sitting still, but was moving her hands about, feeling for her stick.

It grew darker and darker, and somehow it seemed to Merle as if some one outside the hall were shouting. She felt sure she heard some voice in the distance—what could it mean? She was getting more and more frightened. She turned again to Bo-peep, but Bo-peep was fast asleep, and evidently dreaming, for from time to time she turned in her sleep and muttered something about her sheep. Darker and darker!

Merle at last could bear it no longer, and she started to her feet with the intention of getting down from the platform and running out of the hall. But instead of running away, she stood perfectly still, for there shining at the end of the hall were the fiery letters "G.G." They came closer and closer to her, and she knew it was Grunter Grim. Then she remembered all that Goosey Goosey Gander had said to her, how she was to defy the tyrant, and banish him from Endom. She summoned up her courage and began to speak.

"I de——" but got no further, for just then the clocks outside began striking one, and as the red letters came closer and closer to her, she heard a voice saying—

"Once more in strife now ends your hour,
Once more I have you in my power."

All thought of finishing her sentence and banishing Grunter Grim went out of Merle's head. She was terrified.

As the fiery letters came closer to her, she screamed at the top of her voice, "Topleaf—somebody—help! help!"

She quite expected to feel Topleaf's arms round her, but instead, something seemed to come between her and the horrible letters, and she heard beautiful music, and a soft voice singing a lullaby gently and slowly.

Merle knew the tune, but somehow she could not think of the words. Gradually the lullaby grew louder and louder, and the voice appeared to come nearer and nearer. At the same time the fiery letters on Grunter Grim's cap became fainter and fainter, until at last they faded away. Then the darkness lifted, and once more it became light.

G——G——

By the time that Grunter Grim's cap had disappeared, and the darkness with it, Merle's courage had returned. As soon as it was quite light again, she stood up and prepared to speak to Bo-peep; but, strange to say, Bo-peep, Mistress Crispin, Jack and Jill—all the Nursery Rhymes, in fact, and even the Hall—had entirely vanished. Merle could scarcely believe her eyes, but it was indeed the case. She herself was the only thing that had not disappeared.

All this time the lullaby was still going on, though now it was fainter— so faint that Merle scarcely noticed it, as she had so many other things to think about. She was now standing out of doors, in the middle of a road, or rather at a place where four roads met.

Not far from her stood a sign-post, with each of its four arms pointing towards one of the four roads.

Merle walked up to the post to see what was written on it. On the arm pointing to the road on her right was written—

G——G——

Merle felt quite frightened when she saw the dreadful letters, and was going to hurry on to see if anything better were written on the next arm, when she heard some one speaking to her.

"Look closer before you run away, my dear," said the some one.

Merle could not in the least understand where the voice came from, but

she once more looked at the sign-post, and then found that there were other letters besides the two G's. Carefully she spelt it out, and found, after some trouble, that

To Grumbling Greatly

was written there.

"That doesn't sound very inviting," said Merle.

"Of course not," said the some one again; "look at the next."

On the next Merle discovered—

To Gliding Giddily

written in the same way as the first, with the G's large and the other letters small. Very disappointed, she turned to the third, and on that was written, just in the same way—

To Gossiping Grandly

"This is too provoking," said Merle. "I shan't trouble to look at the other. That horrid Grunter Grim is everywhere. I hate the sight of those wretched letters G——G——."

"Don't lose your temper, my dear, that never does any good," said the some one.

By this time Merle was quite angry.

"I wish you would show yourself, whoever you are," she said.

"Look up, and you will see."

Merle looked up, and to her surprise saw that it was the sign-post itself that was talking to her. It was not like an ordinary sign-post, for right at the top, some distance above the arms, there was a head. It looked as if it were only carved wood, but it was quite as able to talk as Merle herself.

"Don't apologise," said the post, "you are only making the mistake that other people have made before you. They only look at a sign-post; if they talked to it they would get much more information, for have we not stood in our places for a very long time? And do we not know a great deal more about the country than we can possibly put on our arms?"

Merle determined that she would no longer make the mistake of only looking at the post, and decided to get as much information as she could. She was rather ashamed of herself, so she said, humbly—

"Would you mind telling me why you have those horrid letters G G on your arms?"

"Do you think I wrote them?" said the sign-post, very indignantly, and he got so excited that his arms shook. "Is it likely that I should write such stuff?"

"Then I suppose Grunter Grim has power over you, as well as over every one else. Did he write them?" asked Merle, hoping to calm the excited post.

"Of course he did," said the post, sulkily.

"What do they mean, please?" said Merle; "surely there isn't really a place called 'Grumbling Greatly.' I wish you would tell me, because I must go some-where, and I don't know which way to go, and you said I was to talk to you, because you know so much. Please help me."

The sign-post had been getting calmer and less sulky as Merle spoke, and when she reached the end of her long speech he said, quite mildly—

"Well, I will help you. Now listen. A long time ago, when we had our own king, I was a sensible sign-post, with proper directions written on my arms."

"Then you quarrelled with some one, I suppose?" said Merle, "and so Grunter Grim got power over you. It is the same story over again."

"Not quite," said the post, sadly, "I did not quarrel with any one. I suf-fer because of other people's wickedness. Every one *would* quarrel with me."

"That is pretty much the same thing, isn't it?" asked Merle.

"Not at all, not at all, but it had the same effect. Grunter Grim came and spoiled all my arms, and now every one goes the wrong way."

"Well, help me to go the right. What does 'To Gliding Giddily' mean?" asked Merle.

"That means really, 'To Jack and Jill's Hill.' Jack and Jill spend all their time 'gliding giddily,' you know, so instead of writing on my arms 'To A—— Hill,' Grunter Grim has put 'To Gliding Giddily.' He likes that name, partly because it misleads every one, and partly because he can use his favourite letters, G G."

"Oh, I understand now. Then, 'To Grumbing Greatly,' let me think— now, what does it mean? I know—the way to Mistress Crispin's of course, and 'To Gossiping Grandly' is the way to the Hall."

"That's right, my dear," said the post. "You really are a clever girl, though you have only two arms."

"Why, of course I've only two arms," said Merle. "However many did you expect me to have?"

"Four, of course," said the post. "How can you point each way if you haven't four? Why, you wouldn't be any good at all on a cross road."

Merle felt that this was unanswerable, and decided to turn the conversation, so she said—

"You haven't told me now which way I am to go. It's no use my following those three roads, for I know all about them."

"Try the fourth, then," said the post.

Merle remembered that she had not even looked at what was written on the fourth arm of the sign-post, so she walked round to it.

It was quite as difficult to understand as the other three, for on it was written—

B—— B——

"That is not much help; I don't know what that means. Who is B—— B——?" said Merle.

There was no answer. Merle looked up at the sign-post, but it seemed to have lost the power of speech—it only stared at her.

"Well, this *is* stupid," said Merle.

The sign-post took no notice, but the arm pointing to B—— B—— shook slightly. It might have been the wind, it might have been fancy, but Merle certainly thought the arm shook. She at once decided that at any rate she would go along the road leading to B—— B——, and try to find out who B—— B—— was. Directly she had come to this conclusion she heard the voice singing the lullaby once more. It seemed, too, as if some one were holding her hand, and she felt as if she were floating along in the air rather than walking.

The farther she got from the four roads and the sign-post, the louder the lullaby grew and the firmer her hand was held, and at last the lullaby stopped, and a voice said—

"Merle, I am delighted to see you. Will you come in and see the claimants to the throne? for you must find a king of Endom."

Imaginary Twins

Merle looked about her. She could not see any one, and, what was worse, she could not see anywhere to go in. But she was getting used to queer things by this time, so she simply said—

"Show me the claimants, and I will do the best I can."

At once she saw in front of her a long low building. It had not been there before, or rather, Merle had not seen it there before; but she was not at all surprised, and walked straight towards it. The door opened, and Merle found herself in a long room. It was almost entirely filled with babies' cradles.

Babies' cradles of every description! Some quite grand ones, trimmed with rows of ribbon and lace, so grand that you would never have thought of giving them such a simple name as cradle, but would have at once decided that they were "bassinettes." Some quite ordinary basket cradles, some old-fashioned wooden ones that had evidently been used for more than one generation of babies, and some not proper cradles at all. One was an old tin bath, another a big basket, and another a wooden box.

Yet they were all—the grand ones, the ordinary ones, and the funny ones—they were certainly all cradles, for each one contained a baby. There was perfect silence in the long room, although there were so many children and not a single nurse—perfect silence, absolute quiet!

Merle at first thought that all the babies must be asleep, and, fearful of waking them, stepped very quietly up to the cradle nearest to her, and peeped in.

She was most devoted to any baby; she loved the whole baby race, as every girl should do, and, in fact, as every right-minded girl does.

Well, Merle peeped into the first cradle. It happened to be one of the grandly trimmed ones. In it was lying a very small, very thin, very pale, but very clean baby. Any one who was not fond of babies would have said, "What an ugly baby!" Merle only thought, "That poor baby looks ill!" The baby, however, seemed happy enough—it was not asleep, but was lying contentedly on its back. As soon as it caught sight of Merle it gave a delighted crow, and at once from every cot of every kind came a baby's joyful crow or coo.

You know, if you know anything about babies, how enjoyable it is to hear one happy, comfortable baby coo. Just fancy what a glorious thing it would be to hear dozens and dozens of perfectly happy babies gently coo with delight.

Merle smiled, simply because she couldn't help it, and then she laughed, at what she did not know. Then she looked once more at the baby in the gorgeous cradle, and noticed for the first time that there was a ticket fastened to one of the curtains. On the ticket was written—Merle looked twice, she thought she must have made a mistake; but no, there it was plainly written, "The Finest Baby in the World."

She was rather astonished, for she felt sure that she had seen finer babies many a time.

In the next cradle—the tin bath one—lay a very bonnie baby, also wide-awake and perfectly happy. This was quite a different-looking baby. It had rosy cheeks and curly hair, though rather a dirty face. It really was a fine baby. Merle saw a ticket fastened to this cradle, and when she looked at it, she saw written on that too, "The Finest Baby in the World."

Then she looked at the next cradle, and on that was another ticket with exactly the same words on it. She looked at another, and another, and another—it was just the same all the way round—every baby, pretty or plain, clean or dirty, thin or fat, each one was labelled, "The Finest Baby in the World."

Merle stood bewildered. What could it all mean?

"It is simple nonsense!" she said aloud. "There can be only one *finest* baby in the whole world."

"That's just the point," said the voice Merle had heard when she had left the sign-post—the voice that had invited her to look at the claimants. Merle turned round, for now there was something more than a voice. Standing close beside her was a small boy who looked about three years old, but who spoke as if he were very much older.

"Just it," he repeated decidedly; "that's just what we want to find out, which is the finest?"

Merle stared at him, amazed.

"Where did you come from?" she said at last.

"I came in long ago," said the boy, "but I was weak. When Grunter Grim told me, as he told you, I could only come in by leaving my body outside, I left it."

"But you got it back, I suppose?" said Merle.

"No, I didn't," said the boy, indignantly, "not my own body. This one doesn't belong to me. I really am a girl, and I was ten years old when I came to Endom, and when I wanted to go out again Grunter Grim said he had given my own body away, and this was the best he could do for me. That's what he does—gives back the wrong bodies, and then down in that stupid world, every one is astonished because big people are often cowards and little people brave, some girls more like boys, and some boys more like girls. It is easy enough to explain it if they only knew the reason why."

"I suppose it is Grunter Grim's doing," said Merle, thoughtfully.

"Of course it is," said the boy. "Children get to Endom, leave their bodies in charge of Grunter Grim, and enter without them. Of course they are unable to help the poor Nursery Rhymes, and when they go away disgusted Grunter Grim gives them back wrong bodies. I am not going back until I get my own property. He knows where it is."

"But how will you get it—er———" Merle stopped and hesitated. "Would you mind telling me your name? It is so much easier for me to talk to you, if I know your name."

"My name? Certainly," said the boy. "It is Thomas Muriel."

Merle stared.

"Don't you see," he continued, "Muriel is my own proper name, but Thomas is the name of this body that I am now in."

Merle looked still more amazed, but the boy was getting so indignant that she did not like to say any more about his name—so asked how he thought of getting his own body back again.

"Why, *you* will help me do that—any one of these babies could answer that question," said the boy.

Merle did not understand how she was to get the boy's own body for him, but he seemed to know all about it and the babies too, so she thought she would probably find out in good time.

"Now then," said Thomas Muriel, when Merle stood perfectly still, without saying anything, "now then, be quick and decide."

"What am I to decide?" asked Merle.

"Which really *is* the finest baby in the world. You said yourself that there could only be one."

"But why do you want me to decide such a difficult question at all?"

"Because we want a king," said Thomas Muriel. "Before the last king finished his reign the Rhymes were all quite happy, but when he was forced to resign———"

"Why did they make him resign if they were all so happy? How very silly of them!" said Merle. "Oh, I am sorry! I never thought before that Nursery Rhymes could be silly."

Poor Merle was so excited that she almost began to cry.

"Wait a minute, my dear, wait a minute," said Thomas Muriel, not in the least disturbed by Merle's excitement. "You don't know what you are talking about. The last king was not forced by the Rhymes to resign, but he lost all his power. He got to be able to talk and walk."

"Talk and walk?" said Merle.

"Yes, talk and walk. What are you astonished at now? Don't tell me that you don't know about the Kings of Endom—you can't be as ignorant as all that."

"But I am," said Merle. "I don't know anything about it. Do explain."

At first, when Merle made this dreadful confession, Thomas Muriel looked horrified, and turned round as if he were going to leave her, but Merle looked so much ashamed of herself and so humble that he relented, and once more began to speak to her.

"A long time ago, Endom, which you know means Nurserydom or Nurseryland, was the very happiest land in the whole world. All the Rhymes were merry, jolly, and contented, and never even thought of quarrelling. The finest baby in the world who could not walk or talk was always made king."

"Who made him king?" asked Merle; "who chose him?"

"Who chooses your king," said Thomas Muriel—"I mean your King of England?"

"But we haven't a King. We've a Queen," said Merle; "and she isn't chosen a Queen, she's born it."

"Well, it was exactly the same with the Kings of Endom," said Thomas Muriel, getting rather impatient, "they were born it. You can't make a baby the *finest,* it has to be born the finest."

"Well, then, I don't see what was the difficulty," said Merle. "Why is there no King of Endom now? and how is it that all these babies are labelled, 'The Finest Baby in the World?' Who gave them their labels?"

"Their mothers, of course," said Thomas Muriel. "Don't you see, when the Rhymes couldn't decide for themselves which was the finest baby in the world, they sent messengers into the world to find out what the mothers thought. And each mother thought her own baby the finest."

"They might have expected that," said Merle.

"Of course," said Thomas Muriel, "but that doesn't settle the question. It is very easy to be clever now, but then at the time Grunter Grim deceived the Rhymes——"

"How?" asked Merle.

"Twins," said Thomas Muriel. "Twins were at the bottom of it all."

"Twins!" said Merle; "twins!"

"Yes—don't you believe me? I think you are very stupid."

"I think you are very rude," said Merle.

It was beginning to grow dark—but the two children were so busy talking that they did not notice it.

"Of course I believe you; but I can't understand what twins had to do with it."

"Not real ones," said Thomas Muriel, very crossly.—It grew darker. "Imaginary ones."

"Now you are talking simple nonsense," said Merle. "Imaginary twins—that's rubbish."

By this time it was quite dark, and Merle could no longer see Thomas Muriel. All at once it flashed across her mind that darkness meant Grunter Grim. Immediately her anger vanished.

"Thomas Muriel," she began, "don't let us quarrel."

All at once the babies began to coo, and it began to grow light.

For a little time it was quite bright in the room once more—but when Merle looked round for Thomas Muriel, he had disappeared, and she was alone with the babies.

Letters! Letters! Letters!

"Now, what is to be done?" said Merle. "I shall never find out quite all about the Kings of Endom. Grunter Grim is evidently doing his best to stop me. I expect he made Thomas Muriel cross. All the same, I do wonder what he meant by talking about twins. Whatever could twins have to do with the Kings of Endom?" Merle was talking aloud, standing in the middle of the big room; but as she asked the last question she walked slowly towards one of the cots.

To her surprise, the baby in the cot immediately began to talk, and not only that baby, but all the other babies. Every baby in the room was talking hard. The funny thing was that though the babies were using just the same baby language of coos and gurgles and a-goos that they generally use in the world, Merle perfectly understood what they said, and they evidently understood each other.

Merle listened with the greatest attention, for the babies were answering her question about the twins, and telling her the true story about the Kings of Endom. As you cannot understand baby-talk, I must tell you in proper language what the babies said to Merle.

Listen, then—

"The Finest Baby in the World was always made king, and before he was able to walk and talk properly, his successor was chosen. Well, it happened once that Grunter Grim was admitted to the meeting at which the future king was to be chosen. Now you must know that the king's name was always announced by the Messenger from the Leaves—for the Leaves know which is the finest baby, as they hear all that goes on in the world, and only come to Endom when they are old and need rest. When the name of the future king was given, Grunter Grim got up, and asked very quietly and innocently if the

Rhymes were sure that their friends the Leaves had fixed on the finest baby, for he knew that the one named had a twin brother.

"This remark at once upset the meeting. No one ever thought of finding out if what Grunter Grim said was true. They know now that it was false. But at that time they immediately began to discuss what should be done.

"There was, of course, great disagreement. Some thought there ought to be two kings, others declared that idea absurd, but all were agreed that where there were twin-babies, one could not be very much finer than the other.

"Finally, the meeting broke up in the greatest confusion, without any king having been chosen.

"At the next meeting, Grunter Grim spoke still more strongly. As a result, there was more disagreement. At the next, it was worse. Then he suggested that the mothers of all the babies should be asked which was the finest, and, as you know, that only caused greater trouble. Time passed on, and still no king was chosen.

"Then there was not only discontent at the meetings, but before them and after them. The time was taken up in discussion and argument, and nothing was done.

"At last the king was obliged to resign, and no successor had been chosen.

"On that day the last meeting was held. Grunter Grim was present, and when the assembly broke up in confusion, he shouted, 'I will give you a king; I will be your king myself. Henceforward, obey Grunter Grim!' Then all was dark—that was the day on which Mistress Crispin's dinner was changed; that was the day on which Jack and Jill, as they went up the hill quarrelling, were thrown down; that was the day on which Bo-peep's sheeps' tails were cut off and the Man in the Moon burnt his mouth. Every misfortune, every trouble that has come to the Rhymes, dates from that day."

This is the story, as the babies told it to Merle.

When they had finished speaking, Merle waited quietly for two minutes, then nodding to them, she said—"Thank you; at last I understand all about it. Now I must set to work to find a real king for Endom, and he ought to be a king for all time, so that there may never be any more disputes and quarrels."

After she had made this little speech to the babies, she bowed, gave them each a kiss, and then walked out of the room. She felt sure that the future king of Endom was not there, and made up her mind that she ought to begin looking somewhere else for him without wasting any more time.

She passed through several rooms, filled with babies and cradles, and at last came to a very small room. At first she thought that this was quite empty, for there seemed to be nothing in it; but then she noticed that though there was nothing actually in the middle of the room, round the walls there were glass cases. When she looked closely at these cases, she saw that they were filled with rows and rows of letters.

"Very curious," said Merle. "I wonder whose letters they are, and why ever they keep them here?"

Then she looked still closer, and then gave a loud cry of astonishment. It was so loud, that if any one had heard her I am sure they would have come quickly to the rescue, for they would have thought that she was in pain. However, no one did hear, so that it did not matter. After her first surprise, Merle seemed to know exactly what to do. She opened the glass case and took out one of the letters, and then she opened it.

Perhaps you may think it was very wrong of Merle to open somebody else's letter. So it would have been, but this was not some one else's; it was her own, for it was addressed to Merle.

And this was not the only one. Every letter,—and there were hundreds of them—every letter in those cases was meant for Merle to read, although they were not all actually addressed to her.

On some of the envelopes, "To any Human Child who can read" was written, and on others, "Let any child who comes to Endom read this." On a great many Merle's own name was written in very plain letters.

Well, Merle opened one letter, and this is what she found inside—

> *"If you would banish Grunter Grim,*
> *Have not the slightest fear of him."*

"I've heard that before," said Merle, "there's nothing new in that. What is in the next?"

She opened another letter, and found the very same words in that. Then she opened another and another, and about twenty others, and every one was exactly the same.

At last she opened one of the letters directed "to any Human Child who can read," and there she found something different, for in that the following words were written:—

> *"If you'd help us, quickly bring*
> *Unto Endom Endom's king.*
> *Find his name, you'll then find him.*
> *Who has got it? Grunter Grim.*
> *Search his house, you'll find at last,*
> *'Tis written down, but sealed up fast."*

"Grunter Grim's house," said Merle; "why, I haven't seen that; I didn't know he had a house. I will go at once; but perhaps I had better finish reading the letter first, as there may be something more in it."

There *was* more in it, and this is what Merle read:—

> *"If you ask who wrote it down—*
> *'Twas one who never wore a crown.*
> *But the monster Grunter Grim*
> *Stole the secret—shame on him!*
> *If you'd get it back again,*
> *Remember this, I write it plain—*
> *When Grunter Grim says 'Yes'—say 'No';*
> *When he says 'Come'—then quickly go;*
> *When he says 'Fly'—be sure to stay;*
> *When he says 'Stop'—then run away.*
> *Defy, Deride, Desist, Deny,*
> *Heed not a growl, or scowl, or sigh."*

Merle read it all through twice, and put it in her pocket. At last she really understood what she was to do.

She wondered very much who had written all these letters. She was leaving the room when she remembered that she had not yet opened one of the letters that had "Let any child who comes to Endom read this" written on it. She thought she had better do so, and she walked back to the glass case, took out a letter and opened it. This was a very short letter, there were only a few words written on a big sheet of paper.

> *"Beware my fate,*
> *I thought too late,*
> *I'm Kate."*

"Whatever does that mean?" said Merle. "I had better look at another." She found in the next—

> *"Do as the letters say—*
> *Be careful to obey,*
> *Or you will fail in the way*
> *That I did—Maggie May."*

"I wonder if these are from children who have been to Endom, and then have been unable to defy Grunter Grim? I wonder what has become of them, and what will become of me? Well, I can but do my best."

So saying, Merle shut the glass case, picked up all the opened letters, made a little heap of them, and then walked out of the room. She was determined to do her best, determined to try to follow the directions in the long letter which she had put in her pocket. As she left the babies' house she repeated aloud the last words—

"Defy, Deride, Desist, Deny,
Heed not a growl, or scowl, or sigh,"

and somehow she found them very comforting.

A Winding Way and a Crooked House

Outside the house, Merle found herself standing facing a broad pathway, with a high hedge on each side of it. She walked a little way down the path, and found that it divided, and several paths led out of it. Each road was closed in by high hedges, so high that Merle could not see over them, and could only wander aimlessly on and on.

The paths twisted and turned, wound in and out, crossed one another, curved, and sometimes suddenly came to an end.

It was fatiguing work, and Merle soon began to feel very tired. Her feet ached, her legs ached, and her head ached. For she was beginning to feel not only tired, but worried and frightened, for it was evident that she had lost her way. Then it began to grow dark, but she was not at all disturbed by that, for she knew that darkness only meant Grunter Grim. And when she remembered Grunter Grim, she took courage, and began to walk more quickly. She felt sure that this crooked, roundabout way must be connected with him, and she felt convinced that she would soon find herself at his house. She was quite right. The road grew narrower, the hedges higher, and, almost directly after, Merle found herself in front of a dark, dismal house.

Like everything else belonging to Grunter Grim, the house was black. It was not straight up and down. Like the way to it, it was very crooked. The walls leant on one side, they seemed as if they must surely tumble down soon. The few windows—and there were very few—were scattered about, as it seemed, anyhow. One end of the house was very high, and looked as if there might be six or seven storeys, and the other end was quite low, only one storey high. Everything about the house looked crooked, and wrong, and uncomfortable.

Merle was not at all surprised at this, however, for she did not expect to find anything pretty or straightforward in connection with Grunter Grim.

She looked about a long while for the door, and at last discovered it high up, in what seemed like the top attic. You would scarcely have thought that a door could be put in such a funny place, but this evidently was a door, for there was a knocker fastened to it and a door-plate, but certainly it was not the least bit of use to any one inside or outside of the house.

Merle looked about to see if she could find any sign of a side-door or a back-door. They were quickly found, but they were in such queer places that nobody could use them. Since there was no door for her to enter, Merle decided to try a window. She noticed one, quite close to the ground, in the one-storeyed end of the house, and quickly walking to it, she peeped in.

She could not see very much inside, as it was dark, and it was only a little window. After peering in for a few minutes, Merle gently tapped. There was no answer, and no sign of any movement inside the house.

Merle knocked much louder; still no sign. She knocked again, and this time called, "Grunter Grim, Grunter Grim, are you in?"

Still there was no answer, so Merle pushed the window to see if she could open it, but it was fastened very securely.

She did not know at all what to do, so she pulled out her letter of directions, to see if she could find out anything from that.

She opened it out, and began to read aloud from it—

"If you'd help us———"

Merle got no further, for she heard a sudden click. She quickly turned round, but she could see no one. She began reading her letter again. Just as she got to the words "Search his house," she happened to look at the window, and, to her amazement, she saw that it was actually opening, as it seemed, by itself.

For a moment Merle stood still, overcome by astonishment, and then she stepped lightly over the low window-sill, and in at the open window.

She fully expected to find Grunter Grim waiting to receive her, but when she got inside the little room she found no one there, and as soon as she was out of the way, the window quietly shut down.

Merle found herself in a very queer place. The room had no wall-paper—at least, if there was one it was quite impossible to see it, for each of the four walls, as well as the ceiling, was covered with something that looked like a kind of rough woollen material. It was a very light colour, nearly white in some places.

Merle thought it looked rather peculiar, and so went up and touched it. It felt like wool, it *was* wool, but Merle found it was all in loose pieces. She pulled one of the pieces apart from the rest.

"Why, it looks just like——" she began, and then she stopped. She remembered that Grunter Grim might be in the house, and might hear her remarks.

"It looks like sheeps' wool," she continued, in a whisper. "I do believe it is a sheep's tail."

She looked again. Then she very nearly shouted, "Of course, of course, these are Bo-peep's sheeps' tails. I've found them."

She was so pleased with her discovery that she determined to examine the rest of the room very carefully.

It contained a perfect mine of treasures. Evidently it was Grunter Grim's store-room, where he kept everything he had stolen from the Rhymes. In one corner Merle found Little Boy Blue's horn.

"Of course," she said, "this explains it. Little Boy Blue couldn't very well blow his horn when Grunter Grim had it here."

In another corner were some gardening tools, and these were labelled, "Johnny's Tools." Merle stood before them for a long time, wondering who "Johnny" was. Then, all at once, the rhyme came into her head—

> "See-saw, Margery Daw,
> Johnny shall have a new master.
> He shall have but a penny a day,
> Because he can't work any faster."

"Of course Johnny wasn't able to work quickly when Grunter Grim had his tools."

Merle was continuing her examination of the room, when suddenly she remembered her letter. She had forgotten the directions, and instead of looking for the packet in which the future king's name was written, she was amusing herself. She put Johnny's tools down, and began soberly and seriously to hunt in every nook and corner for the sealed packet.

She left the little store-room and went into the other parts of the house, but found no sign of the packet.

At last she returned to the store-room, and once more began to hunt there. She noticed something black in a very dark corner that she had not seen when she looked before. She picked the something black up, and found when she shook it out that it was a long cloak.

"Grunter Grim's cloak," said Merle, with a shudder.

Again she looked in the corner—there was something more in it. This time she pulled out Grunter Grim's big pointed hat. Merle looked at the front of it, wondering if the fiery letters would be there, but there was not a sign of them.

Scarcely thinking what she was doing, Merle wrapped the cloak round her and put the big hat on her head. She began to feel quite queer immediately. A change seemed to be taking place in her character.

Before, she had felt happy, peaceful, and interested, for she was always a very contented girl, even down in the world, where she had to lie in bed all the time. As soon as she put Grunter Grim's clothes on, however, she felt herself growing very miserable. Somehow she felt dissatisfied and unhappy, and yet she could give no reason for it.

If she had given way to this feeling, there is no knowing what would have happened; but she was a sensible girl, and she made an effort, and pulled herself together, shook herself, and said very earnestly—

"Now then, be sensible, Merle."

At once she began to feel stronger, very much stronger. The uncomfortable feeling had almost disappeared, and she was about to take off the cloak and hat, when she heard a very loud noise. The whole house seemed to shake—the sheeps' tails waved in the air, Boy Blue's horn stood up and made a bow, the window opened, and Merle saw a dark little man jump into the room.

It was Grunter Grim, come home at last!

How Merle Found the Stolen Packet

It was Grunter Grim, but for the first minute or two Merle did not recognise him. He looked so much smaller, so much meaner, so much less formidable without his hat and cloak, that Merle did not feel the least bit frightened of him, and was only amused.

He was evidently in a bad temper, for he was no sooner safely inside the room than he began stamping and storming and raging.

Merle was in a dark corner, and he did not notice her at first, so she silently listened to him.

"Jackanapes, Jingles, and Jaguars!" he muttered. "Was there ever in this stupid world any one so stupid, so silly as I? Shall I never learn how very risky it is to go out without my cloak and hat? Fortunately, no one has found me out this time."

Merle shrank farther into her corner.

"But I had a quick run for it. That Thomas Muriel nearly caught me. And if he had, by the toes of all the sardines, what would have become of me? He knows the secret only too well."

The little man was dancing with rage, up and down the room. He looked so small, yet he had such a big voice and talked so quickly. Presently

he looked into the corner. He had evidently come to the conclusion that he would not be without his clothes any longer.

"Beetles, Biscuits, and Bandboxes!" he cried, "has any one been here? Can my cloak and hat be gone? No, they must be in the other room." And he bounced out of the door.

Merle came out of her corner and listened. She could hear him running and jumping all over the house, calling and shouting all the time. Presently, before she could disappear, back he came into the room. Directly he caught sight of her in his hat and cloak, he gave a furious yell, a wild leap into the air, and then began dancing up and down the room—talking and shouting the while.

In spite of the cloak and hat, which had made her feel so brave and strong, Merle began to think that she was just the least little bit frightened. You see, she knew only too well what dreadful things Grunter Grim had done to other people, and she did not know, that as long as she kept the cloak and hat on, he could do nothing to her.

The little man stormed, and the little man raged, and then he began to threaten.

"I'll lock you in a dungeon!" he shouted, at the top of his voice. "I'll make you into mincemeat! I'll, I'll——"

He hesitated what to say next. Then, as he saw the colour going from Merle's face, he screamed—

"Now will you give me back my cloak and hat? Say 'Yes' at once!"

Merle lifted her hand to her head to take off the hat—but she still hesitated, and it was well she did. The little man noticed it, and repeated his last words.

"Say 'Yes,' at once!" he shouted, stamping his foot, "and give me the hat, and you shall go."

But these words reminded Merle of her rhyme—

"When Grunter Grim says 'Yes,' say 'No,'"

and plucking up all her courage, Merle pulled the hat down more firmly on her head, and said—

"No, I won't give you your hat and cloak, Grunter Grim!"

She fully expected to find herself blown into the middle of next week or that something dreadful would happen, and she shut her eyes tightly. When she opened them again she was still in the little room, and Grunter Grim had not gone, but he seemed somehow to be completely changed. He was standing silently in one corner. He looked no longer angry and threatening, but dreadfully, painfully miserable.

He was shivering and shaking from head to foot, and big tears were rolling down his cheeks.

Merle felt inclined to cast the cloak and hat before him, if only to cheer him up.

"What is the matter? Are you very cold, Grunter Grim?" she asked, in a gentle voice.

"Cold! I am shivering so much that I cannot keep still," said Grunter Grim, in the mildest, meekest, softest of voices. "Oh! have pity on me, and give me back my cloak. Have you never been cold yourself? Will you not have some mercy?"

As he spoke Merle began to think she must be a very bad girl to steal some one else's cloak, and let them shiver for want of it.

She looked at Grunter Grim as he stood before her crying and shaking, then a tear rolled down her own cheek, and giving a big sigh, she raised her hand to unfasten the cloak. As she did so she heard a much bigger sigh close beside her, and she noticed that the sheeps' tails were waving up and down, looking somehow very miserable. The room seemed filled up with one big sigh, and outside the winds appeared to have caught it up, and were carrying it onwards with them. Merle stopped and looked at Grunter Grim again, then instead of taking off the cloak, she wrapped it more tightly round her, saying softly to herself—

"Defy, Deride, Desist, Deny,
Heed not a growl, or scowl, or sigh."

Grunter Grim watched her closely, but said not a word. He stopped shivering and crying, his whole appearance seemed to change, and he was again the angry, sullen, mean little man. Then he gave Merle a withering glance of hatred and scorn, and walked out of the room.

Merle did not know what to do next. She did not feel much inclined to follow Grunter Grim, and yet she knew that she could do no good until she had made him give her the sealed packet. She was just making up her mind to have one more really good search, when she noticed that the little window had opened itself again.

"That clearly means that I am to get out of this house, and I am very glad of it," said Merle, and she stepped over the window-sill and out into the garden.

She was preparing to make her way down the crooked road when she heard a low chuckle close to her elbow. It was a very wicked chuckle, and Merle turned quickly round, fully expecting to find Grunter Grim at her side.

Instead of this, however, she found a little man, or rather a boy. He was fat, and looked as if his clothes were much too small for him. He was dressed in bright green, and ugly enough he looked.

As Merle turned round and faced him, he gave a jump, as though he were frightened, and ran against Merle, but as soon as he caught sight of her face, he chuckled again.

"Beg pardon, Miss, I'm sure," he said, "but I thought until you turned round that you were Grunter Grim. However did you manage to get his cloak and hat?"

"Why do you want to know? Who are you?" asked Merle, for somehow she felt suspicious of the boy.

"Beg pardon," said the boy, grinning, "but I'm Johnny Green."

"Johnny Green! I seem to know that name," said Merle. "Are you one of the Rhymes?"

"Of course," said the boy, grinning again.

Merle felt very comforted when she heard that, for when she first saw him she had quite expected to find that he had something to do with Grunter Grim.

All at once the boy began laughing loudly, apparently without reason.

"You seem to be amused," said Merle, politely.

The boy laughed still louder. At last he managed to gasp out—

"It would be such fun, you know!"

Merle ventured to say she did not know what he meant.

"I want to play a trick on Grunter Grim, and you must help me," said the boy.

"I don't like Grunter Grim, and I don't like playing tricks," said Merle, "but tell me what it is. If it will help me to get what I want, and if it will be of use to the Rhymes, perhaps I might do it. Tell me what it is."

"Well, to begin with, you must give me the cloak and hat," said Johnny Green, beginning to laugh again.

"Oh, I am not likely to do that. I don't know enough about you to trust you with anything so precious," said Merle.

"Well, you know I am one of the Rhymes; didn't I tell you I was Johnny Green?"

As he spoke the boy came nearer to Merle, and took hold of the cloak.

"Johnny Green; I do remember the name, of course," said Merle. " '*Who put her in? Naughty Johnny Green.*' Why, you're the boy that put Pussy in the well, ding dong bell. I won't have anything to do with you."

Merle pulled the cloak away from Johnny. It needed a hard pull, for he had taken firm hold of it, and evidently meant to get it.

Merle indeed was only just in time; in another minute he would have had it off her shoulders.

"You're a bad boy, Johnny Green; don't touch me. I won't look at you," she cried.

But something was happening to Johnny Green. He had begun to alter as soon as he touched the cloak. His green clothes became much darker, and he grew thinner. When Merle shouted to him to go away and not touch her, the person who stepped back and stamped his foot was no longer Johnny Green, but Grunter Grim!

"You thought to catch me in that way, did you?" said Merle. "You pretended to be a harmless Rhyme, and hoped to make me help you in your tricks."

"My cloak and hat, give them to me," said the little man.

"I won't give them to you. Now find me the sealed packet which you stole," said Merle, defiantly, for she was not a bit afraid of him.

"I can't find the packet without my hat. Give me my hat, and I promise you I will give you the packet," begged Grunter Grim.

Merle hesitated.

"Well, give me the packet first," she said, "and then you shall have the hat."

There didn't seem to be any way of finding it without Grunter Grim's help, so she determined to sacrifice the hat.

"You promise?" said Grunter Grim.

"Yes," said Merle; but as she said it she shuddered, and then she knew that she had made a mistake, but it was too late now.

"You've got the packet," said Grunter Grim, dancing, "it is in the hat, stuck right in the pointed top. Wasn't it a good place to hide it? Now give me my hat."

He tried to snatch it away from Merle before she was able to get the packet out; but this time she was too quick for him. She just managed to get a very small parcel out from the top of the pointed hat before Grunter Grim snatched it away from her, and giving one big jump, reached the door in the top attic, and disappeared inside the house.

Master Richard Bird

When Grunter Grim disappeared with his hat, Merle felt almost inclined to cry. She fully realised, now that it was too late, how silly she had been. Still, she had acted as she thought for the best, for of course she had no idea that the packet she wanted was concealed in the hat.

"Well," said Merle, "at any rate I have done some good. I have the cloak, and nothing shall get that from me, and I have the packet. Perhaps if I find the king's name in that, he will be strong enough to get Grunter Grim's hat away. Now to see what is in the packet. I wish that I were in the babies' house, so that"—but Merle stopped, something very peculiar was happening.

The cloak which she had wrapped so tightly round her was spreading out. It seemed to be dividing into two at the back. Then one part wrapped itself tightly round one of Merle's arms and the other round the other, and then Merle began without thinking to move her arms out from her side and back again. Suddenly she felt herself lifted from the ground into the air.

"Why, I am just like a bird," she shouted, with great delight. "I can fly! I can fly!"

And she was very much like a bird. If you had seen her as she flew swiftly through the air, you might have mistaken her for a big black crow.

Presently she found that she was above the long, low house in which the babies were, and she decided to go down there, and open the mysterious packet which she still held in her hand. She was anxious also to find Thomas Muriel, and tell him her adventures.

She closed her wings down by her side and gently dropped to the ground. The moment her feet touched the earth the wings became a cloak once more.

She was now standing in front of the babies' house, before the very same door by which she had entered the last time, but now that door was shut, and then it had been open.

At first, however, Merle was not disturbed by this, but when she tried to turn the door handle, to her surprise, she found it would not open, and though she pushed, and pulled, and knocked, and tapped, it was all no good—the door still remained tightly shut.

"This is the queerest thing," said Merle. "I thought with this cloak I could could get anywhere—I don't understand it at all. Never mind, perhaps the packet explains everything, and if I can't get inside why I must open it outside."

As she spoke, Merle began to look more closely at the mysterious packet which she had managed to get from Grunter Grim.

It seemed at first sight very much like a small brown paper parcel, and yet Merle could not find out how it was fastened, for there was no string tied round it, nor was it sealed. She tried to tear it open, but could not. She turned it first one way and then the other, pushed and poked, pulled and fumbled, but could find no beginning or ending to it, and above all, no opening of any kind.

She tried for a long time very patiently, but at last she began to lose her temper.

"This really is too stupid," she said, stamping her foot. "I have the packet, and now I can't get it open. This is one of Grunter Grim's tricks, of course. I wish I could get hold of him. I wish I were at——"

She got no further, for in an instant the cloak had shaped itself into wings, and she felt herself lifted from the ground. "I shall have to be careful," she said, as she rose higher and higher in the air. "It is quite evident that I have only to wish to be at a place, and the cloak will take me there. No wonder Grunter Grim was able to get about so quickly, and to be everywhere at once. Now the only question is, where shall I go?"

She hesitated, but only a second, for just then she felt something touching her nose. She let her wings drop, and began to descend to the ground, to get out of the way; but the something seemed to be following, and she had to flap her wings in front of her face to protect herself. At last, by a good deal of flapping, she managed to get above the something, and as she looked down at it—still following her—she managed to make out that it was a small bird which had been attacking her face.

As soon as she could, Merle dropped to the ground, and just as the wings joined and again became a cloak, the bird also reached the ground, and hopped up to her.

He seemed much astonished when he looked at her, and began to apologise.

"I beg your pardon for attacking you, but I thought you were Grunter Grim, and——" here he paused, and began to flutter his wings as though he were much distressed.

Merle did not know what to say, and waited for him to continue.

At last, after flying rather close to her face, he once more settled down on the ground and began to speak again.

"Would you mind putting your hand over your nose, so that I cannot see it. I am sorry to trouble you, but——"

Merle began to laugh. "What a very queer thing to ask me to do!" she said. "Whatever am I to do that for? Who are you?"

"My name is Master Richard—Master Richard Bird—and unfortunately I am forced by Grunter Grim to attack every nose that I see, and to try to pull it off."

"How curious!" said Merle. "Don't you think it is cruel of you?"

"It would be if I did it, but then, you see, I am only forced to *try* to pull a nose off, so of course I never do it," explained Master Richard.

Merle did not quite understand, but was afraid to ask any more questions, lest the bird should think her rude.

"Would you mind telling me if that is Grunter Grim's cloak? I suppose it must be," said Master Richard, after a minute's silence.

"Of course it is," said Merle, "and I have the packet too. I managed to get them both, but it is not much good, because I can't open the packet."

"Why not?" asked the bird. "You have the hat, I suppose, if you have the cloak. Use the hat to open the packet; it will open anything."

"But I haven't got the hat," said Merle, almost beginning to cry. "I gave the hat back to Grunter Grim."

"Well, that is a pity," said Master Richard. "Didn't you know that the cloak is of no use without the hat; for though the cloak will take you to any house, the hat only will get you inside. If you have the hat, you can open any lock, any door, any window, anything—even the parcel."

"Then I must get the hat as soon as possible," said Merle. "Won't you help me?"

"Yes, indeed, I will, if you will keep your nose out of the way, and I'll get the four-and-twenty blackbirds to help, too," said Master Richard.

Merle stared at him. "Four-and-twenty blackbirds," she said to herself. "Richard Bird and my nose! What does it all mean?"

Master Richard, however, took no notice of her, but flew as high as he could into the air, and began chirruping and whistling.

Close behind her Merle heard an answering chirrup, and in a minute a pert young blackbird perched himself on her shoulder. Then a whistle, and behold there was a bird on the other shoulder; then a bird flew on her head, and another, and another, and another, until black birds seemed flying all round her.

At last Master Richard stopped whistling, and came down to the ground. He placed himself right opposite Merle, called to the blackbirds once more, and they formed a line behind him, and then they began to sing.

Merle only listened for a while, then quite suddenly she too began to sing. She sang simply because she could not help it—she felt obliged to sing at the top of her voice:

"Sing a song of sixpence,
A pocket full of rye,
Four-and-twenty blackbirds
Baked in a pie;
When the pie was opened
The birds began to sing,
Wasn't that a dainty dish
To set before a king?"

The birds did not appear to mind at all; indeed, they seemed to enjoy it. Merle went on with the second verse, about the king being in the counting-house and the queen in the parlour, but when she sang,

"The maid was in the garden, hanging out the clothes;
There came a little dicky-bird, and pecked off her nose,"

she found that the birds had stopped and she was singing alone. When she finished, all the blackbirds began to shout at her, "Shame! Tear her to pieces! It isn't true! Shame!" It was evident that somehow she had offended them, and they were very angry. Merle tried to speak, but there was too much noise. Then she shouted, but it was no good. At last Master Richard stepped forward, and at once there was silence.

"Blackbirds, be quiet, it is ignorance; she means no harm," he said, and then he turned to Merle. "I am sure you would not have sung the last part of that song if you had known how it offends us. I am Dicky Bird. I told you my name was Richard, but sometimes I am called Dicky. I am Dicky, and that day that I hurt the maid—and, by the way, I did not peck off her nose, though I'm sorry to say I tried to—I was very much upset. It was partly Grunter Grim's fault——"

"I understand," interrupted Merle, "and I am so sorry. But I will never sing it again, and you must help me to banish him. The first thing to do is to get the hat. Let us quarrel no longer, but all set to work."

A MYSTICAL RHYME

At the word of command from Master Richard all the blackbirds formed themselves into a circle round Merle, and they were just as quiet and polite as they had been noisy and rude before. They only spoke when they were spoken to, and indeed, took little part in the discussion. Merle and Dicky did all the talking, and at last agreed upon a plan of action.

It was arranged that all the blackbirds, with Dicky at their head, were to fly to Grunter Grim's house, get in, if possible, and look for the hat; and if not, to hover about, find Grunter Grim, and try to get some information from him.

Merle, meantime, was to stay behind and keep out of sight, for fear Grunter Grim should recognise her, and try to get back his cloak.

Everything being thus settled, Dicky Bird flapped his wings and flew upwards, crying "Forward!" All the four-and-twenty blackbirds followed his example, and soon Merle was left alone to await their return.

She made herself very comfortable on the stump of a moss-grown tree. As she sat down, she heard a voice singing softly—

> *"Little Miss Muffet*
> *Sat on a tuffet,*
> *Eating curds and whey."*

Merle sprang to her feet and looked round, but she could see no one. Then she looked again at the stump of the tree, and noticed that there was a small label fastened to one side of it, on which was written—

"MISS MUFFET'S TUFFET."

"This is very interesting," said Merle. "I wonder if the spider will come?"

"Of course he won't," said a voice just behind her. "Grunter Grim is the spider, and how can he come when you have the cloak? He is a prisoner!"

Once more Merle turned round, and this time a girl was standing in front of her. She recognised her as the girl she had seen at the meeting, and anyhow, she would have know who it was, because the girl's name was written on the label fastened on her dress.

"So Grunter Grim was the spider," said Merle. "I thought you didn't look the kind of girl to be frightened by a real spider."

"Frightened by a spider—no indeed. Let me tell you my story," said Miss Muffet.

"I suppose it is like all the others," said Merle. "Grunter Grim is the cause of all your trouble, is he not?"

Miss Muffet was just going to answer, when Merle saw two of the blackbirds flying towards them.

"Look, look!" she cried, "they are coming back. Now we shall get some news."

"News?" said Miss Muffet; "news of what?"

But Merle did not answer her, for by this time the blackbirds had reached the two girls, and had perched themselves on Merle's shoulders.

"Tell me—what have you seen or heard?" said Merle.

"I went to the house," said Blackbird Number One.

"Just like *me*," said Number Two.

"And there I saw a window," continued Number One.

"*Just* like me," cried Number Two.

"And I looked in and saw Grunter Grim," went on Number One.

"Just *like*——" began Number Two; but Merle interrupted him.

"Do tell me a little quicker," she said. "Had he the hat on? Did you see it? Did you ask him anything? And what did he say?"

"'No,' to the first question; 'No,' to the second; 'Yes,' to the third and fourth," shouted both blackbirds.

"I asked him where the hat was," said Number One.

"Just like me," said Number Two.

"And he said, 'Ha, ha, ha!'" said Number One.

"No, he didn't," said Two; "he said, 'The hats,' as if there were six or seven magic hats."

"HA! HA! HA!—THE HATS," said Merle, slowly; "what could he have meant?"

But the two blackbirds made no reply, they seemed to think they had done enough work for one day. They flew down from Merle's shoulder, and perching on Miss Muffet's Tuffet, tucked their heads under their wings, and went to sleep.

Merle was beginning to feel angry with them for being so stupid when she saw quite a number of their brothers flying towards her.

"Ah! here they come," she said to Miss Muffet. "Now, this time I will tell them what they saw, and try to get the news more quickly."

"I believe I begin to see what it all means," said Miss Muffet. "You have the cloak, and you are trying to get the hat."

"Hush!" said Merle, as twenty-two blackbirds flew to the ground and hopped in front of her.

As soon as they were settled, without waiting for them to speak, Merle began—

"You went to the house."

"Just like me!" shouted each blackbird.

"And there you saw a window, and you looked in and saw Grunter Grim," said Merle, very rapidly; "and he had not the hat on, and you didn't see it, and you asked him a question, and he said——"

All the blackbirds shouted at the top of their voices something, but, as they all spoke together, Merle could not understand a word.

"Say it one at a time," said Merle; but the blackbirds took no notice of her, they just hopped on to the tuffet, and went off to sleep.

"Oh dear!" said Miss Muffet, "how tiresome of them. What shall we do?"

"Never mind," said Merle, "here comes Master Richard—he will help us."

"Yes, that he will," said Miss Muffet—"only cover up your nose, my dear."

She only spoke just in time, for Master Richard flew straight at Merle's face, and would certainly have touched her nose had she not covered it up.

"I beg your pardon," he said—"but you know——"

"Never mind," said Merle, "give us the news."

"I have very little to tell, unhappily," said Master Richard. "I haven't found the hat, and though I saw Grunter Grim, he wouldn't answer any questions, and whatever I said to him, he only said, 'No one else can.' What he meant by that I don't know. Have the others come back?"

"Yes, but look at them," said Merle, dolefully. "They have all seen Grunter Grim, and he has said some nonsense or a bit of a sentence to each of them; but as they all shouted together, I couldn't exactly make out what it was."

"Put all the bits together, and see if they make a proper sentence," said Miss Muffet.

"But the birds are fast asleep, they won't say it again," said Merle.

"I'll soon make them," said Master Richard. "That is a good idea, Miss Muffet."

Directly Master Richard called to them, the blackbirds woke up; when he called to them a second time, they all jumped to the ground; and at the third call they formed themselves into a line in front of him.

"Now, Blackbirds," said Master Richard, "tell me what you each heard Grunter Grim say. Speak one at a time, clearly and distinctly."

Without a murmur, or even a "Just like me," the birds began—

"To me Grunter Grim said 'HA! HA! HA!'" said Number One.

"To me he only said 'THE HATS,'" said Two.

"To me 'SAFE,'" answered Three.

"To me he only said 'AWAY,'" said Four.

"When I spoke to him he said 'RIGHT,'" said Five.

"When I asked where the hat was, he said 'WELL HIDDEN,'" said Six.

"And when I said 'Is it lost?' he said, 'FOR EVER AND A DAY,'" said Seven.

"Stop a minute," said Merle, "I see something."

"Yes, so do I," said Miss Muffet. "Put those words together, and you get a rhyme."

"Of course you do," said Master Richard; "it's just what I expected. Listen.

> *"Ha! Ha! Ha! the hat's safe away,*
> *Right well hidden for ever and a day."*

"It doesn't tell us much," said Merle.

"Wait for the rest," said Master Richard. "Now, Number Eight, what did he say to you?"

"'DING, DONG,'" answered Eight.

"He only said 'THE' to me," said Nine.

"And only 'BELL' to me," said Ten.

"When I questioned him, he said, 'OF COURSE I KNOW,'" continued Eleven.

"And he said to me 'NO USE,'" said Twelve.

"I only caught the word 'IN' when he spoke to me," said Thirteen.

"And as far as I could make out, he said 'THAT' to me," said Fourteen.

"I heard him say 'WITHOUT THE CLOAK,'" said Fifteen.

"And he called out 'HO! HO! HO!' to me," said Sixteen.

"Two more lines of the rhyme," cried Miss Muffet, excitedly. "Listen Merle.

> *"Ding, dong, the bell, of course I know,*
> *No use in that without the cloak, Ho! Ho! Ho!"*

"Go on, go on," said Merle.

"To me he said 'MERLE,'" said Seventeen.

"To me he whispered 'STOLE,'" said Eighteen.

"And to me 'THE CLOAK,'" said Nineteen.

"I heard the words 'FROM THE POOR OLD MAN,'" said Twenty.

"He only said 'SHE' to me," said Twenty-one.

"And to me he said 'MIGHT GET,'" said Twenty-two.

"I heard him say 'THE HAT,'" said Twenty-three.

"And to me he said 'BUT,'" said Twenty-four.

"And that's all," said Merle.

"Wait a minute," said Master Richard, "you are forgetting what I heard. He said 'NO ONE ELSE CAN' to me."

"Now say the whole rhyme slowly," said Miss Muffet, getting more and more excited.

Master Richard pointed to one bird after the other, and this is what they said—

> *"Ha! Ha! Ha! the hat's safe away,*
> *Right well hidden for ever and a day.*
> *Ding, dong, the bell, of course I know,*
> *No use in that without the cloak, Ho! Ho! Ho!*
> *Merle stole the cloak from the poor old man;*
> *She might get the hat, no one else can."*

"It isn't a little bit of good; it just tells us what we knew before," said Merle, in a very disappointed tone.

"It's a trick of Grunter Grim's," said Miss Muffet, very sadly.

Even Master Richard looked down-hearted. The Rhyme was, as Merle said, "no good at all."

Presently, however, just as the blackbirds were dropping off to sleep again, Merle called out—

"Stop! Perhaps the words would make another Rhyme if we took them in different order."

"You are clever," said Miss Muffet. "I expect you are right. Try them backwards."

But that was no good, it only made nonsense. Then they tried all kinds of ways, but could not get anything at all sensible. At last, just as Merle had made up her mind to give it up altogether, Miss Muffet had a brilliant idea.

"I expect the Rhyme begins with 'Ding, dong, bell,'" she said, "for that is Grunter Grim's favourite rhyme."

"Why didn't we think of that before?" said Master Richard.

"And perhaps, oh! perhaps," said Merle, excitedly, "the hat's hidden in the well. Do let us try to get the Rhyme once more."

They did try very hard. They made the blackbirds stand first one way, and then the other, they mixed them up, and made them shout until they were nearly hoarse, and at last they placed them side by side in this order, with Master Richard in the middle:—8, 10, 3, 13, 9, 6, 5, 4, 7, 17, 22, 23, Master Richard, 21, 18, 19, 20, 1, 24, 11, 14, 2, 12, 15, 16. Then they each said the word or words they had heard once through, and there was such a cry of delight from Merle, such a shout of joy from Miss Muffet, such a lively chirp from Master Richard, and such a twittering and chirruping from the four-and-twenty blackbirds! The secret was found out!

"Now, say your words once more," said Master Richard, and the birds shouted each in turn, and this is how the Rhyme sounded this time:—

> "Ding, dong, bell,
> Safe in the well,
> Hidden right away
> For ever and a day.
> Merle might get the hat, no one else can;
> She stole the cloak from the poor old man.
> Ha! Ha! Ha! but of course I know
> That the hat's no use without the cloak, Ho! Ho! Ho!"

Then came another cheer, and then Merle, Master Richard, and Miss Muffet set off running, flying, and jumping, to find the well and get the hat.

DOWN THE WELL

Merle found the well quite easily. With her magic cloak she moved through the air so quickly that Master Richard and Miss Muffet could not keep up with her, and they were soon left far behind. The well was surrounded by thick trees—so thick, that Merle could not help thinking, as she dropped gently to the ground, that she would never have been able to make her way through the bushes on foot, and that had she not had the cloak to help her, she would not have found the well at all.

It was very like an ordinary well—indeed, the only difference between it and most wells was that above it was fastened a very large bell, from which dangled a very long rope.

Merle knelt down on the ground and peeped into the well. To her delight, she could not see any water in it.

"Hurrah!" she cried, "it will be easy to search that well thoroughly. I was wondering how I should be able to go underneath the water."

She wrapped her cloak round her, wished, and soon felt herself falling gently down, down, down. She reached the bottom quite safely, and at once began her search.

"It is a very large well," she said, as she felt her way about, for it was much too dark to see anything, "and the walls are certainly very damp."

The walls were very damp, though perhaps that was not strange. Every one expects the bottom of a well to be damp. Every one does not usually, however, expect the walls of a well each time they are touched to send out little jets of water, but that was happening in this well.

The water, too, rose rapidly, and in a little time it reached above Merle's knees as she stood in it.

"I see what is the matter," said Merle, slowly, "Grunter Grim means to try to drown me. It is not a bit of good, I mean to find his hat before I go up."

She moved about quickly, but the well seemed to grow larger, and the water was still rising rapidly.

It reached her waist. Should she give up the search? Just then her foot knocked against something, something pointed. Could it be Grunter Grim's hat?

Forgetting all about the water, she stooped down, seized hold of the point, and pulled. The hat—for it was the hat—was pushed very tightly into a hole in the wall.

"One more tug," said Merle.

But she did not give the one more tug, for she felt something pulling

her from above, and before she could cry out or object in any way, she found herself lifted out of the water, out of the well, and on to the ground.

She struggled to her feet and looked about indignantly, expecting to find Grunter Grim before her.

There was no Grunter Grim, only a very tall, very thin, very stupid-looking boy was standing staring at her. He carried a fishing-rod in one hand and a pail in the other, and he was trying to jerk the fish-hook out of Merle's dress, in which it was tightly fastened.

"Whatever did you do it for?" asked Merle, crossly.

"I thought that I had found the whale at last," said the stupid boy.

"Why, you *are* a Simple Simon," said Merle.

The boy frowned angrily.

"Whose fault is that?" he asked.

Merle looked at his pail, at his rod, and then at the ticket fastened on his coat. Sure enough, on it was written "Simple Simon."

"I beg your pardon," she said; "I didn't know."

"It was all Grunter Grim's fault," said Simon; "I was——"

But Merle interrupted him.

"Then why did you fish me out of the well, just when I was going to find his hat?" she said.

"Oh, I am sorry! I am sorry!" said Simon. "You see usually I spend all my time fishing in this pail, but somehow to day I can do what I like, and fish in other places."

"That is because I have Grunter Grim's cloak," said Merle, "and he has lost some of his power."

"Hurrah!" shouted Simon, and he threw his cap into the air.

As it came down it caught in the bell-rope, and at once the bell began ringing.

Ding, dong, bell! Ding, dong, bell!

"What a noise!" said Merle.

But it did not go on ringing very long, and when Merle looked into the well once more, she found that it was empty again, the water had all run away. She wrapped her cloak round her, and turning to Simple Simon, said—

"Don't pull me out this time. I'm not a whale, you see."

"Then I had better be off," said Simple Simon. "I can't help fishing you out if I stay here."

Merle watched him disappear through the trees, and then went down, down, down to the bottom of the well again.

The walls seemed wetter than ever, and the water had risen to her waist before she had even found the point of the hat. It rose so rapidly that she was beginning to feel rather frightened. In spite of her fears, however, she felt very angry when once more she found herself lifted out, and dropped on to the ground.

"I told you to leave me alone," she said, impatiently. Then forgetting her anger, she began to laugh as she looked at the round smiling face of the boy standing over her.

He took off his cap, made a low bow, and said politely—

"Who pulled her out? Little Tommy Stout."

And then he bowed again.

"I wish you had left her in," said Merle. "I never shall find the hat if you and Simon keep fishing me out of the well."

"So sorry," said Tommy, still smiling; "but the fact of the matter is I thought you were Pussy. And you'll excuse me mentioning it, but you didn't seem to be thoroughly enjoying the water, though you are not as wet as you might have been under the circumstances."

"No," said Merle, "I wasn't enjoying the water, and I am afraid I shall be drowned before I can get the hat, the water rises so quickly."

"You don't mean to say," said Tommy, without even a little bit of a smile, "that you stayed in the well when the water was rising."

Merle nodded.

"Then the only thing I wonder at is that you are not drowned this minute. My dear young lady, it is quite evident to me that you are not in the habit of pulling pussies out of wells. If you went into that well seven or eight times a day, as I do, you would know better than to venture in when it was full of water."

"It was empty when I started," said Merle.

"Then of course you did not ring the bell," said Tommy, "though I thought I heard it ringing just now."

"Is that the way you manage?" asked Merle.

"Of course," said Tommy. "What is the bell put there for? I'll show you how it is done."

He jumped into one of the buckets, and seized hold of the bell-rope.

Ding, dong, bell! Ding, dong, bell!

The bell rang loudly all the time Tommy was in the well, and when he reappeared at the top once more, smiling as usual, he was perfectly dry.

"That's the way," he said, cheerfully; "but I think you are mistaken about the hat. I don't think it is there. I saw no sign of it."

But Merle was certain she was not mistaken, and taking hold of the rope and setting the bell ringing, she jumped into the bucket. In a few moments she reappeared with a smile of triumph on her face and the hat in her hand.

"What do you think of that?" she asked, as she put it on her head. "Now, Grunter Grim, you have indeed lost your power!"

Although she no longer held the bell-rope, the bell was ringing loudly, and all the birds in the wood were singing and trilling. Tommy was laughing heartily and shouting at the top of his voice "Hurrah!" and Merle trembled all over as she drew the parcel from her pocket.

She did not need even to touch the parcel with the hat, for as she drew it out she saw that it was open, and these were the mysterious words she found written inside it:—

"Who shall be Endom's king?
A baby he
Must always be;
For a baby is Endom's king.

"What baby is Endom's king?
A baby that's glad
When others are sad;
For contented is Endom's king.

"How to find Endom's king?
The cloak he must wear,
Yet be free from care;
For not all can be Endom's king.

"Who then is Endom's king?
The baby that's glad
When others are sad;
And his name it is Baby———."

Merle read it through aloud twice. She looked very puzzled, for there seemed to be something wrong with the last verse.

"I see what it is," she said at last.

"So do I," said Tommy.

"It's the same old story," said Merle.

"It's Grunter Grim," said Tommy; "he's scratched out the most important word in the whole rhyme."

"Yes, so he has," said Merle: "the word after 'baby' in the last line."

"Of course that was the name," said Tommy; "Oh dear! Oh dear!" and he seized hold of the bell-rope, and jumping into the bucket, disappeared down the well.

HICKORY, DICKORY, DOCK

As soon as Tommy had disappeared Merle turned away from the well.

"It's no use staying here," she said. "It is quite certain that there are no babies in the well; perhaps I had better go back to the baby-house."

She wrapped the cloak round her, and was going to wish, when she remembered the hat, and determined to try its power.

"If I can get through anything with this hat," she said, "I should think I can get through these trees."

Pulling the hat firmly down on her head, she prepared to push her way into the very thickest part of the wood which surrounded the well; but as soon as she reached the trees they seemed to move away from her. They crowded together on each side until there was quite a clear pathway, and at last there were so few trees that at the end of the pathway Merle could see a very tall tower. As she drew nearer to it, she noticed that there was a large clock at the top of it, and above the clock face were three letters—

H. D. D.

"Well, at any rate, I may as well go up the tower," said Merle. "Perhaps I shall be able to get a good view from the top."

It was easier, however, to say she would go up the tower than to do it, for there did not seem to be any door to it, or any way of getting into it.

"It's a good thing I have the hat," said Merle. "I suppose I must make a door for myself."

She took the hat off her head, and was just going to touch the walls of the tower with it, when she heard a loud booming sound which almost deafened her. Whatever could it be? Then she remembered the clock—perhaps it was only the clock striking.

She walked round to the front of the tower, and stared up at the clock-face. Now she noticed for the first time that instead of figures on the face, there were letters.

She began spelling out the letters slowly, "s M I R G R E T—" But she stopped, for she heard a great noise of scratching and scraping, and a sound of something tumbling, then it seemed as though nearly the whole front of the tower opened, and to Merle's great surprise three kittens came rolling out of the huge door. They rolled over and over until they were at her feet, when suddenly they stood up on their hind legs and bowed solemnly.

They were pretty kittens—so pretty that Merle longed to pick them up and cuddle them.

One was perfectly black, another quite white, and the third was a very handsome tabby. Each had a ribbon tied round its neck, and on the front of each ribbon was worked a name.

Merle tried hard to see what the names were, but she could only make out the shortest—the one tied round the grey kitten's neck, and that was "Dock." She was going to ask the names of the others, when all three bowed once more.

Then the black kitten stepped forward, and said, politely—

"Allow me to introduce myself—I'm Hickory."

"Then of course you are Dickory?" said Merle, pointing to the white kitten.

"Exactly so," said all the kittens together.

"And that's the clock," said Merle, pointing to the tower. "But what do the letters mean? 'S M I R G R E T N U R G'—doesn't seem to spell anything."

Hickory looked at Dickory, and Dickory looked at Dock.

"My whiskers!" said Hickory.

"After all this time she doesn't know," said Dickory.

"Rats and mice! who'd have thought it?" said Dock.

Then they all laughed, as only three little kittens can.

Merle went very red, she thought the kittens were rather rude. She turned round, and was going to walk right away, when Hickory said—

"Excuse me, but whose cloak have you got on?"

"Grunter Grim's," said Merle.

"And to whom does the hat belong?" asked Dickory.

"To Grunter Grim," said Merle again.

"Well, now look at the clock again," said Dock.

"Of course—how stupid of me!" said Merle. "I was reading it backwards. The letters spell 'Grunter Grim's.' I might have guessed that."

"So you might," said Hickory.

"Exactly so," said Dickory.

"Precisely so," added Dock.

Then the three little kittens joined paws and danced in a circle round Merle.

"Well, you are certainly the most remarkable kittens," said Merle. "I'm sure you never lost your mittens, or began to cry."

The kittens stopped dancing immediately, and put their paws behind their backs.

"Oh, you did, did you?" said Merle, beginning to laugh.

"Tell her," said Hickory.

"Was it Grunter Grim?" asked Merle.

"Exactly so," said Dickory.

"And I'm forgetting all about the Rhyme and the King of Endom"; and pulling her packet out of her pocket, she read aloud the Rhyme to the kittens.

"Now," she said, "can you guess the missing word?"

"Of course, it means that the king must be a Rhyme Baby, you see that?" said Hickory.

"A Rhyme Baby?" repeated Merle.

"Exactly so," said Dickory.

"A Nursery Rhyme Baby, not a real world baby," said Dock.

"Well, I never thought of that," said Merle. "Of course it does. 'A baby who'll ne'er be a man' can't be a human baby. I never thought of that."

"And, of course, there are not many Rhyme Babies," said Hickory.

"Exactly so," remarked Dickory. "I've an idea."

"It's the first you ever had, then," said Dock, rather rudely. "You don't usually think for yourself."

"Oh, please don't quarrel," said Merle.

"Let us think," said Hickory.

The three little kittens, without any warning, stood on their heads. Merle was too much astonished to say anything, and waited patiently to see what would happen.

Presently Hickory gave a loud miaow, and immediately all three kittens again stood on their hind legs.

"I see," said Hickory, in a very mysterious ghostly voice, waving his tail in the air, "I see a cradle in a wood on a treetop, the bough is rocking, and the child is laughing.

> *"When the bough breaks, the cradle will fall,*
> *Down will go baby, and cradle, and all."*

"I hear," said Dickory, "a voice singing a lullaby to a baby. Listen to the words."

Swaying from side to side, the three kittens began singing softly—

"Dance a baby diddy,
What shall his mother do wid'e?
Sit in her lap, give him some pap,
And dance a baby diddy."

As the lullaby died away, Merle looked at Dock, and waited eagerly for him to speak.

"And I see," said Dock, excitedly, "a lonely house in a lonely wood, a lonely baby in a lonely cradle, a——"

But just then the loud booming sound was heard once more from inside the clock.

"The mouse is up the clock—away!" cried Hickory.

"Exactly so!" said Dickory.

"Precisely so!" added Dock.

And away up the tower, as fast as their legs could carry them, scampered the three little kittens.

The Rhyme-shop

"Now, that's a pity," said Merle, as she watched the three tips of the three tails disappear. "I wanted to ask them ever so many questions."

She wrapped the cloak round her, once more wished, and immediately felt herself floating in the air.

After flying a short distance, she saw the baby-house beneath her, and to her astonishment she found herself dropping down to the earth.

"This is curious," she said. "I wished to be at the Rhyme Babies' house, but perhaps they all live together."

Directly she reached the ground Thomas Muriel came hastening towards her, and as soon as he had heard the story of her adventures, he began to talk very fast.

"You have only one hour more," he said, "to find the king, then there will be another meeting, and you must go back to the earth. Let me help you, and let us be very quick."

"Shall I give you the cloak?" asked Merle.

"It is no good to me, I cannot wear it," said Thomas Muriel, sadly; "only a contented person can wear it."

"Then I must find a contented baby, I suppose," said Merle.

"Of course, the Rhyme says so," said Thomas Muriel; "but don't waste any more time in talking. Come this way."

Merle followed him down several passages, and at last found herself in a large room.

In one corner of it was a cradle, and in the cradle a baby was jumping up and down energetically.

Some one in the room was singing—

"Dance a baby diddy,"

but Merle had not time to see who it was.

"Put the cloak round him," said Thomas Muriel.

Merle obeyed. The baby was laughing and crowing at the top of its voice, but no sooner did the cloak touch him, than he began to cry and scream loudly.

Such a noise! Merle had never heard anything like it. She did not wait a moment, but snatching away the cloak ran out of the room as fast as ever she could.

"He seemed a very contented baby," she said, as soon as they were safely outside.

"I can't make it out," said Thomas Muriel. "Say the Rhyme again."

Merle repeated it slowly—

"A baby that's glad
When others are sad."

"That's it," said Thomas Muriel, "of course. That baby has never been glad when others were sad."

"Well, let us try another baby," said Merle. "Do you happen to know where the baby in the cradle on the tree-top is to be found?"

"I know where to find her," said Thomas Muriel, "but I am afraid she won't be any good, she hasn't been sad."

"Then don't you think a bough breaking, a cradle falling, and a baby and all tumbling down, would make you sad?" asked Merle, rather indignantly.

"Don't you see it says *when* the bough breaks," said Thomas Muriel; "and of course it never does break. It isn't likely it would. Why the baby would be killed."

"Well, I am very glad of that," said Merle. "All the same, I don't see what we are to do next."

Thomas Muriel looked puzzled.

"I wonder which baby Dock meant?" said Merle, quite suddenly. "Perhaps you know a lonely baby in a lonely house."

"No, I don't," said Thomas Muriel, sadly.

Merle began repeating the last verse of the Rhyme slowly—

"Who then is Endom's king?
The baby that's glad
When others are sad;
And his name it is Baby——"

"Stop!" cried Thomas Muriel, "I see something. The baby's name must rhyme with 'king.'"

"Of course," said Merle. "Oh, don't you know a name that will rhyme with 'king?'"

"I don't," said Thomas Muriel, "but I know some one who does; come along quickly."

He seized hold of Merle, pulled her along, and before she had time even to look round her, pushed her in at the door of a small house, and saying—"Now, be quick, I can't stop any longer," ran away and left her.

Merle felt quite bewildered. She could not speak, because she had lost her breath, but she managed to use her eyes, and found that she was in a small shop.

Behind the counter sat a very small person with a very big head, writing busily. She was so much occupied that she did not seem to see Merle at all.

All round the room were shelves, with sheets and sheets of paper packed tightly into them. Each shelf had a number and a label.

One of these labels was quite close to Merle, and she took it up and looked at it. "Little Jack Horner" was written upon it, and as Merle peeped at the papers inside the shelf, she saw that each one was a copy of the Rhyme about Jack Horner.

She was pulling one out to see what the last line was, when she heard some one speaking to her, and turning round quickly, found herself in the presence of the Rhyme-Fairy.

She had a very small voice, so small that Merle could scarcely hear what she said.

"What do you want, little girl?" asked the Rhyme-Fairy; but before Merle could answer she went on, "There are plenty of rhymes to 'girl'—hurl, whirl, curl, furl, for instance, but the proper one on this occasion is 'Merle.'"

Merle stared at her; then she managed to screw up her courage to say gently—

"If you please, I want a rhyme to 'king.'"

"Certainly," said the Fairy. "Rhymes to Order, you know," and she pointed to the sign above her head, on which was printed in large letters, "Rhymes to Order. Any rhyme found on the shortest possible notice. The trade supplied, wholesale and retail, by the Rhyme-Fairy."

Then she reached down a big fat book, marked "K," and began to turn over the leaves, talking quickly all the time—

"K—Ki—Kin—King. There you are! Plenty of rhymes to 'king.'"

She showed Merle a long list of words, and ran her finger down it quickly.

"Is it comic poetry you are writing?" she said, "because, if so, allow me to recommend 'fling,' the noun, not the verb, you know."

Merle shook her head.

"Oh, something sarcastic! Then try 'sting.' No, something rather tender, perhaps? Then I should strongly recommend 'cling,' or even 'ring.' I find 'cling' in great demand."

Merle turned away, she did not understand what the Fairy was talking about, and her precious minutes were flying fast.

She felt very sad. She did not want to go back to the world, leaving the Rhymes unhappy. But the little Fairy was still speaking to her.

"Won't you let me look at the whole line, Miss?" she was saying. "I feel sure I have something that will suit you, and answer your purpose."

Merle pulled the packet out of her pocket, and began to read the verse.

At once the Fairy's manner completely changed. She got down from her chair, pushed away her books and papers, and listened eagerly.

When Merle finished the first verse, she shouted—

"Go on! Go on! I'll help you. Down with Grunter Grim! I'm sick of Rhymes. Give Endom a king, and I'll make no more Nursery Rhymes. I shall be free."

Merle began the fourth verse, and as soon as she finished the Fairy cried, "I see, I see—

> *'Who then is Endom's king?*
> *The baby that's glad*
> *When others are sad;*
> *And his name it is Baby* BUNTING.'*

That's the word you want."

"Of course it is," said Merle; "Baby Bunting—B——B——. He's always contented, though *his father's a-hunting*."

"*His mother's a-milking*," cried the Fairy, excitedly.

"*His sister's a-silking and his brother's gone to buy a skin*," cried Merle. "He is contented through trouble and care, that is quite certain; only let me find him—

> "*'The baby that's glad*
> *When others are sad;*
> *And his name it is Baby* BUNTING.'*"

But as she said the words she heard a wild shout. It seemed as if there were numbers of people repeating the words after her. She looked up, looked down, the shop had disappeared, and she was back again on the platform in the big hall.

B———B———

But how different the Hall looked! No lamps were needed, for the whole room was flooded with sunlight. In each corner shone a big sunbeam, and in each beam hundreds of fairies were dancing madly. It scarcely looked like the same place, and Merle found it very difficult to believe that she really was in the big hall.

But the clocks were striking and the Rhymes were fast assembling.

Mistress Crispin and Jack and Jill were the first to arrive, and they were so busy talking together that they did not notice Merle.

"Just fancy, Mother," said Jill: "we really carried the pail full of water right up to the top of the hill, and we did not tumble down at all. What can it mean?"

"What can it mean, indeed?" said Mistress Crispin. "What do you think has happened to me? The broth is no longer broth, it is once more———"

"Not roast beef and plum pudding," said Jack.

Mistress Crispin nodded her head.

"Hurrah!" shouted Jack. "We'll all come home!"

"Yes, they have come home," cried Bo-peep, as she came hurrying into the room. "What do you think I've found?"

"Not the sheep's tails?" said Jack Horner, who was just behind her.

"Yes, the sheep's tails—and on the sheep, too, my boy," said Bo-peep, triumphantly.

"Well," said Jack Horner, "to be a good boy I *will* try." Bo-peep stared at him.

"Can you say it?" she said eagerly.

"Indeed I can," said Jack; "not once this morning have I said the other thing."

Just then Mother Hubbard, the Man in the Moon, Miss Muffet, and Boy Blue came into the Hall together.

Each one looked more surprised than the other.

"What does it mean?" said the Man in the Moon. "I ate the porridge, and it didn't burn my mouth."

"What has happened?" said Boy Blue, almost in the same breath. "I've found my horn."

"Look at my tools!" shouted Johnny at the top of his voice, as he rushed into the Hall towards the platform with a hop, skip, and a jump. "I've found my tools, now I'll get more than a penny a day."

The clocks were still striking, and the platform was getting more and more crowded.

And when the last clock struck twelve every Rhyme had arrived, and every one seemed overcome with astonishment and amazement.

On all sides there were heard whispers, cries, and shouts of "What has happened? What does it all mean?" Hickory, Dickory, and Dock were thinking hard, standing on their heads, and Simple Simon was shaking his head solemnly, as much as to say, "I don't understand it a bit."

At last Merle stepped forward and held up one hand. There was a loud cheer, and then perfect silence as she began to speak.

"I have found you a king," she said. "He is contented through trouble and care, and he will banish Discontent, he will banish Grunter Grim, and you will be happy for ever."

The Rhymes began once more to cheer.

"His name——" said Merle.

But at that moment there was a wild shriek, and Grunter Grim, without hat, without cloak, looking small, and mean, and miserable, came bounding into the room.

"My hat, my cloak, my power!" he said.

The Rhymes laughed, they were not a bit afraid of him.

"All gone," said Pollie Flinders; "you'll never spoil any more of my new clothes."

"Gone!" said Tom the Piper. "Yah! who stole the pig? Why, you! And who got beat? Why, me!"

"Quite, quite gone," said Hickory.

"Precisely so," observed Dickory.

"Exactly so," said Dock.

And the three little kittens joined paws, and danced round and round the miserable little man.

"Yes, they are gone," said Merle, "but I have not got them. Behold them there!"

Grunter Grim turned, the kittens stopped dancing, and they and all the Rhymes looked in wonder.

For there, in front of the platform, stood a cradle, and by it stood Thomas Muriel.

Merle stepped forward, lifted the baby out of the cradle, and held him up in her arms. The cloak was wrapped round him, and in his small hand he held the magic hat. Yet he crowed and cooed, and seemed perfectly happy.

The Rhymes cheered and shouted—

> *"The baby that's glad*
> *When others are sad;*
> *And his name it is Baby BUNTING."*

For a few moments there was wild confusion, and then Merle looked round for Grunter Grim. He seemed even smaller than when he first came into the Hall.

"Go, Grunter Grim!" cried Merle.

"Go!" cried Mistress Crispin, "and take that with you," and she threw her birch-rod away from her.

"Yes, go!" cried Jack and Jill, Bo-peep, Humpty Dumpty, Pollie Flinders, Tommy Stout, and all the other Rhymes.

But above the cheers and shouts a clear, silvery voice was heard, and as Merle looked towards the cradle, she saw a beautiful Fairy hovering above it. Her face was the most lovely that Merle had ever seen. It was so sweet, so pure, so calm, and so peaceful.

The Rhymes were hushed. They too were gazing at the beautiful Fairy, and they too were listening to her.

"I am the Spirit of Contentment," she said in her soft silvery voice;

"henceforward Endom shall be the land of contentment, the land of peace. Go, Grunter Grim! Go, live in the world, you are not fit for Endom. Go, live with the people who call Nursery Rhymes nonsense!"

There was a happy "coo" from Baby Bunting, and where Grunter Grim had stood there was only a little black heap.

* * * * * *

The Hall was growing darker. The Rhymes seemed getting smaller.

Crash! Bang! Crash!

Merle rubbed her eyes.

"Such nonsense, nonsense! staring at those Rhymes. No wonder the child dreams uneasily."

Was it Grunter Grim's voice? No, Grunter Grim was banished.

What was it? Merle rubbed her eyes again. The Hall, and the beautiful Fairy, the Rhymes, Baby Bunting, all had vanished. She was in her own little room, and Uncle Crossiter was standing by her bedside. She looked up at him solemnly, and then said slowly—

"I suppose you have a bit of Grunter Grim in you?"

Uncle Crossiter started.

"What is the child talking about?" he said. "I thought she was very much excited when she knocked the screen over. I will fetch her mother."

Merle watched him leave the room, and then looked at the screen lying on the floor. Had she knocked it down? Had she been asleep? and was it only a dream, after all?

She felt quite bewildered.

As her mother came into the room she said solemnly—

"I wonder if the Rhyme Fairy will alter all the Rhymes, and make them end properly now."

Her mother looked at her; she began to think that Uncle Crossiter was right, and that the child was delirious.

But Merle saw the puzzled look on her mother's face, and began to laugh.

"I'm all right, mother," she said, "only I've had a wonderful dream. Let me tell you all about it."

And Merle told her all about it.

"Only you see, mother," she said, when she had finished, "Thomas Muriel never got his right body back again, so that there must be some boy walking about in a girl's body now. I wish I knew him. I mean her—no, I mean him. Don't you?"

But her mother only smiled and kissed her.

A New Alice in the Old Wonderland

ANNA M. RICHARDS

ILLUSTRATIONS BY ANNA M. RICHARDS, JR.

1895

ANNA MATLACK RICHARDS (1835-1900) is generally remembered as the wife of William Trost Richards, a successful pre-Raphaelite painter who was an admirer and acquaintance of John Ruskin. At the time of her marriage to Richards in 1856, however, Anna Matlack had already earned a reputation as a successful poet and playwright. She and her husband eventually had eight children, settling—after extensive travel abroad—in Newport, Rhode Island. Richards published a sequence of sonnets in 1881 entitled *Dramatic Sonnets,* and another in 1891, *Letter and Spirit.* In the 1890s she published comic poems for children in children's magazines such as *Harper's Young People* and *St. Nicholas* magazine and, in 1895, *A New Alice in the Old Wonderland,* an expanded version of the stories she had invented years before for her children about their favorite fantasy heroine.[1]

An anonymous reviewer for the *Dial* describes Richards's work as a "hazardous experiment" because of its daring appropriation and transformation of the settings, characters and themes of the original *Alice* novels.[2] Richards challenges the original books not by reinventing them, but by invading them with her "new Alice," Alice Lee.[3] Alice Lee is, however, a new kind of female hero who maintains power over her own fantasy, rather than allowing herself to become its victim.[4]

---

1. Anna Matlack Richards uses the designation "Sr." in signing the preface to this novel to distinguish herself from her namesake daughter, who provided the illustrations. Anna M. Richards Jr. later became well-known as a landscape painter under her married name, Anna Brewster.
2. *The Dial* 19 (December 1895): 340.
3. When informed by his publishers of a proposal to publish Richards's *A New Alice in the Old Wonderland* in Great Britain, Carroll responded with, in his words, "*absolute* disapproval," and even considered legal action to stop British publication of the book, finally deciding against it to protect his reputation and privacy. See Morton N. Cohen and Anita Gandolfo, eds., *Lewis*

A New Alice in the Old Wonderland

PREFACE

So well they loved the Wonderland of Alice,
Once, those unreasonable children three,
No other land would do; no fairy palace,
No brownie-peopled realms of mystery.

And so, long time ago, this tale was told them,—
Adventures in the land they liked the best;
Woven with many a simple charm to hold them,
Of far-fetched incident and harmless jest.

Now they have all grown up,—a charm perennial
In the old nonsense one of them did find,
And made these pictures; and, though Messrs. Tenniel
And Carroll criticise, they will not mind.

We're not original, nor wise, nor witty;
But, since to amuse the children is our plan,
To weigh us in your balance were a pity;
So spare us, gentle Critic, if you can.

                —A.M.R., Sr.

CHAPTER 1. PEGGY THE PIG

*A*LICE LEE WAS SITTING by the window with her chin resting on her hand looking out, although there was nothing much to see.

It was a cold, rainy day, and she could not go out; neither did anything very interesting occur to her to do in the house. She was thinking, rather unconsciously, that there were a great many children who had a better time than she had.

"Mother," she said, at last, "you know the little girl we saw at Aunt Lucy's yesterday,—her name was May Selwyn, she said. Well, they're all going over to France next week; and she says she is going to live in the most *beautiful* house and have a lovely white pony, all her own."

Carroll and the House of Macmillan (Cambridge: Cambridge UP, 1987) 315, 316, 318.
4. Carolyn Sigler, "Brave New Alice: Anna Matlack Richards's Maternal Wonderland," *Children's Literature* 24 (1996): 55-73.

Her mother did not say anything, and Alice went on,—

"And Nanny Grey is going away, too, next Monday. It's the most charming place that ever was, that she is going to. It's on an island in the sea, she says, and the roses grow there all winter. I wish *we* were going somewhere."

Mrs. Lee knew that Alice was not usually a discontented little girl, and she did not begin by telling her—what was nevertheless quite true—that, while there were really only a very few children who were "going somewhere," there must be a great many who would be delighted to live in the home where Alice was at that moment.

She knew, too, that even grown people sometimes have moods in which they wish something more interesting than usual would happen; so she said, at last,—

"Well, yes. I think myself it would be delightful to be '*going somewhere*'; I should be glad if we were packing up our things to go there this very minute. As to France, it's rather late to be on the sea just now; the end of November isn't a very pleasant time to be travelling *any*where.

"And then," she continued, "I'm quite sure you wouldn't wish to be going South for the reason the Greys have to go. Nanny's mother has been very ill, you remember."

"Well, but, mother, of course I didn't mean *that* exactly," said Alice. "I only meant having some kind of adventure, you know."

"I don't see exactly what I can do about it," said her mother, smiling. "I can promise that if I happen to come across any adventure I will be sure to let you have it. I suppose you are getting rather too old to make them up for yourself, as you used to do not so very long ago. What has become of all the plays you acted once, that were so much fun? Don't you remember?"

Alice did remember very well, although it had been some time since she had taken her old interest in "pretending" things. Once she could be happy for days together in imagining herself a fairy, or a powerful old witch in disguise, or a proud, beautiful princess stolen from her father's palace, or else Cinderella.

Cinderella really *was* fascinating. First of all you fastened on to one of your ordinary frocks—it ought to be a white frock—all the odds and ends of adornment that you could beg or borrow or find for yourself. This took a great while; it was better to begin the day before; and the getting ready was quite as much fun as the play itself. Then you put on over all this some old gown that you could easily find in the garret; it must be very worn and faded, and so large that it would slip off at the least touch of the fairy's wand; and then, if you took the precaution to be standing very near a sofa, this could be easily pushed under out of sight with your foot. It was great fun, too, to dance in the hall, even with an imaginary prince, when her brother did not happen to be in the humor to play. He sometimes did join in these "private theatricals," as he called them, and very often her mother, too, would help a little: she made a capital fairy grandmother, with a yardstick for a wand.

Then her thoughts wandered into the Wonderland of the Alice books, with their little world of people so much more real than the ones in ordinary Wonder books. She recalled the hot summer afternoon that she was lying on the seat under the old tree in the garden, and was so *sure* she was wide awake, when she saw the Duchess and the White Queen walking together in the path before her, talking in a low whisper. But just then her brother Tom came whistling along, and of course they straightway vanished.

"Oh, dear!" she said to herself; "how I did use to wish I could get into Wonderland then!—that very same Wonderland, of course; for all the other books about some other kind were perfect nonsense."

Then she smiled to think of the time when the maids complained that there were sometimes mysterious finger-marks on the large looking-glass over the mantel-piece. The truth had been that Alice used to rub the glass with her fingers sometimes, when she found that the fire in the grate was hotter than usual, in order to see whether it ever showed any sign of melting, so that she could climb through into the room on the other side. She could see this mysterious room just as plainly in their house as the other Alice did in hers; and to go through the looking-glass, provided you could, seemed to her a much pleasanter way of getting into Wonderland than falling down a deep rabbit-hole. Besides, though she was always on the watch every time she took a walk in the country, she never saw anything that looked at all like a rabbit-hole, and even confessed to herself that she did not know what a rabbit-hole ought to look like. She had almost succeeded in persuading herself in those old days that she really believed there *was* such a place as Wonderland.

It had grown quite dark while Alice was thinking of these old times, and she was saying to herself that it would be fun to read the Alice books over again that very evening, for it had been at least six months since the last time, when there was a ring at the door-bell. A parcel was left at the door with Alice's name written on it. When the numerous papers were taken off, it proved to be a charming white box containing a generous slice of wedding-cake, sent by a cousin of hers from a distant city, whose wedding her father and mother had attended the week before.

She felt herself to be a very distinguished person; this was almost an adventure in its way, and the whole family gratified her by looking at it with the proper degree of interest, her brother Tom with some added feeling of envy as well.

When she announced her intention of not eating any of it until the next morning, Tom advised her to keep it all night under her pillow—"Just under the edge of your pillow, you know, so that it won't get all smashed"—and to try and dream upon it. He admitted that he did not know *exactly* what would happen in consequence.

"I believe it makes your dreams come true," he said.

"But suppose," said Alice, "that you didn't want your dream to come true."

"Well, *then*, of course it wouldn't," he said; "it's bound to come right somehow."

"Oh, yes," he added, after a short pause, "*now* I know what happens. It makes you dream exactly the thing you want to. And then you're sure to get it."

This was not very lucid, but Alice thought she remembered having once heard something of the kind herself; and although, of course, neither of them was the least in earnest about any such nonsense, they decided that it would be rather fun to try the experiment for once.

"At any rate," said Alice, "it is a very safe place to keep it in, you know."

"I'm not a bit sure of that," said Tom. "You might get hungry in the night and eat it all up without knowing it. You'd much better let me have it to put under *my* pillow. I say! what *do* you suppose makes it smell so good? I expect you'll chop it up into hundreds of pieces and give it to everybody."

"No," said Alice; "mother said she didn't think that was fair. She said it was just about big enough for us two."

"Mother's a duck!" said Tom; "she knows just the right thing. Fred Brown has to give the whole lot of them some of everything he gets, and there's precious little left for him sometimes. That's to make him generous."

"*Is* he generous?" Alice asked.

"Well, he mostly eats up everything he can out of doors, if you call that generous," said Tom.

"Oh, how *dreadfully* greedy!" said Alice.

"But he has to, you know," Tom insisted; "he *isn't* greedy at all. One day he gave me a lot of candy over the fence, and I wasn't looking at him eating it, either."

Alice now shut the box and tied its white ribbon, and then took it upstairs into her room. She had no lessons that evening, so she brought down the Alice books, and was soon as deeply interested as though she did not almost know them by heart. She had chosen "Through the Looking-glass" to begin with this time; and Tom, neglecting his Latin exercise, was speedily absorbed in the other one. He had formerly despised them both, but in his older and presumably wiser years he had been obliged to confess that they were not such "awful stuff as they used to be," after all.

The striking of nine o'clock reminded them both that it was bedtime. Tom said that he was sleepy, and would do his Latin in the morning; but Alice, although she was rather more willing to go than usual, did not feel the least bit sleepy, she said.

The moon was shining on the wall of her room in a great square of light, and after her mother, who had looked in to say "good-night," had shut the door, Alice sat up in bed, thinking how very bright the room was. She saw the box just under the edge of her pillow, and thought she would open it, so as to be perfectly sure that the cake was there. This was a very unwise thing to do. The cake had been there safe enough, of course, until this very moment, but now it was safe no longer. It looked so uncommonly good to eat, that she really could not put it back under the pillow without taking the least little bite, and then afterwards just one more. The end of it was that there was only about half of it left to go into the box again; and with this restored to its place, she lay down and tried to go to sleep, although still not feeling at all sleepy. She was just beginning to be rather sorry for more than one reason that she had eaten so much cake, and glad that there was at least plenty left for Tom, who need never know the whole story, when a very strange thing happened.

She saw on the moonlit wall opposite that there was a door between the washstand and the table, where there had never been a door before. She sat up in bed again and looked earnestly at the wall for some minutes, and then, feeling perfectly sure of it, she jumped quickly out of bed and crept over very cautiously to see if the door would open.

It was a real door, there was no mistake about it. And it had a knob like any other door, that seemed to turn of itself somehow, for hardly had she touched it when the door flew open, and she found herself going out into a very long and narrow dark entry with clear daylight shining at the end.

A moment more and she was out of doors, standing on a flight of marble steps that overlooked a wonderful old-fashioned garden; there were long alleys going off into the distance, bordered on each side by high box-tree hedges. It was exactly like being in the midst of a painted picture; the sky was almost too blue and the leaves too green to be real. On the bushes were flowers of the most brilliant colors; the ones nearest to Alice she stooped down to examine, and they came off in her hand at the least touch. They were dry, scentless things, and she found that they were really only paper flowers,—and not very well made ones, either,—no better than the ones she had just been making herself a few days before.

She walked slowly down one of the alleys. The hedges were so high that she could not see over the tops, but very soon she found that this alley branched off here and there into others, which in their turn led into others still, and that, in fact, the whole garden was a perfect maze, where it was impossible to help getting lost almost as soon as you entered.

She went on, however, turning corners now and then, always into paths exactly similar to each other, and getting more and more mixed up all the time, but not once wondering how she was ever to get back. Several times she thought she heard a slight rustling noise under the hedges, and she stopped at last to listen, when a little pig—a very pink and clean little pig—with a blue silk cap on its head struggled out through the leaves of the box-trees where they grew close down to the ground and ran with all its might down the path.

Alice jumped up and down for joy. "I believe," she said, "I really and truly believe that this is Wonderland, for I am sure that is the Duchess's little pig-baby." She had lost so much time in jumping for joy, however, that although she ran after the little pig as soon as possible, she could not catch it. Giving little squeals of fright as it went along, it kept just a few steps too far ahead to be overtaken, and at last it crowded itself under the gate of a pig-pen, or at least of a place that sounded like one, for Alice could hear the pigs squealing and grunting in several different-sized voices.

She stood on tiptoe to peep over the top, and was just in time to see the pig-baby carefully take off its little blue bonnet and, standing on its hind legs, hang it on a nail that was almost out of its reach. Then it climbed on a chair, and from that jumped on to a small table apparently laid for dinner, but with a very dirty cloth. There were two or three old plates and a rusty tin pan full of apples on the table, and the little pig at once set greedily to work at eating the apples, making a great noise about it as she did so.

The place was rather tidy considering that it was a pig-pen: it had even been swept after a fashion, for the sweepings were to be seen in one corner, only half hidden by an old broom placed over them. Several other pigs were rooting about, and Alice soon found out that what sounds so much like grunting when you are outside of a pig-pen, is only conversation when you lean over and listen.

"Is that you, Peggy?" she heard one of them say; but Peggy, if it were she, went on munching the apples without making any answer. The other pig then went up to a sort of cupboard in the corner and began scratching with his fore feet on the wire netting of the door.

"Peggy, I say," he went on; "I *say*, Peggy! There's roast beef in here; come help me get it!" Peggy, however, was still occupied with the apples; but another pig came up at this invitation. He was a thin, sly-looking fellow, with a

cricket cap over one ear. Both together they continued to scratch at the door, trying to push the wires far enough apart to get at the roast beef.

"Look out, boys! here's Jem and mother coming home from market!" called Peggy. She had her feet on the top of the pen now, and could see down the road. But just then the wire net had given way, and the sly-looking pig snatched a bone that still had a little meat on it and ran off as hard as he could go, followed by the other one in hot pursuit. They crowded under the gate, Peggy watching them evidently with great delight, and Alice saw them disappear behind some bushes. There was still another small pig in the corner of the pen, tied by the tail, evidently to keep him from getting out; he peeped under the gate with a melancholy air of resignation.

"That is meant to be the pig that stayed at home," she said to herself, with sudden conviction, "and I do believe they are all of them here. One got the roast beef, and one didn't; and Peggy is the one that cried '*wee! wee! wee!* ' all the way home, for that is just what you did, Peggy." There was a road a short distance off, on the other side of the pen, and Jem and his mother could be seen coming home from market with baskets in their mouths. Although Alice was much interested, she was rather afraid of *very* large pigs, so she withdrew behind one of the trees near by until they had both come up, and greeted by a chorus of squeals inside, had gone in and shut the gate.

CHAPTER 2. THE DUCHESS AND HER HOUSE

Alice now saw that she had left the garden far behind while she was running after the pig; for nothing more was to be seen of it anywhere. She was perfectly sure by this time that she was in Wonderland, and she thought the best plan would be to keep along the road, where something interesting would be the most sure to turn up. It was a very pleasant-looking road; there was a thick woodland on the other side of it, and a little farther down was a curious sort of house among the trees, with an open space in front. She took one more look at the pigs, which were now all lying on the ground asleep, and then, climbing down a rather steep bank into the road, she set off on her journey, quite sure that she was going to have some real adventures.

The house in the woods was quite small, not very much higher, indeed, than Alice herself; but she was not at all concerned, as the other Alice had been, by remembering that she was too big. The door was wide open, and with great curiosity she immediately crossed over and went to look in. Nobody was there; the hall was empty and silent, excepting for a few great flies that were buzzing about on the ceiling.

Presently she noticed that there were two white doors in the side of the hall, and that one of them, which seemed to be the door of a closet, kept slowly opening of itself a very little way and then immediately shutting up again. This happened several times, until at last it opened a little wider and the frog-footman stuck out his head sideways. He said nothing, but he winked at Alice, and then quickly shut himself in again, and this time he locked the door. She could hear him flopping about inside and sneezing dreadfully. This reminded her that the hall was delightfully smoky and full of pepper; there could be no mistake about it, this must be the house of the Duchess. She went softly down the hall, and ventured to open a door at the other end that she was certain must go directly into the kitchen.

Sure enough, it did; there was the kitchen, but no one was in it, and everything was arranged in the best of order. There was, of course, a great smell of pepper in the air, but there was no soup cooking on the grate, nor was there even any fire in it. Evidently it was the cook's afternoon out, Alice thought; her apron and ugly old cap, both looking very much like her, were hanging in a corner.

"I'm glad she isn't here herself, though," said Alice, who was beginning to feel delightfully at home, "for now I shall have some fun. How I wish Tom were here! I mean to climb up and look into every one of the shelves and drawers in that dresser."

The kitchen, when she entered it, was a light and rather cheerful-looking place, furnished with a table against the wall, a few chairs, and a dresser with rows of plates on it, looking, indeed, like any other kitchen. But to her great bewilderment, as soon as she began her investigations it all changed at once and became the most mixed-up place in the world. She could not remember how the change began, but suddenly there seemed to be countless rows of dark shelves and mysterious corners crowded with all sorts of indescribable things surrounding her on every side. She began to examine the things before her, but as soon as she took the lid off what seemed to be a jar, the jar turned into a box, and then disappeared altogether when she tried to put the lid on again. And then she found that the thing in her hand was not a lid after all, but a paper bag full of something like seeds. In trying to put this back as carefully as possible she disturbed everything else on the shelf, and all sorts of objects began tumbling down on the floor; she plainly heard something break as it fell, but it was so dark beneath her that she could not see what it was. She looked round her, and saw that the whole room had turned itself into a place that reminded her of that curious old shop in the Alice books, where the old Sheep was sitting with her hands full of knitting-needles. Very soon the walls began to crowd together more and more, and the place became smaller, and had grown so very dark that she lost all interest in what was on the shelves. She climbed down with some difficulty, and as soon as her feet touched the floor everything changed back again. The kitchen looked just as it did at first, only there seemed to be another door in it; there was a door, at least, which she had not noticed at first. It was wide open and led out into a dismal little yard, fenced in, which was all overgrown with weeds and half full of rubbish. Among the miscellaneous collection were conspicuous a great many empty tin boxes with red labels on them. Alice read on one of them

PETER PIPER,
MANUFACTURER OF
PIP-PEP-PEPPER.

Of course she would not have thought of wasting a moment's time over such a place as this in her own country, but here everything was interesting; even the old broken kettles and frying-pans which she was sure must be the ones that the cook used to throw at the Duchess.

"I wish, after all, I could see *some*body, even if it was only the ugly old cook."

Alice thought she said this to herself, but she must have spoken aloud, for a squeaky little voice answered, "You needn't be wanting for to see *her*,

missy." It was the sly-looking little pig with the cricket cap who had run off with the roast beef; he had apparently brought it there to enjoy all by himself.

Just then she thought she heard a little mewing noise behind her that sounded like kittens, and she found that it came from a corner of the kitchen, where some tea-towels were hanging to dry which she had not noticed before. There, to her great delight, was actually the old Cheshire cat curled up affectionately on the floor, purring over three little Cheshire kittens; that is, Alice was sure they *must* be Cheshire kittens, though she could only see their little backs. The old cat looked up with the same delightful grin on its face that she knew so well, and said, as if it guessed what Alice was thinking of,—

"Take one of them up and see, if you've a mind to; but don't swing it round the room by its tail."

Alice thought there was not much danger of *that*. "Oh, thank you!" she said, and carefully taking up one of the little furry things, she tried to see its face, but it sneezed so terribly that it did not seem to have any face at all; and directly, to her utter dismay, it began to grow very thin, and then thinner and thinner, until there was nothing left of it but a soft little piece of fur. What must have been its head looked like a tiny round ball of cotton-wool, but she could see that there was a feeble smile upon the side of it, something like its mother's in expression.

"There's nothing at all the matter with the child; it's only just vanishing, as you'd call it," said the cat. "It's *trying* to vanish, that is, and it don't quite succeed yet. It'll soon learn. Just throw it down here to me."

Alice laid the little bit of fur carefully down on the floor, and was much relieved to see that in a moment it grew as round and fat as ever. It went skipping up to its mother, who immediately began to smooth them all with her great tongue so unmercifully that Alice wondered they did not try to vanish, especially as they did not seem to like it much. She fancied as she watched them that they *did* seem to be growing rather thinner.

"They're more trouble than they're worth," the cat stopped to observe. "Fur always gets in a mess with trying to vanish. I do hope they'll go for good some day, and never get back!"

"Oh, *could* they do that?" said Alice. But the old cat had now begun to wash her own face, and did not seem to think the question worth answering.

"Has the cook gone out?" Alice asked, presently.

"The cook! The fire, you *mean*," said the cat. "Can't you see it's gone out? But you can talk about fires and things, when you haven't said so much as a *word* about my precious children that I've been showing you. The sweetest little cherubs you ever *did* see, too, unless you've seen the Duchess's pig, and that's only a very *little* handsomer. And it's all in the family, besides, so it don't count."

The kittens were now all looking up at Alice with the funniest little grin on their faces. She did not honestly think they were as nice as common kittens.

"I thought you said just this minute that you wanted them to vanish and never get back," she answered. "I'm sure I think your children are a great deal handsomer than that pig,—that is, I mean the baby. But was it a baby or was it a pig? I wish you would tell me."

"Oh, it's six of one and half a dozen of the other," answered the cat.

"But you don't mean," Alice contradicted, "that a pig is the same thing as a baby?"

"Whatever I *do* mean," said the cat, "I mean that a baby is the same thing as a pig."

These last words were spoken in a very low voice, and it added something in a whisper that Alice could not hear. Then she noticed that the cat had grown very much paler; soon the stripes on its back were all that was left of its body, and at last only its head was left, which continued to purr complacently until that too was gone. Alice hoped it would appear again. She stood for some minutes looking at the kittens, which she did not venture to take up again, however, and suddenly, as if somebody had frightened them, they all three set off and scurried across the kitchen, sneezing as they went, and growing thinner and thinner all the time, so that by the time they reached the other side they were thin enough to slip through a rather large crack in the floor, which they did with the greatest ease. She knelt down and was trying to peep through this crack, when suddenly she heard a great racket behind her.

It was the cook, who had come in evidently in the very worst of humors. She was banging at the grate with the poker and tongs, upsetting the coal-scuttle, and flinging kettles and frying-pans about with furious energy. Then she dragged the kitchen table into the middle of the room, managing to upset all the chairs as she did so; then she proceeded to pull out the drawer with such violence that she dragged it out altogether, and it fell to the floor with an immense clatter of iron spoons and ladles. Alice would have been very glad to escape, but as the cook had not yet seen her, she was afraid to call attention to herself by the least movement. So she stood as close to the wall as possible and waited for a convenient chance to slip out unobserved. Presently, however, the cook perceived her, and snatching a broom in one hand and a poker in the other, she stood looking as if she did not know which to use first. Fortunately, the table which she had dragged out was in her way, and served as a protection to Alice, who managed to get on the other side, and so reached the door safely, the cook following, only in time to slam it behind her so hard that it made the whole house rattle.

If Alice had been at home all this would have been a very unpleasant experience, but by the time she was safely out in the hall again, the old cook seemed rather fun than otherwise. The hall looked somehow rather different: there were two more doors in it now than there were before; they were opposite to each other and both painted green. There did not seem to be any harm in peeping through key-holes in Wonderland; and, indeed, Alice did not stop to think much whether there was or not. Through one of these key-holes she could see a steep flight of stairs winding up, full of dust and cobwebs, and through the other nothing but darkness, as she said. One of the white doors that she had seen at first was ajar, leaving a very small crack open, and by going close to this she could see into a curious little three-cornered room, where the old Duchess herself, as ugly as ever, was sitting sound asleep in an arm-chair near the fire. A tea-kettle was boiling furiously on the grate, and a sort of five-o'clock-tea table was spread by her side, on which was an immense plate of bread and butter and a great bowl of eggs. It looked as though she were going to have a comfortable meal when she woke up, or at least Alice thought she would if her nap did not last *too* long; for just then the Cheshire cat suddenly made its appearance and immediately began upon the bread and but-

ter. If its appetite were anything like in proportion to the size of its mouth there was no saying how much would be left for the Duchess.

However, Alice thought it was no concern of hers, so she went out to the front door, where she was surprised to see the Cheshire cat again sitting calmly on the step cleaning its whiskers. Presently the door of the Duchess's room opened behind her and a shower of china cups and saucers came flying into the hall.

"Pray, don't mind that," said the cat, as Alice got quickly out of the way; "it's not meant for *you*, you know: it's *me* she's after."

Soon the sugar-bowl came, full of lumps of sugar that were scattered all over the steps when it broke, for everything broke, of course. At last the Duchess threw out some of the eggs, which, strange to say, did not break, but rolled noisily about in every direction.

"Why, they're nothing but china eggs," said Alice, when she had exam-

ined one of them; "just like the nest-eggs that they had on the farm last summer."

"What nonsense you are talking!" said the cat. "Those eggs were made to match the egg-cups, and a very good idea, too."

Alice could not help thinking so herself, if this was the sort of usage they generally had. There was nothing more coming now, and she heard the Duchess slam her door and turn the key sharply in the lock.

Suddenly the frog footman came round the corner of the house. "The doctor says a *little* of that's temper," he said, and kept alternately swelling himself out and then shrinking up to almost nothing, all the while fixing his eyes on Alice. "Say, would you mind going in and seeing what she wants?"

"Why, I don't quite know," Alice hesitated. "Is she always like this?"

"Most generally when the cook's gone out she is. And she's just the same when the cook's come in. And when the cook's gone out *again*—lackaday!

You just ought to see her!" he said, stretching out his hand to stroke the Cheshire cat's fur the wrong way. "You'd better go straight in at once and have done with it."

"Why should I go?" Alice asked. "Why don't you go yourself?"

"Why, you see, you're the nearest the door, and *that* counts; and then you've called on her—through the crack of the door—and you know she's in, and *that* makes a difference; and then it's your turn, and *that*——"

"Oh, just go right in," interrupted the cat; "she's no end of fun."

"Yes; so she is," said the footman. "So she is."

Thus encouraged, Alice, who really thought it would be fun to see something more of the Duchess, concluded that she might venture. The door was very slightly ajar again as at first, and she was about to knock, when the cat, who had followed her into the house, pushed the door wide open and then disappeared.

The Duchess woke up with a start, and Alice was about to explain that it was not she who had opened the door, but she perceived that the Duchess did not seem to notice the intrusion. She began immediately to eat her eggs, crunching them up, shells and all.

Alice happened to be looking at the plate of bread and butter, and to her amazement she saw a slice lift itself up from the pile and disappear in the air; then another slice did the same thing, and then another. The last time, however, she observed the faint outline of a smile in the air just as the bread and butter was vanishing. "That rogue of a cat," she thought, "can eat just the same when it's invisible!"

The Duchess did not seem to perceive that anything was amiss until Alice spoke.

"I thought your eggs were made of china?" she ventured to say, at last.

"China!" screamed the Duchess. "Why, I declare you've been at my bread and butter!"

"Oh, I *beg* your pardon," Alice began; "I saw——"

"Don't say you saw the cat," she interrupted. "I suppose, while you were about it, you thought my bread and butter was made of china too, hey?"

"If you'll just watch the bread-plate," Alice said, "you'll see what becomes of it"; for at that moment she saw another slice vanish in the air.

"If you'll just watch *me*, you'll see what becomes of *you!*" cried the Duchess, reaching out her hand for a large jug of milk that stood on the table. Alice, who knew that her Grace was not very particular as to the things she threw at people, concluded that her visit had lasted long enough, and she quickly took her leave, shutting the door after her. She listened for a minute outside; she could hear the Duchess going on with her eggs.

The frog footman was waiting outside; he looked at Alice with a foolish smile on his face.

"*Bon jour! Au revoir!*" he said. "Did she say what she wanted?"

"No," Alice replied, "she didn't."

"I thought she wouldn't. She *was* in a pepper-jig, wasn't she, though?" he said. "Drop in again to-morrow and try pot-luck."

Then he winked, and began to dance a hornpipe with both hands in his pockets. Alice passed by him without a word, quite offended at his behavior, and went out into the road again. It ran up-hill a little farther along, with hedges on each side, looking very mysterious and tempting; and she walked on, wondering what would happen next. "If I only don't meet with anything to make my neck grow so long!" she said to herself; for this seemed to her the only unpleasant part of the other Alice's adventures. She concluded not to eat or drink anything at all whilst she was in Wonderland. . . .

CHAPTER II. THE TWEEDLES

It was a charming day. It did not occur to Alice to wonder what had become of the darkness; and as to the Banquet, she entirely forgot all about it. She was looking in at a gate-way by the roadside that seemed to open into some beautifully kept park grounds, and hesitating as to whether she ought to enter them, when she saw no less a personage than the Queen of Hearts standing on the lawn and looking through her hands, which she held up to her eyes after the manner of opera-glasses.

"Come here, child," she called out to Alice, without turning her head, "and see if your eyes can't see better than mine. I believe this is Mr. Tweedle got back already. He's been away, you know."

"Oh, do you mean Tweedle Dee and Tweedle Dum?" said Alice, approaching; "and can you see them from here?"

"See *him,* you mean," corrected the Queen. "You talk as if there were two of him."

"Why, there *are* two of them!" said Alice.

"What do you mean? Off with your head!" cried the Queen of Hearts, with a savage frown.

"But, your majesty," Alice persisted, "*every*body knows there are two Tweedles,—why, there they are now!"

Across a long stretch of meadow that reached to the foot of a little hill Alice was sure she saw two short, plump figures standing side by side. It was a long way off, and they were very small, but she thought she could not be mistaken.

"Now, roll up your hands, and look at them as I'm doing," said the Queen.

Alice did so, and the two figures seemed to join together and grow into one. She could see this figure quite plainly; it was certainly one of the Tweedles, but *only* one. She stood looking alternately in both ways for some minutes without speaking, and at last she said, "Why, it's the strangest *thing!* It's just like a stereoscope!"

"Exactly," said the Queen, "if you mean by that that there's only one Tweedle. Nobody but you ever called it such a name. But your head comes off all the same, just as soon as I can get anybody to do it."

Alice walked on towards the meadow, with the Queen following her.

"Well, but," persisted Alice, not very much concerned about her head, "I thought they once agreed to have a battle, and then—— But look at all these rattles on the ground here!"

Strown about on the grass were a number of the wooden toys that children call watchmen's rattles, and there were also two or three babies' rattles made of basket-work.

"Those are rattlesnakes' rattles," said the Queen.

"What nonsense!" cried Alice. "Rattlesnakes don't have *that* kind of rattles!"

"They can have any sort they choose, I suppose!" replied the Queen, in an angry voice. "By the way, I will *send* some one after your head."

Alice was so interested in Tweedle Dum, or Tweedle Dee ("I don't know which it is," she thought), that she hardly noticed that the Queen had departed. She decided at once that she would follow a path that she saw went straight on across the meadow, and find out all about the Tweedles if she could.

It seemed a very short walk, for in a few minutes she found herself going straight in at the door of a little house.

There was a very small tea-table in the room, and seated before it on a little chair was one of the Tweedles, with a mug in his hand. He looked up at her for a moment without showing any surprise, and then went on drinking. The table was set with dolls' tea-things; there were tiny dishes of jam and biscuits and cakes, and Tweedle was evidently having his supper.

"Come in, or else get out; but don't stand there in my light," he said, presently.

"Will you please tell me who you are?" Alice asked.

"I'm Tweedle," he said, watching her very closely as she came in and took the only empty chair in the room, a seat opposite to him at the table. He immediately removed the jam and cakes to his own side of the table, out of her reach as he thought.

"I shall want all these myself," he said.

"I don't want any, I'm sure," said Alice. "You're not very polite, certainly."

"I know it," said Tweedle; "but this is *my* supper; contrariwise, if it was yours, I'd ask you to take some. But are you really sure you don't want any?"

"Really and truly," answered Alice.

"Well, then,—thanks," he said, putting the dishes back, "for you see I'm rather crowded here. And now, if there's anything you want that's *not* on the table, do ring for it."

"Will the maid bring it?" asked Alice.

"No," replied Tweedle, "I expect not. I have no maid. Contrariwise, if you don't want anything, what do you sit down to the table for? I didn't invite you, and I don't mean to."

"There's no other seat in the room," replied Alice; "but I'll go away, I'm sure, if you really don't want me."

"I really don't," answered Tweedle, "nohow."

There was nothing else to do after this but to go at once; and though Alice had a great mind to be vexed, she reflected that she had been *rather* rude herself in coming into his house in such a very unexpected manner.

"I shall be coming out for a bit of a walk myself when I've done supper," he called after her, as she went out the door.

The foot-path led round the side of the house and went straight up the hill behind it. She had not gone far before she heard Tweedle coming up the hill, panting and puffing like a small engine; and he called to her to wait. He had a heavy umbrella with him.

"You *might* have had a little of that jam, after all; it was uncommon nasty and sticky!" he said, as soon as he could speak.

"Couldn't you eat it all yourself?" she asked.

"No, I couldn't, nohow," he answered. "I knew you wanted it, too, all the time."

"You're the rudest person I've seen here!" said Alice.

"I dare say I am," he replied. "I hope so. My brother tries to be ruder than I am, but he can't be, nohow."

"Oh, that's what I want to ask you!" she cried, forgetting all about his rudeness. "Then there are really and truly two of you after all. And so the Queen of Hearts was wrong?"

"No, she was right," he contradicted; "there *is* only one of us,—one of him and one of me. We used to go together so much that we got mistaken for two."

This was not very clear to Alice, but she asked, "And don't you go together any more?"

"No, indeed," replied Tweedle, decisively.

"Why not?" she asked.

Tweedle was rather slow in replying, but at last he muttered, in an angry voice, "Of all the *nas*ty, *self*ish, *greed*y things———" and then stopped as if overcome by some recollection.

"I dare say you were just as bad," said Alice.

"So I was," said Tweedle; "but so was he."

"You haven't got your name on your collar, I see," said Alice, changing the subject. "Which one are you?"

"Oh, those names were just fancy. If you see me first, then I'm Dee; contrariwise, if you see him first, he's Dum. You can see us from the top of this hill. He lives one side and I live t'other; or, I live one side and *he* lives t'other. It's just as it happens, whatever."

"I saw one of you a little while ago," Alice remarked.

"Did you?" asked Tweedle. "Which one?"

"That's what I don't know," said Alice. "At first I thought it was both of you."

"If you don't know which one you saw, you can't tell which one I am," he said, "nohow."

Alice was decidedly puzzled; she kept thinking about it until they came to the top of the hill, without understanding it any better. They walked on a few steps and came to where they could look down on the other side of the hill, and there she saw a little house at the bottom exactly like the one which they had just left, and which was now out of sight. There was no sign of the other Tweedle, however. Alice said she had hoped they might see him, too.

"Oh, we don't want to see him," said Tweedle. "He's a very deserving fellow, he is."

"Is he?" said Alice. "I thought you didn't like him. What makes you say he's *deserving,* all of a sudden?"

"Because he *is,*" Tweedle replied. "He deserves a dozen good whacks; and he'll get 'em, too, if we ever fight again." And he went "Grr-r-r-r-rr," with a snarling gesture, at the thought of his brother.

"There *must* be two of them," Alice said to herself, with conviction.

"He's in bed now," said Tweedle. "He always goes to bed when I'm up. Contrariwise, just as I get snugly tucked up, house and all, out *he* comes."

"That's something like the little man and woman in the barometer that we have," Alice said. "The woman goes in when it rains."

"There you're wrong," said Tweedle. "*He* goes in when it rains, because he hasn't any umbrella."

Here Tweedle looked at his umbrella with great complacency, and pretty soon he raised it over his head, and spent a few minutes in admiring it. There was a small rustic seat by the side of the pathway here on the hill, just large enough for two, and Tweedle sat down upon it.

"Come under this umbrella," he said, "and I'll tell you the rest of that poetry."

"Oh, that will be delightful!" exclaimed Alice, taking a seat. "But you haven't told me *any* poetry yet."

"Haven't I?" said Tweedle; "that's very curious. I don't understand it. For you've *heard 'The Walrus and the Carpenter,'* I'm sure."

"Yes," said Alice, "but *you* didn't say it to *me,* and it wasn't *I* who heard you, and——" She was getting almost as mixed up as the Wonderland people, but Tweedle seemed to understand.

"Just as I thought," he interrupted her. "The other one of *me* said it to the other one of *you.*"

"*Was* there any more of that?" she asked.

"There wasn't then," he replied, "because we didn't know any more. But we know nearly all of it now. What was the last you heard?"

Alice was quite prepared for examination in Wonderland literature. She repeated the lines:

> *"Only the shells were left, because*
> *They'd eaten every one!"*

"That ain't right, nohow," said Tweedle.

"Of course not," Alice assented. "It isn't right to deceive even oysters, like that."

"I mean the *verse* isn't right," he said. "You've got it all wrong. But no matter; have it so if you like. This is the way it goes on:

> *"They flung the oyster-shells away*
> *As far as eye could reach;*
> *And then they both went back again*
> *Along the briny beach.*
> *The Carpenter right sadly gazed*
> *Upon the neighboring shore:*
> *The Walrus did not care a bit;*
> *He wished he had some more.*
>
> *'How many do you think,' he said,*
> *'Could we have had apiece?'*
> *'Too many,' said the Carpenter;*
> *'And here comes the police.'*
> *The Walrus laughed a scornful laugh.*
> *'Well, let them come!' said he.*
> *Yet still he flung their knife away*
> *Into the deepest sea.*
>
> *They walked together hand in hand,*
> *As harmless as they could;*
> *They gazed upon the distant ships:*
> *It did no sort of good.*
> *They took the Carpenter along*
> *And put him into prison;*
> *And this was only right, because*
> *Those oysters weren't his'n.*
>
> *The Walrus, too, was taken off;*
> *They put him in the Zoo;*
> *They kept him in a little pond*
> *Exposed to public view.*

He sometimes wished he could get off
To frolic in the sea;
He often wished that he had let
Those little fellows be."

"Oh," Alice exclaimed, as soon as he had finished, "how perfectly splendid, wasn't it?"

"Well, no, not *splendid,* I should say," said Tweedle. "Nohow."

"Well, but it served them right," said Alice.

"The Carpenter was a relation of mine," he observed.

"Was he? Really?" she asked, in surprise.

"Yes, he was," answered Tweedle, "and the Walrus was my uncle."

"I don't believe you at all," said Alice, detecting a mischievous look on Tweedle's face.

"I don't care," replied Tweedle. "Have him for *your* uncle, then, if you like. It suits me just the same."

"You said you knew *nearly* all of that poem," said Alice, not noticing his last remark. "Is there any more of it?"

"Yes," answered Tweedle. "The Carpenter soon got out of prison, and then he got the Walrus away, too, and so they both went down to the seashore and got some *more* oysters."

"Oh, dear!" cried Alice. "Why, I thought they were both so sorry about it."

"Well, so they were. But oysters are very good. I wish *I* could get some, I know. But how sleepy I am!" he said, with a yawn. "I don't want to talk to you any more."

He suddenly rose from his seat, and shutting his umbrella, he turned and ran back down the hill,—very awkwardly, but at a pace so rapid that Alice could not keep up with him. By the time she had reached his house he had gone in, and he shut the door in her face.

"What am I to do?" she asked, as he appeared at the window.

"Just what you like," he said, shutting the window and pulling down a blind.

Alice had grown accustomed to the abrupt manners most of the Wonderland people had, but Tweedle was certainly the very rudest of them all. He was very diverting, though, and she wished she could see more of him. She walked slowly up to the top of the hill again, and then seeing at a glance that the window of the other house was now open, she concluded to go down and make a visit to the other Tweedle, "For there isn't the least doubt about there being two of them," she said to herself. "I wonder what the Queen of Hearts could have meant."

The path leading down to his house was exactly like the other, and went round to the front door just as that did. She found herself entering at the door in the same abrupt manner in which she had entered the first house. There was *precisely* the same tea-table spread, and Alice could hardly believe it *was* another Tweedle, so exactly like the first one was the figure seated in the little chair with a mug in his hand. He looked up at her for a moment without showing any surprise, and then went on drinking.

"Come in, or else get out; but don't stand there in my light," he said, presently.

"Will you please tell me who you are?" Alice asked.

"I'm Tweedle," he said, watching her very closely as she came in and took the only empty chair in the room, a seat opposite to him at the table. He immediately removed the jam and cakes to his own side of the table, out of her reach as he thought.

"I shall want all these myself," he said.

"I don't want any, I'm sure," said Alice. "You're not very polite, certainly."

"I know it," said Tweedle; "but this is *my* supper; contrariwise, if it was yours, I'd ask you to take some. But are you really sure you don't want any?"

"Really and truly," answered Alice.

"Well, then,—thanks," he said, putting the dishes back, "for you see I'm rather crowded here. And now, if there's anything you want that's *not* on the table, do ring for it."

"Will the maid——"

Here she suddenly became aware that *exactly* the same scene was going on between them; that even she herself was saying the same things she had said before, and she was overcome by a sense of bewilderment. Her eye fell, too, on the umbrella in the corner, just as she remembered seeing it in the other Tweedle's house.

"Well, I can't stand this," she said, after pausing for a moment to think it over; and just as this Tweedle was saying, "No, I expect not. I have no maid," she turned, and left the house at once, walking away as quickly as she could, without noticing whither she was going.

"Of all the curious things I've seen *yet!* " she exclaimed to herself, without finishing the sentence. "And now I shall never know which was which, and I won't ever be sure whether there were two of them or not, after all!"

Chapter 12. The Pageant

On stopping to look round her, she saw that she had come to a very different sort of country, and had entirely lost sight of the little house and its

surroundings, and even of the pathway that led from it, so that she could not have found her way back to it. There was no path in the grassy woodland around her, and she walked on and on among the trees, the landscape slowly changing until it grew to be that of a well-kept park, with old trees in groups, and beautiful deer around them feeding on the soft grass. She walked slowly for fear of disturbing them, but they were very tame, and some of them came up and thrust their noses in her hands. It became more and more charming every moment; never in her life had Alice seen anything so beautiful. Suddenly she came out between two groups of dark foliage into an open space, and beyond this space was a high, close hedge. A wide opening in this hedge made a gate-way, the pillars on each side of which were Castles, one of them Red, the other White. Through this gate-way could be seen the most wonderful garden, with myriads of flowers, and bright-colored birds, and marvellous fountains sparkling in the sun.

The Castles had deep Gothic door-ways, and just at the entrance of the White one stood a White horse that Alice recognized at once as the one belonging to the White Knight, though the Knight was not there. At the other door-way was a Red Knight on his horse, standing, as if on guard, in a stiff attitude, with his helmet on. He looked rather solemn, and seemed to take no notice of Alice, but she summoned courage enough to approach him.

"May I go into that beautiful garden?" she asked.

"No, not just now," he said, in a decided but not very stern voice. "You mustn't go in there without special permission, because the royal family are in residence. But perhaps you can get permission."

"I know some of the Kings and Queens quite well," she said. "I'll ask them as soon as I see any of them. Do they come in and out of this gate?"

"No. The Kings and Queens you've seen are not the same ones who live in the ivory palace that is in these grounds. I'm only an outside gate-keeper myself, and *I* don't go in except I'm invited. There's another gate-way inside there, with pearl and ivory castles; and the Knights there are carved out of ivory. The Kings and Queens have precious stones in them."

"How very grand and proud they must be!" Alice said, thinking aloud.

"No, indeed," the Knight replied, quickly. "They're very kind and good. They're very glad to have any one come into their beautiful grounds, if they're sure that it's somebody who won't do any mischief there."

"The White Knight isn't on his horse," Alice remarked, after a long pause.

"Oh, have you made his acquaintance already?" he asked.

Alice said that she had, and that she liked him very much.

"Well, he's a rather good sort, even if there *is* a little nonsense about him. He wouldn't hurt a fly. And he can fight well enough when he has a chance, too. And then there's the Red Bishops. Have you seen either of them?"

"I saw the one that has no head," Alice replied. "I thought he had a great deal of sense, and I was very sorry about his head."

"Well, then," he said, dismounting and taking off his helmet so that he could talk better, "you'll be very glad. That Bishop is a great friend of mine, and I've been away a long time on my trusty steed, up and down the land, searching for his head. And I've found it. I've only just got back with it."

"Oh," said Alice, delighted, "does he know you've got it?"

"Not yet. He don't even know I went for it, because I thought maybe I wouldn't get it, and then he would be disappointed. I found it not so very far from the spot where he lost it, in a place where I'd looked for it twenty times before."

"Will it make any difference in him?" Alice asked. "Will he be like the White Bishop?"

The Red Knight laughed. "Not a bit of it. Their heads don't make any difference," said he, repeating what the Red Queen had said. "Only it makes them look much better. And I'm very glad that I've happened to come back with the head in time for to-day, because there's going to be a Pageant, and he will be glad to have his head then, so as to look like other people. I hope you'll see him in the Pageant with his head on."

"Oh, how very, *very* much I should like to see the Pageant!" cried Alice, much impressed by the name. "Will you please tell me what it is, and how I could get there?"

"It's a sort of procession," he said, "that we have every year. All the Kings and Queens and their courts, and foreign guests from other kingdoms, have a grand march with all the magnificence they can get. They will wind in and out through all these groups of trees, around and around, and then when they're all collected they will march through the forest until they come to the great Royal Sport Grounds, where there will be games and tournaments for two or three weeks. Perhaps you'd like to be in the Pageant yourself? I think I could manage it. There's a tame white pony wandering about here somewhere; you may ride on him if you like."

Alice was silent. She could not find any words to express her rapture, but the Knight seemed to take it for granted.

"Well, then," he said, "when you hear a horn blowing through the wood, just come here to this gate and wait until you see me."

"By the way," he continued, "I ought to be off now. It won't be long before the Pageant begins, and I ought to be going this very minute, to be in time to give the Bishop his head. How I *wish* the White Knight would come back! He went to get his helmet mended."

"Oh, *must* you wait for him?" asked Alice, anxiously.

"Yes. One of us, at least, must be always here on guard, excepting when we're fighting or else in a procession, and then the Gryphons come. We have to watch the Ivory Gardens, you know."

"Couldn't you get the Gryphons?" she said.

"No; they never come unless they hear the horn blowing," he answered. "I don't know what I shall do!"

"I wish I could watch in your place," Alice said. "But I suppose, of course——"

"That's a capital idea," he interrupted. "I believe you could well enough. I can get the white pony for you at once, and then you'll only have to give me your high word of honor that you'll stay here until the White Knight comes, and that you'll not let anybody pass these gates."

"Well!" cried Alice, joyfully.

The Knight set off immediately, and in a few minutes came back leading a very tame white pony. He helped Alice to mount, and placed her in exactly the position she must keep, and then put a sword in her hand.

"Now," he said, "you'll be all ready for the Pageant; besides, I won't be gone very long even if the White Knight don't come; but I expect he will. I wouldn't go if it weren't so *very* important. You're not afraid, are you?"

"Oh, no indeed!" Alice cried; and the Knight turned to go, looking back to wave his hand. She saw that he had a small box tied on the saddle behind him; no doubt it contained the Bishop's head, she thought.

The moment after, she was alone in that beautiful solitude, seeming to make part of it, so still was her pony and so motionless did she feel obliged to keep herself.

"I never heard of anybody else in the whole world having such a glorious adventure as this," she thought. Her mind went over all the scenes of her every-day life. She remembered even the conversation with her mother the evening before, and her talk with Tom about the wedding-cake, and the new door in her chamber. How long ago that all seemed! The light and shade of the charmed landscape lay around her; she wished she dared turn her pony's head so that she could look into the palace gardens; but she could at least hear the birds singing and the splashing of the fountains. She could not have told how long she stood thus as in an entrancing dream, when a slight noise on one side made her turn her head.

The White Knight was there, sitting on his horse looking towards her. He had his helmet on, which made him look quite unlike himself. Alice explained to him how she had come to be there instead of the Red Knight, and he said that he had supposed that was the way of it.

"I'm very glad to see you again," he added. "I'm sorry I couldn't have come sooner, but the man had my helmet, you see, and I couldn't come without it. I had tried to mend it myself, and that only made it worse; so that's why it took him so long. You can go now, if you like."

"Oh, it has been delightful!" she answered. "I think I should like to stay until the Red Knight comes back."

"I see you have a fine crown on your head now; so I suppose you feel like a queen," he said.

Alice had entirely forgotten the crown that the White Queen had so recklessly given her, and indeed thought that she must have lost it directly afterwards, for she was quite sure that it was not on her head at the great Kindergarten Occasion. But now it had somehow come back again.

"I don't think," she said, in answer to the White Knight, "that you *could* feel like a queen, unless you really were one."

Still, she was very glad now that she would have a crown to wear at the Pageant. She looked down at her every-day dress, and wished very much that some fairy godmother were there to change it into shining silk.

"Do you think it will be much longer before the Pageant begins?" she asked.

"No; they are preparing now," he said. "Don't you see them gathering in the wood yonder?"

Alice changed the position of her pony a little so that she could see better into the woods, and here and there through the trees she could see gleaming figures of Kings and Queens and Knights appear in openings through the foliage.

"I don't remember ever seeing any of these before," she said, after watching them for some time.

"There are a great many strangers come," he said; "new ones every year; whole sets of chess and families of cards that we don't know ourselves. I'm always glad when it's over."

"Do the carved ivory ones come?"

"Oh, never! They never leave their own gardens. But here come all our people, and now we must begin to form into line."

Alice was quite excited. The Red Knight was approaching; the two Bishops that she knew were just behind him, and they all soon came up. The Red Bishop had on his newly-found head, and he gave a merry smile when he saw Alice, but there was no time to say anything. The others were all coming up; she was pleased to see that the Red King had had his feet restored to him, and was walking in a very dignified manner. Already they were forming into a procession, walking two and two. A horn was sounding through the wood, and then Alice saw two Gryphons come up and take the places of the two Knights at the castle door-ways; they were so exactly alike that she could not tell which of them was her old friend. Although Alice was so delighted to be in the procession, she wished she could be standing down under one of the trees at the same time, so that she could see them all go by.

But it was time for her to take her place, which was just after the Kings and Queens and Bishops. The White Rabbit in his herald's dress came and took a place by her side; he had a most serious and important air. It was much too solemn an occasion for any exchange of greeting, and he did not even look at Alice. Then, as the Red Knight had said, they all began to wind slowly round and round among the groups of trees, other parts of the procession coming up continually from the distance and joining themselves wherever they could find a place in the long Pageant.

It got more and more imposing as they went on. Very soon the blowing of the horn of summons changed into the most ravishing music, and gold and jewels began to gleam on the royal personages. Alice found that her plain frock was slowly changing into a magnificent white robe embroidered with golden flowers, and the Knights behind her were transformed with shining armor and waving plumes. The Bishops, too, were in splendid embroidered robes, and had gold and silver inlaid mitres. It was most wonderful. Every now and then they stopped for a few minutes to allow spaces in the ranks behind them to close up; and when the procession was entirely formed, the King in front gave a signal, and they all turned slowly into a dark forest. Then some voices before them began a strange song that blended with the music, and when they stopped, voices behind took up the song in a different key. Alice noticed that the Bishops before her were singing, too, in a very low voice. The forest path seemed to be like a great cathedral, with long shafts of sunlight coming through the high leafy windows here and there between the trees, and making the gems and gold suddenly flash in the darkness.

As the Pageant went on Alice thought that gradually they were moving more and more slowly, so that it seemed to take them a long while to reach a small square pond that she could see by the side of the road just before them. It shone clear and still in the dim woods. When they came to the edge of it she could see, just as in a looking-glass, the reflections of the trees in it, and part of the Pageant. She leaned over a little to see if she could not catch the image of herself on the pony, and just at this minute,—Alice could hardly tell how it happened, for she was sure she had not moved upon her seat,— she began slowly sliding off the pony's back. She saw the Knights come forward and stretch out their arms to help her, but she kept on sliding and sliding, trying all the time as hard as she could to hold on, until she fell gently into the pond.

All the Pageant had vanished. She rubbed her eyes and looked around, and could not imagine what sort of place she had come into. At first she thought the shining pond was still there; but gradually it became plain that the light was only from a large looking-glass, with a mantel-piece below it. There was a fire burning in the grate, and a lamp turned quite low on the centre-table. Suddenly, as her eyes became accustomed to the light, she saw that it was their own drawing-room, and that she was sitting on the floor just at the foot of the large sofa, from which she seemed to have fallen along with all the cushions. She gave a little cry of surprise, and instantly her mother, who had been sitting in the library close by, came in.

"Alice, my dear child, what is the matter?" she asked in some alarm.

"Why, I don't know," said Alice, "only I've had the most wonderful time!"

"You must have been walking in your sleep, my dear," her mother said. And then, fearing that Alice might feel rather frightened, she added, smiling, "I used to do that myself when I was young, but I never knew such a thing to happen to you before. Come, I will go up with you; it is eleven o'clock. You shall tell us all about your dream in the morning."

So Alice was very soon tucked up in bed once more, with another good-night from her mother, and was soon asleep again. Fragments of her strange adventures haunted her sleep all through the rest of the night; some of the scenes she seemed to see over again, and the old characters appeared before her in new combinations. But it was only in the full sunlight of the morning, when she was wide awake in her own little room where there was no new door now to be seen, that she realized the whole significance of her dream, and knew that she too had had some real adventures in Wonderland.

THE END

Justnowland

E. Nesbit

1912

*E*DITH NESBIT (1858-1924) has been described as the first modern children's writer. She published a number of fantasy stories and novels for children including *Five Children and It* (1902), *The Phoenix and the Carpet* (1904), and *The Railway Children* (1906), most of which are still in print and widely read. She and her husband, Hubert Bland, were good friends with the writers George Bernard Shaw and H.G. Wells and were founding members of the socialist Fabian Society. Nesbit's socialism is often reflected in her work for children, as in this dream-fantasy. Cruelly imprisoned in the attic by her aunt, "Justnowland"'s heroine Elsie travels up the chimney to rescue a fantasy land that has been enchanted for being "unkind . . . unjust, and ungenerous" to its workers. Gore Vidal wrote that "[a]fter Lewis Carroll, E. Nesbit is the best of the English fabulists who wrote about children . . . and like Carroll she was able to create a world of magic and inverted logic that was entirely her own."[1]

---

1. "E. Nesbit's Magic," *New York Review of Books* (3 Dec. 1964): 16.

Justnowland

"AUNTIE! NO, NO, NO! I will be good. Oh, I will!" The little weak voice came from the other side of the locked attic door.

"You should have thought of that before," said the strong, sharp voice outside.

"I didn't mean to be naughty. I didn't, truly."

"It's not what you mean, miss, it's what you do. I'll teach you not to mean, my lady."

The bitter irony of the last words dried the child's tears. "Very well, then," she screamed, "I won't be good; I won't try to be good. I thought you'd like your nasty old garden weeded. I only did it to please you. How was I to know it was turnips? It looked just like weeds." Then came a pause, then another shriek. "Oh, Auntie, don't! Oh, let me out—let me out!"

"I'll not let you out till I've broken your spirit, my girl; you may rely on that."

The sharp voice stopped abruptly on a high note; determined feet in strong boots sounded on the stairs—fainter, fainter; a door slammed below with a dreadful definiteness, and Elsie was left alone, to wonder how soon her spirit would break—for at no less a price, it appeared, could freedom be bought.

The outlook seemed hopeless. The martyrs and heroines, with whom Elsie usually identified herself, *their* spirit had never been broken; not chains nor the rack nor the fiery stake itself had even weakened them. Imprisonment in an attic would to them have been luxury compared with the boiling oil and the smoking faggots and all the intimate cruelties of mysterious instruments of steel and leather, in cold dungeons, lit only by the dull flare of torches and the bright, watchful eyes of inquisitors.

A month in the house of "Auntie" self-styled, and really only an unrelated Mrs. Staines, paid to take care of the child, had held but one interest—*Foxe's Book of Martyrs*. It was a horrible book—the thick oleographs, their guarding sheets of tissue paper sticking to the prints like bandages to a wound . . . Elsie knew all about wounds: she had had one herself. Only a scalded hand, it is true, but a wound is a wound, all the world over. It was a book that made you afraid to go to bed; but it was a book you could not help reading. And now it seemed as though it might at last help, and not merely sicken and terrify. But the help was frail, and broke almost instantly on the thought—"*They* were brave because they were good: how can I be brave when there's nothing to be brave about except me not knowing the difference between turnips and weeds?"

She sank down, a huddled black bunch on the bare attic floor, and called wildly to someone who could not answer her. Her frock was black because the one who always used to answer could not answer any more. And her father was in India, where you cannot answer, or even hear, your little girl, however much she cries in England.

"I won't cry," said Elsie, sobbing as violently as ever. "I can be brave, even if I'm not a saint but only a turnip-mistaker. I'll be a Bastille prisoner, and tame a mouse!" She dried her eyes, though the bosom of the black frock still heaved like the sea after a storm, and looked about for a mouse to tame. One could not begin too soon. But unfortunately there seemed to be no mouse at liberty just then. There were mouse-holes right enough, all round the wainscot, and in the broad, time-worn boards of the old floor. But never a mouse.

"Mouse, mouse!" Elsie called softly. "Mousie, mousie, come and be tamed!"

Not a mouse replied.

The attic was perfectly empty and dreadfully clean. The other attic, Elsie knew, had lots of interesting things in it—old furniture and saddles, and sacks of seed potatoes,—but in this attic nothing. Not so much as a bit of string on the floor that one could make knots in, or twist round one's finger till it made the red ridges that are so interesting to look at afterwards; not even a piece of paper in the draughty, cold fireplace that one could make paper boats of, or prick letters in with a pin or the tag of one's shoe-laces.

As she stooped to see whether under the grate some old match-box or bit of twig might have escaped the broom, she saw suddenly what she had wanted most—a mouse. It was lying on its side. She put out her hand very slowly and gently, and whispered in her softest tones, "Wake up, Mousie, wake up, and come and be tamed." But the mouse never moved. And when she took it in her hand it was cold.

"Oh," she moaned, "you're dead, and now I can never tame you," and she sat on the cold hearth and cried again, with the dead mouse in her lap.

"Don't cry," said somebody. "I'll find you something to tame—if you really want it."

Elsie started and saw the head of a black bird peering at her through the square opening that leads to the chimney. The edges of him looked ragged and rainbow-coloured, but that was because she saw him through tears. To a tearless eye he was black and very smooth and sleek.

"Oh!" she said, and nothing more.

"Quite so," said the bird politely. "You are surprised to hear me speak, but your surprise will be, of course, much less when I tell you that I am really

a Prime Minister condemned by an Enchanter to wear the form of a crow till
. . . till I can get rid of it."

"Oh!" said Elsie.

"Yes, indeed," said the Crow, and suddenly grew smaller till he could
come comfortably through the square opening. He did this, perched on the
top bar, and hopped to the floor. And there he got bigger and bigger, and
bigger and bigger and bigger. Elsie had scrambled to her feet, and then a black
little girl of eight and of the usual size stood face to face with a crow as big as
a man, and no doubt as old. She found words then.

"Oh, don't!" she cried. "Don't get any bigger. I can't bear it."

"*I* can't *do* it," said the Crow kindly, "so that's all right. I thought you'd
better get used to seeing rather large crows before I take you to Crownowland.
We are all life-size there."

"But a crow's life-size isn't a man's life-size," Elsie managed to say.

"Oh yes, it is—when it's an enchanted Crow," the bird replied. "That makes
all the difference. Now you were saying you wanted to tame something. If
you'll come with me to Crownowland I'll show you something worth taming."

"Is Crow-what's-its-name a nice place?" Elsie asked cautiously. She was,
somehow, not so very frightened now.

"Very," said the Crow.

"Then perhaps I shall like it so much I shan't want to be taming things."

"Oh yes, you will, when you know how much depends on it."

"But I shouldn't like," said Elsie, "to go up the chimney. This isn't my
best frock, of course, but still . . ."

"Quite so," said the Crow. "I only came that way for fun, and because
I can fly. You shall go in by the chief gate of the kingdom, like a lady. Do
come."

But Elsie still hesitated. "What sort of thing is it you want me to tame?"
she said doubtfully.

The enormous crow hesitated. "A—a sort of lizard," it said at last. "And
if you can only tame it so that it will do what you tell it to, you'll save the
whole kingdom, and we'll put up a statue to you; but not in the People's Park,
unless they wish it," the bird added mysteriously.

"I should like to save a kingdom," said Elsie, "and I like lizards. I've seen
lots of them in India."

"Then you'll come?" said the Crow.

"Yes. But how do we go?"

"There are only two doors out of this world into another," said the Crow.
"I'll take you through the nearest. Allow me!" It put its wing round her so
that her face nestled against the black softness of the under-wing feathers. It

was warm and dark and sleepy there, and very comfortable. For a moment she seemed to swim easily in a soft sea of dreams. Then, with a little shock, she found herself standing on a marble terrace, looking out over a city far more beautiful and wonderful than she had ever seen or imagined. The great man-sized Crow was by her side.

"Now," it said, pointing with the longest of its long black wing-feathers, "you see this beautiful city?"

"Yes," said Elsie, "of course I do."

"Well . . . I hardly like to tell you the story," said the Crow, "but it's a long time ago, and I hope you won't think the worse of us—because we're really very sorry."

"If you're really sorry," said Elsie primly, "of course it's all right."

"Unfortunately it isn't," said the Crow. "You see the great square down there?"

Elsie looked down on a square of green trees, broken a little towards the middle.

"Well, that's where the . . . where *it* is—what you've got to tame, you know."

"But what did you do that was wrong?"

"We were unkind," said the Crow slowly, "and unjust, and ungenerous. We had servants and workpeople doing everything for us; we had nothing to do *but* be kind. And we weren't."

"Dear me," said Elsie feebly.

"We had several warnings," said the Crow. "There was an old parchment, and it said just how you ought to behave and all that. But we didn't care what it said. I was Court Magician as well as Prime Minister, and I ought to have known better, but I didn't. We all wore frock-coats and high hats then," he added sadly.

"Go on," said Elsie, her eyes wandering from one beautiful building to another of the many that nestled among the trees of the city.

"And the old parchment said that if we didn't behave well our bodies would grow like our souls. But we didn't think so. And then all in a minute they *did*—and we were crows, and our bodies were as black as our souls. Our souls are quite white now," it added reassuringly.

"But what was *the* dreadful thing you'd done?"

"We'd been unkind to the people who worked for us—not given them enough food or clothes or fire, and at last we took away even their play. There was a big park that the people played in, and we built a wall round it and took it for ourselves, and the King was going to set a statue of himself up in the middle. And then before we could begin to enjoy it we were turned into big black crows; and the working people into big white pigeons—and *they* can go where they like, but we have to stay here till we've tamed the . . . We never can go into the park, until we've settled the thing that guards it. And that thing's a big, big lizard—in fact . . . it's a *dragon!*"

"*Oh!*" cried Elsie; but she was not as frightened as the Crow seemed to expect. Because every now and then she had felt sure that she was really safe in her own bed, and that this was a dream. It was not a dream, but the belief that it was made her very brave, and she felt quite sure that she could settle a dragon, if necessary—a dream dragon, that is. And the rest of the time she thought about *Foxe's Book of Martyrs* and what a heroine she now had the chance to be.

"You want me to kill it?" she asked.

"Oh no! To tame it," said the Crow.

"We've tried all sorts of means—long whips, like people tame horses with, and red-hot bars, such as lion-tamers use—and it's all been perfectly useless; and there the dragon lives, and will live till someone can tame him and get him to follow them like a tame fawn, and eat out of their hand."

"What does the dragon *like* to eat?" Elsie asked.

"*Crows,*" replied the other in an uncomfortable whisper. "At least *I've* never known it eat anything else!"

"Am I to try to tame it *now*?" Elsie asked.

"Oh dear no," said the Crow. "We'll have a banquet in your honour, and you shall have tea with the Princess."

"How do you know who is a princess and who's not, if you're all crows?" Elsie cried.

"How do you know one human being from another?" the Crow replied. "Besides . . . Come on to the Palace."

It led her along the terrace, and down some marble steps to a small arched door. "The tradesmen's entrance," it explained. "Excuse it—the courtiers are crowding in by the front door." Then through long corridors and passages they went, and at last into the throne-room. Many crows stood about in respectful attitudes. On the golden throne, leaning a gloomy head upon the first joint of his right wing, the Sovereign of Crownowland was musing dejectedly. A little girl of about Elsie's age sat on the steps of the throne nursing a handsome doll.

"Who is the little girl?" Elsie asked.

"*Curtsey!* That's the Princess," the Prime Minister Crow whispered; and Elsie made the best curtsey she could think of in such a hurry. "She wasn't wicked enough to be turned into a crow, or poor enough to be turned into a pigeon, so she remains a dear little girl, just as she always was."

The Princess dropped her doll and ran down the steps of the throne to meet Elsie.

"You dear!" she said. "You've come to play with me, haven't you? All the little girls I used to play with have turned into crows, and their beaks are *so* awkward at dolls' tea-parties, and wings are no good to nurse dollies with. Let's have a doll's tea-party *now,* shall we?"

"May we?" Elsie looked at the Crow King, who nodded his head hopelessly. So, hand in hand, they went.

I wonder whether you have ever had the run of a perfectly beautiful palace and a nursery absolutely crammed with all the toys you ever had or wanted to have: dolls' houses, dolls' china tea-sets, rocking-horses, bricks, nine-pins, paint-boxes, conjuring tricks, pewter dinner-services, and any number of dolls—all most agreeable and distinguished. If you have, you may perhaps be able faintly to imagine Elsie's happiness. And better than all the toys was the Princess Perdona—so gentle and kind and jolly, full of ideas for games, and surrounded by the means for playing them. Think of it, after that bare attic, with not even a bit of string to play with, and no company but the poor little dead mouse!

There is no room in this story to tell you of all the games they had. I can only say that the time went by so quickly that they never noticed it going, and were amazed when the Crow nursemaid brought in the royal tea-tray. Tea was a beautiful meal—with pink iced cake in it.

Now, all the time that these glorious games had been going on, and this magnificent tea, the wisest crows of Crownowland had been holding a council. They had decided that there was no time like the present, and that Elsie had better try to tame the dragon soon as late. "But," the King said, "she mustn't run any risks. A guard of fifty stalwart crows must go with her, and if the dragon shows the least temper, fifty crows must throw themselves between her and danger, even if it cost fifty-one crow-lives. For I myself will lead that band. Who will volunteer?"

Volunteers, to the number of some thousands, instantly stepped forward, and the Field Marshal selected fifty of the strongest crows.

And then, in the pleasant pinkness of the sunset, Elsie was led out on to the palace steps, where the King made a speech and said what a heroine she was, and how like Joan of Arc. And the crows who had gathered from all parts of the town cheered madly. Did you ever hear crows cheering? It is a wonderful sound.

Then Elsie got into a magnificent gilt coach, drawn by eight white horses, with a crow at the head of each horse. The Princess sat with her on the blue velvet cushions and held her hand.

"I *know* you'll do it," said she; "you're so brave and clever, Elsie!"

And Elsie felt braver than before, although now it did not seem so like a dream. But she thought of the martyrs, and held Perdona's hand very tight.

At the gates of the green park the Princess kissed and hugged her new friend—her state crown, which she had put on in honour of the occasion, got pushed quite on one side in the warmth of her embrace—and Elsie stepped out of the carriage. There was a great crowd of crows round the park gates, and every one cheered and shouted, "Speech, speech!"

Elsie got as far as "Ladies and gentlemen—Crows, I mean," and then she could not think of anything more, so she simply added, "Please, I'm ready."

I wish you could have heard those crows cheer.

But Elsie wouldn't have the escort.

"It's very kind," she said, "but the dragon only eats crows, and I'm not a crow, thank goodness—I mean I'm not a crow—and if I've got to be brave I'd like to *be* brave, and none of you to get eaten. If only someone will come with me to show me the way and then run back as hard as he can when we get near the dragon. *Please!*"

"If only one goes *I* shall be the one," said the King. And he and Elsie went through the great gates side by side. She held the end of his wing, which was the nearest they could get to hand in hand.

The crowd outside waited in breathless silence. Elsie and the King went on through the winding paths of the People's Park. And by the winding paths they came at last to the Dragon. He lay very peacefully on a great stone slab, his enormous bat-like wings spread out on the grass and his goldy-green scales glittering in the pretty pink sunset light.

"Go back!" said Elsie.

"No," said the King.

"If you don't," said Elsie, "*I* won't go *on*. Seeing a crow might rouse him to fury, or give him an appetite, or something. Do—do go!"

So he went, but not far. He hid behind a tree, and from its shelter he watched.

Elsie drew a long breath. Her heart was thumping under the black frock. "Suppose," she thought, "he takes me for a crow!" But she thought how yellow her hair was, and decided that the dragon would be certain to notice that.

"Quick march!" she said to herself, "remember Joan of Arc," and walked right up to the dragon. It never moved, but watched her suspiciously out of its bright green eyes.

"Dragon dear!" she said in her clear little voice.

"*Eh?*" said the dragon, in tones of extreme astonishment.

"Dragon dear," she repeated, "do you like sugar?"

"*Yes*," said the dragon.

"Well, I've brought you some. You won't hurt me if I bring it to you?"
The dragon violently shook its vast head.

"It's not much," said Elsie, "but I saved it at tea-time. Four lumps. Two for each of my mugs of milk."

She laid the sugar on the stone slab by the dragon's paw.

It turned its head towards the sugar. The pinky sunset light fell on its face, and Elsie saw that it was weeping! Great fat tears as big as prize pears were coursing down its wrinkled cheeks.

"Oh, don't," said Elsie, "*don't* cry! Poor dragon, what's the matter?"

"Oh!" sobbed the dragon, "I'm only so glad you've come. I—I've been so lonely. No one to love me. You *do* love me, don't you?"

"I—I'm sure I shall when I know you better," said Elsie kindly.

"Give me a kiss, dear," said the dragon, sniffing.

It is no joke to kiss a dragon. But Elsie did it—somewhere on the hard green wrinkles of its forehead.

"Oh, *thank* you," said the dragon, brushing away its tears with the tip of its tail. "That breaks the charm. I can move now. And I've got back all my lost wisdom. Come along—I *do* want my tea!"

So, to the waiting crowd at the gate came Elsie and the dragon side by side. And at sight of the dragon, tamed, a great shout went up from the crowd; and at that shout each one in the crowd turned quickly to the next one—for it was the shout of men, and not of crows. Because at the first sight of the dragon, tamed, they had left off being crows for ever and ever, and once again were men.

The king came running through the gates, his royal robes held high, so that he shouldn't trip over them, and he too was no longer a crow, but a man.

And what did Elsie feel after being so brave? Well, she felt that she would like to cry, and also to laugh, and she felt that she loved not only the dragon, but every man, woman, and child in the whole world—even Mrs. Staines.

She rode back to the Palace on the dragon's back.

And as they went the crowd of citizens who had been crows met the crowd of citizens who had been pigeons, and these were poor men in poor clothes.

It would have done you good to see how the ones who had been rich and crows ran to meet the ones who had been pigeons and poor.

"Come and stay at my house, brother," they cried to those who had no homes. "Brother, I have many coats, come and choose some," they cried to the ragged. "Come and feast with me!" they cried to all. And the rich and the poor went off arm in arm to feast and be glad that night, and the next day to work side by side. "For," said the King, speaking with his hand on the neck of the tamed dragon, "our land has been called Crownowland. But we are no longer crows. We are men: and we will be Just men. And our country shall be called Justnowland for ever and ever. And for the future we shall not be rich and poor, but fellow-workers, and each will do his best for his brothers and his own city. And your King shall be your servant!"

I don't know how they managed this, but no one seemed to think that there would be any difficulty about it when the King mentioned it; and when people really make up their minds to do anything, difficulties do most oddly disappear.

Wonderful rejoicings there were. The city was hung with flags and lamps. Bands played—the performers a little out of practice, because, of course, crows can't play the flute or the violin or the trombone—but the effect was very gay indeed. Then came the time—it was quite dark—when the King rose up on his throne and spoke; and Elsie, among all her new friends, listened with them to his words.

"Our deliverer Elsie," he said, "was brought hither by the good magic of our Chief Mage and Prime Minister. She has removed the enchantment that held us; and the dragon, now that he has had his tea and recovered from the shock of being kindly treated, turns out to be the second strongest magician in the world—and he will help us and advise us, so long as we remember that we are all brothers and fellow-workers. And now comes the time when our Elsie must return to her own place, or another go in her stead. But we cannot send back our heroine, our deliverer." (*Long, loud cheering.*) "So one shall take her place. My daughter—"

The end of the sentence was lost in shouts of admiration. But Elsie stood up, small and white in her black frock, and said, "No thank you. Perdona would simply hate it. And she doesn't know my daddy. He'll fetch me away from Mrs. Staines some day . . ."

The thought of her daddy, far away in India, of the loneliness of Willow Farm, where now it would be night in that horrible bare attic where the poor dead untamable little mouse was, nearly choked Elsie. It was so bright and light and good and kind here. And India was so far away. Her voice stayed a moment on a broken note.

"I—I . . ." Then she spoke firmly.

"Thank you all so much," she said—"so very much. I do love you all, and it's lovely here. But, please, I'd like to go home now."

The Prime Minister, in a silence full of love and understanding, folded his dark cloak round her.

* * * * * *

It was dark in the attic. Elsie, crouching alone in the blackness by the fire-place where the dead mouse had been, put out her hand to touch its cold fur.

* * * * * *

There were wheels on the gravel outside—the knocker swung strongly—"*Rat-tat-tat-tat*—*Tat! Tat!*" A pause—voices—hasty feet in strong boots sounded on the stairs, the key turned in the lock. The door opened a dazzling crack, then fully, to the glare of a lamp carried by Mrs. Staines.

"Come down at once. I'm sure you're good now," she said, in a great hurry and in a new honeyed voice.

But there were other feet on the stairs—a step that Elsie knew. "Where's my girl?" the voice she knew cried cheerfully. But under the cheerfulness Elsie heard something other and dearer. "Where's my girl?"

After all, it takes less than a month to come from India to the house in England where one's heart is.

Out of the bare attic and the darkness Elsie leapt into light, into arms she knew. "Oh, my daddy, my daddy!" she cried. "How glad I am I came back!"

PART TWO

The Didactic Looking-Glass

Ernest

EDWARD KNATCHBULL-HUGESSEN
1869

*E*DWARD H. KNATCHBULL-HUGESSEN, Baron Brabourne (1829-1893) was a great-nephew of Jane Austen and edited a collection of her letters to her sister Cassandra. Politically liberal, he also served for a time as a member of Gladstone's cabinet. In 1869 he released a collection of literary fairy tales, *Stories for My Children,* which contained the following story, "Ernest," and later published a number of other collections of children's tales. His stories were criticized particularly for being violent and macabre—though both *Alice* books received similar criticism from some reviewers who felt that children would find them frightening and confusing. Along with Jean Ingelow's *Mopsa the Fairy,* "Ernest" is one of the earliest works modeled after *Alice in Wonderland* (1865), and in his introduction Knatchbull-Hugessen is quick to point out that "it is difficult to avoid the occasional appearance, if not the reality, of plagiarism." Ernest is, as his name suggests, as polite and anxious to please as Alice, and just as beset by the absurd logic of Toad-land and the demands of its fantastic inhabitants. Though Ernest is—despite Knatchbull-Hugessen's disclaimers—much more an "imitation" than some of the more inventive *Alice* revisions such as *Mopsa the Fairy* or "Amelia and the Dwarfs," it is entertaining and suggestive, particularly in its recreation of Wonderland's darker side of violence and punishment.

Ernest

PREFACE

MOST OF THESE STORIES were originally told to my children in the pleasant half-hours before the arrival of their bedtime and the sound of the dressing-bell interrupted our evening talk.

In travelling upon a path so often trodden before, it is difficult to avoid the occasional appearance, if not the reality, of plagiarism. I believe, however, that the only tale to which such a suspicion might attach is that of "Ernest," which in some points has a family resemblance to "Alice in Wonderland." My excuse must be that both the general idea of the tale, and the parodies of certain familiar rhymes, were conceived and written by me long before the appearance of that admirable child's book.

The Tales are written as they were told; and if they afford to any other children, in reading, some portion of the pleasure which my own have had in hearing them, I shall not regret having been induced to let them go forth to the Fairy-loving Public.

—E.H. KNATCHBULL-HUGESSEN

ERNEST

A little boy named Ernest was once playing at ball by himself in the garden, when his ball suddenly bounded into the well, and fell down with a loud splash. Many boys would have bitten their thumbs with vexation, and given the matter up as a bad job; some might even have cried; and hardly a boy but what would have been more or less put out at losing a new ball in so stupid a manner.

Ernest, however, not being a common boy, and having a particular liking for this ball, immediately splashed in head foremost after it. He knocked himself a little against the sides of the well, but he didn't care for that a bit; and though the water felt rather cold, it only freshened him up, and made him all the more determined to find his ball. Down he went for some distance, and at last got to what he supposed to be the bottom of the well. He wasn't far wrong, either; but the well was much larger at the bottom than the top, and all the water in it seemed to come up like a wall from the ground, leaving a large dry space all round it, into which Ernest crept out of the water, and began to look about him. It wasn't so *very* dry, either, but rather moist, and he could see no ball anywhere; but all round the sides of the kind of cave

in which he was there was a bright substance like crystal, which lighted up the place, and on the floor sat an enormous Toad, smoking a very bad cigar, and evidently thinking himself everybody. He turned upon Ernest directly, and cried out to him in an angry tone—

"You presumptuous fool, how dare you come down here?"

Now Ernest, having been carefully brought up, was well aware that no one loses anything by politeness. Far from being angry, therefore, he replied, with the lowest bow which circumstances enabled him to make—

"Presumptuous, sir, I may possibly be, but it can hardly be the act of a fool which has brought me into the presence of so noble and handsome a Toad as yourself."

"Not so bad," replied the Toad; "I see you have been taught manners. But what do you want?"

"My ball, sir," said Ernest; when instantly a low silvery laugh echoed through the cave, and the Toad, after swelling till Ernest thought he must certainly burst, went into a fit of laughter which rather puzzled the boy.

"Your ball!" at length shouted the Toad. "If you mean that india-rubber affair that came crashing down here some time ago, I should hope it was long since cut up into gaiters for the tame Mice; for it was fit for nothing else, and they were beginning to want new leggings. But as for balls, you shall see such a ball as you've never seen up above Toad-land, if you only wait for a moment."

With that the Toad spat in the air, which was his way of ringing the bell, and immediately a door was thrown open behind him, and several hundred Toadstools came rushing in and stood on their heads all round him.

The Toad then marched solemnly through the door, and the Toadstools after him, two and two, till Ernest had counted about four hundred. Then he got tired of counting, and thought he might as well follow and see what they were all going to do. So he kicked aside several Toadstools that came in his way, and passed on through the door after the procession.

Presently they came to quite a large room, entirely lighted by Glowworms; and here were assembled a great number of Mice, some of whom had gaiters on, which appeared to Ernest to be made of some stuff suspiciously like india-rubber. He had no time, however, to think about it, for as they entered the room the band was striking up a merry tune, and the Mice were asking each other to dance, and forming sets of Lancers just as people do in the world above.

"Will you dance in a sixteen set?" said the Toad to Ernest; but he was so confused that he hardly knew what to say: at last he stammered out—

"If you please, sir, shan't I stamp on somebody? I'm very much afraid I shall never be able to help it."

"That's *their* look-out," replied the Toad. "Now don't be a fool, but get a partner at once."

Ernest was dreadfully puzzled, for he didn't know whether he ought to ask a Mouse, a Toadstool, or the Toad itself to dance; but while he was doubting what to do, a delicate White Mouse came softly up to him, and murmured in a soft but somewhat shrill voice—

"If you would please to dance with me, sir, in a quiet set of eight, I shall be *so* delighted!"

So Ernest bowed civilly, and, as he could not give his arm to the Mouse, he offered her his hand, upon which she sat till the set was formed and they began to dance. Ernest took great care, and all went well until the last figure, when the music went quick, and he was so terribly afraid of hurting somebody that he came to a dead stop, and sat down, as ill-luck would have it, right on the top of a Toadstool, who squashed instantly.

His companions began to abuse Ernest violently, telling him that he was an awkward Fungus, and, in fact, no better than a mere Mushroom. But the White Mouse took his part, and explained that it was all a mistake; and as the squashed Toadstool was not by any means a popular person, he was soon forgotten.

Ernest now asked his partner if he should fetch her some lemonade or a glass of sherry, to which she mildly responded that she felt inclined for a crumb or two of toasted cheese, if he knew where it was to be found. He looked right and left, and seeing a number of the Mice crowding up into one corner, justly guessed that the supper was there: so pushing his way along, with his partner in his hand, he soon discovered a table, on which toasted cheese formed a large part of the eatables. Having placed his partner on this table, he soon saw that she was so fully occupied that he might just as well amuse himself by looking about him. Accordingly, he walked back to the middle of the room, and perceived the Toad seated upon a Toadstool, and making facetious remarks upon everybody about him.

As soon as he saw Ernest, "Halloo, you upper-world boy," he cried; "how do you like the ball?"

"Very much, sir," replied Ernest, respectfully; upon which the Toad rejoined—

"But you must have had enough of it now—at least I know *I* have; so come and feed the gold and silver Fish"; and beckoning Ernest to follow him, he hopped off to a passage in one side of the room, down which he went for some little way, when there appeared more and more light; and Ernest presently found himself in a pleasant garden, in which was a large round pond, full of gold and silver Fish. The Toad knew all these by their names, and they came at his call like dogs to their master. He then began to feed them, his method of doing which was rather peculiar: the Toadstools put crumbs on his back, and then he leaped into the water, and the Fish came swimming round, and took the crumbs off as he told them.

"Come," said he to Ernest, "do as I do, young Worldling."

But Ernest said he was afraid of catching cold, and had rather stay where he was.

"Why *didn't* you stay where you were, then—up above?" said the Toad;

"if you come to Toad-land, you ought to do as Toads do: and as to catching cold, you can't do that here; *our* colds run so fast that nobody ever catches them, and if they do, they are not such fools as to keep them, as you human beings sometimes do, for weeks together."

Ernest bowed silently, for he feared to continue the argument, lest he might be obliged to feed the Fish in the very unpleasant manner adopted by the Toad. The latter, however, soon got tired of his amusement, and, leaping from the pond, told Ernest to come along with him, and hear the Toadstools sing. To this Ernest willingly consented; and the first Toadstool who was in attendance upon the Royal Toad immediately began, in a voice hoarse with emotion—

> "Abroad in the morning to see the bold Toads
> Squat silently down by the side of the roads,
>   With speckles so yellow and bright,
> With their servants behind them, the marsh-loving Frogs,
> Who hurry to follow, from ponds and from bogs,
>   And croak till the coming of night."

"There!" said the Toad, triumphantly, "you won't hear such a singer as *that* every day. What would you do with him, if you had him up above?"

"I think," quietly observed Ernest, "that as he seems so hoarse, I should give him a lozenge."

"Fool!" answered the Toad, angrily, "what would be the use of *that*, when he has got no mouth?"

"No more he has," said Ernest; "I quite forgot that."

"Think before you speak, then," said the Toad. And Ernest began wondering how a creature without a mouth could sing at all, and whether a Toadstool could properly be called a creature; and then he began to say, half aloud, some verses which he remembered to have heard his nurse sing to him:—

> "'Tis the voice of the Toadstool, I heard him complain,
> I came up in the night from a smart shower of rain;
> As a worthless old Fungus, so he in his bed,
> Is left, while the people pick Mushrooms instead."

But these unlucky words were hardly out of his mouth, when a chorus of Toadstool voices began abusing him in the most furious language, and the Toad himself flew into a violent passion.

"Frogs' legs and heads!" exclaimed he; "was ever person so insulted? A common Mushroom, that folks eat upon toast with ketchup, preferred to an

elegant and ornamental Toadstool! Out upon you!—Worldling!—you taste-
less monster!"

Ernest was rather confused at this, and could think of nothing better to
say than that he had meant no harm, and that it was from love and admiration for Toadstools that people in the upper world forbore to eat them. This
statement somewhat calmed the offended followers of the Toad; but a sulki-
ness seemed to pervade the party, until the Toad, who had cooled down quite
suddenly, and appeared as friendly as ever, asked Ernest what he would like
to do next. Wishing to make himself as pleasant as possible, the boy suggested
a game of "leap-frog."

"Leap-toad, I suppose you mean," grumbled the Toad; "but you seem
determined to call everything by its wrong name to-day:—but you shall have
what you want." And ringing the bell again in his usual manner, he directed
the Toadstools to fetch in the leapers; upon which several of them vanished,
and soon returned, ushering in a large number of small Toads, who began
dancing and leaping about in every direction.

"But that isn't what I meant," said Ernest; "don't you know how to play
the real game of leap-frog—I mean leap-toad—down here? One of you stands
still and bends forward, and another jumps over him—like this." And Ernest
imitated the manner in which one boy makes a back and another jumps over
it at leap-frog.

"Don't come down here to teach your betters," shouted the Toad; "that
may be upper-world leap-toad, but this is Toad-land leap-toad. We ought to
know best, being regular toads; and if you don't like it, you may lump it";
and so saying, he sat down again and didn't speak another word for several
minutes, during which time Ernest watched the Toads skipping about as fast
as they could, till, at a signal from the old Toad, they suddenly ranged themselves in a line against the side of the room, and remained perfectly silent and
motionless.

"Now," said the Toad, "you shall see an illumination"; and at the word
of command each of the leaping Toads drew from his pocket a lucifer-match,
lighted it by striking it against the wall, and stuck it into his mouth. This
produced a curious effect, and the Toad appeared highly delighted at it, keeping the leapers there until the matches had burnt so low that their eyes began
to wink, and they trembled visibly; then, at a wave of his cigar, they all got
rid of their matches as quickly as they could, and at a second signal disappeared down the passage out of which they had come.

Ernest now began to recollect that, with all these amusements, he was
no nearer getting his ball, and therefore he politely remarked to the Toad that
he should be much obliged if he would tell him where it was to be found.

"Drat your ball!" angrily answered the Toad; "it's dead—it's burst—it's changed into a mouse—anything you please, only don't bother, but be contented."

"But I would go to the end of the world to get my ball," said Ernest, mournfully.

"Yes, you stupid world-child," remarked the Toad, "and tumble off when you'd got there, as a friend of mine once did, and fell down, and down, till he turned into a star, poor fool, and has stuck there, shining like an idiot of a Glowworm ever since. I should have thought you had had enough of tumbling by this time; but if you really want your ball, you must tumble again."

So saying, the Toad fiercely stamped his foot upon the ground, at the same time taking his eyes out of his head, throwing them up to the ceiling, and catching them again as cleverly as an Indian juggler; after which he replaced them carefully, but took care to put the right eye where the left one was before, and the left in the place of the right. As soon as he had done this, he winked in the most frightful manner, and stamped upon the ground again. Immediately Ernest felt the floor giving way beneath him, and down he sunk, so quickly, that he could not even try to save himself, and all he heard was the voice of the Toad croaking, more and more faintly as he got further and further off—

"*Go* to the end of the world, then, and see how you like it!"

Somehow or other Ernest found this kind of sinking a remarkably easy way of travelling; he went so softly and smoothly that he did not feel the least uncomfortable or giddy; and though he seemed to be passing now through clay, now chalk, and now through something so black that he thought it must be coal, nothing seemed to come off on his jacket, and when he was brought up with a sudden jerk, he was as clean and comfortable, and just as self-composed, as if he had been all the time in his father's garden at home.

He shook himself thoroughly, to be sure that he was awake, and then looked around. Where in the world—or out of the world—was he? On the brink of an enormous precipice, to look over which made him giddy at once; and he felt sure, without being told, that he had really got to the end of the world.

Giddy as he was, he still determined that he must and would peep over to see what there was to be seen; and accordingly he lay down flat on his stomach and looked over. He saw lights at different distances from each other, which he took to be stars; some so large and glaring that they made him wink and shut his eyes when he tried to look at them, others paler and more dim, as if further off. And then he saw, floating all round him in every direction, a quantity of clouds,—at least they looked like clouds at first; but each one had a face, and an uncomfortable sort of anxious expression seemed to rest on every countenance, as it blew first one way and then another, like leaves at the corner of the street which the wind whirls about and catches up and drives in different directions. Still, each Cloud-face seemed to be trying to go its own way, and never to be quite satisfied whichever way it was going.

"What on earth are these?" said Ernest to himself.

"On earth, my child," said a voice near him, "they were undecided people, who spent their time in making and unmaking all their plans, small and great, and could never settle what was best to be done. So now, having left the earth, they are doomed to pursue the same course which they did in life, and are making up their minds—or trying to do it—as you see. The end of the world makes no difference to them, and it will probably be centuries before their minds are finally made up, until which event they blow about here as undecided as ever."

Ernest started at the sound of this voice, and, turning round his head as well as he could, saw to his surprise a venerable Oyster close to him, whose large beard betokened his extreme age. He was open, or else of course Ernest could not have seen his beard; and the sight of him would have reminded the boy at once of vinegar and thin slices of brown bread and butter, had not his voice so surprised him that he could think of nothing else. It was a soft, low voice, sweet to the ear, and not unlike the gentle pattering of the rain against the window when the wind blows it up from the south-west. And Ernest, in spite of his surprise at hearing the Oyster speak, felt a great respect for him at once, and addressed him with the reverence due from youth to age.

"Pray, sir," asked he in a humble tone, "is this the end of the world?"

"Shut me tight if I know," replied the Oyster; "but by all accounts I believe it is, and I wouldn't go too near the edge, if I was you."

"Thank you, sir," replied Ernest; and then, after a moment's hesitation, "How long have you been here, and how did you come?"

"I was born here," said the Oyster, "about a thousand years ago, more or less; but it is very impertinent to ask questions. I thought that nobody did *that*, except the commoner sort of Mussels, or the discarded shell of an old Crab. Pray don't get into such habits."

"But," remarked Ernest, "I am very anxious to find my ball, and I want to know all about the strange places I come to in looking for it."

"Then," solemnly replied the Oyster, "you had better ask somebody else."

"But there *is* nobody else," said Ernest.

"Ah!" sighed the Oyster, "no more there is. I had never thought of *that;* but, you know, one can't go on talking for ever." And without another word he suddenly shut, nor would he open again for anything that Ernest could say.

This was decidedly unpleasant; the more especially as the place on which Ernest was lying was a kind of ledge, with the precipice in front and a wall of chalk behind, and on this ledge he could see nothing but the Oyster. However, he was determined not to be annoyed by trifles: so he crept along the ledge a little way, and presently came to a turning which led away from the precipice right into the chalk. He went down this a few yards, when he suddenly heard a laugh, and looking up saw a little old Man sitting on a shelf above his head. He couldn't have been more than two feet high, and he had a hooked nose, rather like Punch, and a merry eye, and a clay pipe in his mouth, which he had taken out to laugh.

"I hope I don't intrude, sir," said Ernest.

"By no means," answered the little Man; "I am very glad to see you. I am the Man in the Moon, and of course I have come down before my time; and as to asking my way to Norwich, it is quite useless, for I find the people there are frightened at my very name just now; so I have sauntered down here to be out of the way for a time."

"And can you get back again when you please, sir?" said Ernest.

"To be sure I can," replied the little Man, "but I don't want to go just yet. I like to be on the shelf for a little while, now and then; it rests me. And there is a good look-out up here, too. Come up and try!" So saying, he held out his hand to Ernest, and helped him up to the shelf.

There, indeed, was the strangest sight you ever saw. A number of windows, cut in the chalk, enabled you to look out over the whole country around the end of the world, and out of each window you had quite a different view.

Ernest looked through the first one, and saw a number of people pushing and panting with exertion, trying to get through a door which was shut, and which no effort of theirs could force open. They seemed dreadfully disappointed, and their faces were yards long with vexation.

"Who are those?" asked Ernest.

"Oh!" said the Man in the Moon, "those are the people who always declared there was no other world than the one they lived in: so now that they have got to the end of it, they have been taken at their word. They have done with one world, and no other will have anything to say to them; so there they are, pushing and struggling on, unable to go backward or forward."

Ernest looked, and looked again; and then, as it was rather a sad sight, he moved a little way along the shelf and looked through another window. There he saw a number of things like very large leaves of trees, tossing up and down in inextricable confusion, sometimes blown up high as if by the wind, and sometimes sinking down again, each with a curious face to it, on which appeared a restless and unhappy expression.

"Whatever are these?" said Ernest.

"These are Senses," said his companion. "When people up above have lost their senses, they generally blow down here, where they perhaps do less harm than if they had remained with their former owners. They are always, however, trying to get back again; but there is so much nonsense in the world that they hardly ever do so, and not one person out of a hundred in the world gets his senses back when he once loses them, as his brain is instantly stuffed full of nonsense, so that there would be no room for them if they *did* get back."

Ernest turned away and looked through another window, and saw a quantity of birds, of every sort and description, flying about all over the place.

"Ah!" said his friend, "these are the rotten eggs. Don't suppose that a rotten egg in a nest means that there was no bird belonging to it. Only, instead of hatching like a common bird, the rotten-egg birds fly off here to the end of the world, and there, you see, is a regular comfortable place provided for them."

Ernest thought this a very fair arrangement; for why should one egg fare better than another?

He moved on, however, and, looking through another window, saw a number of men walking up and down on a platform, from which they could not move, whilst opposite them were placed a number of large boards, with various inscriptions in large blue and gold and red letters.

"What does this mean?" asked the boy.

"These," said the Man in the Moon, "are railway directors, who have bored people so terribly, when waiting for their trains, by having great staring advertisements put up at their railway stations, that now, whilst *they* are waiting at the end of the world, they are condemned to stay on a platform and have nothing to read but these same advertisements. Look at that stout old gentleman with 'Thorley's Food for Cattle' before him, and that one next him looking up at 'Horniman's Tea.' I warrant they'll never allow such things again if they should ever be directors of an underground railway, or an atmospheric company."

Ernest thought this was all very curious, and rather puzzling; so he didn't look through any more of the windows; but, turning to his pleasant friend, told him the reason why he had come to the end of the world, and asked him where he thought the ball was to be found.

"Found!" said the Man in the Moon; "why, don't you know that india-rubber balls always rebound? Of course, as soon as your ball got to the bottom of the well and struck the ground, it bounded up again as fast as it could, and the wonder is that it didn't strike you in the face as you came down. Your ball is probably waiting for you at the place where you were playing with it when you lost it."

"Dear me!" said Ernest, "I never thought of that. But how am *I* to get up again? *I* can't rebound, you know."

"Of course not," replied his friend; "but there is nothing easier in the world than to do what you wish. I am going back myself directly, and will show you all about it in a minute."

Accordingly, he took his pipe in his left hand, and with the stem of it touched a spring in the chalk rock, when a door immediately opened and disclosed a large cupboard, in which were several enormous tumblers.

"Now," said the Man in the Moon, "have you ever taken a saline draught?"

"Yes," replied Ernest; "you mean the thing that fizzes up when you put water on the powder?"

"Exactly so," rejoined his friend; "but I dare say you never *were* a saline draught, were you?"

Ernest stared, and said he certainly never had been yet; but having long ceased to be surprised at anything, he was quite ready to believe that he might become a draught, or a pill, or even a dose of rhubarb and magnesia, at any moment. The Man in the Moon told him that he must do exactly as he saw *him* do; and he then took two small powders, wrapped in blue paper, out of his waistcoat pocket, and shook one of them into each of two tumblers, which he took out and placed upon the shelf. He then deliberately got into one of the tumblers, and told Ernest to get into the other; after which he took a bottle from the cupboard, which was labelled Double X, meaning, no doubt, that it was a very extraordinary mixture. And so it was; for the Man in the Moon had no sooner poured half of it into Ernest's tumbler and half of it into his own, than they both began bubbling and fizzing like soda-water very much "up." Very much "up" they soon were; for the mixture, carrying them with it, fizzed right up out of the tumblers and through the earth. Everything seemed to give way before them, or else they had hit upon the same passage as that down which Ernest had come, or one very like it. Up, up they went, past coal, and clay, and chalk, as comfortably and as easily as possible; and the last thing Ernest remembered was seeing the Man in the Moon nodding, and smiling, and kissing his hand to him, as he mounted far above him. Then Ernest lifted up his head, opened his eyes wide, and looked around. Where was he? Why, under the mulberry trees that grew near the well in his own father's garden! The cool air was blowing on his face, and the pleasant sunlight was shining down upon him, and there was a gentle rustling of the mulberry leaves above his head, and he sat up and rubbed his eyes in astonishment. Close to him, on the ground, uncut and unhurt, dry and safe, was his india-rubber ball.

"Then the Toad told a story," cried he, "and the tame Mice have *not* got new leggings!"

"New leggings, indeed!" said a voice near him. "What's all that nonsense about mice and leggings? I think we poor maids shall be wanting new legs soon if we have to run about after you children so long. Why, Master Ernest, I've been hunting for you this half-hour. There have your sisters gone in to tea, and Miss Jones has been asking after you, and here you are fast asleep under the mulberry trees!—I declare it's enough to worrit one to death; and all because of that apple-pie and custard you ate such a lot of at dinner, I'll be bound! *Do* come along, there's a good boy."

So Ernest got up and looked the maid straight in the face, and said—

"Jane, were you ever down a well?"

"Down a well, Master Ernest!—no, to be sure not; who ever heard of such a thing? But I shall be up a tree if I don't bring you in to Miss Jones pretty soon!"

Ernest said no more, but went quietly with the maid, who told his sisters and their governess that he had been asleep under the mulberry trees all the afternoon. You and I know better, but it does not always do to tell all one knows out aloud. But, as the Toad, and the Oyster, and the Man in the Moon all knew too, it is no wonder that the real truth came out in spite of Ernest's silence; and in fact, if one of them hadn't told me, *I* should never have known all the wonderful things that I have been telling you, for I don't believe the India-rubber Ball would ever had said a word about it!

From Nowhere to the North Pole

A Noah's Ark-Æological Narrative

TOM HOOD

ILLUSTRATIONS BY W. BRUNTON AND E.C. BARNES

1875

BRITISH WRITER, EDITOR, AND HUMORIST TOM HOOD (1835-1874) was the son of the renowned poet Thomas Hood. Hood the Younger edited the humor magazine *Fun,* a rival of *Punch,* and wrote a number of books for children, including *Petsetilla's Posy* (1870), an imitation of William Makepeace Thackeray's *The Rose and the Ring* (1855), and *From Nowhere to the North Pole,* an imitation of Carroll's *Alice in Wonderland.* Ironically, in 1887 Edward Salmon suggested that *Alice in Wonderland* was probably inspired by *From Nowhere to the North Pole* (apparently not realizing that Carroll's book had been published ten years earlier), asserting that "there is nothing extraordinarily original about either."[1] Carroll wrote a testy letter to the editor in response, asserting that his book had been written first and denying that he had ever read Hood's, and even inserted an announcement in the back of *The Nursery Alice* (1889) further denying Hood's influence. The vehemence of Carroll's response to both Hood's and Richards's *Alice*-like novels suggests that—as Carroll himself strove to capitalize on his own success with such efforts as *Through the Looking-Glass, The Nursery Alice,* and *Sylvie and Bruno*—he may in turn have sought inspiration from others who were also attempting to imitate, revise, or critique the *Alice* books.

Though very much "a fantastic story in the style of *Alice's Adventures,*"[2] as another reviewer described it, *From Nowhere to the North Pole* is also very much in Hood's own comic style, full of puns, grotesque imagery, and wild slapstick humor. Like Amelia in Ewing's "Amelia and the Dwarfs," Hood's spoiled and destructive protagonist, Frank, is whisked away to Fairydom by Prince Silverwings to face the results of his thoughtless selfishness in such places as Teumendtland, where broken toys recuperate, the land of the Wild

---

1. "Literature for the Little Ones," *Nineteenth Century* 22.128 (Oct. 1887): 571-72.
2. *Athenaeum* (12 Dec. 1874).

Wallpaperites, where Frank meets the grotesque creatures with which he has adorned his bedroom wallpaper, and Frog-land, the domain of a pompous and opinionated frog (reminiscent of the admonishing toad in Knatchbull-Hugessen's "Ernest"). These early chapters relate Frank's continuing adventures in the realms of Fairydom.

From Nowhere to the North Pole

CHAPTER 5. HOW FRANK FARED IN TEUMENDTLANDT

WHEN FRANK CAME TO HIMSELF again, he still heard the noise of his pursuers, and looking up above him, saw them still hovering above the edge of the precipice over which he had fallen. They did not, however, make any attempt to follow him, though they shouted all sorts of threats after him.

"Stick a pin through him and glue his wings!" cried one.

"Paste him up against a wall!" said another.

"Drop hot sealing-wax on his paws!" suggested a third.

"Pour thick gum down his throat!" screamed a fourth.

"You had better some of you come down here, and I'll serve you out!" croaked a queer thick voice close behind Frank, who, turning round, saw a very strange figure approaching.

Its head was shaped like one of those conical gum-bottles one sees now-a-days; and to make the resemblance more complete, it wore a tin helmet with a hole in the top, from which the handle of a brush protruded. The body looked like a gallipot, and was all smeared with spillings and tricklings of paste; its legs and arms seemed to be sticks of sealing-wax, and in its hand it carried a steaming glue-pot. It was shaking its fist vigorously at the insects overhead.

"Horrid things!" it said, in an explanatory manner, seeing Frank's bewilderment; "they creep into one's head so, to suck one's brains, and it gives one such a buzzing headache. I caught that fellow at it only the other day when I woke up from a nap."

Following the direction of the new-comer's finger, Frank saw a dead insect pasted up against the side of a rock as a sort of scarecrow to the others, and he then understood why his persecutors had stayed outside the ravine.

"Please, who are you?" said Frank.

"Why, of course, you know I'm Gloogumpehst, or you wouldn't have come here. How did you come?"

"Well, I fell"——

"Yes, to be sure! And what did you break?"

Frank felt his legs and arms, and said,

"Nothing!" adding, "you see, that tree caught me and broke my fall."

"Broke your fall, did it? Then where *is* your fall?"

Frank stared in bewilderment.

"Where am I?" he gasped.

"In Teumendtlandt, of course!" said the other.

"That sounds like German," observed Frank.

"To be sure! A little while ago all toys that came here to be repaired were Dutch or German, and of course they gave the place a name in their own language. What sort of a toy are you?"

"I'm not a toy—I'm a boy," answered Frank.

"H'm! toy or boy, there isn't much difference. I suppose they spell toy with a 'b' in your country, that's all."

"I beg your pardon," said Frank, with dignity. "I'm not a toy at all. I'm alive."

"Oh, come! that won't do here!" said Gloogumpehst, with a knowing wink. "That's like the mouse that came here for a new tail."

"What was that?" inquired Frank.

"Oh! he said he was alive; and he ran round and round several times till he caught on a pebble, and fell over on his side, and then he began to whizz as if a big insect had got inside him. He had just strength enough to say, 'Wind me up!' before he stopped, or he would never have run about any more. He was clockwork. Where are you wound up?"

The little oddity approached Frank, and began to feel his face, apparently taking his mouth to be the place to wind him up. Frank then saw, for the first time, that instead of four fingers and a thumb on each hand, Gloogumpehst had four slugs and a snail; and when the cold slimy things touched his skin, he could not repress a shudder.

"Where's your box, then?" said Gloogumpehst, suddenly.

"Box! What box?" asked Frank.

"Oh, nonsense! I felt your springs quiver then. You are only a Jack-in-the-box that's come loose. But how can I mend you if you haven't brought your box with you?" Frank dissented.

"Oh, not a jack-in-the—not—not a—a—a"——said Gloogumpehst, drowsily.

Frank had noticed that his companion had been growing gradually heavy and dull. Now he kept on repeating "a" in various keys and intonations, which sounded like talking but wasn't sense. It was a sort of tune something like this:

Frank opened his eyes in wonder. Gloogumpehst by a great effort checked himself, and murmured, in a faint voice, "Stir!"—indicating at the same time the brush-handle in his helmet. Frank took it, and stirred it round and round. Gloogumpehst instantly brightened up.

"Ah, that's better!" said he. "You see it settles down after a time—the thick of one's brains. Let me see—what was I saying? Oh! *are* not you a Jack-in-the-Box?"

"No!" said Frank, sturdily. "I'm a boy—a—a human child."

Gloogumpehst bounded towards him, and clapped his slimy hand on his mouth.

"Hush!" he said, looking round anxiously. "Don't say that again. They'd kill you."

"Who would?" asked Frank.

"The toys, of course."

"What toys?"

"Then you really don't know?" said Gloogumpehst, looking at Frank with wonder. "Why, this is where all the broken toys come to be mended. And, as most of their sufferings and fractures are caused by"—here he whispered in Frank's ear, "human children," and then he raised his voice to its natural pitch again—"of course they hate them; and if they caught one here, would certainly kill it. You'd better pass yourself off as a new sort of doll. You haven't as nice a pink and white complexion as most dolls have—but I might paint you up a bit."

Frank declined the offer.

"Well, it's a matter of taste," said his companion; "but *I* think it would be an improvement."

"So this is a sort of dolls' hospital," observed Frank, to change the subject.

"Yes, of course! Yes, you might call it that; and I am the surgeon, to be sure: yes."

"It must be very curious," Frank observed.

"Would you like to see it?" asked his friend.

"Very much indeed!"

"But you must be very careful. Don't you mention that—*that* word, you know, because it's bad for their health, and stops their recovery. And if they were to suspect you were a—you know, *that* word—they would certainly kill you."

"They're very revengeful," said Frank.

"Ah, of course! But then think what tortures they undergo, quite unnecessarily for the mere cruelty or caprice of—of *that* word."

Frank's conscience pinched him as he recalled the collection of wooden legs that he had left at home, and felt alarmed at the prospect of what might happen to him if he was discovered to be a human child, and especially one that had committed such terrible havoc among the doll community.

"Well, of course. Come along!" said Gloogumpehst, but he didn't move, all the same: "come—a—long—long—come—and—we"—

We WE we WE we we we WE we we we we we we WE

Frank saw what was the matter, and seizing the brush-handle, proceeded as before, with the same effect.

"Capital! Quite refreshing, to be sure!" said Gloogumpehst. "Now we'll start."

They proceeded on their way, and presently came in sight of a large building.

"That's it," said Gloogumpehst, "and now, as I shall have my duties to attend to, I'd better take some refreshment."

He sat down by the road, and taking a handful of glue, stuffed it into his mouth, and then put his feet into the glue-pot. Frank sat down on a box that was close by, but in a few seconds the lid flew up with a pop that threw

Frank over backwards. A figure with a shock of rough hair, two goggly eyes, and a fiery complexion, sprang out of the box, trembling with excitement.

"How dare you sit down on a gentleman?" he shouted; "how dare you? and you only a common doll, and badly painted too! What do you mean by coming and sit—" here he suddenly collapsed and the lid closed on him.

"He does that to recruit his strength," said Gloogumpehst, hurriedly, and as he finished the lid flew up, and the figure reappeared, continuing his speech as if it had not been interrupted.

"—ting on a gentleman and his palatial residence, as if he were a common chair. The auda"—here the box closed again.

"He's out here taking the air," explained Gloogumpehst.

"—city!" continued the Jack-in-the-Box, reappearing, "of a mere sixpenny doll to take such a liberty. If I were not an in"—here the lid fell again.

"Let's go," said Frank.

"That wouldn't be polite," answered his companion.

"—valid, I'd frighten you into fits, I would—I would—I would!" shrieked the reappearing figure, and then, exhausted by his efforts, he lolled over the side of his box, shaking feebly.

"Now apologize," whispered Gloogumpehst to Frank, who at once did so, and was graciously pardoned as the old man slowly sank back in his box and the lid fell.

They now entered the building, where, on low beds, lay hundreds of toys in various stages of mending. Gloogumpehst stopped at the bed-side of a kite which had a large rent in it. A card hung above with the words, "A paste plaster every morning after breakfast, and three drops of gum at bed-time."

"You'd better take your drops now," said Gloogumpehst, bending down his head.

The kite took the brush out of the surgeon's head, and dropped three drops on his wound, replacing the brush.

"Wonderful stuff that gum!" said the surgeon to Frank, as they were crossing a courtyard to the next ward. "I suppose you haven't got such a thing where you live?"

Frank explained that it was in common use, adding that he had a bottle of mucilage of his own.

"Who?" said Gloogumpehst, stopping short.

"Mucilage!" said Frank.

"Mucilage!" mused the other: "what a pretty name. Is she very beautiful? Is she married?"

Frank said he could not tell; it was a kind of gum. Gloogumpehst sat down on a bench, and meditatively put his feet into the glue-pot.

"Mucilage!" he murmured. "I—I wonder if she would marry me?"

Frank said he would ask if he ever got back.

"Ah, if you ever get back! I'm afraid you won't: that's it. If you—ever—back—ever—if, if"——

If if *if* IF *if* IF *if* *if* *if* IF *if* *if* *if* IF *if*

Frank stirred the brush again, and Gloogumpehst recovered his wits.

"Well, you'll ask for me if you *do* get back!—so, now come along. To be sure! if you get back, of course."

Frank felt rather depressed in spirits at his friend's doubt of his return home. He had rather feared to contemplate the possibility, and now that Gloogumpehst seemed to think his chance so very uncertain, his heart sank within him.

"This is the musical ward. It is not in my charge as a rule; but the regular surgeon, Twangletoo, is away for his holiday, and I am doing his work for him. You'll find it a little noisy, of course. To be sure, that's only natural."

Here he opened the door, but, to Frank's astonishment, not a sound could he hear. The fact seemed to surprise Gloogumpehst too. Strangely enough, there was plenty of movement, but it was all silent.

There was a white rabbit with a tambourine. It was twitching its ears, and rolling its eyes uncomfortably, but it did not raise its sticks from the parchment. There was a soldier vigorously beating a side-drum, but without producing the ghost of a tap. There was a little figure turning the handle of an organ, without eliciting the slightest tinkle. There were musical carts running round and round, but as mute as mummies; and there were babies' rattles shaking their bells furiously, but the bells were dumb.

Frank drew nearer and examined the patients. The rabbit's sticks were glued to the parchment; the head of the soldier's drum had been removed, and the drum was filled with paste. The grinder's organ was choked with gum; the wires of the musical carts were covered thickly with glue, and the bells on the rattles oozing over with gum. Frank saw how it was at a glance. Gloogumpehst's treatment was capital for torn kites, broken dolls, and ragged picture-books, but it was not suited for the repair of musical instruments. Gloogumpehst himself seemed impressed with the same idea, for, saying hurriedly something about the treatment not having had time to do its work yet, he took Frank by the arm and hustled him out of the place.

"It's a great responsibility undertaking another doctor's duties," he observed, when they were outside: "one has very difficult cases of one's own that puzzle one quite enough. Now, there's a gazelle out of a Noah's ark there": he pointed to a paddock in which the creature was propped up against the railings: "it has got a leg broken off, and the limb is so slender there's no hold for glue."

"Why don't you make a false leg with a pin?" asked Frank, remembering how at times he had resorted to that method of making his broken animals stand.

"I don't understand," said Gloogumpehst.

"Oh, look here," said Frank, taking a pin out of his waistcoat, and sticking it into the gazelle, and so enabling it to stand without leaning against the rails.

"Wonderful!" said Gloogumpehst, examining the artificial limb. "Have you any more?"

Frank, of course, always had a lot of pins stuck in the corner of his waistcoat, to provide for tears and rents, so he took out his stock and presented it to his friend.

"Very good! excellent!" said Gloogumpehst. "It's—it's a sort of wire, isn't it?"
Frank assented.

"I wonder," said Gloogumpehst to himself, "if it would do those musical toys any good to stick a few into them. I don't think paste or glue or gum seems to suit their consti—constit—suit—their—constitutions. I—I"—

Frank revived him with a stir.

"Excellent! Thank you. Yes, of course, quite right again!" said Gloogumpehst. "And now you must be very careful, for this is the Dolls' Ward; and if you are not prudent, they may suspect that you are not a doll."

Frank followed the surgeon with grave apprehension. The first beds were occupied by wax dolls. One had lost her sight: you could hear her eyeballs rattle inside her head when she moved. The other had been held against the hot bars of a grate, and was scored with deep scars across her face. A china doll had a large crack down her cheek and across her neck; and another had had all her hair torn off.

"It's very odd," said Gloogumpehst, as they were entering the next ward, "how many wooden dolls have come here lately that have lost legs. It seems to be quite an epidemic."

Frank turned with the intention of fleeing. But it was too late! He was recognized. There lay a whole regiment of his sister's dolls, whose limbs he had heartlessly torn off. With a loud shriek, they all leapt up in their beds, and began scrambling after him as best they could with their arms and single legs, or swinging their trunks between their hands.

"A child! a cruel child!" was the cry, and it was taken up from ward to ward, as all the disabled toys that were not hopelessly bedridden rushed out in pursuit.

Frank bolted as fast as his legs could carry him—but he could see little chance of escape, for the steep walls of the ravine closed in on both sides, and the winding way before him seemed to stretch away into space. All at once his eye caught sight of a stout creeper that climbed up the perpendicular cliff. Forgetting in the present peril that he might reach the top only to fall a prey to his insect foes, he scrambled up the trailing stem, and, after a sharp struggle, reached the top, and flung himself down breathless on the greensward.

Presently he was startled by the sound of detached stones rolling down the cliff. He looked over in alarm, and saw Gloogumpehst climbing up by the aid of his snail and slug hands.

"Don't be afraid," said Gloogumpehst. "I'm a friend. I want just to say 'good bye.'"

It was pleasant to Frank to have a friend, even though such an uncouth one; so he waited till the little man reached the top and sat down, wiping from his forehead the drops of gum that oozed out in the form of perspiration.

"You must be—must—you—you—be—be"—

BE BE be be *be* be be *be* BE be BE be *be* BE BE

Frank applied the usual restorative.

"All right! Thank you! Of course. To be sure. I'm all right again now!" panted Gloogumpehst. "But what a cruel boy you must be to break up dolls like that!"

Frank expressed his penitence, and promised never to be so wicked again.

"All right! No, you won't, of course. Well, good bye! I hope you'll get away all safe. But I doubt it—I do indeed! But if you do, you won't forget my message to Mucilage, will you? No, of course. To be sure, you won't! Good bye!"—and he slid over the edge—but before disappearing, he bent his head down again: "You wouldn't care for one parting stir? You would, of course. To be sure: I thought so!"

So Frank took a parting stir, and the next minute found himself all alone again in a strange land.

Chapter 6. What Happened to Frank in Quadrupedremia

Left to himself, Frank began to survey the scene around him. The country seemed pleasantly varied. There were woods and pastures, hills and valleys, rocks and streams, on every side. There did not appear to be any birds or insects, but, to judge from various sounds which he heard in the distance, he fancied there must be a good many wild animals about. This did not minister to his peace of mind, for he had been to the Zoological Gardens very often, and had a lively remembrance of bears, tigers, and lions, and other ferocious beasts. Once he had ventured too close to the cage of a big monkey, and it had caught hold of him; but luckily the keeper pulled him away. But he had dreamt for nights afterwards of all kinds of extraordinary brutes, and had been almost afraid to sleep in consequence.

So you may guess he went onward in fear and trembling, looking cautiously on all sides for fear of meeting some savage monster that would gobble him up. He started at the rustle of a leaf, and once when he heard something give a loud splash in a pool he was passing, he gave such a jump that he hit his head against an overhanging bough.

Presently he heard somebody singing, and hoping to fall in with some human being, he hastened in the direction of the sound. But as he got nearer, the voice sounded so strange—something between a grunt and a whistle—that he stopped awhile to listen. This is what he heard. Some of the words puzzled him, but the air seemed familiar:

SONG.

He dreamt that he saw the Buffalant,
   And the spottified Dromedaraffe,
The blue Camelotamus, lean and gaunt,
   And the wild Tigeroceros calf.
      Yes, the Ca-amelotamus, le-ean and gaunt,
      And the Ti-ti-geroceros ca-a-a-alf,
      And the Ti-i-geroceros calf!

The maned Liodillo loudly roared,
   And the Peccarbok whistled its whine,
The Chinchayak leapt on the dewy sward,
   As it hunted the pale Baboopine.
      Yes, the Chi-inchayak on the dew-ewy sward,
      It hu-unted the pale Baboopi-i-i-ine,
      It hu-unted the Ba-aboopine!

He dreamt that he met the Crocoghau,
   As it swam in the Stagnolent Lake;
But everything that in dreams he saw
   Came of eating too freely of cake.
      Yes, e-everything that in dre-eams he saw
      Was e-eating too freely of ca-a-a-ake—
      From e-ating too-oo much cake!

The voice came from behind a rock. Frank crept quietly up and peeped over. A most extraordinary sight met his gaze.

In the centre of an amphitheatre of rocks was gathered together the queerest assembly of four-footed creatures you ever saw. Frank, fresh from his experiences of Teumendtlandt, thought to himself that it was as if you had shaken up the Zoological Gardens and the Natural History collection at the British Museum in a bag, until you broke everything into bits, and had then glued the pieces together haphazard in the dark.

In the centre a Zecamelobra was playing at cards with a Batonkey and an Armaskullamus, while an Elegoapard was tossing-up with a Bob-tailed

Walboon. A Kangarillo was seated on the head of a Monkape, watching the card party, with a Gazelroo looking over its shoulder. A Pigorselope stood farther off, and just below Frank, a Pumag, with a pair of noble antlers, was talking gravely with a Lepunicorn.

"Fifteen two and a pair are ninety-four, and ten are thirty-one, and eight are three hundred, and a flush twenty-two. That's a rub," said the Armaskullamus.

The Zecamelobra sat thinking it over solemnly, evidently being a bad hand at scoring. But the Batonkey said,

"Pooh! Two-and-two-are-six-and-two-are-eight-and-two-are-twelve-and-a-pair-forty-all-told." And then he paused for breath.

"Oh, my poor head!" said the Armaskullamus.

"I don't think you're right, either of you," said the Zecamelobra, who had been counting on his stripes just as some people count on their fingers. "I make it twelve, and it can't be more!"

"Why can't it be more?" asked the Batonkey, spitefully.

"Why, look here," said the Zecamelobra, simply, "I've counted it on the stripes of my left foreleg, and there are only twelve stripes on *that;* so it must be twelve. It can't be more."

"But I've counted it on my teeth!" said the Armaskullamus; "and there are twenty-four of them, not counting tusks!"

"Oh, bother!" broke in the Elegoapard; "what's the use of disputing? Toss up for it."

"What shall we toss?" asked the Gazelroo, lowering its horns.

"That boy," grunted the Kangarillo, pointing to Frank, who turned to fly, but found his path cut off by a ferocious Racoodrill, which was something between an opossum and a big baboon. In a moment he was conducted into the centre of the assembled quadrupeds in the rocky amphitheatre.

There was a tremendous gnashing of teeth, tossing of horns, and waving of trunks going on, to the accompaniment of various discordant noises, that painfully reminded Frank of the Zoological Gardens at feeding-time.

"Pinch him!" said the Pumag to the Racoodrill. "Is he fat?"

The Racoodrill gave Frank a grip that made him writhe.

"Dee-licious!" said the Racoodrill, licking his lips.

"Tender?" asked the Armaskullamus, whose teeth were evidently rather loose and carious.

The Racoodrill gently bit Frank's cheek; but not so gently as not to make Frank wince.

"Soft—like lamb!" said the Racoodrill.

"Then let's dine," said the Walroon, sharpening his big tusks against a handy rock.

"Thank you, I've d—dined," said Frank, in desperation.

"All the better; you'll be nicer to eat," growled the Pigorselope.

"But what do you want to eat *me* for?" asked Frank.

"Why did you dream, then?" said the Armaskullamus, fiercely.

"Please, I can't help dreaming now and then," expostulated Frank.

"Why did you eat too much plum cake?" said the Elegoapard, snappishly.

"Please, I don't think I did!" was Frank's reply.

"And when you *do* dream," growled the Armaskullamus, "why, the British Museum, don't you finish things off properly?"

"I don't understand you!" said Frank, completely bewildered; "and what have my dreams or my cake got to do with your eating me?"

"Look at us!" said the Lepunicorn. "Did you ever see anything like us alive before?"

"N—no! I don't think I ever did," Frank was obliged to confess.

"That's an untruth!" bellowed the Walroon.

"No, it isn't," said Frank, though at the same time he felt a conviction creeping over him that these strange creatures were not altogether unfamiliar to him.

"But it is, though, all the same," said the Zecamelobra, who was apparently less ferocious than the others.

"Would you be kind enough to explain it all to me?" said Frank, in his most persuasive tones.

"Well, well, it can't do any harm to tell him," said the Zecamelobra to the others, who gave a grudging assent.

"Look here," said the Zecamelobra, "do you recollect when the big monkey got hold of you at the Zoological Gardens?"

"Yes, I do," said Frank, with a shudder.

"That night when you went home very much frightened, you were made a great fuss of, and had a glass of currant wine and some cake given you."

"Yes," assented Frank, "I remember it;—plum cake."

"Well, you ate a great deal too much of it, and made yourself ill, and had bad dreams."

"Certainly, very bad dreams."

"Very well. And then you dreamt *us!*" said the Zecamelobra.

And thereupon Frank remembered that the horrors of his dreams had been something of the kind, and could account for the apparent familiarity of these extraordinary brutes.

"Yes!" grumbled the Armaskullamus; "but the worst of it is you didn't dream us out complete. Why, the British Museum, couldn't you finish us off properly?"

"What do you mean?" inquired Frank.

"Look at my head," said the creature; "it's only a skull! And the brains inside have shrivelled up into a little dry lump, and roll about into odd corners, where they can't always be found when wanted. That's why they can cheat me in scoring at cards!" and he ground his teeth and scowled at the Zecamelobra. The Batonkey laughed.

"Look at my legs," broke in the Elegoapard; "they are only bones! Why, the Taxidermy, didn't you dream a skin to them?"

"Yes, and look at my tail!" growled the Walroon. "These knobs are always catching in the forks of trees and clefts of rocks. My backbone aches with the constant jerks it gets."

"And what's the use of my horn?" said the Lepunicorn, sullenly; "it's stuck on the top of my head where I can't see it, and so I'm never sure of hitting anything with it."

Of course Frank was conscious that he was not to blame for incongruities arising from a dream; but he could not but remember that, when he had laughed at the animals in Noah's Ark, and fancied he could invent better ones, he had not proceeded to construct them with any regard to the mutual fitness of the various portions he had designed to join together. He was silent.

"Come! dinner's ready!" said the Armaskullamus.

"No, it isn't though!" said Frank.

"Anyhow, we're ready for dinner!" cried the Pumag.

"Gentlemen," said Frank, catching at a straw as a last despairing effort, "when I came here somebody was singing."

"It was the Zecamelobra," said the Batonkey, with a sneer.

"It was very beautiful," said Frank.

"I *was* singing, certainly," said the Zecamelobra, with diffidence.

"Well, before you eat me," urged Frank, "I should like to hear one more song."

"Would you, really?" said the Zecamelobra, eagerly.

"Will it make you more tender?" inquired the Armaskullamus.

"It will soften me to tears," declared Frank.

"That will give him a nice salt flavour," said the Gazelroo.

"Well, then, sing," said the Walroon, reluctantly, "but look here: don't let it be too long."

"No: by Crackling! if it is," said the Pigorselope, "we'll eat you too, Mr. Zecamelobra!"

The Zecamelobra put on a plaintive expression, and with his head on one side commenced rocking to and fro gently, while he sang the following ditty:

A Lullaby.

The little tigers are at rest,
Coiled within their cozy nest;
The sympathetic crocodile
Is sleeping with a placid smile;
The all-embracing bounteous bear
Dreams sweetly in his lowly lair;—
    Only the purple-nosed baboon,
    Who loves the pale inconstant moon,
      Snores in his throat
      His plaintive note—
Gug-gug-gug-gug, aroo, garoon!
      Lullaby!
      Lullaby!
Glug-gug-gug-gug, aroo, garoon!

The snapping turtle softly shrinks
Within its shell, for forty winks;
The ringed and rufous ocelot
Is slumbering in its leafy cot;

The vampire has its graces hid
Beneath the sleeper's coverlid,
   Only the bandy-legged baboon,
   The lover of the fickle moon,
     Wails through his nose
     Sonorous woes—
Gug-gug-gug-gug, aroo, garoon!
     Lullaby!
     Lullaby!
Glug-gug-gug-gug, aroo, garoon!

The effect of this lugubrious lay upon the various creatures was a surprise as well as a delight to Frank. The Walroon, after beating time for awhile with his tail, dropped off into a nap. The Elegoapard snored audibly through his trunk. The Lepunicorn leant up against the Pumag, and their two heads began to nod in time together. The Gazelroo stretched his long legs beside the Pigorselope, and both were soon asleep. The Batonkey, after making some wonderful faces, followed their example; and the Armaskullamus, giving one or two prodigious yawns, resigned himself to slumber. In short, by the end of the second verse all were in a state of unconsciousness, except the Zecamelobra, who still rocked to and fro, and kept singing the chorus over and over again.

Presently he turned to Frank, and, without ceasing his melody, signed to him to go away. Frank didn't want two hints, but as he turned to leave, he couldn't resist whispering his thanks to his preserver.

The Zecamelobra smiled—opened his mouth wide—and pointed to his teeth.

"All right! I'm graminivorous," he chanted in a slow voice, and then stretching himself on the grass, pretended to fall asleep like the others. But the last that Frank saw of him as he plunged into a thick wood, to conceal himself from pursuit, was that he had raised his head to see the fugitive safely away. When Frank turned, he waved his fore foot and pointed once more to his teeth.

Down the Snow Stairs
Or, From Good-Night to Good-Morning

ALICE CORKRAN

ILLUSTRATIONS BY GORDON BROWNE

1887

ALICE CORKRAN (d. 1916) was a British novelist who wrote a number of *Alice*-like fantasies—including *Down the Snow Stairs, Mrs. Wishing-To-Be* (1883), and *Joan's Adventures at the North Pole and Elsewhere* (1889)—as well as domestic fiction for girls such as *Margery Merton's Girlhood.* She also served as the editor of a children's magazine called *The Bairn's Annual. Down the Snow Stairs* opens on Christmas Eve with Kitty feeling sad and guilty over the illness of her crippled brother Johnnie, whom she had innocently taken out into the cold to see a snowman. Much like Flora in Rossetti's *Speaking Likenesses,* Kitty is spirited away by the snowman to confront her "naughty self in the form of a sprite," but ultimately she receives comfort from a "guardian child" who appears in the form of her brother, and who assures her of the power of love to heal. Awakening from her dream, she finds Johnnie recovering on Christmas morning.

One reviewer for the *Christian Leader* characterized *Down the Snow Stairs* as "a Little Pilgrim's Progress," and Kitty's journey is indeed one of self-improvement. Corkran's revision of the dream-fantasy plot construction is strongly moral and didactic, and she is clearly interested in utilizing the idea of a dream "Wonderland," which she has turned into such realms as "Naughty Children Land" and "Punishment Land," for the purposes of self-improvement; however, her work offers fascinating insights into some of the ways that evangelical Victorian women writers—such as Corkran, Susan Warner, Harriet Beecher Stowe, and Hesba Stretton—appropriated and transformed domestic literary conventions as a means to larger social reform, and as part of what Jane Tompkins has called "a monumental effort to reorganize culture from the woman's point of view."[1]

---

1. Tompkins, *Sensational Designs: The Cultural Work of American Fiction, 1790-1860* (Oxford: Oxford UP, 1985) 124.

Down the Snow Stairs

CHAPTER 4. NAUGHTY CHILDREN LAND

IT WAS AN EXTRAORDINARY looking place. Kitty thought it was the queerest place she had ever seen. It had a tumbled-about, pulled-about appearance, for the ground was all in mounds and holes, and the roots of the trees bulged bare from the sides of the banks. Presently there came a sound of screaming and shouting. Above these dismal cries Kitty fancied she heard the sound of smacking.

"Is that Naughty Children Land?" she asked.

Her play-fellow did not answer.

She turned to look for him, but the queer creature was gone. Kitty was alone. "Extraordinary!" muttered Kitty. "It must be Naughty Children Land," she continued. It was not at all difficult to get into Naughty Children Land; just a step down a bank, a jump over a ditch, and Kitty was in it.

She made a few steps forward. The ground was covered with broken toys. Battered, smashed, noseless, eyeless, hairless dollies; tops without a spin in them; whips without handles, drums without heads; torn picture-books, blotted copy-books, mangled lesson-books, their pages miserably fluttering about.

Queer dull little birds, with one feather only for a tail, flew here and there, uttering melancholy chirps. "Tweet—tweet!" they cried. "Hi—ss—hiss" shrieked a cat, making an ∼ of his thin body, and waving a tail that appeared to have been pulled and pulled till it was more like a bell-rope than anything else.

But what attracted Kitty's attention was a group of little girls, sitting with their shoulders up to their ears, their chins in their hands, their hair falling over their eyes. They would have been very pretty but for their frowning eyebrows, their puckered foreheads; their tumbled hair, their under-lips, that had stuck out so long that now they always stuck out. Every now and then these dismal children gave a big spiteful sob, and their faces were smeared with dirty tears.

"What is the matter? Why do you look so miserable?" asked Kitty.

At first the woebegone children drew down their eyebrows more closely, and stuck their under-lips further out. Then in a sing-song sob-broken voice, raising their shoulders still nearer to their ears, burying their chins deeper in their hands, making wryer faces, they sang in a chorus:

> "Yes we can, we shall, we will.
>   Who's to make us smile and play?
> No—we must be wretched still.
>   Sulky are we?—So you say.
>   No we will not, no we shall not,
>   No we will not laugh or play.

> "Do we mope and do we scowl?
>   What a lot you seem to know.
> P'r'aps you'd like to hear us howl;
>   Pray, if you don't like it—go
>   No we will not, no we shall not,
>   No we will not laugh or play.

"If it suits us best to mutter,
    Lift the shoulders, hang the head;
All that you will hear us utter
    Is what we've already said.
        No we will not, no we shall not,
        No we will not laugh or play."

"Well, I never heard of anyone yet liking to be miserable all the day long," said Kitty with a smile that grew broader and broader as she looked at the dismal, dejected group. But they took no further notice of her. She stood hesitating and watching. Should she jump back over the ditch and go to look for that elf, or should she go on?

The children still kept up their doleful chant.

"I am sure I shall find the naughtiest child in this place," thought Kitty, "and I should so like to see it. Of course I'll find my way back. It will be quite easy. Those broken toys will guide me, and those little girls," she went on, with a twinkle in her eyes, "who are determined to be wretched will still be here. They do not seem inclined to run away."

Kitty walked on. Certainly it was the most extraordinary place that could be imagined. Through the trees she could see houses. All the windows seemed to have broken panes; fat, cross children looked out; the gardens seemed to be a tangle of thistles and weeds.

More broken toys, more blotted copy-books, more torn picture-books; everywhere weeping, howling, shouting. She could see no one here; probably all were sitting at home crying. It was as if everybody was crying in the place. There were plaintive cries, and angry cries, and lazy, nothing-else-to-do cries. There were cries like old street organs that had lost the beginnings and ends of their tunes, and still went round and round, *"piano, crescendo, piano, crescendo,"* as the music-books have it. There were cries like bagpipes in a rage, shrill, blustering, furious; there were cries like bagpipes that had caught a cold and were going to sneeze.

Kitty's blue eyes twinkled as she listened to these weepings. "Those children ought all to be whipped and put to bed," she said severely. "That would brighten them up."

Through that chorus of cries she distinguished barks—not jovial, satisfied, inquisitive barks—but snarls, and growls, and angry frightened yappings. She heard fierce mews and hissings also—every now and then lean cats ran along at full speed, their ears lying back, their eyes full of a wild hunted light.

"Pussy, pussy!" said Kitty softly as a black creature dashed past her. It whisked up a tree, and glared at her with eyes like green lanterns. Kitty thought of the pussy at home, of his sleek fur coat, of his comfortable ways.

"Pussy, pussy!" she said again in her most winning voice.

"Hi—ss!" answered the cat, ruffling up all his fur and glaring at her spitefully.

"A most unamiable, disagreeable cat! He ought to be whipped and put to bed also," said Kitty, and she marched on with an offended air.

Birds which looked as if they were always moulting watched her as she passed, presenting a most dejected appearance with their heads very much on one side.

"Poor birdies—birdies!" whispered Kitty softly.

At the first step she made in their direction they flew off with as much flutter as their feeble wings could make.

"I wonder have I grown *horrid* to look at, that they are all so frightened at me!" muttered Kitty. She felt her cheeks, her nose. Her nose seemed to be the same round little nose inclined to point upwards, her cheeks felt plump and soft.

All at once something cold dropped on the nape of her neck, just behind her ear. Kitty put up her hand and took hold of a goggle-eyed frog. "Oh,
oh, oh!" she cried with a shiver, throwing it away.

"Ha, ha, ha!" shouted a little boy, dancing round and round.

He was the queerest little lad she had ever seen. He had short legs, and
a queer little fat figure, and queer little pointed ears, queer little curls fell over
his forehead, and he had queer yellow eyes.

He looked so funny, putting one in mind of something between a monkey, a squirrel, and a boy, that Kitty after a moment began to laugh. It seemed
to her that Cousin Charlie might look like that at his very naughtiest.

"Make friends," said the boy, stopping his dance. "Give me a kiss."

"Certainly not," answered Kitty; "but *perhaps* I may shake hands with
you."

She put out her hand, cautiously watching the boy, who had a gleam in
his eyes she did not quite like. He approached with a hop and a jump.

"There's a sweet for you," he cried, depositing a spider on Kitty's palm.

"Oh, oh, oh!" she shivered, gathering herself into a little trembling mass of disgust, skipping about and shaking her finger tips to make sure she had dropped the spider.

The boy laughed louder and louder; that was evidently his idea of fun.

"You are the disagreeablest, mischievousest boy," said Kitty, turning away, and trying to make her words sound as long and severe as she could. "You deserve to be where you are, in Naughty Children Land. I am going to leave it."

She blinked her eyes to prevent the tears from falling. She would not for all the world that the boy should see he had made her cry.

As she turned away he sang lustily after her:

> "Up and down, and round and round,
>   Turn to left and turn to right,
> Never will the way be found
>   By weary walking day and night."

Kitty pretended not to hear. She walked back the way she fancied she had come. Before, behind, on every side of her stretched the tumbled-about land, and every untidy side looked exactly like the other. Was she really going only round and round? Presently she found herself standing once more close to the queer little boy. There were a number of other children about the place now. They were having high games, throwing each other into a duckweed pond, full of frogs that loudly croaked their vexation; or they were trying to make each other slip into a bed of nettles, or sit down on a wasp's nest.

Bu—uzz! bu—uzz! went the wasps in a rage.

The children laughed louder and louder, till they fairly screamed with merriment.

The queer little boy sat by himself, striking one stone against another. Out of the dark, dull stones the sparks flew, golden and beautiful. As they flew up he laughed.

"Listen, I'll tell you a secret," he said, winking one yellow eye at Kitty. "I am practising to set the world on fire."

"The world—on—fire!" she repeated quite breathless.

The queer boy nodded his head.

"Listen; the sparks will catch the trees in the wood. There will be a hiss, a flame. How the people will run, scamper, and tumble! They will tumble about like ninepins in their fright; and how their hair will catch fire! But the flames will run faster. Hurrah, what a bonfire that will be!"

He sprang to his feet, he leaped about, swinging his arms; his teeth flashed. Kitty thought he looked like a small tiger.

"But you would be burned yourself," she said, with a gleam in her eyes.

"Oh, I am brave! I don't mind pain!" said the boy, beginning to strike the stones once more with a fine flourish. Bang went the uplifted stone down upon his thumb, and hit it with a great thump. The boy set up a roar, like that of forty cross babies.

"Oh! o-oh! O-o-o-h-h! Daddy Coax—Da-addy Coax!" he shouted, flinging down the stones and running off with all the speed of his legs.

"Daddy Coax! I wonder who Daddy Coax is? It sounds a nice name!" thought Kitty. Then she continued: "Setting the world on fire! with the dear little birds, and the pussies, and the faithful dogs in it! And there would be the old people, and the cripple children who can't run!"

The thought of Johnnie seemed to knock at her heart, yet she did not remember distinctly. She seemed to hear the eager, uneven thump of his crutch. Again her little heart ached with the confused sense of pain. She walked on faster.

She made her way towards a wood that seemed the only pretty spot near. As she approached it she nearly fell over a wee girl who was kneeling, watching a lovely butterfly with wings like quivering flowers, twinkling and hovering near the ground. As it rested to stretch its bright body for a moment, down came the clenched little fist and crushed the happy winged creature.

"Oh, how could you?" cried Kitty.

"Don't you love to kill fies and butterfies and see them wiggle?" asked the child. She was so small she could not speak plain yet; but her bright black eyes twinkled, and she showed her wicked little teeth.

Before Kitty could answer she heard the tramp of small feet running. The next moment she was surrounded by a crowd of children, who cried: "Come along, come along! We are going to rob a nest. There are two newborn birds with yellow beaks, and there are three blue-speckled eggs. The mother bird is sitting on them. The father bird is watching. We'll kill him with a stone."

"We'll blow the eggs and string them for a necklace," cried a girl.

"I won't come!" exclaimed Kitty indignantly. "How can you be so wicked?"

A pitiless hand seized hers. It was so strong in its unkindness it pulled her along.

"Let me go! let me go!" entreated Kitty as the cruel children pushed and pulled her.

Run she must; run with the children. Oh! the cruel children, with hands strong to hurt, with feet nimble to give pain, with shrill voices to jeer and mock.

Presently Kitty saw a hedge, and in it a pretty nest, so cunningly built.

It lay among the fresh green leaves. A baby prince could not have a daintier cradle, set among shadier curtains, than had those callow birds. The father bird was fluttering above uttering cries of reproach. A thousand other birds were singing; Kitty understood their song.

They sang of their love for their pretty nestlings, of their pride in the nest they built in the sweet spring weather.

"Twe—et! twe—et! bur—rrr!" sang the father bird, with all his heart in his throat. "Shame upon the boys and girls who find sport in robbing the homes we and our mates make so patiently!"

"Twe—et! twe—et! Save my little ones," piteously cried the mother bird.

Her head showed just above the border of the nest. Brave mother bird! she did not stir as the children came nearer. Out of the green twilighty hedge her watching eyes shone wistfully. Kitty thought they turned upon her. Their light seemed to burn into her heart.

"Twe—et! twe—et! Save my little ones! Save my little ones!" entreated the mother bird.

Then Kitty sprang from the children. She placed herself between them and that part of the hedge where stood the nest. She defended its approach with all her might. She waved her brave little arms like the sails of a windmill in a tempest, pushing down the children as they came. Pitiful little arms, eager to comfort, not to hurt. The father bird did his best to help in the battle. He flew against the invaders. He fluttered his wings in their faces. He pecked at their noses, at their hair.

"Twe—et, bu—urr, bu—urr! Shame, shame!" he cried louder and louder.

The mother bird kept up that piteous twe—et.

This touching little noise, that sounded between a sob and a prayer to be delivered from the cruel children, seemed to give Kitty strength. But what could she do against so many? Alone against a crew of spoilers!—She shut her eyes as the children dragged her from the place she had defended. She heard them clambering through the hedge and the crack of the twigs. She heard the sorrow of all the birds—the screech of the father, the wail of the mother. Then came a wild hurrah! and she knew the children had their hands on the nest. The hurrah stopped all of a sudden.

Kitty looked up. Two severe-looking old dames, carrying birch rods, had suddenly appeared on the scene.

Whack, whack! went the rods.

"Oh, oh, oh! Daddy Coax! Daddy Coax!" cried the children, running away. They might be very brave laying siege to birds' nests; but they could not run away fast enough from these birch rods.

The stern-looking old ladies pounced upon the leaders of the gang, and held them firmly tucked under their arms. Kitty saw the black-eyed child who liked to kill "fies" and "butterfies."

As she stood looking, the severe dames suddenly disappeared, carrying off the children as they vanished.

"Extraordinary!" muttered Kitty, rubbing her eyes.

She looked to the right, to the left; they were gone! "I can't understand it! They were here a moment ago—and who is Daddy Coax? How shall I find out where he lives?"

PART THREE

Sentimental Re-Creations

Davy and the Goblin
Or, What Followed Reading
"Alice's Adventures in Wonderland"

Charles E. Carryl

Illustrations by E.B. Bensell

1885

CHARLES E. CARRYL (1841-1920) made his career as a director of railroad companies and as a New York stockbroker. He was inspired by his son Guy to write a fantasy in the style of his near-namesake, Lewis Carroll. Dedicated to Guy, *Davy and the Goblins* was first serialized in *St. Nicholas* magazine in 1884 before being published in book form. Enthusiastically received as an American *Alice in Wonderland, Davy and the Goblins* and the 1892 fantasy *The Admiral's Caravan* (which introduced an adventurous young heroine named Dorothy a decade before L. Frank Baum's *Oz* books) clearly show the influence of Lewis Carroll; however, both works are memorable and original as well, and were highly praised by reviewers as works of truly *American* fantasy at a time when American children's literature was largely realistic and didactic. Davy's "Believing Voyage" with his goblin companion reacquaints him with some of the heroes of his imagination, including Robinson Crusoe, Jack and the Beanstalk, Mother Hubbard, and Robin Hood, and introduces him as well to many new fantastic characters such as the Cockalorum and the Hole-Keeper. The importance of an ongoing faith in the power of imagination and the possibility of wonders is at the heart of Carryl's fantasy. This fast-paced chapter from early in the book demonstrates Carryl's love of rapid, almost surreal, transitions and his affinity for punning and word-play.

Davy and the Goblin

CHAPTER 7. THE MOVING FOREST

"OH, DEAR!" CRIED DAVY, speaking aloud in his distress, "I do wish people and things wouldn't change about so! Just so soon as ever I get to a place it goes away, and I'm somewhere else!"—and the little boy's heart began to beat rapidly as he looked about him; for the wood was very dark and solemn and still.

Presently the trees and bushes directly before him moved silently apart and showed a broad path beautifully overgrown with soft turf; and as he stepped forward upon it the trees and bushes beyond moved silently aside in their turn, and the path grew before him, as he walked along, like a green carpet slowly unrolling itself through the wood. It made him a little uneasy, at first, to find that the trees behind him came together again, quietly blotting out the path; but then he thought, "It really doesn't matter, so long as I don't want to go back"; and so he walked along very contentedly.

By and by the path seemed to give itself a shake, and, turning abruptly around a large tree, brought Davy suddenly upon a little butcher's shop, snugly buried in the wood. There was a sign on the shop, reading, "ROBIN HOOD:

VENISON," and Robin himself, wearing a clean white apron over his suit of Lincoln green, stood in the door-way, holding a knife and steel, as though he were on the lookout for customers. As he caught sight of Davy he said, "Steaks? Chops?" in an inquiring way, quite like an every-day butcher.

"Venison is deer, isn't it?" said Davy, looking up at the sign.

"Not at all," said Robin Hood, promptly. "It's the cheapest meat about here."

"Oh, I didn't mean that," replied Davy; "I meant that it comes off of a deer."

"Wrong again!" said Robin Hood, triumphantly. "It comes *on* a deer. I cut it off myself. Steaks? Chops?"

"No, I thank you," said Davy, giving up the argument. "I don't think I want anything to eat just now."

"Then what did you come here for?" said Robin Hood, peevishly. "What's the good, I'd like to know, of standing around and staring at an honest tradesman?"

"Well, you see," said Davy, beginning to feel that he had, somehow, been very rude in coming there at all, "I didn't know you were this sort of person at all. I always thought you were an archer, like—like William Tell, you know."

"That's all a mistake about Tell," said Robin Hood, contemptuously. "*He* wasn't an archer. He was a crossbow man,—the crossest one that ever lived. By the way," he added, suddenly returning to business with the greatest earnestness, "you don't happen to want any steaks or chops to-day, do you?"

"No, not to-day, thank you," said Davy, very politely.

"To-morrow?" inquired Robin Hood.

"No, I thank you," said Davy again.

"Will you want any yesterday?" inquired Robin Hood, rather doubtfully.

"I think not," said Davy, beginning to laugh.

Robin Hood stared at him for a moment with a puzzled expression, and then walked into his little shop, and Davy turned away. As he did so the path behind him began to unfold itself through the wood, and, looking back over his shoulder, he saw the little shop swallowed up by the trees and bushes. Just as it disappeared from view he caught a glimpse of a charming little girl, peeping out of a latticed window beside the door. She wore a little red hood, and looked wistfully after Davy as the shop went out of sight.

"I verily believe that was Little Red Riding Hood," said Davy to himself, "and I never knew before that Robin Hood was her father!" The thought of Red Riding Hood, however, brought the wolf to Davy's mind, and he began to anxiously watch the thickets on either side of the path, and even went so far as to whistle softly to himself, by way of showing that he wasn't in the least afraid. He went on and on, hoping the forest would soon come to an end, until the path shook itself again, disclosing to view a trim little brick shop in the densest part of the thicket. It had a neat little green door, with a bright brass knocker upon it, and a sign above it, bearing the words:—

"SHAM-SHAM: BARGAINS IN WATCHES."

"Well!" exclaimed Davy, in amazement. "Of all places to sell watches in that's the preposterest!"—but as he turned to walk away he found the trees and bushes for the first time blocking his way, and refusing to move aside. This distressed him very much, until it suddenly occurred to him that this must mean that he was to go into the shop; and, after a moment's hesitation, he went up and knocked timidly at the door with the bright brass knocker. There was no response to the knock, and Davy cautiously pushed open the door and went in.

The place was so dark that at first he could see nothing, although he heard a rattling sound coming from the back part of the shop; but presently he discovered the figure of an old man, busily mixing something in a large iron pot. As Davy approached him he saw that the pot was full of watches, which the old man was stirring with a ladle. The old creature was very curiously dressed, in a suit of rusty green velvet, with little silver buttons sewed over it, and he wore a pair of enormous yellow-leather boots; and Davy was quite alarmed at seeing that a broad leathern belt about his waist was stuck full of old-fashioned knives and pistols. Davy was about to retreat quickly from the shop, when the old man looked up, and said, in a peevish voice:—

"How many watches do you want?"—and Davy saw that he was a very shocking-looking person, with wild, staring eyes, and with a skin as dark as mahogany, as if he had been soaked in something for ever so long.

"How many?" repeated the old man, impatiently.

"If you please," said Davy, "I don't think I'll take any watches to-day. I'll call"—

"Drat 'em!" interrupted the old man, angrily beating the watches with his ladle; "I'll never get rid of em—never!"

"It seems to me"—began Davy, soothingly.

"Of course it does!" again interrupted the old man, as crossly as before. "Of course it does! That's because you won't listen to the why of it."

"But I *will* listen," said Davy.

"Then sit down on the floor and hold up your ears," said the old man.

Davy did as he was told to do, so far as sitting down on the floor was concerned, and the old man pulled a paper out of one of his boots, and, glaring at Davy over the top of it, said, angrily:—

"You're a pretty spectacle! I'm another. What does that make?"

"A pair of spectacles, I suppose," said Davy.

"Right!" said the old man. "Here they are." And pulling an enormous pair of spectacles out of the other boot he put them on, and began reading aloud from his paper:—

> *My recollectest thoughts are those*
> *Which I remember yet;*
> *And bearing on, as you'd suppose,*
> *The things I don't forget.*
>
> *But my resemblest thoughts are less*
> *Alike than they should be;*
> *A state of things, as you'll confess,*
> *You very seldom see.*

"Clever, isn't it?" said the old man, peeping proudly over the top of the paper.

"Yes, I think it is," said Davy, rather doubtfully.

"Now comes the cream of the whole thing," said the old man. "Just listen to this":—

> *And yet the mostest thought I love*
> *Is what no one believes—*

Here the old man hastily crammed the paper into his boot again, and stared solemnly at Davy.

"What is it?" said Davy, after waiting a moment for him to complete the verse. The old man glanced suspiciously about the shop, and then added, in a hoarse whisper:—

> *That I'm the sole survivor of*
> *The famous Forty Thieves!*

"But I thought the Forty Thieves were all boiled to death," said Davy.

"All but me," said the old man, decidedly. "I was in the last jar, and when they came to me the oil was off the boil, or the boil was off the oil,—I forget which it was,—but it ruined my digestion, and made me look like a gingerbread man. What larks we used to have!" he continued, rocking himself back and forth and chuckling hoarsely. "Oh! we were a precious lot, we were! I'm Sham-Sham, you know. Then there was Anamanamona Mike,—he was an Irishman from Hullaboo,—and Barcelona Boner,—he was a Spanish chap, and boned everything he could lay his hands on. Strike's real name was Gobang; but we called him Strike, because he was always asking for more pay. Hare Ware was a poacher, and used to catch Welsh rabbits in a trap; we called him 'Hardware' because he had so much *steal* about him. Good joke, wasn't it?"

"Oh, very!" said Davy, laughing.

"Frown Whack was a scowling fellow with a club," continued Sham-Sham. "My! how he could hit! And Harico and Barico were a couple of bad Society Islanders. Then there was Wee Wo,—he was a little Chinese chap, and we used to send him down the chimneys to open front doors for us. He used to say *that* sooted him to perfection. Wac—"

At this moment an extraordinary commotion began among the watches. There was no doubt about it, the pot was boiling, and Sham-Sham, angrily crying out, "Don't tell *me* a watched pot never boils!" sprang to his feet, and, pulling a pair of pistols from his belt, began firing at the watches, which were now bubbling over the side of the pot and rolling about the floor; while Davy, who had had quite enough of Sham-Sham by this time, ran out of the door.

To his great surprise he found himself in a sort of underground passage, lighted by grated openings overhead; but as he could still hear Sham-Sham, who now seemed to be firing all his pistols at once, he did not hesitate, but ran along the passage at the top of his speed.

Presently he came in sight of a figure hurrying toward him with a lighted candle, and, as it approached, he was perfectly astounded to see that it was Sham-Sham himself, dressed up in a neat calico frock and a dimity apron, like a house-keeper, and with a bunch of keys hanging at his girdle.

The old man seemed to be greatly agitated, and hurriedly whispering, "We thought you were *never* coming, sir!" led the way through the passage in great haste. Davy noticed that they were now in a sort of tunnel made of fine grass. The grass had a delightful fragrance, like new-mown hay, and was neatly wound around the tunnel, like the inside of a bird's-nest. The next moment they came out into an open space in the forest, where, to Davy's amazement, the Cockalorum was sitting bolt upright in an arm-chair, with his head wrapped up in flannel.

It seemed to be night, but the place was lighted up by a large chandelier that hung from the branches of a tree, and Davy saw that a number of odd-looking birds were roosting on the chandelier among the lights, gazing down upon the poor Cockalorum with a melancholy interest. As Sham-Sham made his appearance, with Davy at his heels, there was a sudden commotion among the birds, and they all cried out together, "Here's the doctor!" but before Davy could reply the Hole-keeper suddenly made his appearance, with his great book, and, hurriedly turning over the leaves, said, pointing to Davy, "*He* isn't a doctor. His name is Gloopitch." At these words there arose a long, wailing cry, the lights disappeared, and Davy found himself on a broad path in the forest, with the Hole-keeper walking quietly beside him.

The Wallypug of Why

G.E. Farrow

Illustrations by Harry Furniss and Dorothy Furniss

1895

GEORGE EDWARD FARROW (1866?-1920?)[1] was a popular and commercially successful British author of at least thirty works for children, including *Alice*-like fantasies and adventure stories, as well as poetry. He wrote a number of *Wallypug* books after *The Wallypug of Why*, including *Adventures in Wallypugland* (1898) and *In Search of the Wallypug* (1903). Like Lewis Carroll, who authorized such *Alice*-related merchandise as an *Alice* biscuit tin and an *Alice* postage stamp case, Farrow capitalized on his books' success through such items as "The Wallypug Birthday Book." Like Carroll, Farrow also encouraged his young audience to write to him, and responded with long prefaces to his readers explaining how they had influenced his writing of the current novel (and often hinting about the contents of the next). Girlie's adventures in the land of Why ("where all the questions and answers come from") feature His Majesty the Wallypug ("*a kind of king*, governed by the people instead of governing them") and are not only lively and engaging, but full of comic inventiveness.

Many of the *Wallypug* books were illustrated with lovely, energetic drawings by Harry Furniss, who had done the illustrations for Carroll's *Sylvie and Bruno* (1889) and *Sylvie and Bruno Concluded* (1893), as well as those for Maggie Browne's *Wanted—A King* (1890). Furniss's female characters are vigorous and vital, as indeed Girlie is (despite her unfortunate name).

---

1. Little information remains about Farrow's life, and his birth date has been variously recorded as 1862, 1866, and 1868. Some evidence, however, suggests that 1866 is the correct date. In the preface to *The Wallypug in London* (1898), Farrow jokes with an eight-year-old reader who wants him to wait for her to grow up so she can marry him, observing that "it would take nearly twenty-five years for her to catch up to me" (xiii). In his introduction for *To the Land of Fair Delight* (London: Gollancz, 1960), an anthology of children's fantasies that includes Farrow's *The Little Panjandrum's Dodo* (1899), Noel Streatfield observes sadly the lack of information about Farrow's life: "I think he must have met a Snark who turned out to be a Boojum, for he certainly has 'softly and suddenly vanished away'" (7).

Journeying through the land of Why
You'll meet the strangest company,
Various creatures, great and small,
And something odd about them all—
A socialistic Cockatoo;
A most mysterious thing—a Goo;
The quaintest men; a charming maid
Two ancient ladies, prim and staid;
The Wallypug——Pray, who is he?
I mustn't tell you; read and see.

The Wallypug of Why

CHAPTER I. THE WAY TO WHY

IT WAS A VERY WARM afternoon, and Girlie was sitting by the play-room window watching the gold fish idly swimming about in her little aquarium. She was feeling very "sigh" as she called it, that is, not very happy, for her brothers were all away from home, and she had no one to talk to. Even Boy, her youngest brother, was staying with some friends at Broadstairs, and she thought it very hard that she should have to wait at home for another week before joining him there. Her aunt, with whom she was staying, had received a letter from him that morning and had brought it up to Girlie to read.

"But it will only make me more sorry than ever that I am not there," thought poor Girlie. She had the letter in her hand and was trying to decide whether she should read it or not when she caught sight of a few words at the bottom of the first page, which was half drawn out of the envelope:—

I have found a Goo,

was written in Boy's big, sprawling handwriting.

"Whatever is a Goo?" thought Girlie; and, instead of reading the rest of the letter as most people would have done, she shut her eyes and tried to think whether she had ever heard of, or seen such a thing. She was trying hard to remember whether there was such a creature mentioned in her Natural History book, and had just come to the conclusion that she had never read of one, when she heard a little cough from the other end of the room, and, opening her eyes, she saw Dumpsey Deazil, her favourite doll, struggling up

244

from the very uncomfortable position in which she had been lying, with her head in a domino box and her feet on Noah's Ark.

Girlie stared with amazement, and the more so when Dumpsey Deazil, having succeeded in getting on to her feet, walked awkwardly up to where she was sitting, and holding out a stiff, sawdust-stuffed hand, said in a squeaky little voice:

"So you want to know what a Goo is, do you?"

"Oh, you dear old thing!" cried Girlie, jumping up excitedly, and catching Dumpsey Deazil up in her arms. "I always *knew* that you could talk if you only *would,* and now at last you are going to do so, just as dolls always do in fairy tale books."

"Of course *all* dolls can talk if they like," said Dumpsey Deazil; "only they never do so, except when they wish. But about the Goo, do you really want to know what it is?"

"Yes, I do," said Girlie, "because I don't remember ever having heard of such a thing."

"Well, I don't quite know what it is myself," said Dumpsey Deazil, "but I can take you to the land of Why if you like, where all the questions abd answers come from, and then you can find out for yourself, you know."

"Oh! that would be splendid!" exclaimed Girlie. "Is it a very long way off though?"

"Yes, it is rather a long way," admitted Dumpsey Deazil; "but it would not take us long to get there by the way in which we should go."

"How is that?" asked Girlie. "By train?"

"Oh dear, no!" cried Dumpsey Deazil; "by a *much* quicker way than that. You have just to take hold of one of my hands and, shutting your eyes very tightly, count up to one hundred aloud, and then when you open them again you will find yourself there."

"What a funny way to travel," said Girlie. "I am sure, though, that I should like it very much indeed. Can we go now, this very minute?"

"Yes," said Dumpsey Deazil; "but, before we start, you must promise me that you will be very kind to the Wallypug, for he is a kind of relation of mine."

"The Wallypug! Good gracious!! Whoever is he?" exclaimed Girlie.

"You will see when you get to Why," said Dumpsey Deazil mysteriously. "Now then, are you ready? Remember, though, you must *be sure* and not let go of my hand till you have counted up to one hundred, or you will lose me."

"All right!" promised Girlie, taking hold of Dumpsey Deazil's hand and screwing up her eyes very tightly. "One, two——"

She was sorely tempted to open her eyes, however, when she felt herself

being carried off her feet; still, she felt very comfortable and it seemed to her that she was floating rapidly through the air.

* * * * * *

"Eighty-five, eighty-six! Oh dear! somebody has taken hold of my other hand now," cried Girlie. "I really *must* look."

And, opening her eyes, she found herself in a country lane.

A benevolent-looking little old gentleman, dressed in knee breeches and wearing a huge broad-brimmed hat, was holding her wrist with one hand, while in the other he held a toy watch.

Dumpsey Deazil was floating rapidly away in the distance, frantically waving her arms and screaming out in an agonised voice,—

"I told you not to open your eyes until you had got to one hundred!"

Girlie watched her disappear over the hedge, and then turned in dismay to the little old gentleman, who was still holding her hand and beaming upon her with a reassuring smile.

"Your friend was taking you through the air rather too quickly to be good for your health, so I thought that I had better stop you," he said.

"Well, then, I think it was very rude of you," said Girlie, who felt greatly alarmed at having lost Dumpsey Deazil. "I don't know, I am sure, however I am going to get home again now," she continued, feeling half inclined to cry.

"Excuse me, you should never say '*I don't know*,'" said the old gentleman. "It is a very bad plan. If you really do not know anything, you should always pretend that you do. I invariably do so, and I ought to know, for I am the Wallypug's Doctor-in-law."

"Oh! Who *is* the Wallypug, please?" asked Girlie curiously, "and I'm afraid I don't know what a doctor-in-law is, either."

"One question at a time, my child," said the old gentleman. "Who the Wallypug is you will soon find out for yourself; and a doctor-in-law is something between a father-in-law and a step-father, a sort of half-a-step-father, in fact. That will be six-and-eightpence, please," and the Doctor-in-law held out his hand with a smile.

"What for?" exclaimed Girlie.

"Professional advice," said the Doctor-in-law blandly.

"What advice?" asked Girlie; "I don't know what you mean."

"Didn't I *advise* you never to say, 'I don't know'?" explained the Doctor-in-law.

"But I didn't ask you to give me any advice at all," cried Girlie in dismay.

"Oh! if I waited till people *asked* me for advice I should never get any clients!" said the Doctor-in-law; "and you might as well give me the other guinea at the same time," he continued.

"What other guinea? What *do* you mean?" asked Girlie.

"The guinea for professional attendance when you first arrived here," said the Doctor-in-law. "I always charge a guinea for that."

"But I didn't want you to attend to me," said Girlie indignantly. "I wish you hadn't."

"If I waited till people *wanted* me to attend to them I should get no patients," admitted the Doctor-in-law; "so I always attend to people when I think they require it, whether they wish me to do so, or not. I must really insist on the fee, please. Let's see, that will be three pounds seven altogether, won't it?" he continued, making a calculation in his pocket-book.

"Certainly not!" said Girlie; "how can you make that out?"

"Well, you see, if you add them together they come to about that," said the Doctor-in-law.

"I am sure they don't," cried Girlie.

"It's very rude to contradict your elders," remarked the Doctor-in-law severely. "I am surprised at you. Give me the money at once, please."

"But I have no money with me," said Girlie, getting rather frightened.

"Dear me, this is very serious," said the old gentleman, looking genuinely grieved. "Do you really mean to tell me," he continued, "that you are travelling about the country without any money at all in your pocket?"

"Yes," said Girlie. "You see, I didn't know that I was coming here, or that I should require any."

"Oh! that's an absurd excuse, my dear," said the Doctor-in-law. "But what's that in your hand?" he continued, staring at her right hand.

Girlie opened it, and found a crumpled piece of paper in it, though how it came there she could never tell. Smoothing it out, she found it to be a kind of money-order with the words, "Please to pay the bearer the sum of five pounds. Signed, THE WALLYPUG," written on it.

"Oh! a Wallypug order for five pounds; that will do very nicely," said the Doctor-in-law, taking it from her and putting it into his pocket. "And now you will only owe me the odd sixpence," he said.

"What odd sixpence?" asked Girlie. "I don't remember anything about a sixpence."

"Well," said the Doctor-in-law, "if you don't remember it, *it's very odd,* therefore it must be an odd sixpence; don't you see, my dear?" and he held out his hand again.

"But I've already given you five pounds instead of three pounds seven," said Girlie, getting hopelessly muddled.

"Well, my dear, don't let *that* worry you in the least," said the Doctor-in-law kindly; "I'll overlook it this time, and, if you can't find the sixpence, I don't mind taking your watch instead. I see that you have a very pretty one."

"I think it's very unkind and greedy of you, then!" said Girlie, turning very red and feeling greatly frightened; for her watch had been given to her by her aunt, and she was allowed to wear it only now and then as a great treat.

"Not at all, my dear; you don't look at these things in the right light," said the Doctor-in-law. "Don't you see that, if you can't pay me the money, it is only fair that you should give me your watch?"

"But it is worth a great deal more than sixpence," argued Girlie.

"Not at all!" said the Doctor-in-law, flourishing his watch about at the end of the chain. "Mine only cost a penny."

"Yes, but yours doesn't go," objected Girlie; "mine does, you know."

"Does what?" asked the Doctor-in-law.

"Go!" said Girlie.

"Oh, well, then, I don't want it," said the Doctor-in-law hurriedly. "I don't want a watch that will *go,* I want one that will stay. Why, if my watch was to *go,* I should always have to be going after it! and, talking about going, I must be off or I shall be late for the Wallypug. You can pay me the half-crown when we meet again." And, with a nod and a smile, the little old gentleman pocketed his watch and hurried off.

"Oh! if you please!" cried Girlie, running after him, "could you direct me to——"

"Can't stop!" interrupted the Doctor-in-law; "my time is far too valuable, and besides, you have no money." And walking rapidly away, he got over a stile and disappeared into a field beyond.

"Oh dear me! whatever *shall* I do now?" thought poor Girlie, looking about her in dismay.

There was nobody in sight, so she decided to sit down on the bank and wait until some one came past who would direct her to somewhere or other.

"For I haven't the remotest idea where I am," she thought. "I don't even know how many miles I am from home. I wonder," she went on, "how many miles one can travel through the air while you count eighty-five. I suppose it depends upon how quickly you are travelling. Perhaps I could make a sum of it and do it by rule of three. Let's see! If it takes one girl one minute to count sixty, how many miles can a girl and a doll travel through the air while you count eighty-five? I suppose you have to multiply the minutes by the miles, and divide by the number of people," she thought; and was so very busy trying to *do this sum in her head,* as she described it, that she did not notice a young man walking down the lane, till he had nearly reached her.

Girlie could scarcely keep from laughing when she first saw him, for he looked such a *very* comical person; he had long hair, and wore glasses, and carried his hands dangling in front of him. ("For all the world like a kangaroo," thought Girlie.)

He came and sat down quite close to her, and after staring at her for some time, smiled in a patronising kind of way.

"Don't you think me very handsome?" he said at last.

"Well, I am afraid not," stammered Girlie, who did not like to hurt his feelings by telling him what she really did think about him.

"Dear me! then your eyes must be seen to, decidedly," said the young man. "Why, you must be nearly blind not to see that I am very, *very* beautiful; and I am a very *important* person, too," he continued impressively.

"Are you really?" asked Girlie, who could scarcely keep serious.

"Yes, I am a very superior individual indeed. I am the King's Minstrel, enormously rich, and I am going to marry the Wallypug's niece. I *compose* better than any one else in the world."

"Really!" said Girlie. "What do you compose?"

"Draughts," said the King's Minstrel. "Of course you have heard of composing draughts."

"Yes," said Girlie. "They are things to send you to sleep, aren't they?"

"Sometimes," said the King's Minstrel. "Mine keep you awake, though, and that's why they are so much better than anybody else's."

"Isn't it very difficult to compose?" asked Girlie.

"Yes; it requires a great brain like mine to do it properly," replied the King's Minstrel conceitedly. "Would you like to hear my latest composition?" he asked.

"Yes, please," said Girlie, folding her hands in her lap and preparing to listen.

The King's Minstrel took a roll of music from under his arm and, after coughing importantly, began to sing in a very harsh and discordant voice—

> " 'Won't you walk into my parlour?' said the spider to the fly,
> How I wonder what you are, up above the world so high.
> 'I'm going a-milking, sir,' she said,
> And when she got there the poor dog was dead.
>
> "Four and twenty blackbirds baked in a pie,
> Gin a body, kiss a body, need a body cry.
> Humpty-dumpty sat on a wall,
> And if I don't hurt her she'll do me no harm."

"There! isn't it lovely?" he asked when he had finished.

"Why, it's perfect *nonsense!*" cried Girlie; "it's just a lot of separate lines from nursery rhymes all strung together; and, besides, there's no sense in it," she added.

"That shows you don't know anything at all about it," said the King's Minstrel contemptuously. "Any respectable person knows that there never *should* be any sense in really good poetry; the less you are able to understand it the better it is; and it wouldn't be a composition," he went on, "if it wasn't *composed* of several bits of other poems. The great thing is to get it to rhyme. You see this all rhymes beautifully."

"I'm sure the last two lines don't!" said Girlie decidedly.

"Oh!" said the King's Minstrel, looking rather confused, "you see, you have to pronounce '*harm*' as near like '*wall*' as you can; you often have to do that in poetry, you know. Besides, people always pardon little slips of that kind in really clever people, like myself. Good-bye! You *may* have the honour of meeting me again later," he continued, preparing to go.

"Oh, I was going to ask you," cried Girlie hurriedly, "whether you could kindly direct me to Why, or tell me the way to get home again."

"I beg your pardon, but I make it a point *never* to do anything useful. I am purely *ornamental*," said the King's Minstrel, bowing politely and then strutting away with a conceited air, leaving Girlie once more alone in the lane. . . .

CHAPTER 3. BREAKFAST FOR TEA

When she reached the top of the stairs, Girlie found herself in a courtyard, surrounded by high railings and some massive iron gates. There was a lodge by the gates, at the door of which stood an old crocodile with a white bandage around his head. He came slowly towards Girlie, carrying some enormous keys in his hand.

"Have you had your tea?" he queried anxiously.

"No!" said Girlie, thinking that she should very much like some after all those stairs.

"Very well, then," said the Crocodile, "we will have some together; step this way." Girlie followed him into the lodge, the door of which opened directly into a cosy little room. A table stood in the centre, covered with a white table-cloth.

"Will you have some eggs with your tea?" asked the Crocodile kindly.

"Yes, please," replied Girlie.

"And some cake and jam?" continued the Crocodile, smilingly.

"I should like some very much indeed, thank you," said Girlie, who thought him very kind.

"Wait a minute," said the Crocodile; "I had better put it down so that I don't forget"; and he took down a slate that was hanging behind the door.

"Let's see," he continued, writing it down, as he went on, "thin bread-and-butter, eggs (boiled, I suppose?)," he enquired, looking at her.

Girlie was just going to nod her head, when she suddenly remembered that, if she did so, she might turn into a Mandarin; so she hastily said "Yes, please," instead.

"Tea, cake, and jam," continued the Crocodile, putting it all down on his slate.

"Are you sure you won't have anything else?" he asked.

"Oh no, thank you," said Girlie, "that will do very nicely."

"All right," said the Crocodile; "where are the things?"

"What things?" asked Girlie in a surprised voice.

"Why, the things for tea, of course," said the Crocodile.

"But I *haven't* any," said Girlie; "I thought that you asked me to take tea with *you*," she continued.

The old Crocodile burst into tears.

"I think it most cru-cru-cruel of you," he sobbed, "to raise my ho-ho-ho-hopes in this way only to dis-dis-dis-ap-ap-ap-point me. You said you were going to have eggs," he cried tearfully, referring to the slate, "and ca-ca-cake, and ja-ja-jam"; and the poor old thing was quite overcome with grief.

"Oh, *please* don't cry," said Girlie, who felt quite sorry for him; "I am disappointed, too, you know."

The Crocodile dried his eye (the other one was covered with the bandage) and began to brighten up a little.

"I know what we'll do," he said at length. "Do you ever have tea for breakfast?"

"Yes," said Girlie, "I don't care for coffee."

"Very well, then, let's have *breakfast* for *tea* instead," suggested the Crocodile.

"But how can we do that if we haven't the things?" asked Girlie.

"Oh! I have enough for *breakfast*," said the Crocodile, going to the cupboard and bringing out a basket of eggs, a loaf of bread, some butter, a large iced cake and a pot of jam.

"Why, they're the same things that we were going to have for tea," thought Girlie.

"Let's see, one for you, one for me, and one for the pot," remarked the Crocodile, putting three spoonfuls of tea into the teapot. "You will find some hot water in the next room," he continued, handing it to Girlie.

Girlie took the teapot and went to the door; she found that it led into a large kitchen paved with red bricks. The room was filled with steam and, at the further end of it, Girlie could just see three large washtubs at which three seals were washing table-cloths. They had coloured handkerchiefs tied over their heads, and were singing when Girlie entered. She could not hear all the words, but just caught the end of the verse:—

"Most beautiful suds that e'er were seen,
Of colours red, and blue, and green,
Tra-la-la, tra-la-la, tra-la-lee."

It finished on a very high note, which none of the seals could reach, so that it ended in a kind of squeal.

"What do you want?" asked the largest Seal, catching sight of Girlie; "some hot water?"

"Yes, please," said Girlie.

"Are you going to have *tea* or *breakfast*?" asked the Seal anxiously.

"Breakfast, I believe," said Girlie, though she couldn't at all see why it should be called breakfast any more than tea.

"Ah! I was afraid so," said the Seal in a disappointed voice, while the other seals sighed heavily. "We haven't had tea here for weeks and weeks. How many spoonfuls did he put in, dear?" he continued, taking the teapot from her.

"Three," said Girlie.

"One each," said the Seal to the others, who nodded their heads, then turning out the tea into a cup, he filled the teapot with boiling water from a kettle on the fire, and handed it back to Girlie.

"Aren't you going to put the tea back again?" she asked.

"Certainly not," said the Seal; "that's for us."

"How do you know?" said Girlie.

"Because there were three spoonfuls and there are only *two* of you, so it must be for us; now hurry back to the Crocodile, or he will think you are lost," said the Seal.

Girlie took the teapot doubtfully, and went back to the other room. She found that the Crocodile had set the table while she had been gone.

"Will you pour out, please?" he said, seating himself, and motioning Girlie to the head of the table. "Did you hear how he is to-day?" he continued in an anxious tone when she had taken her place.

"Who?" asked Girlie.

"The *tea*," said the Crocodile; "he has been very poorly lately. Ah!" he continued, while Girlie poured out the hot water, "poor little thing! poor little thing! How dreadfully pale and weak he is, to be sure!" and, taking the tea-cup from her, he gazed down into it anxiously. "Do you think a little milk would do him any good?" he asked at last.

"I don't think it could possibly do any harm," said Girlie, who felt very much inclined to laugh.

"Pass the milk-jug, then," said the Crocodile.

Girlie did so, and the Crocodile poured a little milk into his cup.

"Gracious!" he cried, in an alarmed voice, after he had done so. "It's worse than ever; he is turning paler than he was before. Pray run into the next room and ask how the seals' tea is getting on."

Girlie got up again and went into the kitchen.

The Seals had left their washtubs, and were sitting around the fire on little three-legged stools, eating rather thick bread-and-butter; and the eldest Seal was just pouring out tea.

"The Crocodile wishes to know how your tea is, if you please," said Girlie.

"Oh! give him our compliments," replied the Seal, "and say that he is very well, thanks; getting quite strong, and is learning to draw very nicely. How is his poor tea, do you know, dear?" he added.

"Very weak," said Girlie ("and likely to be so," she thought).

"Do you mean to say you haven't brought us any cake?" said the youngest Seal.

"No," said Girlie. "I didn't know you wanted any."

"Well, go and fetch some then, and bring your teacup back with you," said the Seal. "You shall have some of our tea, if you like; it will be better for you."

Girlie thought so, too, and ran back to the other room to ask for some cake for the seals.

She found the Crocodile with his hat and gloves on. At the door stood a perambulator, in which was the weak cup of tea, propped up with pillows, and carefully wrapped in a little woollen shawl.

"I can't enjoy my breakfast till I have taken the poor little thing out for a breath of fresh air," said the Crocodile when she came in. "Did you hear how their tea is?" he asked anxiously.

"Oh, quite strong and beginning to draw very nicely," said Girlie.

"I'm sure I'm very glad to hear it," said the Crocodile, wiping his eye and looking ruefully at his own weak tea. "I shall probably not be back for some time," he continued, "so, perhaps, I had better say good-bye. Pray make yourself at home." And, after shaking hands with her, the poor old creature went out, looking very mournful, and tenderly wheeling the perambulator with the weak cup of tea in it.

"How absurd!" said Girlie to herself; and, after watching him out of sight, she took her cup and saucer with her, and went back to the seals.

"I say," said the eldest Seal when she entered the door, "there's a letter for you in the post."

"How do you know?" asked Girlie, putting down the cake, and passing her cup over for some tea.

"Because I put it there," said the Seal.

"Put it where?" asked Girlie.

"In the post," said the Seal in a tone of surprise.

"What *do* you mean?" asked Girlie.

"Go and see for yourself," said the Seal, pointing to the door at the other end of the kitchen.

Girlie walked across and saw that the door-post had a number of little slits in it, in one of which was a letter.

Drawing it out, she found it addressed to herself:

"Miss Girlie,
   "c/o The Crocodile,
      "The Lodge,
         "Why."

Very curious to know what it was about, she hastily opened the envelope, and was greatly disappointed to find a plain sheet of paper with only the letter "C" written on it.

"Wasn't it kind of me to send it?" asked the Seal when she walked slowly back.

"But there's nothing in it," said Girlie.

"Isn't there a letter?" asked the Seal.

"No," said Girlie; "nothing but a plain sheet of paper with a big 'C' on it."

"Well," said the Seal, "that's a letter, isn't it, stupid? I didn't say that I had sent you a *lot* of letters, did I? I thought you would like the letter 'C'; it's such a useful one."

"What is it good for?" asked Girlie, who didn't see how it *could* be of much use to her.

"Why, to *suggest* things, of course," said the Seal. "You have only to look at it in order to think of all kinds of lovely things—*cakes* and *carpets, calico* and *crockery,* for instance, to say nothing of *chocolate creams* and *crumpets.*

"Of course there are *some* uncomfortable things, too, such as *caterpillars, centipedes,* and *castor-oil*; but, on the whole, it's a most useful letter."

"Yes; very different from some," said the middle-sized Seal, who had not spoken to Girlie before.

"I had the letter 'M' sent to me once," he continued, "and immediately had the *measles,* the *mumps,* and the *megrims,* and did not get over them till somebody kindly sent me the letter 'T,' so that I could have *travelling* with *tranquillity,* and *Turkish delight.* I wish some one would send me 'G,'" he went on, "so that I could have *gooseberries* and *greengages* and *grapes.* I'm so fond of fruit."

"Then I should think 'F' would be the best letter to have, wouldn't it?" asked Girlie. "'F' stands for *fruit,* you know."

"Yes, and *frogs* and *freckles* and *five-finger* exercises, too," said the Seal. "No, thank you—not for me. One has to be very careful, I can tell you."

Just then a great bell began to ring, and the seals got up hastily and went back to their washtubs.

"What's that?" asked Girlie.

"The public meeting is about to commence next door," said the eldest Seal. "Wouldn't you like to go?"

"What is it about?" asked Girlie.

"To settle questions," replied the Seal. "All the questions and answers are decided at these meetings. The Wallypug will attend in state," he continued.

"Oh! I *should* like to see the Wallypug," said Girlie eagerly. "And I have an important question to ask, too," she thought, remembering the Goo. "May any one go?" she asked aloud.

"Yes," said the Seal. "Only you must make haste or you will be too late. You can go through the garden, if you like," he suggested, opening the door for her, and pointing to a green gate at the end of the path.

Girlie thanked him and, hastily bidding them all good-bye, ran down the pathway and opened the gate.

Chapter 4. Girlie Sees the Wallypug

"Late again!" called out the Hall Porter when Girlie hurried up the broad stone steps leading to a great building opposite to the little green gate.

"How can I be late *again*," asked Girlie angrily, "when I've never been here at all before?"

"If you've not been here *before,* then you must have been *behind*," said the Hall Porter; "and, if one is behind, they are late, don't you know? You are fined sixpence," he added, taking sixpence from his pocket and handing it to Girlie.

"What is this?" she asked.

"The sixpence that I fined you, of course," replied the Hall Porter.

"But what am I to do with it?" asked Girlie in surprise.

"Oh! findings', keepings," muttered the Hall Porter, walking away. "Put it in your pocket; you'll want it soon."

And, sure enough, before she had gone many steps along the stone corridor, Girlie came to a great door with the words "Admission, sixpence" written on it.

After knocking timidly, she waited awhile, till it was, at last, opened by a policeman, who, silently taking the sixpence which she offered him, motioned her to a seat near the door.

"Well, it's a good thing that I *was* fined, or I should never have got in here," thought Girlie; and she sat down and looked about her curiously.

She found herself in a long Gothic hall with low seats against the wall on each side. At one end was a raised dais, on which was a throne with a canopy over it. The centre of the room was quite bare. On the seats against the wall were sitting a number of animals, and Girlie could see that the Fish with a cold and his companion the Calf were sitting near the throne. The Fish had his tail in a tub of hot mustard-and-water; and by his side was a small table, on which were a basin of gruel, some cough mixture and a packet of lozenges. And near him, at a low desk, sat a Lobster writing rapidly; Girlie afterwards discovered that he was a Reporter. None of the animals had taken the slightest notice of her on her entrance, except an old white Cockatoo in a Paisley shawl, carrying a huge market-basket, and who, as soon as Girlie sat down, made some remark to two Monkeys who were sitting near her. The Monkeys laughed, and one of them, leaning forward so that he could see Girlie more distinctly, made a grimace at her.

"Don't take any notice of them, dear," said a motherly-looking Penguin, who sat next to her knitting a very curiously-shaped stocking. "They are always rude to strangers; and I think you have not been here before, have you?" she asked smilingly.

"No, never," replied Girlie, smiling back again, for she quite took to this kindly-looking creature.

"You're what they call a Proper Noun, aren't you?" asked the Penguin after a pause.

Girlie thought the matter over, and then replied that she supposed she was, although usually spoken of as a little girl.

"It's all the same, my dear," said the Penguin. "All girls are nouns, you know, although all nouns are not girls, which is very funny when you come to think of it, because——"

Before she could finish the sentence, there was a stir amongst the animals, when a severe-looking gentleman in black velvet and steel buckles and buttons entered, carrying a long wand.

"Silence!" he cried in a loud voice, and the talking, which had been going on all over the room, immediately ceased.

"The Husher," whispered the Penguin, hastily putting away her knitting.

"Silence!" again called out the Husher, glaring fiercely at Girlie.

"I didn't speak, sir," said Girlie nervously.

"Yes, she did! yes, she did!" screamed the Cockatoo. "She's been talking ever since she came in," she went on noisily.

"Silence, both of you!" said the Husher, frowning severely first at Girlie and then at the Cockatoo, and then walking to the other end of the room, as a door at the top of some steps near the throne opened, and two Heralds entered, blowing a blast on their trumpets.

"Here comes the Wallypug!" said the Penguin, and everybody stood up as a kind of procession filed into the room.

Girlie and the Penguin moved a little nearer the door, in order to see more distinctly.

First in the procession came the Doctor-in-law, smiling blandly; then the King's Minstrel came strutting in, looking more conceited than ever, and carrying a large roll of music under his arm. He was followed by an elderly gentleman carrying a microscope.

"The Royal Microscopist," said the Penguin in answer to an inquiring glance that Girlie gave her.

"What is the microscope for?" asked Girlie in a whisper.

"To see the jokes with," replied the Penguin. "Some of them cannot be seen at all without it."

Following the Royal Microscopist came an old lady in a poke bonnet and black lace shawl, who turned out to be the Head Mistress of the High School at Why. She was a very sharp-featured person and wore blue glasses.

There was a slight pause, and then the Wallypug entered. He was a meek-looking little creature, splendidly dressed in royal robes, which, however, fitted him very badly, and his crown was so much too big that it came quite over his head and just rested on the tip of his nose. He carried an orb in one hand and a sceptre in the other. His long velvet cloak, lined with ermine, was held by two pages, who were giggling and occasionally giving the cloak a tug which nearly upset the poor Wallypug, who seemed to have great difficulty in getting along as it was.

"Now then, Wallypug, sparkle up!" called out the Husher, giving him a poke with his wand as soon as he entered the door.

Girlie was greatly surprised to see him treated so disrespectfully, and was quite indignant when, the Wallypug having reached the steps of the dais, the pages gave an extra hard pull at his cloak and caused him to fall awkwardly forward on to his hands and knees, dropping his orb and sceptre and knocking his crown further over his face than ever.

Everybody else, however, seemed to think it a great joke, and even the Wallypug smiled apologetically while he scrambled nervously up to the throne.

During the time that the animals were settling into their places, Girlie found out from the Penguin that the Wallypug was a *kind of King,* governed by the people instead of governing them. He was obliged to spend his money as *they* decided, and was not allowed to do *anything* without their permission. He had to address every one as "Your Majesty," and had even to wear such clothes as the people directed. The state robes he now wore had belonged to the previous Wallypug, who had been a much larger man, and that was why they fitted him so badly.

So soon as the room was quiet, the Husher announced in a loud voice, "The Speech from the Throne"; and the Wallypug immediately stood up, nervously fumbling at a sheet of parchment which he held in his hand. His crown being quite over his eyes, he had to hold the parchment nearly up to his nose in order to see what was written on it. However, he soon began in a feeble voice,—

"May it please your Majesties——" when he was immediately interrupted by the Cockatoo, who screamed out,—

"We don't want to hear all that rubbish! Let's get to business."

"Yes, yes," cried several voices; "business first."

The Husher called out "Silence! silence!" in a dignified way. "I think you *had* better sit down, though," he added, turning to the Wallypug.

"Very well, your Majesty," said the Wallypug, looking greatly relieved and sitting down immediately.

The Husher then walked over to the Fish and seemed to be asking him some question, to which the Fish evidently replied in the affirmative, for the Husher looked very pleased and immediately announced,—

"Ladies and gentlemen——"

"What about us?" screamed the Cockatoo.

"And others," continued the Husher, giving a glance in her direction. "You will be pleased to hear that the Lecture to-day will be given by A. Fish, Esq., and the subject is one which will no doubt interest you all. It is '*The Whichness of the What as compared to the Thatness of the Thus.*'"

A storm of applause followed this announcement, in the midst of which

the Fish arose, assisted by his friend the Calf, who, so soon as he had helped him to stand, ran hurriedly out of the room, returning almost immediately with a large kettle of boiling water and some more mustard. These he poured hastily into the tub, stirring it round and round and gazing up anxiously into the Fish's face.

The Fish gasped once or twice, and then, after swallowing a little gruel, he began in a very choky voice:

"O-o-o-b, o-o-o-b, o-o-o-b, Ladles ad Geddlebed——"

The Reporter looked up with a puzzled air. "May I trouble you to repeat that?" he asked, putting his claw to his head. "I didn't quite catch the last part of the sentence."

"O-o-o-b, o-o-o-b, I said, Ladles ad Geddlebed," repeated the Fish, looking rather put out.

"Latin quotation?" asked the Reporter of the Doctor-in-law, who stood near him.

"Partly," replied the Doctor-in-law. "'Ladles' is English, 'ad' is Latin, and 'Geddlebed' is Dutch, I think. It's a very clever remark," he continued.

The Reporter looked greatly impressed, and made a note of what the Doctor-in-law had said, and then waited for the Fish to go on.

The Fish, however, was taking some more gruel, and saying "O-o-o-b" between every spoonful. Presently he choked dreadfully, and, amidst great excitement, had to be helped from the room by the Calf and the Doctor-in-law, who kept thumping him violently on the back all the way to the door.

So soon as they had gone out, the King's Minstrel jumped up and rapidly began undoing his roll of music.

"I will now oblige you with one of my charming songs," he said.

There was immediately a great commotion in all parts of the room.

"No, you won't!" "Turn him out!" "We don't want to hear it," was heard on all sides, while the old Cockatoo got positively frantic, jumping madly up and down, and screaming out as loudly as she could, "Down with him! *Down with him!* DOWN WITH HIM!"

The Husher rushed wildly about calling out "Silence! silence!" and it was not until the King's Minstrel had sulkily rolled up his music and sat down again that order was restored.

CHAPTER 5. WHAT IS A GOO?

"Let's have some Questions and Answers now," suggested somebody, when they had all settled down into their places again.

"All right," said the Husher. "Who has any questions to ask?" he continued.

Several animals held up their paws.

"Let's have yours first," he said, turning to a large black French poodle.

The Poodle at once got up and made a very polite bow. "It's a 'Question of Etiquette,'" he said, "and I've taken the liberty of putting it into verse."

"No one should be allowed to write poetry but me," said the King's Minstrel sulkily.

"Silence," called out the Husher, frowning severely at him. "Go on with your question, Poodle."

The Poodle bowed again, and placing his feet in the first position for dancing, read the following lines:—

"The people of Japan, I've heard,
    Are really *most* polite;
To compliment all sorts of things
    Is daily their delight;
They speak in terms of courtesy
    Of an '*Honourable* table,'
And flatter other household things
    Whenever they are able.

"Determined not to be outdone
    In manners so genteel,
I now express to all *my* goods
    The deep respect I feel.
The system I've adopted, though,
    Is really most confusing,
And circumstances oft arise
    More serious than amusing.

"An instance recently occurred
    Which leaves me much distressed,
For I fear I used expressions
    Which I ought to have suppressed.
On my '*most distinguished table*,'
    Was a '*well connected* dish,'
And reposing gently on it
    Was an '*influential* fish.'

"My '*honourable* cat' (a-hem)
    Was unfortunately there,
And she very quickly got up
    On my '*educated* chair.'

* * * * * *

When seeking somewhat later
    For that '*influential* fish.'
I discovered not a particle
    On my '*well connected* dish.'

"The question now arises,
    And I think I ought to know,
How far this fulsome flattery
    Expects a dog to go.
Am I compelled by Etiquette,
    Now please to tell me that,
To call a cat that steals my fish
    An 'honourable cat?'"

"Family Coach," called out the Husher when the Poodle had finished, and every one immediately rushed across the room and changed places with the one sitting opposite to him.

"What's that for?" asked Girlie breathlessly, so soon as she reached the other side.

"So that we can hear *both* sides of the question," replied the Penguin, waddling awkwardly to her seat.

"Silence," called the Husher. "Now repeat the question," he added, turning to the Poodle.

The Poodle repeated the last verse.

"Now then, what's the verdict?" asked the Husher, looking all around the room.

A small Guineapig at the further end held up his paw.

"Well?" said the Husher.

"I should like to put a few questions to the Poodle before replying," squeaked the Guineapig.

"Certainly," said the Poodle politely.

"First of all," said the Guineapig, referring to some notes that he had made, "you said you had *heard* that the people of Japan were most polite; now where did you hear it?"

"I *read* it in a book," explained the Poodle.

"Then you didn't *hear* it at all, so you are not telling the truth," said the Guineapig severely.

"It's the same thing," argued the Poodle.

"It's not!" said the Guineapig decidedly. "Now attend to me," he continued; "has your cat *left*?"

"No," said the Poodle, "she returned after she had eaten the fish."

"Then," said the Guineapig triumphantly, "if she's not *left* she must be *right*, so you see you must call her '*Right honourable*' in future."

This answer seemed to give general satisfaction, and there was some attempt at applause, but the Husher called out severely, "Silence: next question," and the Schoolmistress stood up.

"Mine's French," she said importantly. "Does any one here understand French?"

"I do, a little," said Girlie, feeling quite proud of her knowledge.

Several animals on the same side of the room as herself leaned forward and stared at her curiously.

"Bah! down with the foreigners!" screamed the Cockatoo.

"Silence," called out the Husher, and every one listened attentively while the Schoolmistress asked the following question.

"Has the son of the miller the mustard of the daughter of the gardener?"

"*That's* not French," said Girlie contemptuously.

"I'm *sure* it is," said the Schoolmistress; "isn't it?" she asked, turning to the Husher.

"I've seen questions very much like it in my French lesson book," he replied.

"Then, of course, it's French," said the Schoolmistress, while the Cockatoo screamed out, "Yah! who said she knew French and didn't! *laugh at her, laugh at her!*" Before Girlie, who felt very indignant, could reply, the Husher had called out "Family Coach" again, and they all had to change places once more.

"Now does any one know the answer?" asked the Husher, after the Schoolmistress had repeated the question.

"Please, sir, I do," said a meek-looking Donkey. "I work for the son of the miller, you know."

"Well, has he the mustard of the gardener's daughter?" asked the Husher.

"Please, sir, yes," said the Donkey.

"How do you know?" queried the Husher.

"Because he is so hot-tempered, sir," replied the Donkey ruefully.

"Ah! then I expect he *has* got it," said the Husher reflectively. "What's the next question?"

Girlie suddenly remembered about the Goo, and jumped up, excitedly saying, "Oh! I have a question, if you please."

"Well, let's have it," said the Husher.

"Could you kindly tell me what is a Goo?" asked Girlie.

"A what?" said the Husher, frowning.

"A Goo," replied Girlie.

"How do you spell it?" he asked.

"G-o-o, I think," said Girlie.

The Husher looked perplexed. "Family Coach," he called at last, and they all scrambled across the room again.

"Now then, what's a Goo?" he asked anxiously.

No one spoke.

"I don't believe she knows herself," at last called out the Cockatoo.

"Of course I don't," answered Girlie, "or I shouldn't have asked the question."

"It's no use whatever asking questions," said the Husher crossly, "if you can't tell us whether we give you the correct answer or not; and how can you do that if you don't know yourself? Well, you'll *all* have to know by next week," he continued, "or I shall send you all to sea."

"What good will that do?" asked Girlie of the Penguin, who was still sitting next to her.

"Oh! we always have to go to sea, if we don't know things," replied the Penguin dolefully.

Girlie was just going to ask a further question about this, when she looked up and saw that the Wallypug was wriggling nervously about on the throne, and that the Husher was glaring fiercely at him.

"Don't jiffle," said the Husher, "you make me giddy; what's the matter with you?"

"I'm afraid, your Majesty," said the Wallypug, standing up and speaking in a frightened voice, "that I shall have to present another petition."

"Good gracious!" said the Husher, "what do you want now? you're always wanting something or other; last week it was to have your boots mended, and the week before you wanted your hair cut, and now you want something else."

"No, your Majesty," said the Wallypug meekly, "it's the same thing. If you remember, you know, you couldn't all agree as to whether I might have it cut or not, so I had to have *part* of it cut, and now it really looks so very ridiculous, that I humbly beg that you will allow me to have the rest taken off."

There was a murmuring in the room, and then some one called out, "Take your crown off."

The Wallypug did so, and showed that on one side of his head his hair hung over his ear, while, on the other, it was quite short.

"Well, it certainly does look rather silly," said the Husher. "How much will it cost to have it cut?"

"Threepence, your Majesty," replied the Wallypug meekly.

"Too much! too much!" screamed the Cockatoo angrily. "Down with the Wallypug, down with the barbers, down with everybody and everything."

"Hold your tongue," shouted the Husher. "Well, what shall we say to the Wallypug's petition," he continued, addressing the meeting.

There was a great argument in which everybody seemed to take part at once, and, at last, it was decided that the Wallypug should wait until the *short hair* grew the *same length as the other,* and then he might have it all cut together.

Girlie thought this did not seem a very satisfactory arrangement for the Wallypug, and she felt quite sorry for him when, sighing disconsolately, and pulling his crown over his head, he sat meekly down on the throne again, looking very unhappy.

"Now," said the Husher briskly, "I beg to propose that the Wallypug invites us all to dinner."

"Hear, hear!" shouted all the animals.

"Oh! please, no," said the Wallypug nervously. "My cook would be so *very* angry with me; he can't bear me to bring a lot of people home unexpectedly."

However, the animals would take no denial, so the poor Wallypug left the hall to make arrangements with his cook while the rest of the company went home to dress for dinner, leaving Girlie alone in the room.

New Adventures of "Alice"

JOHN RAE

ILLUSTRATIONS BY THE AUTHOR

1917

JOHN RAE (1882-1963) was best known as an American illustrator and painter who painted the portraits of such luminaries as Carl Sandburg and Albert Einstein. Rae also wrote and illustrated a number of works for children. A student of the renowned author/illustrator Howard Pyle, Rae created detailed illustrations and decorations for *New Adventures of "Alice"* that are reminiscent of Pyle's ornate, Pre-Raphaelite style. Rae's sequel, like Richards's, is framed by a domestic scene in which a young girl, Betsy, longs for "more Alice." In an ensuing dream Betsy discovers a stack of "Wish There Were More Books" in the attic, including one titled "More Adventures of Alice," which comprises the rest of the novel. Alice's new adventures begin as she's reading Mother Goose Rhymes to her kittens, and include encounters with conventional nursery rhyme characters, though Rae's version of Alice's dream-world is often more chaotic and surreal than Carroll's. These new Alice adventures also contain humorous commentary on artistic and literary subculture as Alice encounters a peevish printer, a poet who speaks only in verse and writes with self-steering pens, and an artist whose "lifelike" drawings assume lives of their own.

New Adventures of "Alice"

FOREWORD

PROBABLY YOU, LIKE MYSELF, have often wished that Lewis Carroll might have found time to write another book about "Alice." Certainly most of the children who have delightedly followed her through "Wonderland" and the "Looking Glass" country have sighed regretfully when Mother finished reading the last chapter to them.

After reading the marvelous tale for perhaps the tenth time when I was a little boy, I started trying to imagine what Lewis Carroll would have written had he continued the "Adventures," and it has been great fun for me to go on with these imaginings from time to time and finally to write them down.

The children "with dreaming eyes of wonder" to whom I have related some of these "New Adventures" have frankly enjoyed them and their accompanying nonsense verses, and have helped with many stimulating questions and suggestions. This leads me to hope that even Lewis Carroll, himself, might have enjoyed some of these added "doings" of his adventurous "Alice."

And so I make no excuse or apology for what to some may at first seem my shocking assurance, and if any of my love for the dear old dog-eared volume of "Alice's Adventures in Wonderland" and "Through the Looking Glass" has crept—as I meant it should—between the lines of this humble supplement, that is excuse enough for its being. It is offered as a loving gift from thankful children to the sweet spirit of the immortal Lewis Carroll who has always seemed to me a dear, indulgent, story-telling Uncle to all children.

Caldwell, N. J.   JOHN RAE

CHAPTER I. FOUND IN THE ATTIC

"But the provoking Kitten only began on the other paw, and pretended it hadn't heard the question. Which do *you* think it was?"

Mother closed the book and Sister Betsy and Brother Billy both sighed.

"Oh dear, I wish there were more of it," said Betsy, "Isn't there another book about Alice, Mother?"

It was the fifth or sixth time that Mother had read "Alice's Adventures in Wonderland" and "Through the Looking Glass" to them out of the fat red book, and every time they had reached the end, Betsy had asked this same question.

"I'm just as sorry as you are, Dears, that there isn't," said Mother. "But even if there were we couldn't read any more tonight. It's your bed time!"

And sure enough, the old fashioned hall clock had begun to buzz and grind and click as it always did before striking the hour. "As though it were chuckling wickedly to itself," Betsy thought.

Betsy must have been thinking of "Alice" and making up for herself more Adventures and wishing there were another book all the time she was getting undressed and brushing her nice little white teeth, for when she said her prayers she added, "And please send me another book about Alice."

She had hardly got comfortably snuggled and settled into the pillow and kissed Mother and called "Good night" to Dick, the canary (who answered with a sleepy little thrill), when she found herself up in the attic looking for things "to dress up in."

The bed clothes seemed to have turned into dusty old dresses and coats which she was pulling over, looking for a little dress her Mother had worn when Mother herself was only eight years old. She knew it was somewhere in the pile of things in the attic, and would be just what she wanted to dress the part of "Alice," in a little play which she and Brother and some of the other children were going to give, perhaps, the next Saturday afternoon.

Somehow or other the dresses and coats as she handled them became smaller and stiffer and smaller still and flat, and pretty soon she realized that they weren't dresses and coats at all, but a pile of neat little books, none of which Betsy had ever seen before and which seemed to come in a sort of set. They were called "Wish There Were More" books or the "Sequel Series"— "Oh, if I only had them all on my shelves."

"Now," said Betsy to herself, "P'raps I'll find another Alice book"; and she took them up one by one with eager hands.

There was "More Robinson Crusoe!" "More Arabian Nights!" "More Grimm's Fairy Tales!" "More Wonder Clock Stories!" and oh, dreams come true! there was the book she had longed for:— "More Adventures of Alice!"

She turned the pages with trembling fingers, afraid that she might find that it was a cruel joke: but no! There were exactly the same kind of stiff little

pictures of Alice that she had loved in the battered old red book, from which Mother had just been reading. Alice doing this, or Alice doing that, and usually surrounded by strangely dressed people or creatures.

With a sigh of complete contentment, she settled herself comfortably and cosily on a moth-eaten old buffalo robe in a corner nearest the half-moon attic window and started to read. In her dream she seemed to change and become dear, quaint little Alice herself, and be *living* and *acting* in the story, instead of simply reading it.

What follows is what she read, and the pictures that follow are those she looked at in that "Wish There Were More" book. For Betsy has often and often told me all about that wonderful dream of hers.

CHAPTER 2. TO BUNBERRY CROSS, OR ALONG CAME A SNIPE
(Really Chapter I of the book Betsy found in the attic, in her dream)

It was a sleepy, spring-time Sunday afternoon.

Alice was lying on the grass near the garden-house reading Mother Goose Rhymes to her kittens who were tumbling about near her in the slanting yellow sunshine. (She often pretended the kittens were small children.) Just now she was reading "Ding Dong Bell, Pussy's in the Well."

"I'm sure you'll like this one and it *may* prove a warning to you," she said.

Her sister was sitting on the garden-house step making a pretty little sketch of a blossoming hawthorne tree which stood in the corner of the hedge at the foot of the garden.

Over the hedge they could see the church spire across the river. Somewhere far off a bell was ringing. Its sweetly sleepy sound mingled with the scent of blossoms and the droning of Alice's voice very harmoniously.

She had just come to the line "What a naughty boy was that"—when she noticed a bird with a straw in its beak alighting on the hedge nearby. Alice stopped reading to watch him for she always liked to find out where nests were being built. The bird was a very sprightly little fellow, cocking his head from side to side and looking directly at Alice with remarkably intelligent bright eyes.

"Why," thought Alice, "he looks as if he were actually going to speak!" And sure enough, he did!

"Wonderful view from here," said the bird casually in a rather muffled voice. Alice now saw it was a Snipe, much larger than she had at first supposed, and that instead of a straw he held in his beak a long clay pipe from which a thin wisp of bluish smoke was curling, and which probably caused the indistinct mumbling voice.

The hedge, too, seemed to be changing strangely, it was growing higher and higher, and soon she saw it was a hedge no longer, but a grove of tall oaks, and the muffled voice of the Snipe now sounded very far away indeed.

"I've something important to ask you. Do you—" she thought she heard him say and then she could not catch any more. Though he was still to be seen on one of the topmost branches of the tree nearest her.

Now Alice was a very polite little girl, and it seemed to her that the only right thing for her to do was to climb the tree and find out what it was that the Snipe wished to know. So she was very pleased to see a narrow spiral stairway, which she had certainly not noticed before, winding up around the trunk. She placed her foot upon the lowest step and grasped the rail, and was greatly surprised to find that the railing seemed to be moving spirally upward; pulling her along, at first slowly and gently but getting faster and faster, so that by the time she was half way up the tree her feet were no longer touching the steps at all. Somehow though, the sensation was rather pleasant and she felt no alarm. She even kept calm enough to notice that, as the trunk apparently slid down past her, little bird faces appeared at open, curtained windows here and there, and one old-lady black-bird in a blue sunbonnet called out as Alice shot past—"Hoity, toity, my dear child, there's *really* no such hurry, you know."

Faster and faster she went, so that when the tree-top was reached she could not seem to stop, but went right on up into the air quite a ways and then gently floated down (her skirt spreading out like a parachute and supporting her) and finally alighted on the topmost branch, right beside the Snipe.

Talking to the Snipe was a curious little fellow with a big, round, shiny face and very slender little legs and arms. In one hand he carried a covered basket and in the other a big blue handkerchief, decorated with little white stars. In his belt was a great cheese knife. His round face was shining with perspiration and from time to time he mopped it with the blue handkerchief.

"He looks as though he had come a long way," thought Alice.

As she settled herself on the swaying branch and smoothed out her skirt, the Snipe was saying thoughtfully, puffing hard on his pipe, "Norrich, Norrich?—Now—let—me—see—I *should* know, and that's a fact—Perhaps *she* can tell you!" he exclaimed, brightening.

The Man in the Moon (for of course Alice knew now that it must be he) turned respectfully to her. "Your pardon, Miss, but could you, perhaps, tell me as how I could get to Norrich? I'm anxious to get there before night-fall, that I am, Miss."

"He speaks exactly like the nice old farmer who comes around to sell us cheese," thought Alice.

"And that's just what he does," put in the Snipe, just as if she had said it aloud. "Of course, you know," he continued, "the moon's made of green cheese and," pointing to the Man in the Moon, "he peddles it. Give her a sample."

"Certainly, Miss, to be sure," beamed the Man in the Moon, "and no obligation to buy neither, Miss."

He opened his basket and taking his knife from his belt cut off a thin slice of the most beautiful and curious cheese that Alice had ever seen. It was soft and glowed with a greenish-silver light, and when she bit into it! "It was like eating marshmallows dipped in moonlight," she said afterwards.

Alice was just about to take a second bite when she remembered that the Moon Man's courteous question had not been answered, and she started to direct him as well as she could; but somehow her geography lessons and some directions she had heard the gardener give a wagon driver the day before became hopelessly mixed in her mind and she found herself saying, "Norrich is a town of seven thousand inhabitants in the north eastern part of Norfolk on the river Yare. You take the road to the right as far as Earle's Bridge and follow the river to the old Exton Mill—settled in the year thirteen hundred and forty—turn to the left and the principal exports are—" She stopped, realizing how absurdly she was talking and intending to say, "No, that's not at all what I meant."

But the jolly little man had already started. He was not flying, but stepping briskly along "on nothing at all," swinging his basket, and Alice could just hear him anxiously repeating part of her ridiculous directions—"to old Exton Mill, settled in thirteen hundred and forty—"

She called after him, but he evidently did not hear for he kept straight ahead and soon disappeared behind a great flock of black-birds.

The Snipe shook his head sadly and blew tremendous puffs of whirling smoke from his pipe in silence for a while, but finally he sighed—"Poor fellow! *Poor* fellow, but I dare say he'll happen on the finger-post and then he can get to *Babylon* anyhow; that is, of course, if he has a candle about him."

"What good would *that* do him?" asked Alice, anxiously, for she was quite worried about the Man in the Moon. She naturally felt responsible and guilty. Of course, she hadn't really meant to give him those absurd directions. "I don't believe I even got the population right," she said to herself, helplessly.

"Why, Silly, you can always get to Babylon by candle light," replied the Snipe, severely. "And you ought to know it." "Great view," he added absently, as if to change the subject.

Now for the first time Alice looked down. How changed everything was! The gravel garden path had become a dusty road winding under the oaks, and in place of her sister there was a strange little man in very baggy clothes and a flowing necktie so long that the ends hung down almost to the ground. He was busily sketching just as her sister had been.

Alice, although she was ever so high up in the tree-tops, could somehow or other see just what he was drawing on his little pad. This was what she saw—

"Why, it's the Old Lady 'with Rings on her Fingers and Bells on Her Toes,' just like the picture in my Mother Goose," she exclaimed delightedly.

"Yes, he drew us all, drat him," murmured the Snipe, crossly. "He made one of my wings shorter than the other, too!"

When the artist's picture was finished it seemed immediately to grow to natural size and come to life.

By this time Alice was quite used to unusual happenings, and about the only thing that could have startled her very much would have been for something to look "just everydayish" or act in a perfectly normal manner. She was not at all surprised, therefore, to see the white hobby horse start off down the road with a rocking sort of gait, the old lady in her familiar spotted dress and strange bonnet jouncing up and down on his back and in a cloud of dust.

Alice could just catch the faint jingling of the "bells on her toes."

"This must be the road to Banbury Cross, then," said Alice, half aloud.

"*Bun*berry Cross," corrected the Snipe, kindly. "No fault of yours, my child, the Printer ran out of U's, that's all. You see it's where they make the hot cross berry-buns. You'd never say, 'hot cross *bans*.' No, certainly not! In the first place it would never rhyme with *sons*, and in the second pla—but no matter. What do you think of the view?"

And pointing to the artist with his pipe, "He drew it all—all the houses and trees and the hills just as he had to draw all of us, birds and animals and people."

Now Alice knew why it was that the landscape looked "strangely familiar"; it, too, was like the pictures in her Mother Goose! But also quite a little like Wonderland and the strange Looking Glass country that she had once dreamt about.

"Isn't it hilly?" Alice began; "and what's that——"

"Of course! It has to be hilly," interrupted the Snipe, impatiently. "There's got to be Jack and Jill's Hill and Blackbird's Hill and the Hill the Old Woman lived under and Pippin Hill and all the rest of the Hills."

Now, ever since Alice had reached the tree-top, a far-away bell had been ringing, just as one had rung before she left the garden and her Sister and the Kittens. (And Dear, Dear! how long ago that did seem.) Alice wondered idly what the bell could be.

"It's the bellman over at Bunberry Cross, I'm pretty sure," said the Snipe, who always seemed good at guessing just what one was going to say. "Probably somebody's stolen something or other and the King has offered a reward for the capture of the thief. There's lots of thieves among 'em, Tom, the Piper's Son, who stole the pig, and dozens more. Why, even one of their Kings, years ago, stole some barley meal for a bag pudding!"

"What a bad example," exclaimed Alice.

"Let's go and see what the row's about," suggested the Snipe. "I've got to return this pipe anyway. Of course that pipe business was just a practical joke. I hope you didn't think *I* was a thief." He looked anxiously at Alice, then added more brightly, "Bombay's the next village beyond and the Old Man's a great friend of King Cole's—in fact, he's Prime Minister.

"Let's start—Ever fly?"

Before Alice realized what was happening, the Snipe had given her a gentle push and she found herself awkwardly floundering about in the air, not exactly frightened but a bit cross that the Snipe should have given her no warning.

"Well, I don't think *that* was very nice, and I did so want to see what the artist was going to draw next," said she.

"It's the only way to ever learn to fly or swim," said the Snipe, amiably but decidedly; "try it more this way,—that's better." And then as if to put her in a better humor he began to sing—as well as possible with the pipe still in his mouth—

> "You never know what you can do till you try;
> A girl like a bird may be able to fly;
> A bird like a fly may be able to buzz;
> Things stranger have happened and every day does.
> I've heard many times (I have proofs if you wish)
> A deaf and dumb oyster can sing like a fish!—"

"But fish can't sing," interrupted Alice, who by this time was managing to fly fairly well and was going remarkably fast—she had to keep a little ahead of the Snipe, as the smoke trailing from the pipe was very choking and blinding.

"What's their scales for then, I'd like to know?" snapped the Snipe; and after a moment he added, triumphantly, "Some of 'em fly anyhow! But don't interrupt again or we'll never get there."

Alice couldn't see just what the Song had to do with getting them there, but said nothing, and the bird continued—

> "Why how, let me ask you, my
> dear, do you s'pose
> I learned to smoke pipes, and
> to eat with my nose?
> There's one thing, however,
> that cannot be done
> With all of your trying, that's
> this—
> Have a bun."

The strangest thing had happened! They were "bumping into a flock of buns" as the Snipe expressed it. The air was full of hot cross buns which seemed to be floating up from an open window of a house on the outskirts of the village far below them.

"That's the baker's shop and there's the butcher's and there's the candlestick maker's," said the Snipe.

Alice saw that they were now right over a little village. She had been too busy listening to the Snipe to realize how fast they had approached it.

"Drop 'em a penny, drop 'em a penny!" called the Snipe, and then in his effort to snatch one of the floating buns with his beak lost the pipe which fell through the air, leaving behind it a trail of blue smoke.

"Now I'm in a pretty pickle and no mistake," he mumbled in a scared voice. "I didn't mean to keep the old pipe, it was just a joke—"

"But here we are!" cried Alice between bites—she had caught two of the buns which were still very warm and wonderfully light. "Perhaps that's why they float away," she thought.

"Yes, here we are!"

And, sure enough, they were hovering directly over the village green where a may pole stood decked out with streamers and flowers ready for the dance. It was just like one Alice had seen a few days before on their village green at home.

Then she saw that the bell, whose ding donging had been growing louder and louder as they had approached the village, was being rung by the Bellman or "Town Crier" who stopped his ringing now and then to bawl out:

"Has anyone seen Master Thomas B. Green?
Be he dead or alive, the reward is two 'n five!"

"Let's stop here," said Alice, clutching at the may pole to stop her flight. (You see she had never practiced alighting gracefully.)

She swung 'round and 'round and 'round and 'round. Petals from the blossom wreaths were shaken off and floated down all about her. When she softly struck the ground after her long spiral descent no one seemed to have noticed her, for the Bellman was the center of attraction. All the strange townsfolk and animals were crowding about him listening to his bawling, or talking together in excited groups.

When she looked about her for the Snipe he was nowhere to be seen, but finally she spied him perched on the very top of the may pole. He seemed agitated and was whispering something hoarsely to her, but she could only make out the words— "Don't dare to come down," and "They'll put me in jail" and "I'll see you some time again"—Then he flapped heavily away and Alice suddenly felt very lonesome and just a little "scared."

Chapter 3. The Peevish Printer

"It makes me sick! Absolutely sick!" exclaimed a small peevish voice at Alice's elbow. "They ought to have let me print 'em some neat hand bills to stick up at every corner instead of having all this hubbub."

Turning, Alice saw a little spectacled man almost bald, with a very inky apron and the dirtiest hands she had ever seen. She simply couldn't help looking at them a little disapprovingly, as her Mother looked at *hers* sometimes.

He did not seem to notice her reproving glance, however, but continued to exclaim, "It makes me sick!" more bitterly than before, now putting his hands over his ears as if to shut out the din made by the Town Crier's bawling and the noisy bell. Of course when he did this his ears and cheeks became almost as dirty as his hands, and Alice found herself saying, "Now just look at your face!"

"Don't be ridiculous," said the little man. "How can I look at my face? That's for *you* to do! There are no mirrors in this town anyhow, even if I *wanted* to look at my face, which I don't. You see King Cole—but that's a long story, perhaps I have it with me."

"I'm a Printer, as you may have guessed; that is, I'm a Printer *most* of the time. *Fair time* I sell pies—have to make a living *somehow*, you know."

"Oh, then you're the Pieman!" exclaimed Alice.

"Yes—but Pastry Purveyor would have sounded much better, don't you think so? Looked well in print, too."

He had been fumbling in his pocket and now fished out a folded sheet of very soiled paper which he carefully spread out on the grass.

"This isn't it, I'm afraid," he murmured, "but it will do *pretty* well."

It was the strangest page of print Alice had ever seen. She could make nothing of it except the title at the top which was Printer's Pi—in very black capital letters.

"But even that's spelled wrong," she said to herself. "It should be PI*E*."

The rest was a jumble of letters and figures and punctuation marks of all kinds and sizes, something like this:—

```
        Printer's Pi
:7xumllq  ,,ffneosn6uri  fussiop
8—..  4pa55  n%@W  (h;TP #9
:beic?SI.   —S pvhr—5.   X ufram
tuPL#7.–)-vdgsyainby   PT.;$£
tcb yjO : ; bfhySRVTGY#3—4(7
.a,Ohf6%cRVhin#2.yuth43′/:p
.19n?b6h5g4c$2x  —invbg
```

"Perhaps it's a puzzle?"

"It looks very interesting and like some foreign language," said Alice, doubtfully. "But what *does* it mean?"

"That's what I was hoping *you'd* be able to tell *me*," said the Printer, thoughtfully tapping the paper as though to shake the jumble of letters into some more readable arrangement.

"Children usually know all about pie. You see, I have to print this sort of thing now and then just to keep busy now that they have a Town Crier," he added apologetically.

"I wish I had a piece of *apple* pie right this minute," sighed Alice, suddenly reminded that she was very hungry in spite of the two flying buns she had eaten.

"You *ought* to've come at Fair time you know," said the Printer; "but perhaps we can manage it, it's only a matter of spelling after all."

He drew from the huge pocket in his apron a very compactly folded up little printing press and some small sheets of paper; found an E—which he inked with the palm of his hand—and printed it carefully after the PI of the title, making it PIE.

"They're kicking up such a noise I almost forgot how to spell," he muttered to himself. "Don't want to see you go hungry, though, and I'll do the best I can for you. But show me first your penny," he added absent-mindedly.

While he talked he had been tearing the paper into the form of scalloped circle like this

—and finally handed it to her.

Alice was somehow not in the least surprised that the paper pie had become brown and warm and fragrant and the letters P I E had turned into the usual row of cuts in the crust.

She handed him a penny which he took and examined with great inter-est turning it over and over and murmuring in a hoarse whisper,—"Very pretty,—very pretty—a good likeness, too—very good indeed."

Alice had noticed that his voice had been growing hoarser and hoarser as he talked. It was now scarcely audible.

When he had thoroughly examined the coin he put it back into her hand, pushing it away without a word when she tried to return it to him. He then started setting type with great rapidity and slipping a small piece of pa-per into the press he jammed down the lever, raised it again and pulled out this neatly printed little slip:

> I said, "*show* me your penny".
> Not, "*give* me your penny."

"Oh!" said Alice, "so you did."

This seemed to her a strange way of carrying on a conversation but, "After all," she said to herself, "it's really a very nice sort of a game. I wonder if he usually talks this way?"

The Printer seemed to have read her thoughts, for in the twinkling of an eye he had printed another little slip like this:

> Well, in the first place, as you see, my voice is rather weak;
> It very rapidly becomes a whisper, so to speak.
> Just think how handy it might be to print, instead of talk,
> If I should fall into the sea:
> "Help! Help!" I'd never squawk.
> Not I, I'd print some circulars
> (In bold faced type display)
>
> **"Your kind assistance is required;**
> **I'm sinking in the bay."**
> Or, if I took to me a wife,
> Stone deaf; of course, you see
> In converse, then, how indispensable my press would be!

"That sounds very reasonable, I must say," mused Alice.

> Of *course* it's reasonable

said (or rather printed) the peevish Printer, petulantly; then something seemed to occur to him. He smiled mysteriously and printed this—("That tiny type looks just like a whisper," thought Alice).

This is a secret!
I'm the man who printed Mother Goose! This is a rhyme the Poet   wrote about me.

> Printer Man, Printer Man, print me a book;
> Tell what a great Man am I;
> Make me a Hero, by hook or by crook,
> Or I'll beat you and blacken your eye!

I didn't just like that one (especially the part about beating me) so I simply left it out. You see I might have been twice as famous. There's just that Pie-Man rhyme about me now. Then, too, I wasn't anxious to be known as the Printer of the book either. The Poet who wrote the rhymes has had to live in hiding for years. (Some folks didn't like what he said about 'em and wanted to kill him) and they might have felt the same about me for printing what he wrote. I don't know as I'm exactly proud of being classed with that Mother Goose crowd anyway, they're a mixed lot; beggars, pigs, and pipers and very few gentlemen among 'em, you'll notice.

Alice *had* noticed that the crowd gathered about the Town Crier in the street was a strangely assorted lot (though all looked familiar), tall and short, fat and thin, beggars and fine folk, and a great many quaintly dressed old women and children. Pigs, cats, dogs and crows and other beasts and birds seemed to mingle with the rest on equal terms. One neatly shaven pig she noticed coming out of a shop, over the door of which hung a sign—

> I. SHAVEM
> Barber and Wig-maker.

She had been so interested in the printed conversation game that she had almost forgotten to eat her pie which lay on the grass beside them. Now she took it up.

"What a dear little brown pie! How good it will taste!" she thought. "Um, um! I'd better eat it before it's all cold," she thought, and politely started to offer a bite to the Printer, but saw that he was furiously busy printing a lot of little circulars on bright red paper!

When he had printed fifty or more he gathered them up and jumped to his feet. Then thrusting one into Alice's hand so excitedly that he caused her to drop the pie, he dashed off into the crowd distributing his red circulars right and left in mad haste. Even the Bellman stopped his din in amazement.

Alice looked at the scarlet sheet and read in huge capitals—

FIRE!!   FIRE!!!
FIRE!!!!

CHAPTER 4. FIRE!!

All was confusion and excitement! Some of the Mother Goose people were running in one direction and some in another. Most of the crowd were trying to squeeze through the town-gate and seemed to be hopelessly stuck in the narrow opening.

While Alice stood wondering in which direction the fire really lay, she noticed nearby a little man in green pointing excitedly with a long flute. Looking in the direction in which he was pointing she saw, through an opening between the bakery and the barber shop a thin column of smoke which seemed to come from behind a barn in a field about half a mile away.

"That must be it," thought Alice, "for where there's smoke there must be fi——."

Just then somebody collided with her so violently that she was almost knocked off her feet!

"I beg your pardon, Miss, but really you know, Miss, you should be more careful 'ow you stands about staring—that was, as you might say, a close shave. I might 'ave cut yer hear off."

It was the Barber. He held a large nicked razor and a mug of lather in one hand and an unfinished wig in the other. He was very much confused and flustered by the collision and began to mutter, "I'll never get it done. I'll never get it done, that I won't. Something halways hinterrupts."

He seemed *so* unhappy that Alice, wishing to divert his mind, bethought herself of the pie and politely offered him a bite. "Thankee Miss"—said the Barber, brightening, "a pinch or two,—a pinch or two—it's just wot I needs."

Puzzled by his words, Alice looked down at the pie and saw to her surprise that it was a pie no longer but a very large round snuff box, the cover of which still slightly resembled a piecrust, being made of yellow ivory, inlaid with flying blackbirds; the edge was scalloped.

"You're werry kind, Miss, I'm sure, you're werry kind indeed. Though I'm bound to say," he added, "as how *ladies* doesn't *usually* carry—" "Look!!" cried Alice, "who are *they*?"

Two quaint figures, a boy and a girl, were coming down the street in long leaps. It seemed to be a sort of race and the strange girl, who had just cleared the may pole in a tremendous jump, was slightly in the lead. "It'll be Jumping-Joan and Jack-be-Nimble, of course, Miss, they always gets to fires first," muttered the Barber complainingly. And then, struck by a bright idea, he shouted at the fast approaching figures, "Give us a lift! Give us a lift!" And turning to Alice, "'Itch on and 'old tight!"

The next moment Alice found herself clinging to Jack-be-Nimble's hand and leaping with him over the candlestick maker's shop. "Just like big grass-hoppers," she said to herself.

Soon they could see the fire distinctly.

"It's the King's haystack, just as I thought!" said Jack, excitedly, "and we ought to be the first ones there. I hope that big barn near the stack doesn't catch fire, for all the King's horses are in *there*."

"Maybe Boy Blue has been playing with matches," ventured Alice. "That looks like the pictures of the haystack he always takes his nap in."

"Listen! there's the new fire-alarm," cried Jack, bounding along in his excitement faster than ever, so that they really seemed not to touch the ground at all. "It's the Cat, you know. He's paid by the town according to the amount of noise he makes, and," he added with a happy sigh, "he *can* make a *deli-cious* amount when he really tries—he plays a fiddle and a pair of bagpipes at the same time!"

"Oh, there he comes now, out of the barn!" cried Alice as the caterwaul-ing din rose louder and more piercing. "And *look* at the fire *now!* Do you think——"

"It was all our fault, too," interrupted a familiar voice at her elbow, in a hoarse stage-whisper. She turned to see the Snipe who was flying along by her side; he seemed very much agitated and there was an air of mystery about him. "That is to say," he continued, "it's *really* the Baker's fault you know, for if *he* hadn't let those buns escape and fly away, *we* never would have dropped that dratted pipe." Here the Snipe hesitated a moment, looked this way and that, then getting very close to Alice's ear whispered louder than before, "*It must have been that pipe that set fire to the King's haystack!* If the Prime Minis-ter finds it out *we'll* go to the dungeons, of course."

"I don't quite see why he says, '*We* shouldn't have dropped the pipe,' and '*We'll* go to the dungeons,'" thought Alice. "*I* had nothing to do with it, I'm sure." She had begun to feel very impolite not to have introduced Jack-be-Nimble to the Snipe. Then too it seemed extremely rude for the Snipe to continue whispering to her and ignoring her companion.

"Have you met my friend,"—she began; but when she turned it was quite a different person from her leaping partner of a few moments before whose hand she now held. He was a strange little spindle legged man, rather shabby, with *very* long hair, large wistful eyes and a friendly smile.

"I'm the Poet. Jack was only a disguise. Have to do it, or they'd get me, I surmise," said he, pointing back at the crowd they had left far behind.

Alice, the Snipe, and the Poet were now walking hurriedly across a broad stubbly field toward the burning haystack. As they approached, a cloud of Lady Bugs passed over them, coming from the direction of the fire. "Poor things," said the Snipe, remorsefully to himself, "they probably lived in that haycock."

"Let's watch the blaze awhile from here, until the townsfolk get too near," suggested the Poet smiling at Alice and added, "Then we must skip, you know, my dear, all three of us have cause to fear!"

Alice now noticed for the first time that the little man wore a brass chain about his neck with a metal tag, numbered 333; she wondered what it could possibly be, but was, of course, far too polite to ask on such short acquaintance.

"My Poet's License—as you see, my number is three-thirty-three," the Poet remarked pleasantly, noticing her curiosity. "A thing I'm very proud of too,—becoming, *quite,* I think. Don't you?"

All this time the smoke from the hay was growing blacker and thicker, and the din of the fire-alarm bag-pipes was getting louder and wilder and the scraping of the cat's fiddle more shrill and piercing.

Now from the big barn nearby came sounds of trampling feet and ungrammatical shouts of "That's him! That's him! There he is!" And what seemed to Alice like *hundreds* of archers, each with a big gold crown embroidered on his left sleeve, rushed pell-mell out of the big barn door.

"We're lost! Alack a day, friends, we must flee! All the King's men! I know they're after me," exclaimed the Poet.

"It's *me* they're after, neighbor, if you must know," said the Snipe a little jealously. "*I* dropped the pipe that caused this fire in the King's hay."

Alice was a little frightened, it must be confessed, and *very* impatient at the Poet and the Snipe for waiting to talk when it did seem as though they should all have been running for their lives!

The Archers had drawn up in line in front of the barn and one who seemed to be their captain stepped forward and gave the commands, "Ready! * * * * Aim! – – – – – –"

The Poet turned to Alice excitedly and whispered very rapidly, "I have a plan. We'll wait until they shoot; each grab a shaft and out of danger scoot, then"—

"Fire!" yelled the captain of the King's men, and the air was full of flying arrows.

"All aboard! Don't be slow. Hold on tight! Home we go," shouted the Poet.

Whirrrr—an arrow whizzed by close to Alice's head, and following the suggestion of the Poet, she grasped it as it flew past and scrambled aboard. "An *arrow* escape," she heard the Snipe chuckle. The goose feather tip made a very comfortable springy seat and she could hold firmly to the shaft near the head.

The arrow was going at a frightful speed, and the Wind whistled behind Alice's ears; in fact, it whistled a real tune, "London Bridge." "And very prettily too," thought Alice. "I wonder if 'Blue Bells of Scotland' comes next, as it does on my music box?"

She had just turned to see if the Poet and Snipe were anywhere near her when suddenly everything grew black as night and she realized that they had dived into the thick cloud of smoke from the fire. Alice clutched the arrow tighter. "For," she said to herself, "it *would* be nasty to fall into the fire with this clean pinafore on."

Somehow the shaft of the arrow had grown softer and feathery and when Alice looked down she saw that it was now a fat grey goose she rode! The goose seemed to have lost her way in the dense smoke and was flying hither and thither in an aimless fashion.

The smoky darkness was full of sparks. "Or are they stars?" she wondered. "And isn't that the light from a little window way off there?" The goose seemed to have seen the lighted window too, for she stopped darting about and flew very rapidly in that direction, murmuring half under her breath, "That's the house I'm sure, I smell the cakes aburning."

As they came nearer Alice saw that the light came from a tiny little thatched cottage, built high in the air, on four tremendously long poles.

"Why it's all upstairs," she exclaimed.

"To prove that I'm erratic, I built my house all attic," said a voice near at hand; and there was the Poet flying along beside her on a goose exactly like hers.

Uncle Wiggily in Wonderland

HOWARD R. GARIS

ILLUSTRATION BY EDWARD BLOOMFIELD

1916

HOWARD R. GARIS (1873-1962) was a prolific inventor, entrepreneur, and children's writer, originator not only of the well-known Uncle Wiggily stories, games, and toys, but of many other popular novels and novel series for children. These range from science fiction and boys' adventure stories to animal fantasy and domestic tales, including the *Curley Top, Rocket Rider,* and *Teddy* series. Garis also worked for more than fifty years (from 1896 to 1947) as a reporter and feature writer for the *Newark (N.J.) Evening News,* where he first began publishing his "Uncle Wiggily Longears" stories in 1910. The tales, for which Garis coined the term "bedtime stories," were immensely popular, and gained an even wider audience when they were syndicated in other newspapers and again, later, when Garis began reading them over the radio. Altogether, Garis was the author of over three hundred books, including more than thirty-five Uncle Wiggily books (producing a total of almost fifteen thousand Uncle Wiggily stories). It is little wonder, then, that Garis often turned to the work of other writers for inspiration, including that of Lewis Carroll. Uncle Wiggily, like Alice, has remained an important and enduring icon in children's literature. Though the tales in *Uncle Wiggily in Wonderland* are not as complex and original as many of the other literary responses to Carroll's *Alice* books, they are notable in their reworking of the *Alice* tales to agree with Garis's and Uncle Wiggily's lively optimism and good humor, as well as with Garis's consciousness of the war in Europe, which the United States would enter the next year.

Uncle Wiggily in Wonderland

UNCLE WIGGILY AND WONDERLAND ALICE

ONCE UPON A TIME, after Uncle Wiggily Longears, the nice bunny rabbit gentleman, had some funny adventures with Baby Bunty, and when he found that his rheumatism did not hurt him so much as he hopped on his red, white and blue striped barber pole crutch, the bunny uncle wished he might have some strange and wonderful adventures.

"I think I'll just hop along and look for a few," said Uncle Wiggily to himself one morning. He twinkled his pink nose, and then he was all ready to start.

"Good-bye, Nurse Jane! Good-bye!" he called to his muskrat lady housekeeper, with whom he lived in a hollow stump bungalow. "I'm going to look for some wonderful adventures!" He hopped down the front steps, with his red, white and blue striped crutch under one paw, and his tall, silk hat on his head. "Good-bye, Miss Fuzzy Wuzzy!"

"Good-bye!" answered Nurse Jane. "I hope you have some nice adventures!"

"Thanks, I wish you the same," answered Uncle Wiggily, and away he went over the fields and through the woods. He had not hopped very far, looking this way and that, before, all of a sudden, he came to a queer little place, near an old rail fence. Down in one corner was a hole, partly underground.

"Ha! That's queer," said Uncle Wiggily to himself. "That looks just like the kind of an underground house, or burrow, where I used to live. I wonder if this can be where I made my home before I moved to the hollow stump bungalow? I must take a look. Nurse Jane would like to hear all about it."

So Uncle Wiggily, folding back his ears in order that they would not get bent over and broken, began crawling down the rabbit hole, for that is what it really was.

It was dark inside, but the bunny uncle did not mind that, being able to see in the dark. Besides, he could make his pink nose twinkle when he wanted to, and this gave almost as much light as a firefly.

"No, this isn't the burrow where I used to live," said Uncle Wiggily to himself, when he had hopped quite a distance into the hole. "But it's very nice. Perhaps I may have an adventure here. Who knows?"

And just as he said that to himself, Uncle Wiggily saw, lying under a little table, in what seemed to be a room of the underground house, a small glass box.

290

"Ha! My adventure begins!" cried Uncle Wiggily. "I'll open that glass box and see what is in it."

So the bunny uncle raised the cover, and in the glass box was a little cake, made of carrots and cabbage, and on top, spelled out in pink raisins, were the words:

"Eat Me!"

"Ha! That's just what I'll do!" cried jolly Uncle Wiggily, and, never stopping to think anything might be wrong, the bunny gentleman ate the cake. And then, all of a sudden, he began to feel very funny.

"Oh, my!" exclaimed Uncle Wiggily. "I hope that cake didn't belong to my nephew, Sammie Littletail, or Johnnie or Billie Bushytail, the squirrel brothers. One of them may have lost it out of his lunch basket on his way to school. I hope it wasn't any of their cake. But there is surely something funny about it, for I feel so very queer!"

And no wonder! For Uncle Wiggily had suddenly begun to grow very large. His ears grew taller, so that they lifted his tall silk hat right off his head. His legs seemed as long as bean poles, and as for his whiskers and pink, twinkling nose, they seemed so far away from his eyes that he wondered if he would ever get them near enough to see to comb the one, or scratch the other when it felt ticklish.

"This is certainly remarkable!" cried Uncle Wiggily. "I wonder what made me grow so large all of a sudden? Could it have been the cake which gave me the indyspepsia?"

"It was the cake!" cried a sudden and buzzing voice, and, looking around the hole Uncle Wiggily saw a big mosquito. "It was the cake that made you grow big," went on the bad biting bug, "and I put it here for you to eat."

"What for?" asked the bunny uncle, puzzled like.

"So you would grow so big that you couldn't get out of this hole," was the answer. "And now you can't! This is how I have caught you! Ha! Ha!" and the mosquito buzzed a most unpleasant laugh.

"Oh, dear!" thought Uncle Wiggily. "I wonder if I am caught? Can't I get out as I got in?"

Quickly he hopped to the front of the hole. But alas! Likewise sorrowfulness! He had grown so big from eating the magical cake that he could not possibly squeeze out of the hole through which he had crawled into the underground burrow.

"Now I have caught you!" cried the mosquito. "Since we could not catch you at your soldier tent or in the trenches near your hollow stump bungalow,

I thought of this way. Now we have you and we'll bite you!" and the big mosquito, who with his bad friends had dug the hole on purpose to get Uncle Wiggily in a trap, began to play a bugle tune on his wings to call the other biting bugs.

"Oh, dear!" thought Uncle Wiggily. "I guess I am caught! And I haven't my talcum powder pop gun that shoots beanbag bullets! Oh, if I could only get out of here!"

"You can get out, Uncle Wiggily," said a soft little voice down toward the end of his pink, twinkling nose. "You can get out!"

"Oh, no, I can't!" the bunny said. "I am much too large to squeeze out of the hole by which I came in here. Much too large. Oh, dear!"

"Here, drink some of this and you'll grow small just as I did when I drank from it before I fell into the pool of tears," the soft and gentle voice went on, and to Uncle Wiggily's surprise, there stood a nice little girl with long, flaxen hair. She was holding out to him a bottle with a tag that read:

"DRINK ME."

"Am I really to drink this?" asked the bunny.

"You are," said the little girl.

Uncle Wiggily took a long drink from the bottle. It tasted like lollypop ice cream soda, and no sooner had he taken a good sip than all of a sudden he found himself shutting up small, like a telescope. Smaller and smaller he shrank, until he was his own regular size, and then the little girl took him by the paw and cried:

"Come on! Now you can get out!"

And, surely enough, Uncle Wiggily could.

"But who are you?" he asked the little girl.

"Oh! I'm Alice from Wonderland," she said, "and I know you very well, though you never met me before. I'm in a book, but this is my holiday, so I came out. Come on, now, before the mosquitoes catch us! We'll have a lot of funny adventures with some friends of mine. Come on!" And away ran Uncle Wiggily with Wonderland Alice, who had saved him from being bitten. So everything came out all right, you see.

And if the teacup doesn't lose its handle and try to do a foxtrot waltz with the soup tureen, I'll tell you next about Uncle Wiggily and the March Hare.

UNCLE WIGGILY AND THE MARCH HARE

"Well, Uncle Wiggily, you certainly did have quite a time, didn't you," said Nurse Jane Fuzzy Wuzzy, the muskrat lady housekeeper for the rabbit gentleman as they both sat on the porch of the hollow stump bungalow one morning. It was the day after the bunny rabbit had been caught in the mosquito hole, where he swelled up too big to get out, after eating cake from the glass box, as I told you in the first story.

Then Alice from Wonderland happened along and gave Uncle Wiggily a drink from a magical little bottle so that he grew small enough to crawl out of the hole again.

"Yes, I had a wonderful time with Alice," said the rabbit gentleman. "It was quite an adventure."

"What do you s'pose was in the cake to make you swell up so large?" asked Nurse Jane.

"Cream puffs," answered Uncle Wiggily. "They're very swell-like, you know."

"Of course," agreed Nurse Jane. "And what was in the bottle to make you grow smaller?"

"Alum water," Uncle Wiggily made reply. "That's very shrinking, you know, and puckery."

"Of course," spoke Nurse Jane again, "I might have guessed it. Now I suppose you're off again?"

"Off to have another adventure," went on Uncle Wiggily, with a jolly laugh. "I hope I meet Alice again. I wonder where she lives?"

"Why, she's out of a book," said Nurse Jane. "I used to read about her to Sammie Littletail, when he was quite a little rabbit chap."

"Oh, yes, to be sure," said Uncle Wiggily. "Alice from Wonderland is like Mother Goose, Sinbad the Sailor and my other Arabian Night friends. Well, I hope I meet some of them and have another adventure now," and away he hopped down the front steps of his bungalow as spry as though he never had had the rheumatism.

The bad mosquitoes that used to live over in the swamp had gone away on their summer vacation, and so they did not bother the bunny rabbit just at present. He no longer had to practice being a soldier and stand on guard against them.

Pretty soon, as Uncle Wiggily hopped along, he came to a little place in the woods, all set around with green trees, and in the center was a large doll's tea table, all ready for a meal.

"Ha! This looks like an adventure already!" said the bunny uncle to himself. "And there's a party," he went on, as he saw the little girl named Alice, a March Hare (which is a sort of spring rabbit), a hatter man, with a very large hat, much larger than Uncle Wiggily's, on his head, and a dormouse. A dormouse (or doormouse) is one that crawls out under a door, you know, to get away from the cat.

"Oh, here's Uncle Wiggily!" cried Alice. "Come right along and sit down. We didn't expect you!"

"Then if I'm unexpected, perhaps there isn't room for me," spoke Uncle Wiggily, looking at the March Hare.

"Oh, yes, there's plenty of room—more room than there is to eat," said the spring rabbit. "Besides, we really knew you were coming."

As this was just different from what Alice had said, Uncle Wiggily did not know what to believe.

"You see, it's the unexpected that always happens," went on the March Hare, "and, of course, being unexpected, you happened along, so we're glad to see you."

"Only there isn't anything to eat," said Alice. "You see, the Hatter's watch only keeps one kind of time—"

"That's what I do when I dance," interrupted Uncle Wiggily.

"We haven't come to that yet," Alice spoke gently. "But as the Hatter's watch only keeps tea-time we're always at the tea table, and the cake and tea were eaten long ago."

"And we always have to sit here, hoping the Hatter's watch will start off again, and bring us to breakfast or dinner on time," said the March Hare, who, Uncle Wiggily noticed, began to look rather mad and angry. "He's greased it with the best butter, but still his watch has stopped," the hare added.

"It's on account of the hard crumbs that got in the wheels," said the Hatter, dipping his watch in the cream pitcher. "I dare say they'll get soaked in time. But pass Uncle Wiggily the buns," he added, and Alice passed an empty plate which once had dog biscuits on, only Jackie and Peetie Bow Wow had eaten them all up—I should say down, for they swallowed them that way.

Uncle Wiggily was beginning to think this was a very queer tea party indeed, when, all of a sudden, out from the bushes jumped a great, big, pink-striped Wabberjocky cat, who began singing:

"London Bridge is falling up,
    On Yankee Doodle Dandy!
As we go 'round the mulberry bush
    To buy a stick of candy."

"Well, what do you want?" asked the Mad March Hare of the Wabberjocky. "If you've come to wash the dishes you can't, for it's still tea time and it never will be anything else as long as he keeps dipping his watch in the molasses jug! That's what makes it so sticky-slow," and he tossed a tea biscuit at the Hatter, who caught it in his hat, just like a magician in the theater, and turned it into a lemon meringue pie.

"I've come for Uncle Wiggily!" cried the Wabberjocky. "I've come to take him off to my den, and then—"

Uncle Wiggily was just going to hide under the table, which he noticed was growing smaller and smaller, and he was wondering if it would be large enough to cover him, when—

All of a sudden the Mad March Hare caught up the bunny uncle's red, white and blue striped rheumatism crutch, and cried:

"You've come for Uncle Wiggily, have you? Well, we've no time for that!" and with this the March Hare smashed the crutch down on the Hatter's watch, "Bang!" breaking it all to pieces!

"There, I guess it'll go now!" cried the March Hare, and indeed the wheels of the watch went spinning while the spring suddenly uncurled, and one end, catching around Uncle Wiggily's left hind leg, flew out and tossed him safely away over the trees, until he fell down on his soft soldier tent, right in front of his own hollow stump bungalow. So he was saved from the Wabberjocky.

"Well! That was an adventure!" cried the bunny uncle. "I wonder what happened to the rest of them? I must find out." And if the laundry man doesn't let the plumber take the bath tub away for the gold fish to play tag in, I'll tell you next about Uncle Wiggily and the Cheshire Cat.

Uncle Wiggily and the Cheshire Cat

Uncle Wiggily Longears, the rabbit gentleman, was hopping along through the woods one day, wondering what sort of an adventure he would have, and he was thinking about Alice in Wonderland and what a queer tea party he had been to the day before, when the Mad March Hare smashed the Hatter's watch because the hands always stayed at 5 o'clock tea time.

"If anything like that is going to happen to me today," said the bunny uncle to himself, "I ought to have brought Nurse Jane Fuzzy Wuzzy along, so she could enjoy the fun. I'll just hop along and if anything queer starts I'll go back after her."

So he went on a little farther, and, all of a sudden, he saw, lying on the woodland path, a piece of cheese.

"Ha!" cried Uncle Wiggily. "I wonder if Jollie or Jillie Longtail, the mouse children, dropped that out of their trap? I'll take it to them, I guess."

He picked up the bit of cheese, thinking how glad the mousie boy and girl would be to have it back, when, all at once, he heard behind him a voice asking:

"Oh, did you find it? I'm so glad, thank you!" and from under a bush out stepped a cat wearing a large smile on the front of its face. The cat stretched out its claw and took the bit of cheese from Uncle Wiggily.

"Oh! Is that yours?" asked the bunny gentleman, in surprise.

"It's Cheshire cheese; isn't it?" asked the cat.

"I—I believe so," answered the bunny. "Yes," he added as he looked and made sure, "it is Cheshire cheese."

"Then, as I'm the Cheshire cat it's mine. Cheshire cat meet your cheese! Cheese, meet your cat! How do you do? So glad to see you!" and the cat shook paws with the cheese just as if Uncle Wiggily had introduced them.

"I dare say it's all right," went on the bunny uncle.

"Of course it is!" laughed the cat, smiling more than ever. "I'm so glad you found my cheese. I was afraid the March Hare had taken it for that silly 5 o'clock tea party. But I'm glad he didn't. At first I took you for the March Hare. You look like him, being a rabbit."

"My birthday is not in March, it is in April," said Uncle Wiggily, bowing.

"That's better," spoke the Cheshire cat. "You have done me a great favor by finding my cheese, and I hope to be able to do you one some day."

"Pray do not mention it," spoke the bunny uncle, modest like and shy, as he always was. He was just going to ask about Alice in Wonderland when the cat ran away with the cheese.

"Never mind," thought Uncle Wiggily. "That was the beginning of an adventure, anyhow. I wonder what the next part will be?" He did not have long to wait.

All of a sudden, as he was walking along through the woods, sort of leaning on his red, white and blue striped barber pole rheumatism crutch, there was a rustling in the bushes and out popped a whole lot of hungry rats.

"Ah, there IT is!" cried one rat, seizing hold of Uncle Wiggily by his ears.

"Yes, and just in time, too!" cried another, grabbing the bunny by his paws. "Into our den with IT before the mouse trap comes along and takes IT away from us!"

With that the rats, of which there were about five hundred and sixteen, began hustling Uncle Wiggily down a hole in the ground, and the first he knew they had him inside a wooden room in an underground house and they locked the door, taking the key out.

"What does this mean?" cried the bunny uncle. "Why do you treat me this way?"

"Why, IT can speak!" cried several of the rats, in surprise.

"Of course I can!" cried Uncle Wiggily, his pink nose twinkling. "But why do you call me IT?"

"Because you are a piece of cheese," said one rat, "and we always call cheese IT."

"Cheese? I, cheese?" asked astonished Uncle Wiggily.

"Of course," cried the biggest rat of all. "You're Cheshire cheese. Why, you perfume the whole room! We're so hungry for you. We thought the grocer had forgotten to send you. But it's all right now. Oh, what a delightful meal we shall have. We love Cheshire cheese," and the rats in the room with Mr. Longears looked very hungrily at the bunny uncle—very hungrily indeed.

"Oh, what shall I do?" thought Uncle Wiggily. "I see what has happened. When I picked up the Cheshire cat's piece of Cheshire cheese some of the perfume from it must have stuck to my paws. The rats smelled that and think I'm it. IT!" murmured the bunny gentleman. "As if I were a game of tag! IT!"

The rats in the locked room were very busy, getting out their cheese knives and plates, and poor Uncle Wiggily hardly knew what to do with this most unpleasant adventure happening to him, when, all of a sudden, right in the middle of the room, there appeared a big, smiling mouth, with a cheerful grin spread all over it. Just a smile it was, and nothing more.

"Oh!" cried Uncle Wiggily in surprise. "Oh!"

With that all the rats looked up and, seeing the smile, one exclaimed:

"I smell a cat! Oh, woe is me! I smell a cat!"

Then, all of a sudden the smile grew larger and larger. Then a nose seemed to grow out of nothing, then some whiskers, then a pair of blazing eyes, and then ears—a head, legs, claws and a body, and finally there stood the Cheshire cat in the midst of the rats.

"Scat, rats," meaouwed the Cheshire cat. "Scat!"

"How did you get in here?" asked one rat.

"Yes, tell us!" ordered another. "How did you get in past the locked door?"

"Through the keyhole," said the Cheshire cat. "I sent my smile in first, and then it was easy for my body to follow. Now you scat and leave Uncle Wiggily alone!" and with that the cat grinned larger than ever, showing such sharp teeth that the rats quickly unlocked the door and ran away, leaving the bunny uncle quite safe.

"Alice in Wonderland, most magically knew of the trouble you were in," said the Cheshire cat, "so she sent me to help you, which I was glad to do, as you had helped me. My Cheshire cheese, that you found for me when I had lost it, was very good!"

Then Uncle Wiggily hopped back to his bungalow, and the cat went to see Alice; and if the paper cutter doesn't slice the bread board all up into pieces of cake for the puppy dog's party, I'll tell you next about Uncle Wiggily and the Dormouse.

David Blaize and the Blue Door

E.F. Benson

ILLUSTRATIONS BY H.J. FORD

1919

Edward Frederic Benson (1867-1940) was the son of Archbishop Edward White. Benson was one of the most prolific and popular writers of the Edwardian era, flourishing in the same period as Oscar Wilde, Saki (H.H. Munro), and P.G. Wodehouse. The author of more than one hundred books and two hundred short stories, as well as poetry, drama, biography, and social commentary, Benson is best remembered for his chilling tales of the supernatural and for his Mapp and Lucia books—acerbic social comedies set in the village of Tilling.

Benson wrote three books about David Blaize. The first, *David Blaize* (1916), a semiautobiographical novel about the friendship between two boys at boarding school, is one of six novels Benson considered to be his best and became a classic in the British gay community, for whom David Blaize was an icon. *David at Kings* (1924) continues David's school experiences at Cambridge. *David Blaize and the Blue Door* is an imaginative fantasy that departs radically from the more traditionally structured David Blaize school stories. After discovering a small blue door beneath his pillow, six-year-old David Blaize goes in search of "the real world lying somewhere just below the ordinary old thing in which his father and mother and nurse and the rest of the fast-asleep grown-up people lived." Searching for answers to important questions that adults dismiss as nonsense, David finds behind the door a Wonderland-like realm where nonsense is taken seriously by the inhabitants. *The Times Literary Supplement* notes similarities to the *Alice* books, but observes that Benson "carries the sincerest form of flattery just far enough to be clear of any charge of attempted concealment; and he weaves it into a story that is, in its main lines, his own invention."[1] Benson's inventive dream-fantasy anticipates some of his later supernatural fantasies, exploring the nature of "nonsense" in order to question the limitations of conventional notions of "sense."

---

1. *Times Literary Supplement* (December 19, 1918): 642.

David Blaize and the Blue Door

CHAPTER I

EVER SINCE HE WAS FOUR years old, and had begun to think seriously, as a boy should, David Blaize had been aware that there was a real world lying somewhere just below the ordinary old thing in which his father and mother and nurse and the rest of the fast-asleep grown-up people lived. Boys began to get drowsy, he knew, about the time that they were ten, though they might still have occasional waking moments, and soon after that they went sound asleep, and lost all chance of ever seeing the real world. If you asked grown-ups some tremendously important questions, such as "Why do the leaves fall off the trees when there is glass on the lake?" as likely as not they would begin talking in their sleep about frost and sap, just as if that had got anything to do with the real reason. Or they might point out that it wasn't real glass on the lake, but ice, and, if they were more than usually sound asleep, take a piece of the lake-glass and let you hold it in your fingers till it became water. That was to show you that what you had called glass was really frozen water, another word for which was ice. They thought that it was very wonderful of them to explain it all so nicely, and tell you at great length that real glass did not become water if you held it in your fingers, which you must remember to wash before dinner. Perhaps they would take you to the nursery window when you came in from your walk, and encourage you to put your finger on the pane in order to see that glass did not become water. This sort of thing would make David impatient, and he asked, "Then why don't you put ice in the window, and then you could boil it for tea in the kettle?" And if his nurse wanted to go to sleep again, she would say, "Now you're talking nonsense, Master David."

Now that was the ridiculous thing! Of course he was talking nonsense just to humour Nannie. He was helping her with her nonsense about the difference between ice and glass. He had been wanting to talk sense all the time, and learn something about the real world, in which the fish put a glass roof on their house for the winter as soon as they had collected enough red fire-leaves to keep them warm until the hot weather came round again. That might not be the precise way in which it happened, but it was something of that sort. Instead of pinching herself awake, poor sleepy Nannie went babbling on about ice and glass and sap and spring, in a way that was truly tedious and quite beside the real point.

Yet when the sleepy things tried to awake to the real world, they could not get their grown-up dreams out of their heads. Sometimes his mother would come up to the nursery before he went to bed, and take him on her knee, which was a soft, comfortable place, and tell him a story, which often began quite well and seriously. David always asked that the electric light should be put out first, because then the flame-cats would come out of their holes, and play puss-in-the-corner all over the nursery. They always helped the story to seem true and serious, for they were real, only the electric light must be put out first, because it gave them shocks, and naturally you could not play when you were being shocked. He knew that to be true even in the sleepy grown-up world, because once when his mother was playing with him, he had put out his tongue at Nannie when she came to say it was bed-time, and his mother couldn't play any more, because she was shocked. That was why the flame-cats must have the electric light put out.

Well, there were the flame-cats dancing (sometimes they had a ball instead of puss-in-the-corner), and here was he very comfortable and wide-awake, and sometimes, as I have said, the story began quite well, with an air of truth and reality about it. There was a little green man with whiskers who lived in the pear-tree, and washed his hands with Pears' soap. Or there was a red-faced old woman who lived in the apple-tree, and kept a sharp look-out for dumplings coming round the corner, for these were her deadliest enemies, and pulled pieces off her, and made them into apple-dumplings. Sometimes they pulled her nose off when they caught her, or a finger or two, which never grew again till next spring, and often, if spring was late, from going to sleep again after Nannie Equinox had called him, there was practically nothing left of her. So when the regiment of dumplings came round the corner, Grand-mamma Apple-tree hid in the grass, and pretended she was Mr. Winfall, the tailor, who had made David's new sailor clothes. Then Colonel Dumpling would stumble over her, and sometimes he did not know whether she was Grandmamma Apple-tree or Mr. Winfall. So he began very politely, like a subscription paper with a half-penny stamp in case it proved to be Mr. Winfall, who had the habit of eating Colonel Dumpling whenever he saw him, and often some privates as well, cleared his throat and said in his best suetty voice:

"Dear Sir or Madam."

He never got further than that because, if it proved to be Mr. Winfall, Mr. Winfall ate him whether he had an apple inside or not, and if it was Grandmamma Apple-tree, she was so indignant, as every proper female should be at being taken for a man, that she began abusing Colonel Dumpling in a red voice, if she was ripe, and a green one if she wasn't and gave the whole show away. So she lost an arm or a leg if there were many people in the house, or a finger or two if father and mother were alone, and Colonel Dumpling said to his regiment:

"Attention! Slow fatigue March! Right-about Kitchen Turn!"

Now all this sort of thing was clearly true, and belonged to the real world, but too often, unfortunately, David's mother got grown-up and sleepy again, and began talking the most dreadful nonsense. A little girl with golden hair and blue eyes made her unwelcome presence known by singing, or a baby would be found underneath a gooseberry bush (David always hoped that it got frightfully pricked), or a sweet lovely fairy would fly in, just when everything was getting on so nicely, and make rubbish out of it. He was too polite to let his mother know how boring she had become, and so whenever the golden-haired little girl or the sweet fairy appeared, he would try to go on with Colonel Dumpling's part of the story in his own mind, or watch the flame-cats getting tired as the fire burned low.

Nannie was not so good at stories, but she had flashes of sense, as when, one night, when David preferred to sit up in bed instead of lying down to go to sleep, she hinted that a black man *might* possibly come down the chimney, unless he put his head properly on the pillow. David knew that it was not likely, for it would have to be a very small man indeed, and fireproof, but there was some glimmering of a real idea in it. So he was not the least frightened, and asked, with interest, if he would be like bacon or beef before he got through the fire. This exploded any sense there might have been in Nannie's original idea at once, because she threatened to go downstairs and tell his mother if he wouldn't lie down. A very poor ending to the black man coming down the chimney! Nannie clearly knew nothing about him really if she so quickly got sleepy and talked about fetching his mother. Nobody grown-up ever woke to the real world for more than a minute or two at a time, except perhaps his father, who spent so many hours in a big room called "The Laboratory." There he seemed to dabble in realities, for he could put a fragment of something on the water, and it began to blaze, or he could mix a powder out of certain bottles, and when it was lit it burned with so red a flame that his father looked as if he was illuminated inside like a turnip-ghost. Or he could, by another mixture, produce a smell that he said was "Tincture of Rotten Eggs," and was really made of the ghosts of bad eggs ground up and exorcised. But then, poor man, he got grown-up, and when, subsequently, David wanted to know what the ghosts of bad eggs looked like when they were exorcised, he muttered in his sleep something about sulphuretted hydrogen.

* * * * * *

David was now just "turned six," as Nannie expressed it, and knew that he had only about four years more in front of him before he began to lapse into that drowsy state of grown-uppishness which begins when boys are ten or thereabouts, and lasts, getting worse and worse, till they are twenty or seventy or anything else. If he was going to find the real world of which he caught glimpses now and then, he must do so without losing much time. There was probably a door into it, and for a long time he had hoped that it was the door in the ground by the lake. But one day he had found that door open, and it was an awful disappointment to see that it only contained a tap and a round opening, to which presently the gardener fixed a long curly pipe. When he turned the tap, the pipe gave some jolly chuckling noises, and began to stream with water at its far end. That was very delightful, and consoled David a little for the disappointment.

Then one night he had a clue. He had just lain down in his bed, when he heard a door beginning to behave as doors do when they think they are quite alone, and nobody is looking. Then, as you know, they unlatch themselves, and begin walking to and fro on their hinges, hitting themselves against their frames. This often happened to the nursery door when he came downstairs in the morning after he was quite sure he had shut it. His mother therefore sent him up to shut it again, and sure enough the door was always open, having undone itself to go for a walk on its hinges. But on this night he thought that the sound of the door came from under his pillow, but he very carelessly fell asleep just as he was listening in order to make sure, and the next thing he knew was that Nannie was telling him it was morning. Again, on the very next night he had only just put his head on the pillow when the door began banging. It sounded muffled, and there was no doubt this time that it came from under his pillow. He sat up in bed, broad awake, and pulled his pillow away. By the light of the flame-cats who were dancing to-night, he could see the smooth white surface of his bolster, but, alas, there was no door there.

David was now quite sure that somewhere under his pillow was the door he was looking for. One time he had allowed himself to go to sleep before finding it, and the other time he had got too much awake. So on the third night he took the pin-partridge to bed with him, in the hope that it would keep him just awake enough, by pricking him with the head of its pin-leg. The pin-partridge had, of course, come out of Noah's Ark and in the course of some terrible adventures had lost a leg. So Nannie had taken a pin, and driven it into the stump, so that it could stand again. The pin-leg was rather longer than the wooden one, which made the partridge lean a little to one side, as if it was listening to the agreeable conversation of the animal next it.

* * * * * *

Sure enough, on this third night, David had only just lain down, with the pin-partridge in one hand, and the pin ready to scratch his leg to keep him just awake enough, when the door began banging again, just below his pillow. He listened a little while, pressing the pin-head against his calf so that it hurt a little, but not enough to wake him up hopelessly, and moved his head about till he was sure that his ear was directly above the door. Then very quietly he pushed his pillow aside, and there in the middle of his bolster was a beautiful shining blue door with a gold handle, swinging gently to and fro, as if it was alone. He got up, pushed it open and entered. For fear of some dreadful misfortune happening, like finding his mother on the other side of it, who might send him back to shut it, he closed it very carefully and softly. He found that there was a key hanging up on the wall beside it, and to his great joy it fitted the keyhole. He locked it, and put the key back on its nail, so that when he came back he could let himself out, and in the meantime nobody could possibly reach him.

Chapter 2

The passage into which the blue door opened was very like the nursery passage at home, and it was certainly night, because the flame-cats were dancing on the walls, which only happened after dark. Yet there was no fire burning anywhere, which was rather puzzling, but soon David saw that these were real cats, not just the sort of unreal ones which demanded a fire to make them dance at all. Some were red, some were yellow, some were emerald green with purple patches, and instead of having a band or a piano to dance to, they all squealed and purred and growled, making such a noise that David could not hear himself speak. So he stamped his foot and said "Shoo!" at which the dance suddenly came to an end, and all the cats sat down, put one hind-leg in the air, and began licking themselves.

"If you please," said David, "will you tell me where to go next?"

Every cat stopped licking itself, and looked at him. Some cat behind him said:

"Lor! it's the boy from the nursery."

David turned round. All the cats had begun licking themselves again, except a large tabby, only instead of being black and brown, it was the colour of apricot jam and poppies.

"Was it you who spoke?" said David.

"Set to partners!" said the tabby, and they all began dancing again.

"Shoo, you silly things," said David, stamping again. "I don't want to stop your dancing, except just to be told where I'm to go, and what I'm to do if I'm hungry."

The dancing stopped again.

"There is a pot of mouse-marmalade somewhere," said the tabby, "only you mustn't take more than a very little bit. It's got to last till February."

"But I don't like the mouse-marmalade," said David.

"I never said you did," said the tabby. "Where's the cook?"

"Gone to buy some new whiskers," said another. "She put them too close to the fire, which accounts for the smell of burning."

"Then all that can be done is to set to partners, and hope for the best," said the tabby.

"If any one dances again," said David, "before you tell me the way, and where I shall find a shop with some proper food in it, not mousey, I shall turn on the electric light."

"Fiddle-de-dee!" said the tabby, and they all began singing

> "Hey diddle-diddle
> The cat and the fiddle"

at the top of their voices.

David was getting vexed with them all, and he looked about for the electric light. But there were no switches by the door, as there ought to have been, but only a row of bottles which he knew came out of his father's laboratory. But the stopper in one of them was loose, and a fizzing noise came out of it. He listened to it a minute, with his ear close to it, and heard it whispering, "*It's me! it's me! it's me!*"

"And when he's got it, he doesn't know what to do with it!" said the tabby contemptuously.

David hadn't the slightest idea. He was only sure that the bottle had something to do with the electric light, and he took it up and began shaking it, as Nannie did to his medicine bottle. To his great delight, he saw that, as he shook it, the cats grew fainter and fainter, and the passage lighter and lighter.

The tabby spoke to him in a tremulous voice.

"You're shocking us frightfully," she said. "Please, don't. You may have all the mouse-marmalade as soon as the cook comes back with her whiskers. She's been gone a long time. And if you don't like it, you really know where everything else is. There's the garden outside, and then the lake, and then the village. It's all just as usual, except that everything is real here. But whatever you do, don't shock us any more."

The passage had grown quite bright by now and there were only a few of the very strongest cats left. So, as he was a kind boy, he put down the bottle again, which began fizzing and whispering:

"*Pleased to have met you: pleased to have met you: pleased to have met you.*"

"I don't know why you couldn't have told me that at first," said David to the tabby.

"Nor do I. It was my poor head. The dancing gets into it, and makes it turn round and square, one after the other. May we go on?"

The cats began to recover as he stopped shaking the bottle, and he walked on round the corner where the game cupboard stood against the wall. All the games were kept there, the Noah's Ark, and the spillikins, and the Badminton, and the Happy Families, and the oak-bricks, and the lead soldiers; and, as usual, the door of it was slightly open, because, when all the games were put away, even Nannie could not shut it tight. To-night there was an extraordinary stir going on in it, as if everything was slipping about inside, and, as David paused to see what was happening, a couple of marbles rolled out. But, instead of stopping on the carpet, they continued rolling faster and faster, and he heard them hopping downstairs in the direction of the garden door.

"I don't want to play games just yet," he said to himself, "when there is so much to explore, but I must see what they are doing."

He opened the door a little wider, and heard an encouraging voice, which he knew must be Noah's, come from inside.

"That's right," it said; "now we can see what we're doing. Is my ulster buttoned properly this time, missus? Last night, when you buttoned it for me, you did it wrong, you did, and I caught cold in my ankle, I did. It's been sneezing all day, it has."

"I never saw such trouble as you men are," said Mrs. Noah. "Get up, you silly, and don't sit on Shem's hat. I've been looking for it everywhere."

David stooped down and looked in. He had a sort of idea that he was invisible, and wouldn't disturb anybody. There was the ark, with all its windows open, and the family were dressing. It consisted of two compartments, in the second of which lived the animals, one on the top of each other right up to the roof. There was no door in it, but the roof lifted off. At present it was tightly closed and latched, and confused noises of lions roaring and elephants trumpeting and cows mooing, dogs barking, and birds singing came from inside. Sometimes there was ordinary talk too, for the animals had all learned English from David as well as knowing their own animal tongue, and the Indian elephant spoke Hindustanee in addition. He was slim and light blue, and was known as the "Elegant Elephant," in contrast to a stout black one who never spoke at all. All this David thought that he and Nannie had made up, but now he knew that it was perfectly true. And he stood waiting to see what would happen next.

The hubbub increased.

"If that great lamb would get off my chest," said the elegant elephant, "I should be able to get up. Why don't they come and open the roof?"

"Not time yet," said the cow. "The family are still dressing. But it's a tight fit to-night. I'm glad the pin-partridge isn't here scratching us all."

"Where's it gone?" said the elephant.

"David took it to bed; more fool he," said the cow.

"He couldn't be much more of a fool than he is," grunted the pig. "He knows nothing about us really."

At this moment David heard an irregular kind of hopping noise coming down the passage, and, just as he turned to look, the pin-partridge ran between his legs. It flew on to the roof of the ark, and began pecking at it.

"Let me in," it shouted. "I believe it's the first of September. What cads you fellows are not to let me in!"

"You always think it's the first of September," said the cow. "Now look at me; I'm milked every day, which must hurt me much more than being shot once."

"Not if it's properly done," said the partridge. "I know lots of cows who like it."

"But it's improperly done," said the cow. "David knows less about milking than anybody since the flood. You wait till I catch him alone, and see if I can't teach him something about tossing."

This sounded a very awful threat, and David, who knew that it was best to take cows as well as bulls by the horns, determined on a bold policy.

"If I hear one word more about tossing, I shan't let any of you out," he said.

There was dead silence.

"Who's that?" said the cow in a trembling voice, for she was a coward as well as a cow.

"It's me!" said David.

There was a confused whispering within.

"We can't stop here all night."

"Say you won't toss him."

"You can't anyhow, because your horns are both broken."

"Less noise in there," said Noah suddenly, from the next compartment.

The cow began whimpering.

"I'm a poor old woman," she said, "and everybody's very hard on me, considering the milk and butter I've given you."

"Chalk and water and margarine," said the pin-partridge, who had been listening with his ear to the roof. "Do say you won't toss him. I can't see him, but he's somewhere close to me."

"Very well, I won't toss him. Open the roof, boy."

David was not sure that Noah would like this, as he was the ark-master, but he felt that his having said that he would keep the roof shut unless the cow promised, meant that he would open it if she did, and so he lifted the roof about an inch.

At that moment Noah's head appeared. He was standing on Shem's head, who was standing on Ham's head, who was standing on Japheth's head, who was standing on his mother's head. They always came out of their room in this way, partly in order to get plenty of practice in case of fire, and partly because they couldn't be certain that the flood had gone down, and were afraid that if they opened the door, which is the usual way of leaving a room, the water might come in. When Noah had climbed on to the top of the wall, he pulled Shem after him, who pulled Ham, who pulled Japheth, who pulled Mrs. Noah, and there they all stood like a row of sparrows on a telegraph wire, balancing themselves with great difficulty.

"Who's been meddling with my roof?" asked Noah, in an angry voice. "I believe it's that pin-partridge."

The pin-partridge trembled so violently at this that he fell off the roof altogether, quite forgetting that he could fly. But the moment he touched the ground, he became a full-sized partridge.

"No, I didn't," he said. "There's that boy somewhere about, but I can't see him. He got through the blue door to-night."

David now knew that he was invisible, but though it had always seemed to him that it must be the most delicious thing in the world to be able to be visible or invisible whenever you chose, he found that it was not quite so jolly to have become invisible without choosing, and not to have the slightest idea how to become visible again. It gave him an empty kind of feeling like when he was hungry long before the proper time.

"The cats saw me," he said, joining in, for he knew if he couldn't be seen, he could be heard.

"Of course they did," said Noah, "because they can see in the dark when everything is invisible. That's why they saw you. You needn't think that you're the only thing that is invisible. I suppose you think it's grand to be invisible."

"When I was a little boy," said Ham, "I was told that little boys should be seen and not heard. This one is heard and not seen. I call that a very poor imitation of a boy. I dare say he isn't a real one."

"I've been quite ordinary up to now," said David. "It seems to have come on all of a sudden. And I don't think it's at all grand to be invisible. I would be visible this minute if I knew how."

"I want to get down," said Mrs. Noah, swaying backwards and forwards because her stand was broken.

"You'll get down whether you want to or not, ma," said Shem irritably, "if you go swaying about like that. Don't catch hold of me now. I've got quite enough to do with keeping my balance myself."

"Why don't you get down?" asked David, who wanted to see what would happen next.

"I haven't seen the crow fly yet," said Noah. "We can't get down till the crow has flown."

"What did the crow do?" asked David.

"It didn't. That's why we're still here," said Japheth.

"Some people," said Noah, "want everything explained to them. When the cock crows it shows it's morning, and when the crow flies it shows it's night. We can't get down until."

"But what would happen if you did get down?" said David.

"Nobody knows," said Noah. "I knew once, and tied a knot in my handkerchief about it, so that I could remember, but the handkerchief went to the wash, and they took out the knot. So I forgot."

"If you tied another knot in another handkerchief, wouldn't you remember again?" asked David.

"No. That would not be the same knot. I should remember something quite different, which I might not like at all. That would never do."

"One, two, three," said Mrs. Noah, beating time, and they all began to sing:

"Never do, never do,
Never, never, never do."

Most of the animals in the ark joined in, and they sang it to a quantity of different tunes. David found himself singing too, but the only tune he could remember was "Rule Britannia," which didn't fit the words very well. By degrees the others stopped singing, and David was left quite alone to finish his verse, feeling rather shy but knowing that he had to finish it whatever happened. When he had done, Noah heaved a deep sigh.

"That is the loveliest thing I ever heard in my life," he said. "Are you open to an engagement to sing in the ark every evening? Matinées of course, as well, for which you would have to pay extra."

This was a very gratifying proposal, but David did not quite understand about the paying.

"I should have to pay?" he asked.

"Why, of course. You'd have to pay a great deal for a voice like that. You mustn't dream of singing like that for nothing. It would fill the ark."

"I should say it would empty it," said Mrs. Noah snappishly.

"I don't know if I'm rich enough," said David, not taking any notice of this rude woman.

"Go away at once then," said Mrs. Noah. "I never give to beggars."

Just then there was a tremendous rattle from the ark, as if somebody was shaking it.

"It's the crow," shouted Ham. "The crow's just going to fly. Get out of the way, boy."

The crow forced its way through the other animals, balanced itself for a moment on the edge of the ark, and flew off down the passage, squawking. The moment it left the ark it became ordinary crow-size again, and at the same moment David suddenly saw his one hand still holding up the lid of the ark, and knew that he had become visible. That was a great relief, but he had no time to think about it now, for so many interesting things began happening all at once. The Noah family jumped from the edge of the ark, and the moment their stands touched the ground, they shot up into full-sized human beings, with hats and ulsters on, and large flat faces with two dots for eyes, one dot for a nose, and a line for a mouth. They glided swiftly about on their stands, like people skating, and seemed to be rather bad at guiding themselves, for they kept running into each other with loud wooden crashes, and into the animals that were pouring out of the ark in such numbers that it really was difficult to avoid everybody. Occasionally they were knocked down, and then lay on their backs with their eyes winking very quickly, and their mouths opening and shutting, like fish out of water, till somebody picked them up.

David got behind the cupboard door to be out of the way of the animals and all the other things that came trooping from the shelves. Luckily the nursery passage seemed to have grown much bigger, or it could never have held everybody, for the animals also shot up to their full size as soon as they left the ark. But they kept their colours and their varnish, and though David had been several times to the Zoological Gardens, there was nothing there half so remarkable as the pale blue elephant or the spotted pigs, to take only a few examples. Every animal here was so much brighter in colour, and of course their conversation made them more interesting. On they trooped with the Noahs whirling in and out, towards the steps to the garden door, and when they were finished with, the "Happy Families," all life-size, too, followed them. There were Mrs. Dose, the doctor's wife, with her bottle, and Miss Bones, the butcher's daughter, gnawing her bone in a very greedy manner, and Master Chip, the carpenter's son, with his head supported in the pincers. He had no body, you will remember, and walked in a twisty manner, very upright and soldier-like, on the handles of them. The lead soldiers followed them with the band playing, and the cannons shooting peas in all directions, only the peas were as big as cannon-balls, and shot down whole regiments of their own men, and many of the hindmost of the happy families. But nobody seemed to mind, but picked themselves up again at once. Often the whole band were lying on their backs together, but they never ceased playing for a moment. The battledores and shuttlecocks came next, the shuttlecocks hitting the battledores in front of them, which flew down the passage high over the heads of the soldiers, and waited there, standing on their handles till the shuttlecocks came up and hit them again. After this came David's clockwork train, which charged into everything that was in its way, and cut a lane for itself through soldiers, happy families, and animals alike. It had a cow-catcher in front of the engine, which occasionally picked people up, instead of running over them, and when David saw it last, before it plunged down the stairs, it had Mr. Soot, the chimney-sweep, and the Duke of Wellington, and the llama all lying on it, jumbled up together, and kicking furiously.

While he was watching this extraordinary scene, the cupboard doors banged to again, and he saw that there was a large label on one of them:—

No Admittance Except by Presenting
Your Calling-card and Very Little Then.

And on the other was this:

No Bottles or Followers or Anything Else.
Ring Also.

David studied this for a minute or two. He did not want to go in, but he wanted to know how. He hadn't got a calling-card—at least he never had before he came through the blue door, but so many odd things had happened since, that he was not in the least surprised when he put his hand in his pocket to find it quite full of calling-cards, on which was printed his name, only it was upside down. So he naturally turned the card upside down to get the name un-upside-down, but however he turned it, his name was still upside down. If he looked at it very closely as he turned it, he could see the letters spin round like wheels, and it always remained like this:

ᴅᴀᴠɪᴅ ʙʟᴀɪᴢᴇ

The other trouser-pocket was also quite full of something, and he drew out of it hundreds of other calling-cards. On one was printed "The Elegant Elephant, R.S.V.P.," on another "Master Ham, P.P.C.," on another "The Duke of Wellington, W.P." on another "The Engine Driver, R.A.M.C.," on another "Miss Battledore, W.A.A.C." Everybody had been calling on him.

"Whatever am I to do?" thought David. "Shall I have to return all these calls? It will take me all my time, and I shall see nothing. Besides"—and he looked round and saw that the passage was completely empty, and had shrunk to its usual size again—"Besides, I don't know where they've all gone."

He looked at the cupboard doors again, and found that they had changed while he had been looking at the cards. They were now exactly like the big front door at home, which opened in the middle, and had a hinge at each side. In front of it was a doormat, in the bristles of which was written:

Go Away.

Now David was the sort of boy who often wanted to do something, chiefly because he was told not to, in order to see what happened, and this doormat made him quite determined to go in. It was no use trying the left-hand side of the door, partly because neither bottles nor followers nor anything was admitted, and partly because you had to ring also, and there wasn't any bell. But there seemed just a chance of getting in by the right-hand part of the door, and he went up to it and knocked. To his great surprise he heard a bell ring inside as soon as he had knocked, which seemed to explain "ring also." The bell did not sound like an electric bell, but was like the servants' dinner bell. As soon as it had stopped, he heard a voice inside the door say very angrily:

"Give me my tuffet at once."

There was a pause, and David heard the noise of some furniture being moved, and the door flew open.

"What's your name?" said the butler. "And have you got a calling-card?"

David gave him one of his cards, and he looked at it and turned it upside down.

"It's one of them dratted upside-downers," he said, "and it sends the blood to the head something awful."

He gave a heavy sigh, and bent down and stood on his head.

"Now I can read it," he said. "Are you David or Blaize? If David, where's Blaize, and if Blaize, where's David?"

"I'm both," said David.

"You can't be both of them," said the butler. "And I expect you're neither of them. And why didn't you go away?"

"You've given me too much curds," said a voice behind the door. "I've told you before to find some way to weigh the whey. It's a curd before. Take it away!"

"That must be Miss Muffet," thought David. "There's a girl creeping into it after all. I wonder if she makes puns all the time. I wish I hadn't knocked."

"No, I'm rationed about puns," said Miss Muffet, as if he had spoken aloud, "and I've had my week's allowance now. But a margin's allowed for margarine. Butter—margarine," she said in explanation.

"I saw that," said David.

"No, you didn't: you heard it. Now, come in and shut the door, because the tuffet's blowing about. And the moment you've shut the door, shut your eyes too, because I'm not quite ready. I'll sing to you my last ballad while you're waiting. I shall make it up as I go along."

Accordingly David shut the door, and then his eyes, and Miss Muffet began to sing in a thin cracked voice:

"As it fell out upon a day
When margarine was cheap,
It filled up all the grocers' shops
In buckets wide and deep.
　　Ah, well-a-day! ah, ill-a-day!
Matilda bought a heap.

And it fell out upon a day
When margarine was dear,
Matilda bought a little more
And made it into beer.
　　Ah, well-a-day! ah, ill-a-day!
It tasted rather queer.

As it fell out upon a day
There wasn't any more;
Matilda took her bottled beer
And poured it on the floor.
　　Ah, well-a-day! ah, ill-a-day!
And that was all I saw."

"Poor thing!" said Miss Muffet. "Such a brief and mysterious career. Now you may open your eyes."

David did so, and found himself in a large room, with all the furniture covered up as if the family was away. The butler was still standing on his head, squinting horribly at David's card, and muttering to himself, "He can't be both, and he may be neither. He may be either, but he can't be both." In the middle of the room was a big round seat, covered with ribands which were still blowing about in the wind, and on it was seated a little old lady with horn spectacles, eating curds and whey out of a bowl that she held on her knees.

"Come and sit on the tuffet at once," she said, "and then we'll pretend that there isn't room for the spider. Won't that be a good joke? I like a bit of chaff with my spider. I expect the tuffet will bear, won't it? But I can't promise you any curds."

"Thank you very much," said David politely, "but I don't like curds."

"No more do I," said Miss Muffet. "I knew we should agree."

"Then why do you eat them?" asked David.

"For fear the spider should get them. Don't you adore my tuffet? It's the only indoor tuffet in the world. All others are out-door tuffets. But they gave me this one because most spiders are out-of-doors spiders. By the way, we haven't been introduced yet. Where's that silly butler?"

"Here," said the butler. He was lying down on the floor now, and staring at the ceiling.

"Introduce us," said Miss Muffet. "Say Miss Muffet, David Blaize—David Blaize, Miss Muffet. Then whichever way about it happens, you're as comfortable as it is possible to be under the circumstances, or even above them, where it would naturally be colder."

"I don't quite see," said David.

"Poor Mr. Blaize. Put a little curds and whey in your eyes. That's the way. Dear me, there's another pun."

"You made it before," said David.

"I know. It counts double this time. But as I was saying, a little curds and whey—oh! it's tipped up again. What restless things curds are!"

She had not been looking at her bowl, and for several minutes now a perfect stream of curds and whey had been pouring from it over her knees and along the floor, to where the butler lay. He was still repeating, "Miss Muffet, David Blaize—David Blaize, Miss Muffet." Sometimes, by way of variety, he said, "Miss Blaize—David Muffet," but as nobody attended, it made no difference what he said.

"It always happens when I get talking," she said. "And now we know each other, I may be permitted to express a hope that you didn't expect to find me a little girl?"

"No, I like you best as you are," said David quickly.

"It isn't for want of being asked that I've remained Miss Muffet," said she. "And it isn't from want of being answered. But give me a little pleasant conversation now and then, and one good frightening away every night, and I'm sure I'll have no quarrel with anybody; and I hope nobody hasn't got none with me. How interesting it must be for you to meet me, when you've read about me so often. It's not nearly so interesting for me, of course, because you're not a public character."

"Does the spider come every night, or every day, whatever it is down here?" asked David.

"Yes, sooner or later," said Miss Muffet cheerfully, "but the sooner he comes, the sooner I get back again, and the later he comes the longer I have before he comes. So there we are."

She stopped suddenly, and looked at the ceiling.

"Do my eyes deceive me?" she whispered, "or is that the s——? No; my eyes deceive me, and I thought they would scorn the action, the naughty things. Perhaps you would like to peep at my furniture underneath the sheets. It will pass the time for you, but be ready to run back to the tuffet, when you hear the spider coming. Really, it's very tiresome of him to be so late."

David thought he had never seen such an odd lot of furniture. Covered up in one sheet was a stuffed horse, in another a beehive, in another a mowing-machine. They were all priced in plain figures, and the prices seemed to him equally extraordinary, for while the horse was labelled "Two shillings a dozen," and the mowing-machine "Half a crown a pair," the beehive cost ninety-four pounds empty, and eleven and sixpence full. David supposed the reason for this was that if the beehive was full, there would be bees buzzing about everywhere, which would be a disadvantage.

"When I give a party," said Miss Muffet, "as I shall do pretty soon if the spider doesn't come, and take all the coverings off my furniture, the effect is quite stupendous. Dazzling in fact, my dear. You must remember to put on your smoked spectacles."

David was peering into the sheet that covered the biggest piece of furniture of all. He could only make out that it was like an enormous box on wheels, and cost ninepence. Then the door in it swung open, and he saw that it was a bathing-machine. On the floor of it was sitting an enormous spider.

"Does she expect me?" said the spider hoarsely. "I'm not feeling very well."

David remembered that he had to run back to the tuffet, but it seemed impolite not to ask the spider what was the matter with it. It had a smooth kind face, and was rather bald.

"My web caught cold," said the spider. "But I'll come if she expects me."

David ran back to the tuffet.

"He's not very well," he said, "but he'll come if you expect him."

"The kind good thing!" said Miss Muffet. "Now I must begin to get frightened. Will you help me? Say 'Bo!' and make faces with me in the looking-glass, and tell me a ghost story. Bring me the looking-glass, silly," she shouted to the butler.

He took one down from over the chimney-piece, and held it in front of them, while David and Miss Muffet made the most awful faces into it.

"That's a beauty," said Miss Muffet, as David squinted, screwed up his nose, and put his tongue out. "Thank you for that one, my dear. It gave me quite a start. You are really remarkably ugly. Will you feel my pulse, and see how I am getting on. Make another face: I'm used to that one. Oh, I got a beauty then: it terrified me. And begin your ghost story quickly."

David had no idea where anybody's pulse was, so he began his ghost story.

"Once upon a time," he said, "there was a ghost that lived in the hot-water tap."

"Gracious, how dreadful!" said Miss Muffet. "What was it the ghost of?"

"It wasn't the ghost of anything," said David. "It was just a ghost."

"But it must have been 'of' something," said Miss Muffet. "The King is the King of England, and I'm Miss Muffet of nothing at all. But you must have an 'of.'"

"This one hadn't," said David firmly. "It was just a ghost. It groaned when you turned the hot water on, and it squealed when you turned it off."

"This will never do," said Miss Muffet. "I'm getting quite calm again, like a kettle going off the boil. Make another face. Oh, now it's too late!"

There came a tremendous cantering sound behind them, and Miss Muffet opened her mouth and screamed so loud that her horn spectacles broke into fragments.

"Here he comes!" she said. "O-oh, how frightened I am!"

She gave one more wild shriek as the spider leaped on to the tuffet, and began running about the room with the most amazing speed, the spider cantering after her. They upset the bathing-machine, and knocked the stuffed horse down, they dodged behind the butler, and sent the beehive spinning, and splashed through the curds and whey, which formed a puddle on the floor. Then the door through which David had entered flew open, and out darted Miss Muffet with the spider in hot pursuit. Her screaming, which never stopped for a moment, grew fainter and fainter.

The butler gave an enormous yawn.

"Cleaning up time," he said, and took a mop from behind the door, and dipped it into the pool of curds and whey. When it was quite soaked, he twisted it rapidly round and round, and a shower of curds and whey deluged David. As it fell on him, it seemed to turn to snow. It was snowing heavily from the roof too, and snow was blowing in through the door. Then he saw that it wasn't a door at all, but the opening of a street, and that the walls were the walls of houses. It was difficult to see distinctly through the snowstorm, but he felt as if he knew where he was.

CHAPTER 3

The snow cleared as swiftly as it had begun, and David saw that he was standing in the High Street of the village near which he lived. It was all quite ordinary, and he was afraid that he had somehow been popped back through the blue door during the snowstorm, and was again in the stupid dull world. Just opposite him was the post and telegraph office, and next to that the bank, and beyond that the girls' school. There were the same old shops too, Mr. Winfall the tailor's, and the confectioner's and the bootmaker's, and at the bottom of the street was the bridge over the river.

"Well, if I am back in the world again," said David, "it would be a pity to let all this good snow go to waste without its being tobogganed on. I'll go home, I think, and get my toboggan. I wonder how they did it."

He started to go down the street to the bridge across which was the lane which presently passed by the bottom of the field beyond the lake, on the other side of which was the garden, where was the summer-house in which he had left his toboggan yesterday. But he happened to look a little more closely at the bootmaker's shop, and instead of the card in the window which said, "Boots and shoes neatly repaired," there was another one on which was written "Uncles and Aunts recovered and repaired."

"I suppose they recover them when they're lost, and repair them when they're found," thought David. "But it's not a bit usual."

He found it no more usual when he looked at the girls' school, for instead of the brass plate on which was written, "Miss Milligan's School for Young Ladies," he saw written there "Happy Families' Institute," and in the window of the bank a notice "Sovereigns are cheap to-day."

"I'll go in there at once," thought David, "and buy some. I wonder how much money I've got."

He found four pennies in his pocket, and went in with them to the bank. The manager was there talking in a low voice to a very stout gentleman with a meat-chopper in his hand, whom David knew to be the Mint-man from London, just as certainly as if he had had it written all over him. What made it absolutely sure was the fact that sovereigns kept oozing out of his clothes and dropping on the floor. There was quite a pile of them round his feet, which the porter who opened the door to David kept sweeping up, and putting down his neck again.

"So it's only the same sovereigns all over again," thought David, "but there must be a lot of them. No wonder they're cheap."

He walked up to where they were standing.

"Please, can you let me have four penny-worth of sovereigns," he said.

The Mint-man blew his nose before he answered, and some thirty or forty sovereigns rattled out of his handkerchief. "Do you want them new-laid or only for cooking?" he asked.

David had no intention of cooking them, so he said:

"New-laid, please."

The Mint-man picked off one that was coming out of his right elbow, another from his tie, another from his bottom waistcoat button, and the fourth from his knee, and gave them to David.

"It'll never do if other people get to know about it," he said. "We shall be having all the happy families in, though I don't suppose they've got much money. Have another notice put up at once."

The manager took an enormous quill pen from behind the counter. It reached right up to the ceiling of the room, and he had to hold it in both hands. Up the side of it was printed, "Rod, pole or perch."

"What shall I say?" he asked.

"You may say whatever you like," said the Mint-man, "but you must write whatever I like. Now begin—

"Sovereigns are five pounds two ounces each to-day, but they'll be dearer to-morrow."

"Then will you please give me five pounds for each of my sovereigns?" asked the greedy David. "Never mind about the ounces."

The Mint-man and manager whispered together for a little while, and David could hear fragments of their talk like "financial stringency," "tight tendency," "collapse of credit," which meant nothing to him. All the time the porter was shovelling sovereigns down the back of the Mint-man's neck.

"The only thing to be done," he said, "is to write another notice. Write 'The Bank has suspended payment altogether. The deposits are therefore forfeited by square root, rule of three, and compound interest.' What do you make of that?" he asked David triumphantly.

David knew that compound interest and square root came a long way on in the arithmetic book, and that he couldn't be properly expected to make anything of it. Evidently they were not going to pay him five sovereigns for each of his, but he had done pretty well already, with his four sovereigns instead of four pence.

"I don't make anything of it yet," he said, "because I haven't got so far."

"When I was your age," said the manager severely, "I'd got so far past it that it was quite out of sight."

The Mint-man nudged him, and said behind his hand:

"Never irritate the young. Keep them pleased and simmering."

He turned to David with a smile, and patted him on the head. Two cold sovereigns went down the front of David's jersey.

"We have read your references," he said, "and find them quite satisfactory. You are therefore appointed honorary errand-boy, and your duties begin immediately. So go straight across to the shop where they repair uncles and aunts, and see if there's a golden uncle being repaired. If there is, tell him that his nephew—that's you—wants him to come out to tea—that's here—and that the motor will be round immediately—and that's where?"

David felt that he didn't want to be errand-boy to the bank at all, but somehow he seemed to remember having sent in references. What was even more convincing was that he found his sailor clothes had disappeared, and that he was dressed in a jacket that came close up to his neck, and was covered with brass buttons. He had black trousers, rather tight, and a peaked cap, round the rim of which was written: "David Blaize, Esquire. To be returned to the bank immediately. This side up."

But after he had received his appointment as honorary errand-boy, nobody attended to David any more, for they were all most busily engaged. The manager wheeled in a tea-table and began arranging tea-things and muffin-dishes on it, then when he had done that, brought in easy chairs, and a piano and all the things that you usually find in drawing-rooms, while the Mint-man made up a huge fire in the fire-place, and put a large saucepan as big as a bath upon it, into which he dropped the sovereigns that oozed out of him. Meantime, the porter had gone out carrying a ladder and a pot of paint, and when David went out too on his errand, he had already painted over the signboard outside the house, which said it was the bank, and had written on it:

"This is the house of David Blaize, the nephew of Uncle Popacatapetl."

"So that's the uncle who's coming to tea with me," thought David. "I wonder if he knows who he is yet."

The snow had already melted, so that he did not again consider whether he should go tobogganing. It had gone very quickly, but everything seemed to happen quickly here. It could hardly have been five minutes since he had gone into the bank with fourpence in his pocket, and here he was with four sovereigns instead, a complete suit of new clothes, an uncle, and a position as honorary errand-boy. He crossed the street, and entered the shop where boots and shoes used to be repaired, but where now they repaired uncles and aunts.

On the counter there lay a very odd-looking old gentleman, dressed in rags and tatters in about equal proportions. His hands and face were quite yellow, and wherever there was a tatter, or there wasn't a rag, and he showed through, he was yellow there too. His boots were in very bad repair, and a great golden toe stuck out of one, and a golden heel out of the other: in fact, there could be no doubt at all that he was made of pure gold, and as he was being repaired, he was also either an aunt or an uncle. But though one of David's aunts had a slight moustache, he had never yet seen an aunt with a long beard and whiskers, and so without doubt there was Uncle Popacatapetl.

The bootmaker and his wife were repairing him, which they did by driving nails into him, so as to tack down the rags over the tatters. If there was a very big tatter, which they could not cover with the rag, they nailed on anything else that was handy. In some places they had filled up the gaps with pieces of newspaper, match-boxes, and bits of leather and sealing-wax, and balls of wool, and apples and photographs. While this was going on, Uncle Popacatapetl kept up a stream of conversation, interspersed with laughing.

"Anyhow it can't hurt him much," said David to himself.

"Delicious, delicious!" said Uncle Popacatapetl. "Nail the toe of my boot a little more firmly on to the toe of me. Put a paper-knife there if you can't cover up the hole. Now my gloves."

He put on a pair of thick white woollen gloves that came up to his elbow.

"Would you like them nailed on too, sir?" asked the shoemaker.

"By all means. Put a nail in each finger, and three on the wrist, and ninety-eight round my elbows. Did you gum the gloves inside, before I put them on?"

"I glued them well," said the shoemaker's wife.

"That'll glue then," said Uncle Popacatapetl. "I think when I've put my mask on the disguise will be complete. What fun it all is. To think of the Mint-man having traced me all the way here, only to find I'm not in the least like me any more. Or is it ever more?"

"Never more, ever more, any more," said the shoemaker, with his mouth full of nails.

"It's every-more. I *think*," said Uncle Popacatapetl, "though it does matter. When I'm finished, and when you're finished, they won't think I am anything, still less an uncle. I don't suppose they ever saw anything the least like me, so *why*," he added argumentatively, "should they pitch upon uncle?"

They had none of them appeared to notice David at all as yet, and, as he was an errand-boy, he thought he had better proceed with his errand.

"If you please," he said, "I think you're my uncle, and I should like to have you come to tea with me. It's quite a short way, in fact it's only across the road, but the motor will be here in a minute, so that you can get in at one door and out at the other."

Uncle Popacatapetl sat up so suddenly that David knew he must have a hinge in his back. He looked at David, but he couldn't speak, because the last nail the shoemaker had driven into him had fixed his beard to his chest, which naturally prevented him moving his mouth. But he wrenched off the pair of scissors which had been nailed into his knee, and cut a piece of his beard off, so that he could talk again. He had turned quite pale in the face, which was the only part of him visible, just as if he had been made of silver.

"Say it again," he said.

David said it again, upon which Uncle Popacatapetl jumped up and looked out of the window.

"It's a plot," he said. "That used to be the bank. Now it's David Blaize. Has it been disguising itself too? Because if so, we're as we were, and I've had all the trouble and hammering for nothing."

He began to cry in a helpless golden sort of manner. The shoemaker had followed him to the window to repair an enormous tatter with very little rag on his shoulder, and was nailing bananas on to it to cover it up. But he was so much affected by Uncle Popacatapetl's misery that he hit his fingers instead of the nail and began to cry too, sucking his injured finger and dropping nails out of his mouth. As for his wife, she gave one loud sob, and tore out of the room, leaving the door open. They heard her falling downstairs, bumpity, bumpity, bumpity, till she came BUMP against the cellar door.

"Bumpity, crumpity, rumpity, numpity, squmpity, zumpity," said the shoemaker, with a sob between each word. "There she goes! I don't rightly know if it's her crying that makes her fall down, or her falling down that makes her cry, but it don't make home happy, and it's a great expense in sticking-plaster. The sticking-plaster that's come into this house would be enough to paper it."

David was determined not to cry whatever happened, for it never did any good to cry, and besides something must be done at once, only he had not the least idea what that something was. It was perfectly clear that the Mint-man wanted to get Uncle Popacatapetl into the bank, and no wonder, since he was worth his weight in gold, with all the bananas and match-boxes thrown in. And he thought with a shudder of the meat-axe and the saucepan heating over the fire. Without the least doubt Uncle Popacatapetl was going to be chopped up and melted down into sovereigns.

"It's all too sad," sobbed Uncle Popacatapetl, "and too true and too tiresome. I knew they had tracked me down here—wow—wow—but when I saw that there was this nice respectable shop, where uncles and aunts—wow—wow—wow—could be recovered and repaired, I thought I could have myself recovered and repaired out of all knowledge—wow—wow—wow—wow—and diddle the whole lot of them. Instead of which, they send in my beastly nephew to ask me to tea, and then they'll chop me up, and make sovereigns of me. I've seen their signs and notices. They tried to put me off the scent by saying that sovereigns were cheap, and make me think they didn't want me. And then that was changed, and they said sovereigns were dearer. And then that was changed, and they suspended payment to make me think that they weren't collecting gold any more, never more at all. Oh, I know their cussedness. And just when everything was going so well, and I was going to walk across the street as cool as carrots or cucumbers, and I should have left by the next telegram that was sent from the office. Look at them all flying in! And there's one going out with its mackintosh on, and I could have caught it as easy as a subtraction sum if it hadn't been for this upset. Wow, wow, wow, wow, wow."

David felt dreadfully sorry for him, but what he said about telegrams was quite as dreadfully interesting, and he looked out.

It was quite true: there was a whole string of telegrams rushing down the wires towards the post-office, each in a neat mackintosh. It had begun to snow again, and was getting dark.

"But why have they got mackintoshes on?" he asked.

"Well, of all the silly nephews that ever I had," said Uncle Popacatapetl, who had stopped crying as suddenly as if a tap had been turned off, "this one takes the cake. Why do you wear a mackintosh?"

"To keep me dry," said David.

"Well, and mayn't telegrams do the same?" asked his uncle. "They come from America and Australia and Jerusalem, and did you ever see a wet telegram, though it had gone for hundreds and billions and millions and thousands of miles under the sea?"

"No, they all seem dry," said David.

"And there you are, sitting there," said the golden uncle, "and wanting to deprive them of their mackintoshes. Crool, I call it. They puts them on when they starts, and they takes them off when they arrive and cools themselves."

Uncle Popacatapetl had begun to talk so like David's father's gardener, that again he was afraid he had got back into the stupid world.

"I sees them coming, and I sees them going," said his uncle, "and who so free I arsk, as a little ninepenny telegram? They're cheap at the price, they are, going where they please like that——"

He gave a wild shriek, like Miss Muffet when the spider came, and snatched the mask that the shoemaker was holding.

"There's the motor come for me," he sobbed, "and what is a poor old man to do? Nail my mask on quickly. Don't mind my eyes or my ears or anything."

He lay down in the window-seat, and David and the shoemaker drove nails in all over his face. Sometimes the mask, which was that of a young lady with pink cheeks, tore, and then they tacked on buttons from David's jacket, or bits of the window-curtain.

"Don't mind me," Uncle Popacatapetl kept whimpering. "There goes one eye, and there goes the other, but make it safe whatever you do. Cut off my head, if that would make me look more like a young lady—but I won't, I won't, I won't look like anybody's uncle. They may take me for an aunt if they like, or a nephew, or a niece, but I won't be a golden uncle."

The mask was nailed on at last, and Uncle Popacatapetl sat up.

"Now go outside, David," he said, "and find out exactly what sort of motor-car it is."

David very obediently went out into the street. It looked quite different now, for there were flags flying from every house with the inscription, "David Blaize, the fireman's son," which was very gratifying, and showed a pleasant interest in him on the part of the happy families. He felt that he had seen a card of himself as the fireman's son, but he could not remember his mother as Mrs. Blaize, the fireman's wife, or his father as Mr. Blaize, the fireman.

But that was not the immediate business in hand. As the whole street was decked out in honour of himself, he naturally bowed right and left, but since nobody was there, it did not matter much whether he bowed or not. Still it was better to be polite. Then he looked in front of him. There stood an immense motor-car, that buzzed in a most sumptuous manner. It was pointing down the street towards the bridge over the river, but it did not much matter which way it pointed, because the bank was immediately opposite. There were two cords attached to the roof of it, and attached to the cords were a couple of aeroplanes, which were pointing in the opposite direction. On the pavement were standing the chauffeur and two pilots of the flying-corps. They all saluted smartly as David came out.

"Three cheers for David Blaize," said one of them. "Hip, hip, hip—I'm blowed if I know how it goes on."

"You must all say 'Hurrah,'" said David.

They all said "Hurrah," in a very depressed sort of voice, and one of the airmen said, "Lor', these civilians."

"Lor', yourself," said David, rather rudely. "I want to hear about the motor-car."

The chauffeur stroked the side of the bonnet which contained the engines.

"She's a good thing," he said. "She's a good going concern. But throttle her up never so, she won't go less than a hundred miles an hour. So I made so free, your honour, since that was above speed-limit, to harness these two silly aeroplanes which between 'em go ninety miles an hour in the other direction. That brings she down to ten miles an hour, and no one can say a word against her."

And then the two airmen threw their caps in the air, and shouted "Hurrah."

This was all very clever on the part of the chauffeur, but as the bank was just opposite, and all that the motor-car had got to do was to stand quite still while Uncle Popacatapetl stepped in at one side and got out at the other, it seemed a little superfluous. But David appreciated kind intentions, and next minute he found himself hand-in-hand with the chauffeur and the airmen, and they were all dancing in a circle, singing.

"Ninety miles one ways, and a hundred miles the others,
And some of us are nephews, and all of us are brothers."

"Then are you ready to start, your honour," said the chauffeur, when they had finished dancing.

David pulled himself together.

"Yes, but I am taking an invalid with me," he said. "It's my uncle, who is far from well, like the spider!"

"The one that sat down next that old woman," asked the chauffeur, pointing over his shoulder with his thumb. "He's all right again, he is."

"It's that sort of illness," said David. "He's coming to tea with me, but he had better have a little drive first, to give him an appetite. We'll go along some road with plenty of telegraph wires. They make him feel better."

The window of the shoemaker's house was thrown open, and David's uncle looked out in his mask.

"Much better," he said. "Better much, much better," and he closed it again so violently that all the glass broke.

"Crash!" said the second of the airmen. He had a very long elastic sort of nose, which David had not noticed before. Then both of them and the chauffeur opened their mouths very wide, as if they were going to sing again.

"There must be no more singing," said David sternly, and they all shut their mouths again with a snap.

There was evidently no time to lose, for David could hear the roaring of the fire in the bank opposite, over which poor Uncle Popacatapetl was to be melted after he had been cut up, and against the red glow of it he could see the heads of the Mint-man and the manager pressed so tightly against the glass that the tips of their noses were quite white, as they looked out and wondered why the motor-car didn't return.

"Come on, uncle," he shouted, "the tea will be spoiled," and he gave him a great wink to show that he had got an idea in his head.

So the chauffeur got into his place, and Uncle Popacatapetl came out covered with apples and match-boxes and things like a Christmas-tree, and at the very last moment David undid the buttons of the cords to the aeroplanes, and away they flew, leaving the airmen gazing up at them. Then he shut the door, and he and Uncle Popacatapetl drove off at a hundred miles an hour down the street to the bridge.

"Turn to the left when you get over the bridge," shouted David, "and drive over the fields till you come to our lake. You'll have to jump that, but after that there's only the garden."

"She ain't been jumping much lately," said the chauffeur.

"It can't be helped," shouted David. "Then go to the garden door. I'll hide you in the game cupboard," he explained to his uncle. "There's lots of room there now all the games have gone."

Suddenly there came an awful crash. They had run into the railing of the bridge, and the whole motor-car flew into several million small pieces, and there were David and his uncle standing in the middle of the road.

Uncle Popacatapetl began whimpering again.

"I'm a poor old man," he said, "and I don't know whether I'm standing on my head or my heels."

David looked at him attentively.

"I think you're standing on your heels," he said, "but it's so dark I can't tell you for certain. Wait till I light a match."

There came a noise of running behind them, and, before David could be sure whether his uncle was on his head or his heels, he saw the porter and the Mint-man and the bank manager rushing down the street towards them.

At that very moment the telegraph wires began to sing, as they always do when a telegram is coming along them, and looking up he saw a very long one with its mackintosh on sliding down the wires. It was so long that it came within six or seven feet of the ground.

"Quick, jump and catch hold of it," said David, "and then you'll be safe."

Twice Uncle Popacatapetl tried to jump, but he couldn't jump far because he was so heavy, and the Mint-man with the meat-chopper in his hand was close upon them. But the kind good telegram, which was reply-paid, reached down a hand, and pulled him up at the very moment the Mint-man and the manager were grabbing at him. They just missed him, and the Mint-man being unable to stop himself flew over the railing of the bridge, followed by the manager and the porter, and they all fell into the river with three splashes, each louder than all the rest put together.

By this time the telegram and Uncle Popacatapetl were far away out of sight, and as the chauffeur had vanished too, there was little use in David's remaining on the bridge all alone. He tried, as long as his match burned, to put together some pieces of the motor-car, but when that went out, it was like doing the most awful jig-saw puzzle in the dark.

So he walked back up the street, for there was a bright light coming out of the door of the bank, which looked cheerful, and besides he remembered that he had been sent to ask his Uncle Popacatapetl to tea, so that probably there would be tea ready.

"It must be time for tea," he thought, "because it has been dark quite a long time, and I haven't had it yet. Tea always comes soon after dark even on the shortest days."

By the bank door were standing the two airmen, whose machines he had unbuttoned. They had got their caps on the side of their heads all right, but they didn't look quite like ordinary airmen. The nose of one had grown enormously since David saw him last, and he waved it about, turning up the end of it in a manner that reminded David not of an airman at all, but of some quite different sort of creature. The other had a large kind face, and kept moving his mouth round and round, and out of his hair there distinctly stuck two horns, both broken.

As soon as they saw David they ran inside the bank, and shut the door in his face, leaving him out in the dark and the cold.

PART FOUR

Political Parodies

The Westminster Alice

SAKI

ILLUSTRATIONS BY F. CARRUTHERS GOULD

1900-1902

*S*AKI was the pen name of Hector Hugh Munro (1870-1916), which he adopted in 1900 before beginning his collaboration with political cartoonist F. Carruthers Gould on the *Alice* sketches for the *Westminster Gazette*. These sketches marked the beginning of a brief but significant writing career; Munro went on to author several short story collections, plays, and three novels. Though the sketches in *Alice in Westminster* specifically reflect British uneasiness with the Boer War in South Africa, they anticipate Saki's later work in a number of respects, satirizing the smug complacency of the English upper class, and—as in many of his short stories such as "Gabriel-Ernest," "Sredni Vashtar," and "The Toys of Peace"—using a child to reveal social hypocrisy and delusion. In his verse introduction, Saki characterizes Alice as—like Ewing's Amelia—"a very observing child," an agent of social insight:

> "Alice," Child with dreaming eyes,
> > Noting things that come to pass
> Turvey-wise in Wonderland
> > Backwards through a Looking-Glass.

In his foreword to a collection of the *Westminster Alice* sketches, former *Westminster Gazette* editor J.A. Spender wrote: "Parodies of the famous original [*Alice in Wonderland*] had several times been submitted to me (as I suppose to most editors) and nearly all had been dismal failures. Such things must either succeed perfectly or fail lamentably, and to succeed perfectly meant not merely copying the form but catching the spirit of the inimitable fantastic original. I cannot imagine any one doubting that 'Saki' is one of the few who have succeeded."[1]

---

1. "The Westminster Alice," *The Novels and Plays of Saki* (New York: Viking, 1944) 293.

The Westminster Alice

Introduction

"Alice," Child with dreaming eyes,
    Noting things that come to pass
Turvey-wise in Wonderland
    Backwards through a Looking-Glass.

Figures flit across thy dream,
    Muddle through and flicker out
Some in cocksure blessedness,
    Some in Philosophic Doubt.

Some in brackets, some in sulks,
    Some with latchkeys on the ramp,
Living (in a sort of peace)
    In a Concentration Camp.

Party moves on either side,
    Checks and feints that don't deceive,
Knights and Bishops, Pawns and all,
    In a game of Make-Believe.

Things that fall contrariwise,
    Difficult to understand
Darkly through a Looking-Glass
    Turvey-wise in Wonderland.

ALICE IN DOWNING STREET

"HAVE YOU EVER SEEN an Ineptitude?" asked the Cheshire Cat suddenly; the Cat was nothing if not abrupt.

"Not in real life," said Alice. "Have you any about here?"

"A few," answered the Cat comprehensively. "Over there, for instance," it added, contracting its pupils to the requisite focus, "is the most perfect specimen we have."

Alice followed the direction of its glance and noticed for the first time a figure sitting in a very uncomfortable attitude on nothing in particular. Alice had no time to wonder how it managed to do it, she was busy taking in the appearance of the creature, which was something like a badly-written note of

interrogation and something like a guillemot, and seemed to have been trying to preen its rather untidy plumage with whitewash.

"What a dreadful mess it's in!" she remarked, after gazing at it for a few moments in silence. "What is it, and why is it here?"

"It hasn't any meaning," said the Cat, "it simply *is*."

"Can it talk?" asked Alice eagerly.

"It has never done anything else," chuckled the Cat.

"Can you tell me what you are doing here?" Alice inquired politely. The Ineptitude shook its head with a deprecatory motion and commenced to drawl, "I haven't an idea."

"It never has, you know," interrupted the Cheshire Cat rudely, "but in its leisure moments" (Alice thought it must have a good many of them) "when it isn't playing with a gutta-percha ball it unravels the groundwork of what people believe—or don't believe, I forget which."

"It really doesn't matter which," said the Ineptitude with languid interest.

"Of course it doesn't," the Cat went on cheerfully, "because the unravelling got so tangled that no one could follow it. Its theory is," he continued, seeing that Alice was waiting for more, "that you mustn't interfere with the Inevitable. Slide and let slide, you know."

"But what do you keep it here for?" asked Alice.

"Oh, somehow you can't help it; it's so perfectly harmless and amiable and says the nastiest things in the nicest manner, and the King just couldn't do without it. The King is only made of pasteboard, you know, with sharp edges; and the Queen"—here the Cat sank its voice to a whisper—"the Queen comes from another pack, made of Brummagem ware, without polish, but absolutely indestructible; always pushing, you know; but you can't push an Ineptitude. Might as well try to hustle a glacier."

"That's why you keep so many of them about," said Alice.

"Of course. But its temper is not what it used to be. Lots of things have happened to worry it."

"What sort of things?"

"Oh, people have been dying off in round numbers, in the most ostentatious manner, and the Ineptitude dislikes fuss—but hush, here's the King coming."

His Majesty was looking doleful and grumpy, Alice thought, as though he had been disturbed in an afternoon nap. "Who is this, and what is that Cat doing here?" he asked, glancing gloomily at Alice and her companion.

"I really must ask you to give me notice of these questions," said the Ineptitude with a yawn.

"There's a dragon loose somewhere in the garden," the King went on peevishly, "and I am expected to help in getting it under control. Do I look as if I could control dragons?"

Alice thought he certainly did not.

"What do you propose doing?" drawled the Ineptitude.

"That's just it," said the King. "I say that whatever is done must be done cautiously and deliberately; the Treasurer says that whatever is done must be done cheaply—I am afraid the Treasurer is the weakest member of the pack," he added anxiously.

"Only made of Bristol board, you know," explained the Cat aside to Alice.

"What does the Queen say about it?" asked the Ineptitude.

"The Queen says that if something is not done in less than no time there'll be a Dissolution."

Both looked very grave at this, and nothing was said for some minutes. The King was the first to break the silence. "What are you doing with that whitewash?" he demanded. "The Queen said everything was to be painted khaki."

"I know," said the creature pathetically, "but I had run out of khaki; the Unforeseen again, you know; and things needed whitewash so badly."

The Cat had been slowly vanishing during the last few minutes, till nothing remained of it but an eye. At the last remark it gave a wink at Alice and completed its eclipse.

When Alice turned round she found that both the King and the Ineptitude were fast asleep.

"It's no good remaining here," she thought, and as she did not want to meet either the Queen or the dragon, she turned to make her way out of the street.

"At any rate," she said to herself, "I know what an Ineptitude is like."

ALICE IN PALL MALL

"The great art in falling off a horse," said the White Knight, "is to have another handy to fall on to."

"But wouldn't that be rather difficult to arrange?" asked Alice.

"Difficult, of course," replied the Knight, "but in my Department one has to be provided for emergencies. Now, for instance, have you ever conducted a war in South Africa?"

Alice shook her head.

"I have," said the Knight, with a gentle complacency in his voice.

"And did you bring it to a successful conclusion?" asked Alice.

"Not exactly to a *conclusion*—not a *definite* conclusion, you know—nor entirely successful either. In fact, I believe it's going on still. . . . But you can't think how much forethought it took to get it properly started. I dare say, now, you are wondering at my equipment?"

Alice certainly was; the Knight was riding rather uncomfortably on a sober-paced horse that was prevented from moving any faster by an elaborate housing of red-tape trappings. "Of course, I see the reason for that," thought Alice; "if it were to move any quicker the Knight would come off." But there were a number of obsolete weapons and appliances hanging about the saddle that didn't seem of the least practical use.

"You see, I had read a book," the Knight went on in a dreamy far-away tone, "written by some one to prove that warfare under modern conditions was impossible. You may imagine how disturbing that was to a man of my profession. Many men would have thrown up the whole thing and gone home. But I grappled with the situation. You will never guess what I did."

Alice pondered. "You went to war, of course——"

"Yes; *but not under modern conditions.*"

The Knight stopped his horse so that he might enjoy the full effect of this announcement.

"Now, for instance," he continued kindly, seeing that Alice had not recovered her breath, "you observe this little short-range gun that I have hanging to my saddle? Why do you suppose I sent out guns of that particular kind? Because if they happened to fall into the hands of the enemy they'd be very little use to him. That was my own invention."

"I see," said Alice gravely; "but supposing you wanted to use them against the enemy?"

The Knight looked worried. "I know there is that to be thought of, but I didn't choose to be putting dangerous weapons into the enemy's hands. And then, again, supposing the Basutos had risen, those would have been just the sort of guns to drive them off with. Of course they *didn't* rise; but they might have done so, you know."

At this moment the horse suddenly went on again, and the Knight clutched convulsively at its mane to prevent himself from coming off.

"That's the worst of horses," he remarked apologetically; "they are so Unforeseen in their movements. Now, if I had had my way I would have done without them as far as possible—in fact, I began that way, only it didn't answer. And yet," he went on in an aggrieved tone, "at Crécy it was the foot-men who did the most damage."

"But," objected Alice, "if your men hadn't got horses how could they get about from place to place?"

"They couldn't. That would be the beauty of it," said the White Knight eagerly; "the fewer places your army moves to, the fewer maps you have to prepare. And we hadn't prepared very many. I'm not very strong at geography, but," he added, brightening, "you should hear me talk French."

"But," persisted Alice, "supposing the enemy went and attacked you at some other place——"

"They did," interrupted the Knight gloomily; "they appeared in strength at places that weren't even marked on the ordinary maps. But how do you think they got there?"

He paused and fixed his gentle eyes upon Alice as she walked beside him, and then continued in a hollow voice:

"They rode. Rode and carried rifles. They were no mortal foes—they were Mounted Infantry."

The Knight swayed about so with the violence of his emotion that it was inevitable that he should lose his seat, and Alice was relieved to notice that there was another horse with an empty saddle ready for him to scramble on to. There was a frightful dust, of course, but Alice saw him gathering the reins of his new mount into a bunch, and smiling down upon her with increased amiability.

"It's not an easy animal to manage," he called out to her, "but if I pat it and speak to it in French it will probably understand where I want it to go. And," he added hopefully, "it may go there. A knowledge of French and an amiable disposition will see one out of most things."

"Well," thought Alice as she watched him settling down uneasily into the saddle, "it ought not to take long to see him out of that."

ALICE AND THE LIBERAL PARTY

Quite a number of them were going past, and the noise was considerable, but they were marching in sixes and sevens and didn't seem to be guided by any fixed word of command, so that the effect was not so imposing as it might have been. Some of them, Alice noticed, had the letters "I.L." embroidered on their tunics and headpieces and other conspicuous places ("I wonder," she thought, "if it's marked on their underclothing as well"); others simply had a big "L," and others again were branded with a little "e." They got dreadfully in each other's way, and were always falling over one another in little heaps, while many of the mounted ones did not seem at all sure of their seats. "They won't go very far if they don't fall into better order," thought Alice, and she was glad to find herself the next minute in a spacious hall with a large marble staircase at one end of it. The White King was sitting on one of the steps, looking rather anxious and just a little uncomfortable under his heavy crown, which needed a good deal of balancing to keep it in its place.

"Did you happen to meet any fighting men?" he asked Alice.

"A great many—two or three hundred, I should think."

"Not quite two hundred, all told," said the King, referring to his note-book.

"Told what?" asked Alice.

"Well, they haven't been told anything, exactly—yet. The fact is," the King went on nervously, "we're rather in want of a messenger just now. I don't know how it is, there are two or three of them about, but lately they have always been either out of reach or else out of touch. You don't happen to have passed any one coming from the direction of Berkeley Square?" he asked eagerly.

Alice shook her head.

"There's the Primrose Courier, for instance," the King continued reflectively, "the most reliable Messenger we have; he understands all about Open Doors and Linked Hands and all that sort of thing, and he's quite as useful at home. But he frightens some of them nearly out of their wits by his Imperial Anglo-Saxon attitudes. I wouldn't mind his skipping about so if he'd only come back when he's wanted."

"And haven't you got any one else to carry your messages?" asked Alice sympathetically.

"There's the Unkhaki Messenger," said the King, consulting his pocket-book.

"I beg your pardon," said Alice.

"You know what Khaki means, I suppose?"

"It's a sort of colour," said Alice promptly; "something like dust."

"Exactly," said the King; "thou dost—he doesn't. That's why he's called the Unkhaki Messenger."

Alice gave it up.

"Such a dear, obliging creature," the King went on, "but so dreadfully unpunctual. He's always half a century in front of his times or half a century behind them, and that puts one out so."

Alice agreed that it would make a difference.

"It's helped to put us out quite six years already," the King went on plaintively; "but you can't cure him of it. You see he will wander about in by-ways

and deserts, hunting for Lost Causes, and whenever he comes across a stream he always wades against the current. All that takes him out of his way, you know; he's somewhere up in the Grampian Hills by this time."

"I see," said Alice; "that's what you mean by being out of touch. And the other Messenger is———"

"Out of reach," said the King. "Precisely."

"Then it follows," said Alice———

"I don't know what you mean by 'it,'" interrupted the King sulkily. "No one follows. That is why we stick in the same place. DON'T," he suddenly screamed, jumping up and down in his agitation. "Don't do it, I say."

"Do what?" asked Alice in some alarm.

"Give advice. I know you're going to. They've all been doing it for the last six weeks. I assure you the letters I get———"

"I wasn't going to give you advice," said Alice indignantly, "and as to letters, you've got too much alphabet as it is."

"Why, you're doing it now," said the King angrily. "Good-bye."

As Alice took the hint and walked away towards the door, she heard him calling after her in a kinder tone: "If you *should* meet any one coming from the direction of Berkeley Square———"

Clara in Blunderland

CAROLINE LEWIS

ILLUSTRATIONS BY STAFFORD RANSOME

1902

"CAROLINE LEWIS" was really the collaborative team of Harold Begbie (1871-1929), J. Stafford Ransome (b. 1860), and M.H. Temple, who together wrote two *Alice*-inspired political parodies, *Clara in Blunderland* and *Lost in Blunderland* (1903). Begbie, who also wrote under the pseudonym "A Gentleman With a Duster," worked as a journalist for a number of British newspapers. He also authored more than twenty-five novels, works of non-fiction and biographies, including *The Political Struwwelpeter* (1899), *The Life of William Booth, the Founder of the Salvation Army* (1920), and an *Alice*-like fantasy novel, *Bundy in the Greenwood* (1902). Ransome, the illustrator as well as partial author of *Clara in Blunderland,* worked as a journalist, and was the author of a number of works on engineering and labor issues. Like Saki's *Westminster Alice* sketches, *Clara in Blunderland* reflects British anger at the government's failure to resolve the Boer war, and uneasiness with the current heads of state:

> Drifting—All o'er the sea of politics
> Full leisurely we glide;
> And Britain's bark, with little skill,
> And little care we guide,
> While little minds make little plans,
> And stronger hands are tied. [ix]

Clara in Blunderland

DEDICATED

With the most profound affection
and respect to the memory of
LEWIS CARROLL,
to whom the author is as much
indebted for the text as the
illustrator to Sir John Tenniel
for the ensuing parodies of his
perfect pictures.

DRIFTING

All o'er the sea of Politics
  Full leisurely we glide;
And Britain's bark with little skill,
  And little care we guide,
While little minds make little plans,
  And stronger hands are tied.

Ah, cruel fate! to make us tell
  This very plaintive story,
Of Clara's trip to Blunderland,
  Of creatures bold and boery;
And clothe in garb of fantasy
  Prosaic Whig and Tory.

A sense of Duty urged us first
  To "hurry and begin it."
Fatuity then whispered low,
  "It won't take half a minute!"
We laughed to scorn the bare idea
  That there was money in it.

So far we have confined our words
  To merely pointless chatter,
As flat as other prefaces,
  Perhaps a trifle flatter;
But, as the reader always skips
  This part, it does not matter.

One serious word—we have to pay
Our tribute to those sages
Who wrote and drew that "Wonderland"
On which are based these pages.
A classic which in nursery land
Will stand the test of ages.

We claim that naught within these leaves
Has been set down in malice,
That certainly against the State
By us there no cabal is—
And, reader, if you've praise to give,
Bestow it all on Alice.

CHAPTER 1. IN A HOLE AGAIN

*C*LARA FELT VERY LISTLESS and stupid that afternoon. You see she had so many governesses and they taught her such very dull lessons. There was Miss Bowles, who tried to instruct her in facts and figures, and all sorts of stupid things of that kind, and Miss Yerburgh, who wanted her to learn about China and other places in which she never could feel any interest, and another lady to teach her the use of the *Globe;* but nobody to give her nice little lessons in kindergarten philosophy, or even to help her and her sister Geraldine in making Irish stew.

No wonder she felt dull; and there was no occasion for surprise when, purely in search of distraction, she went right into a hole on the putting green to fetch out her ball. People do and say such funny things when they are bored at golf.

You may think it wonderful that such a big girl as Clara could get down a hole of this sort, but she had a marvellous gift in that way, and it was said that she could get into a hole when no one else would have found it possible; so you see she had no difficulty about it.

This particular hole, however, appeared to be bottomless, and the moment she got into it she began to fall, which made her say at once to herself, "Dear me! I must be dreaming again, for of course in real life I could never fall at all. My Aunt Sarum would not allow it."

But she fell,
and fell,
and fell.
Down,
down,
down,

until she began to fear that she would fall right down to the level of the Aberrationals, and come out in Ireland, where the inhabitants are all cannibals, and the resources of civilisation have long ago been exhausted.

"I *do* wish," she said, as she was falling, "I had Geraldine with me. Then I could hide in some Cabinet or other where I should never be noticed and, perhaps, when the Aberrationals had eaten her, they wouldn't be hungry for me. I never knew anybody except Auntie for whom one of the family was not *quite* enough."

She was, so she thought, years and years in falling, and once she nearly saved herself by catching hold of an Old Age Pension which was sticking out of a pigeon-hole in the wall, with nobody to look after it. But it pulled itself back and hissed at her, "just," as she said afterwards, "like a Snake in the Grass." So you see it only caused her to slacken in her downward career for the moment.

A little later she saw in another recess a large and very dusty jar labelled PROGRAMME. She snatched it off the shelf eagerly, as she passed, for she was hungry by this time. "This ought to be good," she said to herself; but, alas! it was empty, and with a sigh she placed it on a lower shelf.

And still she went
down,
down,
down.

At last, however, the great fall was over, and Clara found that she was not nearly so much hurt as she expected.

She found herself sitting on a nice little seat which was as safe as you can imagine, and which was situated in a large hall full of green chairs. In the highest of these sat a very sedate White Rabbit, who said, "Order! Order!" in a loud voice; but as nobody brought any refreshments, and as he said he was "now going to read the bill," Clara thought she had better try to find some way out, as she did not wish to pay for food she had not had.

All the doors were locked, but through the key-hole of one (which bore the inscription "Noblesse Oblige. Admittance £20,000 a year. Liberal discount to Successful Brewers and Unsuccessful Generals.") she could see a beautiful garden, carpeted with flowers of hereditary intellect, and filled with hundreds upon hundreds of happy children, of whom three formed a quorum, and of whom some seemed to be more than half awake. "I shall call that the Palace of Sleeping Beauties," cried Clara, in ecstasies, quite forgetting that a garden can't be a palace.

She tried very hard to get through the key-hole into this charming place, but it was of no use, and when she found that she would have to stop in the hall with the green chairs and hear the White Rabbit read the bill, she sat down and cried and cried.

"Must I stop here for ever and ever?" she moaned.

"My dear," answered the White Rabbit, "I am afraid you will never leave this house until it is dissolved."

"Oh dear, oh dear," she said despairingly. "Why *was* it built on such solid foundations?"

"You ought to be very thankful," he added, "after your great come down, to be here at all when you think how many strange creatures are trying to get in and can't."

After the bill was read the serious business began. The hall became full of all sorts of animals. "Both quadrangles and biceps," as she told Geraldine afterwards. There were a good many geese, a very ugly duckling, some saucy monkeys, wolves in sheeps' clothing, parrots in eagles' feathers, guinea pigs looking about for guineas, pigeons, cuckoos, and any quantity of rats. These strangely assorted creatures began at once to wrangle, and insult each other, and soon there was a free fight, which lasted, Clara could not say how long.

At length, however, the White Rabbit rose from his seat, and pulled out his watch, crying, "Time! Time!"

Then the animals and birds trooped out of the hall, and Clara found herself hustled by the crowd out into the lobby.

When the noisy party had thinned down somewhat, a stately Dodo approached Clara diplomatically, and said politely, "I have been watching you for some time in the house, and, if you will excuse my saying so, my dear, admiring your way of looking on while other people did the business. It seems to me that you have grasped the meaning of that policy of masterly inactivity which is the key-note to our Party Tactics."

Clara did not understand the meaning of all these long words, but she smiled prettily.

"You are still a comparatively innocent child," continued the Dodo, with kindly patronage, "and what you want is Protection."

"I do wear a chest protector in the winter," said Clara, "and I don't like it, but Aunt Sarum makes——"

"Tut! tut! my dear, you want more than that, you want protecting everywhere, and against everything. Confide in me. I will protect you. Take this bottle and drink its contents. You must drink it all if you want to be thoroughly protected."

"It would be very nice to be protected," said Clara, "for some of those beasts are rather terrifying." She looked up into the fatherly face of the Dodo and could not help having confidence in him; he was so ponderous and bland.

She took the bottle in her hand. "Is it nice?" she asked.

"Delicious, my dear," he replied. "It is all sugar on the top and there are lots of plums in it."

Clara had noticed the Red Queen, standing by the door and eyeing her narrowly, and every now and then, when the Dodo wasn't looking, she seemed to be signing to Clara not to drink the stuff.

Clara hesitated.

"Come, come, my dear," said the Dodo, persuasively. "It's so nice, besides it will make you grow out of all conscience. Drink it up."

She uncorked the bottle cautiously, and sniffed at the contents. It was quite white, and didn't smell nasty; besides Clara had a vague ambition to become something big. The Red Queen was still beckoning to her, but Clara threw prudence to the winds and took a sip.

Certainly she was growing——

Crash! Bang!!

What was the matter? Clara had shot up so rapidly that her head had struck the chandelier, and the shock had caused her to drop the bottle, which now lay shattered by her far off feet.

"Ah! you foolish girl," cried the Dodo, angrily, "you have lost your chance of becoming one of us. Unless the whole is swallowed the effect will not last. See, you are shrinking again already. You naughty child," he continued, working himself up into a passion, "you have wasted all that old and crusted spirit of conservatism; and there is very little of the genuine article left in the country. We can only get the real thing in China now, and we have found the Chinese article very expensive lately."

"Oh, please!" sobbed Clara, "I'm so sorry—I'm sure, I——"

"What would have happened I really don't know," said Clara, afterwards, "he was *so* angry."

Just then, however, the Red Queen saved the situation by rushing furiously up to the Dodo. "Why can't you leave the girl alone?" she cried, and turning to Clara, she said, "The Dodo's aims are too high for you, my dear. What you want is speed, not height. Come along with me."

Seizing Clara unceremoniously by the hand, she hurried her off the terrace. Out into the country they sped at a terrible rate which was ever increasing. It was not running. It was not flying. It was shooting. On, on, they shot till the little girl was giddy and terrified.

"Stop! stop! I'm a—fraid—I—can't—go—your—pace," gasped Clara.

Alice in Blunderland
An Iridescent Dream

JOHN KENDRICK BANGS
ILLUSTRATIONS BY ALBERT LEVERING
1907

JOHN KENDRICK BANGS (1862-1922) was an American humorist and author of novels, short fiction, essays and drama. Unlike his contemporaries and colleagues Samuel Clemens and Ambrose Bierce, Bangs sought more to entertain and delight with his good-natured wit than to satirize, and his urbane but gentle style of humor was an inspiration for Harold Ross in founding the *New Yorker* magazine in the 1920s. The father of three boys, Bangs was also a writer and collector of fairy tales, legends, and myths, collaborating with Charles Macauley on an *Alice*-like fantasy called *Emblemland* in 1902. His *Alice in Blunderland* pokes fun at familiar issues from high taxes and bureaucratic ineptitude to the greediness of giant business "copperations":

> A copperation is a beast
>   With forty leven paws
> That doesn't ever pay the least
>   Attention to the laws.
>
> It grabs whatever comes in sight
>   From hansom cabs to socks
> And with a grin of mad delight
>   It turns 'em into stocks. [8]

Alice in Blunderland

Chapter 1. Off to Blunderland

*I*T WAS ONE OF THOSE dull, drab, depressing days when somehow or other it seemed as if there wasn't anything anywhere for anybody to do. It was raining outdoors, so that Alice could not amuse herself in the garden, or call upon her friend Little Lord Fauntleroy up the street; and downstairs her mother was giving a Bridge Party for the benefit of the M. O. Hot Tamale Company, which had lately fallen upon evil days. Alice's mother was a very charitably disposed person, and while she loathed gambling in all its forms, was nevertheless willing for the sake of a good cause to forego her principles on alternate Thursdays, but she was very particular that her little daughter should be kept aloof from contaminating influences, so that Alice found herself locked in the nursery and, as I have already intimated, with nothing to do. She had read all her books—The House of Mirth, the novels of Hall Caine and Marie Corelli—the operation for appendicitis upon her dollie, while very successful indeed, had left poor Flaxilocks without a scrap of sawdust in her veins, and therefore unable to play; and worst of all, her pet kitten, under the new city law making all felines public property, had grown into a regular cat and appeared only at mealtimes, and then in so disreputable a condition that he was not thought to be fit company for a child of seven.

"Oh dear!" cried Alice impatiently, as she sat rocking in her chair, listening to the pattering of the rain upon the roof of the veranda. "I do wish there was something to do, or somebody to do, or somewhere to go. The Gov'ment ought to provide covered playgrounds for children on wet days. It wouldn't cost much to put a glass cover on the Park!"

"A very good idea! I'll make a note of that," said a squeaky little voice at her side.

Alice sprang to her feet in surprise. She had supposed she was alone, and for a moment she was frightened, but a glance around reassured her, for strange to say, seated on the radiator warming his toes was her old friend the Hatter, the queer old chap she had met in her marvellous trip through Wonderland, and with him was the March Hare, the Cheshire Cat, and the White Knight from Looking Glass Land.

"Why—you dear old things!" she cried. "You here?"

"I don't know about these others, but I'm here," returned the Hatter. "The others seem to be here, but I respectfully decline to take my solemn daffydavy on the subject, because my doctor says I'm all the time seeing things that ain't. Besides I don't believe in swearing."

"We're here all right," put in the March Hare. "I know because we ain't anywhere else, and when you ain't anywhere else you can make up your mind that you're here."

"Well, I'm awfully glad to see you," said Alice. "I've been so lonesome——"

"We know that," said the White Knight. "We've been studying your case lately and we thought we'd come down and see what we could do for you. The fact is the Hatter here has founded a model city, where everything goes just right, and we came to ask you to pay us a call."

"A city?" cried Alice.

"Yep," said the March Hare. "It's called Blunderland and between you and me I don't believe anybody but the Hatter could have invented one like it. His geegantic brain conceived the whole thing, and I tell you it's a corker."

"Where is it?" asked Alice.

"That's telling," said the Hatter. "I haven't had it copyrighted yet, and until I do I ain't going to tell where it is. You can't be too careful about property these days with copperations lurkin' around everywhere to grab everything in sight."

"What's a copperation?" asked Alice.

"What? Never heard of a Copperation?" demanded the Hatter. "Mercy! Ever hear of the Mumps, or the Measles, or the Whooping Cough?"

"Yes—but I never knew they were called Copperations," said Alice.

"Well, they ain't, but they're no worse—so they ought to be," said the Hatter. "Listen here. I'll tell you what a copperation is."

And putting his hat in front of his mouth like a telephone the Hatter recited the following poem through it:

THE COPPERATION

A copperation is a beast
  With forty leven paws
That doesn't ever pay the least
  Attention to the laws.

It grabs whatever comes in sight
  From hansom cabs to socks
And with a grin of mad delight
  It turns 'em into stocks

And then it takes a rubber hose
  Connected with the sea
And pumps 'em full of H_2Os
  Of various degree

And when they're swollen up so stout
  You'd think they'd surely bust
They souse 'em once again and out
  They come at last a Trust

And when the Trust is ready for
  One last and final whack
They let the public in the door
  To buy the water back.

"See?" said the Hatter as he finished.

"No," said Alice. "It sounded very pretty through your hat, but I don't understand it. Why should people buy water when they can get it for nothing in the ocean?"

"You're like all the rest," groaned the Hatter. "Nobody seems to understand but me, and somehow or other I can't make it clear to other people."

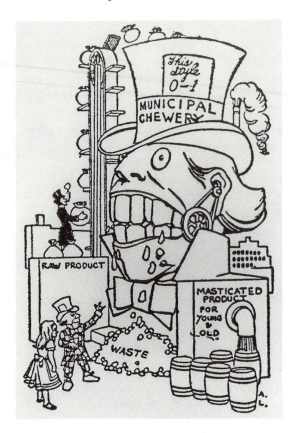

"You might if you didn't talk through your hat," grinned the Cheshire Cat.

"Then I'd have to stop being a public character," said the Hatter. "I'm not going to sacrifice my career just because you're too ignorant to see what I'm driving at. I don't mind telling you though, Alice, that outside of poetry a Copperation is a Creature devised by Selfish Interests to secure the Free Coinage of the Atlantic Ocean."

> "Little drops of water,
> Plenty of hot air,
> Make a Copperation
> A pretty fat affair,"

warbled the March Hare.

"O well," said Alice, "what about it? Suppose there is such an animal around. What are we going to do about it?"

"We're going to gerraple with it," said the Hatter, with a valiant shake of his hat. "We're going to grab it by its throat, and shake it down, and shackle it so that in forty years it will become as tame as a fly or any other highly domesticated animal."

"But how?" asked Alice. "You aren't going to do this yourself, are you? Single handed and alone?"

"Yes," said the Hatter. "The March Hare and the White Knight and I. We've started a city to do it with. We've sprinkled our streets with Rough on Copperations until there isn't one left in the place. Everything in town belongs to the People—street cars, gutters, pavements, theatres, electric light, cabs, manicures, dogs, cats, canary birds, hotels, barber shops, candy stores, hats, umbrellas, bakeries, cakeries, steakeries, shops,—you can't think of a thing that the city don't own. No more private ownership of anything from a toothbrush to a yacht, and the result is we are all happy."

"It sounds fine," said Alice. "Though I think I should rather own my own toothbrush."

"You naturally would under the old system," assented the Hatter. "Under a system of private ownership owning your own teeth you'd prefer to own your own toothbrush, but our Council has just passed a law making teeth public property. You see we found that some people had teeth and other people hadn't, which is hardly a fair condition under a Republican form of Government. It gave one class of citizens a distinct advantage over other people and the Declaration of Independence demands absolute equality for all. One man owning his own teeth could eat all the hickory nuts he wanted just because he had teeth to crack 'em with, while another man not having teeth had either to swallow 'em whole, which ruined his digestion, or go without, which wasn't fair."

"I see," said Alice.

"So it occurred to Mr. Alderman March Hare here," continued the Hatter, "that we should legislate in the matter, and at our last session we passed a law providing for the Municipal Ownership of Teeth, so that now when a toothless wanderer wants a hickory nut cracked he has a perfectly legal right to stop anybody in the street who has teeth and make him crack the nut for him. Of course we've had a little trouble enforcing the law—alleged private rights are always difficult to get around. Long-continued possession has seemed so to convince people that they have inherent rights to the things they have enjoyed that they put up a fight and appeal to the Constitution and all that, and even when you mention the fact, as I did in a case that came up the other day (when a man refused to bite off another chap's cigar for him), that the Constitution doesn't mention teeth anywhere in all its classes, they are not easy to convince. This fellow insisted that his teeth were private property, and no city law should make them public property. He's going to take it to the Supreme Court. Meanwhile his teeth are in the custody of the sheriff."

"And what has become of the man?" asked Alice.

"He's in the custody of the sheriff too," said the Hatter. "We couldn't arrange it any other way except by pulling his teeth, and he didn't want that."

"I can't blame him," said Alice reflectively. "I should hate to have my teeth taken away from me."

"O there's no obfuscation about it," said the Hatter.

"Confuscation," corrected the March Hare. "I wish you would get that word right. It's too important to fool with."

"Thank you," replied the Hatter. "My mind is on higher things than mere words. However, as I was saying, there is no cobfuscation about it. We don't take a man's teeth away from him without compensation. We pay him what the teeth are worth and place them at the service of the whole community."

"Where do you get the money to pay him?" asked Alice.

"We give him a Municipal Bond," explained the Hatter. "It's a ten per cent. bond costing two cents to print. When he cracks a hickory nut for the public, the man he cracks it for pays him a cent. He rings this up on a cash register he carries pinned to his vest, and at the end of every week turns in the cash to the City Treasury. That money is used to pay the interest on the bonds. The scheme has the additional advantage that it makes a man's teeth negotiable property in the sense that whereas under the old system he couldn't very well sell his teeth, under the new system he can sell the bond if he gets hard up. Moreover, the City Government having acquired control has to pay all his dentist's bills, supply tooth powder and so on, which results in a great saving to the individual. It hardly costs the city anything, except for the Tooth Inspector, who is paid $1,200 a year, but we can handle that easily enough, provided the people will use the Public Teeth in sufficiently large numbers to bring in dividends. Anyhow, we have gone in for it, and I see no reason why it should not work as well as any other Municipal Ownership scheme."

"I should love to go and see your city," said Alice, who, though not quite convinced as to the desirability of the Municipal Ownership of Teeth, was nevertheless very much interested.

"Very well," said the Hatter. "We can go at once, for I see the train is already standing in the Station."

"The Station?" cried Alice. "What Station?"

But before the Hatter could answer, Alice, glancing through the window, caught sight of a very beautiful train standing before the veranda, and in a moment she found herself stepping on board with her friends, while a soft-spoken guard at the door was handing her an engraved card upon a silver salver "Respectfully Inviting Miss Alice to Step Lively There.". . .

CHAPTER 7. OWNERSHIP OF CHILDREN

"What time is it?" asked the Hatter, suddenly turning to the White Knight.

"Six o'clock," replied the White Knight, looking at his watch.

"Mercy!" cried Alice. "I had no idea it was so late! I shall have to run along home—it's supper time."

The Hatter laughed.

"O, as for that," he said, "there's no hurry. Under our present system of Municipal Ownership of Everything, I can issue, as Mayor, a general order postponing the Municipal Supper Hour to seven or eight o'clock. Still—if you'd prefer to go home——"

"I don't want to," said Alice courteously, "but I think I'd better. My mother would be worried not finding me in the nursery. You see, I left home without telling anybody where I was going."

Again the Hatter laughed.

"What foolishness!" he ejaculated. "That's the great trouble with the private ownership of children. It worries their poor mothers, keeps 'em from their daily Bridge parties, interferes with that freedom of action which is guaranteed to the individual by the contravention of the United States——"

"Constitution, I guess you mean," suggested Alice.

"It used to be the Constitution," returned the Hatter, "but now it's the Contravention. It has been contravened so often in the past few years that our Reformed Language Commission at Washington has named it accordingly."

"It simply bears out what you said in your message approving the Public Ownership of Children Act passed by the Common Council last November, which I wrote for you, and consequently consider a very able document," said the White Knight.

"The Public Ownership of Children?" cried Alice, with a look of alarm on her face.

"Yes," said the Hatter. "Just as the Nation has gone in for paternalism, we here in Blunderland have gone in for maternalism. The children here belong to the city——"

"But—" Alice began.

"Now, don't bother," said the Hatter kindly. "It works very well. It has

reduced children to a state of scientific control which is as careful and as ef-
fective as that of the street cleaning department or the public parks, and it
has emancipated the mothers as well as materially decreased the financial
obligations of the fathers."

Alice's lip quivered slightly, and she began to feel a little bit afraid of
the Hatter.

"I want to go home," she whimpered.

"Certainly—as you wish," said the Hatter. "We'll take you there at once.
Come along."

Reassured by the Hatter's kindly manner Alice took her companion's
outstretched hand and they walked along the highway together until they
came to a handsome apartment house fronting upon a beautiful park, where
the Hatter pressed an electric button at one side of the massive entrance. The
response to the bell was immediate, and Alice was pleased to find that the
person to answer was none other than the Duchess herself.

"Why, how-di-doo," said the Duchess affably. "Glad to see you again,
Miss Alice."

"Thank you," said Alice. "It is very nice to be here. Do you live in this
beautiful building?"

"Yes," said the Duchess. "You see, I've just been appointed Commissioner of Maternity. I'm what you might call the official mother of the town.
Since that great Statesman, the Hatter"—here the Duchess winked graciously at the March Hare—"devised his crowning achievement in the Municipal
Control of the Children and appointed me to be the Head of the Department, I have been stationed here."

"And a mighty good old mother she is!" ejaculated the Hatter with
fervour.

"Palaverer!" said the Duchess coyly.

"Not at all," said the Hatter. "I speak not as a man, but as a Mayor, and
what I say is to be construed as an official tribute to a faithful and deserving
public servant."

"Servant, sir?" repeated the Duchess haughtily.

"In the American sense," said the Hatter with a low bow. "In the sense
that the servant is as good as, if not better than the employer, Madam."

"That man's a perfect Dipsomaniac," said the March Hare.

"Diplomat, man—diplomat," corrected the White Knight. "A dipsomaniac is a very different thing from a Diplomat. Consuls may be dipsoma-
niacs, but a Diplomat is a man worthy of Ambassadorial honours."

"Oh—I see," said the March Hare. "Well—he's a Diplomat all right,
all right."

"How are things going to-day, Duchess?" asked the Hatter. "Children happy?"

"They will be in time," said the Duchess. "So many of them have been brought up so far on the *Ladies' Home Journal* system that it is hard to introduce the new Blunderland method without friction."

"I was afraid of that," said the Hatter. "How does the compulsory soda-water regulation work?"

"Splendidly," said the Duchess. "Since I started in in January to make the children drink five glasses of Vanilla Cream soda every day as a matter of routine and duty, sixty per cent. of them have come to hate it. I think that by the end of the year we shall have stamped out the love of soda almost entirely. The same way with caramels and other candies in place of beef. We have caramels for breakfast, gum-drops for dinner and marshmallows for tea, regularly, and last night seventeen of the children presented a petition asking for beef-steak, mutton chops and boiled rice. I have a firm conviction that when the new law, requiring beef to be sold at candy stores, and compelling those in charge of the young to teach them that boiled rice and hominy are bad for the teeth, goes into effect, we shall find the children clamouring for wholesome food as eagerly as they do now for things that ruin their little tummies."

"It's a splendid system—and how are you meeting the matinee problem?" asked the March Hare.

"Same way," said the Duchess. "Every Wednesday and Saturday afternoon we make 'em go to a matinee, rain or shine, whether they want to or not, and really it's pathetic to see how some of the little dears pine for a half-holiday with a hoople, and since I forbade the youngsters to even look at the back of a geography, or a spelling book, it is most amusing to see how they sneak into the library and devour the contents of those two books when they think nobody's looking. I caught one of the boys reading an Arithmetic in bed last night, wholly neglecting his Jack Harkaway books that I had commanded him to read, and leaving his 'Bim, the Broncho Buster of Buffalo,' absolutely uncut."

"Fine!" chuckled the Hatter. "And now, my dear Duchess, will you oblige me by taking charge of Miss Alice? She has expressed a desire to go home and so I have brought her here."

"Certainly," said the Duchess. "I'll look after her."

"You'll excuse us, Alice," said the Hatter, politely. "We'd escort you further ourselves, but a question has come before the Municipal Ownership Caucus that we must settle before the meeting of the Common Council to-night. Certain of our members claim that they have a right to sell their votes for $500 apiece——"

"Mercy!" cried Alice. "Why, that is—that is terrible."

"It certainly is," said the March Hare ruefully. "It's more than terrible, it's rotten. Here I've been holding out for $1,250 for mine, and these duffers want to go in for a cut rate that will absolutely ruin the business."

"It's a very important matter," said the Hatter. "After all our striving to elevate the people we don't want them to make themselves too cheap. For my part I don't think they should let go of a vote on any question for less than $2,500."

"That's all right, Mr. Mayor," said the White Knight. "But you don't want to frighten capital, you know."

"Well, you and I disagree on that point," said the Mayor. "Capital isn't at all necessary to the success of our schemes. My watchword is Bonds, and as long as I have a printing press to print 'em, and a fountain pen to sign 'em I'm not going to be influenced one way or another by a feeling of subserviency to the capitalist class. Good night, Miss Alice. Glad to have met you and I hope you will have a pleasant time with the Duchess. Here," he added, taking a beautifully printed green and gold paper from his pocket, "here is a Blanket Mortgage 18% Deferred Debenture Bond on the Main Street Ferry of a par value of $100,000 payable in 3457, as a souvenir of your visit."

"A hundred thousand dollars," cried Alice. "For me?"

"No," corrected the Hatter. "A hundred thousand dollar bond. You don't get the money until 3457, and not then unless you present it in person to the City Treasurer."

With which munificent gift the Hatter respectfully bowed himself away and made off, followed by the March Hare.

"Good-bye, Alice," said the White Knight sympathetically; and then thrusting a paper in her hand, he leaned forward and whispered into the little girl's ear, "If you get into trouble, use this."

"Thank you," said Alice. "What is it?"

"It's a temporary injunction issued by the Chief Justice restraining anybody from interfering with you," said the White Knight. "You may need it."

And the kindly old knight ran madly off up the street after the Mayor and the March Hare, and shortly after disappeared around the corner.

"Now, my little dear," said the Duchess, "we'll take you home."

Seizing Alice by the hand the Duchess led the little traveller into the Municipal Nursery. Entering the elevator, they went up and up and up and up until Alice thought they would never stop. Finally on the 117th floor the elevator stopped. Alice and the Duchess alighted and entered a funny little flat, singularly enough labelled with Alice's own name.

"This is it," said the Duchess. "There is your bedroom, here is your parlour, and that is the bath-room. The apartment has running soda-water, hot and cold; you will find a refrigerator stocked with peanut brittle, molasses candy, and sugared fruits in the pantry. Your reading will consist of Lucy the Lace Vendor, or How the Laundress Became a Lady; the works of Marie Corelli; Factory Fanny, the Forger's Daughter, and any other unwholesome book you may want from the House of Correction Library. Play-time will begin at seven every morning and you will be compelled to dress and undress dolls until one, when your caramel will be given to you, after which you will skip the rope and read fairy stories until six. You must drink five glasses of soda-water every day and will not be allowed to go to bed before eleven o'clock at night. Hurry now, and get your hair mussed and your hands dirty for dinner. The first course of whipped cream and roasted chestnuts will be served promptly at six-thirty."

"But," cried Alice, "I don't want to stay here—I want to go home."

"You are home," said the Duchess. "This is the Municipal Home of the Children of Blunderland."

"But I want my father and mother," whimpered Alice.

"The City is your father, my child, and I am officially your mother," said the Duchess.

"You are not!" cried Alice. "You are trying to kidnap me!—I'll—I'll call the police."

"The police can't arrest a city, my dear child, and as for me, as the Commissioner of Maternity I am immune from arrest," laughed the Duchess.

"Well, I just won't stay, that's all," cried Alice, stamping her foot angrily. "I don't want a city for a father, and I shan't have an official mother in place of a real one."

The child ran toward the door, but the Duchess was too quick for her, seizing her by the arm.

"Let me go!" shrieked Alice.

"Never," snapped the Duchess.

And then the little girl thought of the piece of paper the White Knight had given her.

"I guess that will make you change your mind," she said, handing the injunction to her captor.

The Duchess read it carefully; her face paled, and she too stamped her foot.

"I'll see about this," she roared angrily, and in a moment she had gone, slamming the door so hard behind her that the building fairly shook. A moment later Alice followed, and in a short time was bounding down the stairway as fast as her little legs would carry her toward freedom, when all of a

sudden she tripped and began to fall—down, down, down—O, would she never stop! And then, bump! Her fall was over, and strange to relate the little maid found herself sitting on the floor back in her own nursery in her own real home, with her mother bending over her.

"Dear me, Alice," said her mother. "I hope you haven't hurt yourself."

"No," said Alice. "Why—have I—I really fallen?"

"You most certainly have—off the sofa," laughed her mother. "Where have you been?" she added. "In Wonderland again?"

"No," said Alice. "In Blunderland—this time."

Which struck her father, when he heard the story of her adventures later, as a very apt and descriptive title for the M. O. Country.

Alice and the Stork
A Fairy Tale for Workingmen's Children

HENRY T. SCHNITTKIND
1915

HENRY THOMAS SCHNITTKIND (1886-1970) was the full name of the American author who also wrote under the pen name Henry Thomas. Highly educated, with a doctor of philosophy degree from Harvard University, Schnittkind wrote books ranging in subject from mathematics and politics to biography and philosophy. Indeed, in a *Who's Who* entry from the late 1930s, Schnittkind listed his hobby (with what degree of irony it is impossible to say) as "education of the masses." His satire, *Alice and the Stork,* is particularly interesting in its appropriation of the familiar *Alice* form and character for a strongly socialist and pro-women's suffrage satire of wealthy upper-class inhumanity and greed, a striking contrast to Bang's antisocialist *Alice in Blunderland.* Alice is "the daughter of a rich landlord" who has been led by her parents and nurse to believe that "poor people who cannot buy a house for themselves are lazy and good-for-nothing" (14). Continually struggling to grow beyond the limited ideas of her upbringing, Alice learns compassion for others through a series of dream adventures. In this middle chapter, Alice's adventures continue after she has been scolded for playing with some poor children in the park.

Alice and the Stork

CHAPTER 4. ALICE VISITS THE AMERICAN EAGLE

WHEN ALICE HAD BEEN SCOLDED for playing with the poor children, she sat down near the window and began to pout. She thought that her mother and the nurse were right, but still she felt very miserable because she was not able to play with children whom she liked.

Soon she forgot all about her troubles, for she saw a little swallow on the window-sill.

"Pretty swallow," said Alice, "where are you coming from?"

"I'm coming from the land of Joy, where I go every morning to renew my voice by drinking out of the spring of Pure Thought and Unbought Melody."

"What queer names!" cried Alice. "What do they mean, anyhow?"

"The land of Joy," said the swallow, "is the land that all men dream about when they are unhappy. In that land all faces are as bright as the morning sky and all hearts sing as the waterfalls in the springtime. It is not way up in the clouds, but it is a real land. Some people see it once in a great while, but nobody believes them."

"And what is the spring of Pure Thoughts and Unbought Melody, where you renew your voice?" asked Alice.

"That," said the swallow, "is the spring whose pure water has never been made muddy by the false thoughts of people, for the only thoughts that are found there come from the bottom of the heart. And in that spring there live all the songs that come to the lips of men and women who will not sell their thoughts for money."

"It must be a beautiful place you're telling about," said Alice. "Won't you take me there?"

"No, not now," said the swallow. "No people of your world are able to live there yet, for the air in that land is too pure. You people need heavy air to breathe. Why, my negro relative, the raven, has told me that he remembers how your great-great-grandfathers have killed people for just telling them about this land. Some day, perhaps, your children's children may be able to live there. But before you are ready to know more about the land of Joy, you must make the place you are now living in better."

"How can I do it?" asked Alice.

"First of all," said the swallow, "you must find out some of the things that have to be made better in your world."

"How can I find them out?" asked Alice.

"That's just what I've come here for," said the swallow. "Your guardian bird, the stork, has sent me to take you on a visit to the American Eagle, and he will show you some of the things you ought to improve in America."

"Where does the American Eagle live?" asked Alice.

"You ought to know a simple thing like that," said the swallow. "Why, the American Eagle lives in the place which has been named after the father of our country, of course. The American Eagle lives on top of Mt. Washington. But come along now, for we must not lose any time."

Alice followed the swallow out through the open window, and soon they came to the home of the American Eagle.

When Alice and the swallow came to the American Eagle, they found that he had not a single feather on him.

"Why hasn't he any feathers?" asked Alice.

"I don't know," said the swallow. "Perhaps you had better ask him."

"What has become of your feathers?" said Alice to the eagle.

"They've been taken away from me," answered the eagle.

"Who took them?" asked Alice.

"Oh, everybody who tries to become great," said the eagle.

"I don't understand you," said Alice.

"Well, then," said the eagle, "let me explain. When people want to become great, they don't try to do anything useful for anybody. But instead, they want to stick a feather in their cap, and then everybody will cry hooray."

"Oh, I see," said Alice. "Then a great man is a hooray who sticks a feather in his cap."

"That's right," laughed the eagle. "And now tell me why you have come to me."

"I'll tell you," said the swallow. "This little girl is Alice, and she is seeking for Love-of-the-heart. And the stork, who is Alice's guardian, has sent me with her to you where she may learn something."

"I'm afraid," said the eagle, "that you have come to the wrong place. You know that people have stamped all my eagle relatives on their silver money and their gold money. And when one lives on money, he knows very little about Love-of-the-heart."

"We don't expect you to teach us any thing about Love-of-the-heart," said the swallow. "But we want you to show us how bad it is for people to run after money and get Hate-of-the-heart."

"Let me tell you," said the eagle, "that there are very few who really have Hate-of-the-heart. In my travels I've seen all kinds of people, poor people and rich people, and I find that most of them would like to be good and kind. But almost everybody has *Sleep*-of the-heart. For they are so busy running after money that they forget ever to wake their hearts."

"Well, then," said the swallow, "tell Alice why it is bad to have Sleep-of-the-heart."

"All right," said the eagle. "Look into the valley where the people live."

"I'd like to ask you a question, Mr. Eagle," said Alice.

"What is it?" said the eagle.

"Why do most people live down there in the valley instead of up here, on top of the mountain?"

"This is a very good question," said the eagle. "Most people live in the valley because that is where all the money is to be found."

"Why is most money in the valley?" asked Alice.

"Because it is so heavy that it falls down as far as it can," said the eagle.

"And aren't there any people at all who try to get up on the top of the mountain?" asked Alice.

"Oh, yes," said the eagle. "But if they have any money with them while they are climbing up, it becomes so heavy and the mountain is so steep that they are dragged down again."

"Why don't they throw the money out of their pockets?" asked Alice.

"Some do," said the eagle, "and in that way they reach to the top."

"Then why aren't there any here now?" asked Alice.

"Don't you understand why? Because people can't live if they have no money at all. And so, when these people have reached to the top of the mountain, they die of hunger."

"Oh," said Alice, "that's too bad."

"It is," said the eagle, "but I know how to fix all this."

"Tell me how," said Alice.

"Before I show you that," said the eagle, "I must show how bad it is to live down there in the valley where all people get the terrible sickness called 'Sleep-of-the-heart.'"

"Is Sleep-of-the-heart a sickness?" asked Alice.

"Yes, indeed," said the eagle.

"Do people die of it?" asked Alice.

"No," said the eagle, "but their love dies. But let us look down into the valley now."

Alice looked down, and this is what she saw. In the middle of the valley there was a house made of golden walls. And it had a diamond roof through which the heart could look inside. In the house there sat a man grinding all the time at a large grindstone.

And as he ground, servants brought to him many men and women and children. And they plucked the laughter out of their hearts and the bright-ness out of their eyes, and these they gave to the man at the grindstone. And this man took the brightness and the laughter and the joys of the other people and mixed them together and crushed them. And then the servants came in with golden bowls, and the bowls were filled with mothers' tears. And the man at the grindstone took these and washed the grindstone with them. And then he put everything into a machine and turned a great big wheel, and out of the machine there came huge heaps of money.

When Alice saw this, she wept. And she asked the eagle what this was.

"This," said the eagle, "is the way in which one man makes money out of the life and the happiness of others."

"And who is this man who is sitting at the grindstone?" asked Alice.

"This man," answered the eagle, "is called Riches."

"He is a cruel murderer," said Alice.

"He is not cruel," said the eagle, "only he is blind. Look at his eyes and you will see."

Alice looked at his eyes and saw that he had two five-dollar gold pieces instead of eyes in his forehead.

"I pity him," said Alice. "He really doesn't know what he is doing, does he?"

"No, he does not," said the eagle. "Now look at some of the other people who live in the valley."

Alice looked, and at the other end of the valley she saw old and dark houses with small rooms. And these rooms had low ceilings and hardly any windows in them. And in each room there lived several people, and these people were pale and coughing. And into these houses came the servants from the rich man's house that had the golden walls and the diamond roof. And the servants said to the people who lived in the old houses, "Come, your lives are needed at the grindstone. Our master wants to make more money." And the poor people hung their heads and never said a word and went to the grindstone.

When Alice saw this, she was very much surprised, and she said, "It's very queer how these people let themselves be crushed, and how they give their life and their joys to be ground into gold without even complaining."

"It's not at all queer," said the eagle, "for these people are blind, too."

"Have these no eyes, either?" asked Alice.

"Look, and you will see for yourself," said the eagle.

Alice looked once more, and she noticed that instead of eyes these people had deep holes darker than the night.

"Now tell me who these people are," asked Alice.

"These people," said the eagle, "are working people. And the rich make them work not for the sake of making useful things for everybody, but for the sake of making money for just a few."

"Now tell me," said Alice, as she saw a house with a great many soldiers in it near the big house with the golden walls and the diamond roof. "What is this house, and why is it near the money-maker's house?"

"This house," said the eagle, "is an armory, and the soldiers in it are guarding the rich man's gold."

"Why don't the soldiers guard the poor men's lives instead of the rich man's money?" asked Alice.

"Because," said the eagle, "these soldiers, too, have no eyes, but bullets instead."

"And what is that white building with so many windows in it, as if they wanted the sun to fill the whole house?" asked Alice.

"This is a college," said the eagle. "And do you see the books piled up on the window-sills, keeping out all the light of the sun?"

"Yes, I do," said Alice. "It seems very funny to me. At first they make a lot of windows for the sun, and then they cover up the windows with books. But tell me, why is this college near the rich man's house, and not near the poor men's?"

"Because some of the teachers and some of the students want to be near the rich man. For then they will be able to shine his shoes when the dust of the gold settles too thickly on them."

"Are these men blind, too?" asked Alice.

"Yes, they are," said the eagle. "And they are also suffering from the disease called Sleep-of-the-heart."

"Then all the people in the valley are miserable because most of them are blind, isn't that it?" said Alice.

"That's just it," said the eagle.

"Then what can you do about it?" asked Alice.

"We just need someone to put real eyes into them and awaken their hearts," said the eagle.

"Are there any people who try to do it?" asked Alice.

"Yes," said the eagle. "There are some people who would like to take the sunlight and put it into everybody's eyes. They are brave people, and they fight alone against the whole world. But they do not fight with swords or with guns. Their only weapon is to be kind to those who are weak and to cheer up those whose courage is failing. They want all men to be Comrades, and they are trying to make a world where there will be no grindstones to grind money out of the laughter and life of men and women and children."

"And will everybody then live on the mountain-tops, where the air is so pure and where the hills all around you can echo your laughter?"

"Yes," said the eagle, "for then all will help one another to climb to the top. And when they get there, they will work for one another, and no one will be hungry or unhappy."

"Well, Mr. Eagle," said Alice, "I'm very glad I've visited you, for you have taught me many good things. Good-bye, and I hope next time I come here, you will have your feathers back."

"I do hope so, indeed," said the eagle. "But I shan't get my feathers again until great men stop being hoorays and sticking feathers in their cap. Good-bye, and come again."

Alice left the eagle and was soon back in her house. Here her mother found her and sent her off to bed, reminding her once more never to play with poor children. And again her heart felt weak and miserable.

Alice in the Delighted States

EDWARD HOPE

ILLUSTRATIONS BY REA IRVIN

1928

*E*DWARD HOPE was the pen name of American author and screenwriter Edward Hope Coffey (1896-1958). He began his career in advertising and, in the early 1920s, was invited by the *New York Herald Tribune* to serve as a substitute for Don Marquis, who wrote the popular "The Lantern" column, while Marquis was on vacation. His *Alice in the Delighted States* began, like Marquis's *Archy and Mehitabel,* as comic sketches for the *Tribune,* satirizing such issues as immigration restrictions, Prohibition, the American "trial and error" justice system, censorship, and "the Department of Infernal Revenue," while retaining a charming and urbane sense of whimsy. In a parody of Carroll's "'Tis the Voice of the Lobster" (which is itself a parody of Isaac Watts's moralistic poem "'Tis the voice of the Sluggard") Hope pokes fun at the dilettante self-improver:

> 'Tis the voice of the plugger, I hear him complain,
> "I simply have got to develop my brain."
> As the mouse with the crackers, so he with his books
> Nibbles morsels of learning from volumes de luxe. [77]

The *New York Times* called *Alice in the Delighted States* "the first imitation of Lewis Carroll to convey some of the 'innocent merriment' of the original. It is frankly an imitation, but seems to have caught more of the spirit than of the form of *Alice in Wonderland.* . . . Such harmony with classic originals demands as much of the creative artist as of the copyist."[1]

---

1. "Alice Comes to North Hysteria," *New York Times Book Review* (15 April 1928): 2.

Alice in the Delighted States

CHAPTER I. THROUGH THE DRINKING-GLASS

ALICE PLUMPED HERSELF into the big armchair her Father had risen from. She didn't see why one's Father and Mother had to be forever hurrying off after dinner to go to a theatre or to play Bridge with the So-and-sos. She objected particularly to Bridge because the name of it sounded as if it might be quite fun, but she knew that it was a gloomy sort of game that was played with cards and scowls and very complicated talk.

She wondered why grown-ups were always so serious, anyway, when there were so many things in the world to laugh at, and grown-ups could do just as they pleased without always being pestered with governesses and other people to keep telling them what wasn't Nice.

She wondered why her Father had sat, all through dinner and over his coffee afterward, talking about the book on Permanent Peace he had been reading, when he might have talked about the new puppy that had come to live with the Thomases next door.

She wondered why he drank that tiny glass of nasty-smelling, brownish stuff after his coffee, when he might have had Nora, the new waitress, make him a glass of sweet lemonade.

Alice was always wondering about things. She was never too tired to wonder. In fact, the sleepier she grew, the more she wondered.

Now, when Miss Larraby would be coming any minute to tell her it was bed-time, she took to wondering about the little empty glass on the table beside her. She wondered if the stem of it was hollow, as it looked. And, if it *was* hollow, she wondered if the passage through it didn't connect with another little passage through the leg of the table, which was directly underneath, and if *that* passage didn't go right into the earth and lead to a magic cave, full of gold and precious stones.

She wondered whether a person small enough to get into the glass could slide down through the stem and through the table-leg and into the magic cave. . . .

And just then a curious thing happened. A very small white rabbit came from among the roots of the fern on the table and jumped down from the flower-pot to the lace cover. He seemed to be in a great hurry, for he pulled his watch from his waistcoat pocket, looked at it hastily, and made a *st-st-st* noise with his tongue.

And the next thing Alice knew, he had jumped into the tiny glass and was sliding down through the stem and out of sight.

"So," said Alice, "I was right about it!"

She twisted about in the chair to get on her hands and knees and peer down after the rabbit, but she discovered suddenly that she was shrinking, and that when she stood up on the chair-seat her head reached scarcely higher than the arm. As fast as she could—for fear she would shrink even more and not be able—she scrambled up the arm and jumped from it to the table.

But she was still getting smaller. By this time the glass was nearly twice as high as she. She looked about at the other objects that towered over her, the fern looking like a tall jungle growing out of a fortress, the match-box as big as a trunk.

"Oh, dear!" she cried. "Now that I'm small enough to get *into* it, I'm too small to get *up* to it!"

And then she thought of the cigarette-box. It was made of wood and quite light. She put her shoulder against it and pushed it toward the glass. It took a great deal of puffing and grunting, but it moved, and at last it was placed beside the glass and Alice climbed upon it. This brought her high enough to reach the rim.

"If only," she thought, "it doesn't tip over with me. . . ." And she hesitated for a moment. "Still," she went on, to get up her courage, "nothing ventured, nothing won."

And with that she threw her arms over the side of the glass and swung herself up and over. For a moment she looked down at the table, a dizzy distance below. Then she gritted her teeth and let go her hold on the rim.

"If *he* can do it," she told herself, as she slid down the slippery inside of the glass, "I fancy *I* can!"

* * * * * *

Either the hole was very deep or she fell very slowly, for she had time to look about her, and to wonder what was going to happen next. She looked at the sides and noticed that they were filled with cupboards and bookshelves; here and there she saw maps and pictures hung upon pegs.

She took down a map as she passed. It was neatly divided by lines up and down and lines across, and there were parts in pink and parts in blue and parts in other bright colors. In fact, it was very like school maps, with words and numbers on it, except down in the corner, where it should have said "British Isles," or "Western Europe" it said, in large, neat letters, WHY NOT?

Alice had never heard of a country called Why Not? and she thought that this must be a very curious map indeed. So she rolled it up and put it under her arm, thinking she would take it home with her and show it to her Teacher, if ever she could get out of this hole.

Down, down, down. Would the fall *never* come to an end? "I wonder how many miles I've fallen by this time," she said, aloud. "I must be getting near the center of the earth. I wonder if I shall fall right *through* the earth and come out in—in China. And that would be dreadful because of the—the Evolution. I think it is the Evolution." But her elbow kept bumping against the side of the tunnel and she thought that curious.

"I know," she said to herself suddenly. "It's bent. It's a crooked tunnel and I'm not falling straight down at all. So there's no telling where it comes out." And she wrinkled her nose as she tried to remember the names of all the strange continents in her geography. She said them over to herself.

"Aphasia," she said. "Aphasia, Paprika, North Hysterica, South Hysterica, Stirrup and Nostalgia. Or—or *something* like that, at any rate," she apologized to herself, for she was sure that the words were almost right. And then she went on, changing the unpleasant subject. "Perhaps I shall come out in the Delighted States and see Charlie Chaplin and Sinclair Loos and Mr. Coolish in his cowboy suit. And perhaps I shall get them to show me all the Dollars and the Foreign Debts and—and Exhibition."

And she was so pleased with the idea that she clapped her hands, and did not notice that the tunnel was getting lighter and lighter, the further she went.

"Well," said Alice, "when I get there—if ever I *do* get there," she put in, for there was no wood anywhere in sight that she could knock, "I'll have one friend, anyway. Because, of course, the Rabbit comes right from home, and he'll know me. And he *must* be going wherever I'm going because there isn't any place else to go."

While she was saying this, the tunnel became very bright, all at once. She looked down and saw a round hole with blue sky in it. "But," she said, "then I can't be falling at all, because I'm going *up* toward the sky. And you *can't* fall up. *Really* you can't," she insisted, as if somebody had said you could. "Oh, dear! I do hope I shall stop when I'm out, and not go right on into Space." Alice had heard Father talk about Space, and she thought it was somewhere beyond the sky, where it isn't blue any more.

Before she had more time to worry, she came to the end of the tunnel and went through it with a *whoosh,* because the entrance was small and she nearly filled it as she went by.

Alice stopped falling suddenly and landed sitting at the side of the hole.

CHAPTER 2. JEALOUS ISLAND

She was in a field filled with the brightest and prettiest flowers she had ever seen. They came up to her neck and she could just see over them. And a few yards away was the Rabbit, looking at his watch again and hurrying away as fast as his legs would carry him.

"I—I *beg* your pardon," called Alice in a voice that didn't exactly go with what she was saying, because she wanted to be sure he would hear her. The Rabbit turned his head slightly and looked at her fussily.

"Granted," he called back, and hurried on.

"Oh, *please!*" said Alice, and could think of nothing else to say. The Rabbit stopped and took out his watch again impatiently.

"Please *what*?" he said.

"Please, Rabbit," she said, for she did not know whether that was what he meant or not. And then she added, "Please, Rabbit, what time is it?" for that seemed to be an easy question for him to answer.

"Quota after," he said curtly, and rudely hurried off.

"Don't—don't leave me here," called Alice, but the Rabbit kept on, and when he was nearly out of sight, he turned and said:

"They won't. Don't worry."

"Won't what?" said Alice, but he was gone.

For a minute or two, Alice sat there among the flowers and cried. She did not know exactly *why* she cried, and it didn't help at all, but she cried just the same. And then she spoke to herself.

"Come, this won't do," she told herself. "And you can't blame the Rabbit. *He* didn't ask you to go down the glass, you know."

That struck her as being very true, so she got to her feet and started off for the place where the Rabbit had disappeared. But she found it very hard indeed to force her way through the plants, for by this time they towered over her.

"My!" she said to herself, "how they grow. This *must* be the Delighted States, because I remember everything grows fast there. I'm *sure* that's right. Cotton and wheat and corn and—oh, everything." She rested against the stem of a great flower. "But I wonder whatever these flowers can be," she said a-loud.

"Isms," said a voice from somewhere overhead. Alice looked up and saw a strange Bug peering at her from over the edge of a poppy.

"I beg your pardon," said Alice, for she believed in being polite to bugs that spoke, even if they didn't speak English.

"Isms," the Bug repeated, and withdrew behind the petals of the poppy.

"Did you say 'Isn't'?" asked Alice. "And if you did, what isn't?"

"'Isn't' isn't what I said," answered the Bug curtly. "*Isms,*" he said very plainly. "And as for what isn't, practically everything."

"Practically everything isn't what?" Alice insisted, wishing the Bug would make his meanings clearer.

"Allowed," said the Bug, peeping over the edge of the flower just long enough to say it, and then going out of sight again.

"But," said Alice, trying to be very polite, "if practically everything isn't allowed, what does everybody do?"

"Come up," said the Bug, and the stem of the poppy bent over until the huge flower was at Alice's waist. Alice pulled herself up on the edge of a great petal, and the stem straightened itself again.

It swung up and they were in the warm sunlight, as if they had been in a little crimson boat and the surrounding flowers had been a lake.

Alice looked at the Bug and found he was rather like a red beetle, except that he had long, mussy black hair on top of his head, and wore steel-rimmed spectacles, through which he looked at her intently. Alice did not speak, for she felt that the Bug was her host. She waited and presently he laughed a low, rumbly laugh.

"Practically everything," he said, and laughed again.

"I know. I heard you before," said Alice, growing a little impatient. "You said practically everything wasn't allowed."

"If you would keep up with the conversation," the Bug said unpleasantly, "we shouldn't have to waste so much time. You said, 'If practically everything isn't allowed, what does everybody do?' I answered that."

"Well, if you did, *I* didn't hear you," replied Alice, who did not like to be spoken to crossly.

"Everybody does practically everything," said the Bug, "and I hope you've got *that* straight by this time."

"Yes," said Alice, although she wasn't entirely sure she had. Then she thought it would be better to talk about something else, so she said: "What are isms?"

"Things it is fun to believe in," answered the Bug, "like Paternalism and Americanism and—"

"And Fairies?" asked Alice, who thought it was great fun to believe in Fairies.

"Something like Fairies," said the Bug, "only not so pretty. And of course, Fairies are there, whether you believe in them or not, but Isms aren't there unless you believe in them."

"But I thought you said these flowers were Isms," said Alice. "And I think they're very pretty."

"They are pretty now," the Bug agreed, "because they're new. And, of course, they haven't been taken in yet."

"In *where*?" demanded Alice.

"Into this country, of *course*."

"But that's stupid," said Alice, "because they *are* in this country."

"Oh, no," smiled the Bug, growing very superior, "this isn't this country."

"This isn't *what* country?" Alice felt herself getting rather red and annoyed.

"*This* country," said the Bug. "And it isn't any other country, either. This is Jealous Island."

"But—oh, it's *all* so mixed up," said Alice in despair. "I don't understand at all."

"No," the Bug nodded. "Nobody does. But that's because of Uncle Sam'l. Do you know 'You Are Old, Uncle Sam'l, the Young Man Said'?"

"You are old, *Father William*," corrected Alice.

"Uncle Sam'l," the Bug persisted. "It will help you understand. But you mustn't interrupt. Be very quiet and I'll say it for you."

Alice sat very still and the Bug began (bug-an, Alice thought to herself)—

"You are old, Uncle Sam'l," the young man said,
    "And your hair's growing thin at the crown,
Yet on junket and pasteurized milk you are fed—
    How on earth do you get the stuff down?"

"In my youth," Uncle Sam'l replied to the lad,
    "I drank whisky from morning till night,
And—now I've decided such habits are bad—
    I'm a glutton for Sweetness and Light."

"You are old," said the youth, "as I mentioned before;
    You are old, and you're wrinkled and fat,
And yet you're a Clown, and a Zany, what's more—
    Pray, what is the reason of that?"

"In my youth," said the Sage, with the ghost of a smile,
    "I was forced to stick close to my labors,
So, now that I've leisure to rest for a while,
    I like to play Oaf for the neighbors."

"You are old," said the youth, "and you're rich as the deuce;
    You have more than you'll possibly spend.
Getting richer and richer's no possible use—
    Do you think that it pays in the end?"

"In my youth," said the patriarch, "I was so poor
    I had scarcely enough for my vittles;
So, now that I'm rich, I feel perfectly sure
    I can spend it on sodas and skittles."

"You are old," said the youth. "One would hardly suppose
    That a Book or a Drama could hurt you,
Yet you shut up your eyes and you clutch at your nose—
    How come all this fear for your virtue?"

"I've answered three questions and that is enough,"
    Said his Uncle. "Don't give yourself airs.
Do you think I can listen all day to such stuff?
    Be off, or I'll kick you downstairs!"

"*That's* not right," said Alice.

"No," admitted the Bug, "but it's true, and that's what matters." The

Bug yawned, holding one hand politely before his mouth. "And now you must get along before you miss another quota."

"Another *what*?" asked Alice, noticing that the Bug had produced a pillow and was getting ready to lie down.

"Quota," said the Bug sleepily. "Quota to wait."

"Do you mean 'quarter'?" asked Alice, hoping she wasn't too patronizing.

"No," yawned the Bug. "No quarter asked or given. Sorry you must be going."

"But," said Alice, who didn't want to go at all, "who are you, and what are you doing on Jealous Island, if it isn't any country?"

"Can't you see I'm going to take my nap?" demanded the Bug rudely. "I'm a Red, and I'm waiting here among the dear deported."

"You mean the dear departed, of course," said Alice. "And what is a Red?"

"I do not. And a Red is one of the primary colors, which you get to be if you ask too many questions. There are also Blues and Red-white-and-blues. So now run along."

Suddenly the Bug shook the poppy violently, and Alice toppled out, and down through miles and miles and miles of space, for the Ism in which the Red lived had grown and grown while she was sitting in it.

Chapter 3. Humble Pie

Alice got to her feet and looked about her at the forest of stems. Although each of them had a flower at the top of it, they were really more like tree-trunks, for they were bigger around than her arms and they went straight up into the air almost out of sight. They grew close together, so that a person could scarcely squeeze between them, and Alice had fallen so far and landed with such a bump that she couldn't possibly guess which stem led to the Ism the Red lived in.

"People are always saying one thing leads to another," she said to herself, "but that isn't much good unless you know which thing leads to which other. Anyway, the Red is taking his nap by this time, so it's no use trying to get *him* to help. And goodness knows what lives in the other Isms. Though it can't be very important," she added, "because I'm sure I've heard that there isn't much in Isms."

She looked about again, and this time she saw that two of the near-by stems had signs on them that she hadn't noticed before. Each sign had an arrow marked Jealous Island and both arrows pointed the same way, but under one arrow were the words, Delighted States, This Way In, and under the other the words, Delighted States, This Way Out.

"Well," said Alice, "they agree on one thing. Wherever you want to go, this is the way."

She hadn't gone far before she came to a high wall with a tiny door in it, just about big enough for a very small cat to get through with a very great deal of wiggling. Alice lay flat on her tummy and peeped through the door.

Inside there was a lovely garden and among the flowers were paths paved with gold. At one side there was a river of milk and on the other side a river of honey. And there were tall, handsome people who smiled a lot and looked very happy in their silks and satins.

"This *must* be the Delighted States," said Alice, "even though there are no wild Indians and I don't see any Exhibition Agents. I wonder how one gets in," and she looked about to see if there might be another door. There was none, but there was a small bottle against the wall and Alice picked it up.

The label was beautifully lettered in purple, C_2H_5OH, and underneath in big blue letters, DON'T DRINK ME, but it was perfectly easy to see that some one had put on the "Don't" as an afterthought.

"And anyway," said Alice, "it must be here for some reason," so she raised the bottle to her lips and took a swallow from it. It was nasty-tasting stuff. She started to put the bottle back.

But when she leaned over she found that it was much further to the ground than it had been before. She had to get down on her knees to reach the ground at all. "Oh, dear!" she said. "Now I've grown bigger than ever and I shall never get in!" She was just about to sit down and cry, when a thought struck her. "Unless there's a big door somewhere else," she added, and started off along the wall to look.

* * * * * *

Around a bend she came to a white building with smoke coming out of its chimney. Across the front of it was painted in big black letters, "Jealous Island Bakery, Delighted States of Hysterica." Alice went in.

It was hot inside and smoky and confusing. A man in a baker's white suit and apron and hat was bending over a stove and muttering to himself.

"Oh, dear!" he mumbled. "Will they *ever* be satisfied? *That* should hold them!" and he emptied a large tin of pepper into a pan on the stove. He didn't seem to notice Alice, so she spoke to him.

"I beg your pardon," she said politely.

"It all depends on what the Court thinks you've done," answered the Baker. "And by that I mean the Court of Terror and a Squeal."

"But I haven't done anything," cried Alice, and then she thought of the bottle and added in a very small voice, "except maybe—"

"That is a very bad sentence," said the Baker. "A terrible sentence. 'I haven't done anything except maybe.' If it's a sentence at all you ought to have it commuted," he went on thoughtfully, "and that means you'll have to find a commuter."

"What's a—" began Alice.

"Or a Governor," the Baker continued rudely. "And don't ask me what a Governor is. A Governor is something that keeps the wheels from going around too fast. Except a Wet Governor. There are Wet Governors and Dry Governors, and—"

"Oh, like batteries!" said Alice, delighted to be able to join in.

"Not at *all* like batteries, and don't interrupt," said the Baker, "or you'll never be pardoned or commuted or anything." He stopped and poured a bottle of castor oil into his pan. "Except maybe what?" he demanded.

Alice was so startled she could not answer at once. "Except," she said finally, "I drank out of the bottle of C_2H_5OH." It was hard to say the little numbers off the line.

"In that case," said the Baker, "it's no use asking for a pardon, because you won't get one." He reached into the oven and brought out a smoking pan. "Have some?" he asked.

"It doesn't smell very good," said Alice.

"Smell *good!*" exclaimed the Baker. "I should hope not, after all the trouble I've taken. The question is: Is it *bad* enough for them?"

"Bad enough for who?" asked Alice. "I mean whom."

"Whom is where the heart is," said the Baker, humming a little tune. "Bad enough for the Misrepresentatives and the Ginger-aliens. You see, they're plain Aliens at first, but we make them Ginger-aliens before we let them in."

"In where?" asked Alice.

"Into the Delighted States," answered the Baker. "That's why my pie has to be so bad. They have to eat it before they can get in. And by that I mean that it's Humble Pie. Nothing else served on Jealous Island. Have some?"

"Dear me!" cried Alice, "I don't think I shall like it."

"I don't see why you should," said the Baker. "Nobody does." He held the pie under his nose, and smacked his lips. "My!" he exclaimed. "Now, that *is* Humble Pie. You'll go to a lot of countries before you get pie as humble as we have here."

"But *must* I eat it?" asked Alice, who was liking the Humble Pie less and less, the more she smelled it.

"If you don't like this country," said the Baker, "you can go right back where you came from. That's Rule One on Jealous Island."

"But I didn't say—" Alice protested, feeling her skin getting hot at the insulting tone the Baker was using.

"There," he cried. "You're getting pink. Parlor pink! I shouldn't be at all surprised to find out that you're Red." He bent over the oven and pulled out several other burned and smoking pies.

"I'm not Red," declared Alice. "And I'm only pink because you're so rude."

"Spare the rude and spoil the child," said the Baker. "If you're not Red, eat your Humble Pie as every one else does." He cut a large V from one of the fresh pies and handed it to her.

"Very well," agreed Alice, thinking that if she held her breath and gulped it very quickly it might not taste so bad. She took a big bite and swallowed it

without chewing, but the pie tasted like alum and castor oil and red pepper and quinine and choke cherries, and Alice gasped, "Oh!"

She could feel herself shrinking.

"Finish it!" cried the Baker. "Eat it all. Finish, finish, finish!"

There was no help for it now, so Alice gobbled the rest of the pie and made an awful face. "There," she said. The Baker produced a large pad and a short, stubby pencil.

"Hmm," he said, writing things on the pad, "that'll be—let's see—yes—one point seven seven three. He who eats pie must pay the piper."

Alice suddenly realized that she was only as high as the Baker's knees and that she was still getting smaller. "You mean I have to pay?" she said, for she had no money and she didn't know what to do.

"Naturally," said the Baker. "Pie is worth three point one four one six, but you didn't have a whole pie, so that will be one point seven seven three. That includes discipline, snoopervision, under-cover charges and sports, including passports."

By this time Alice was only three or four inches high, so she slipped behind the leg of a chair for a moment while she thought out what to do next. She heard the Baker clumping about, opening the oven door.

"Come," she thought to herself, "I'm only about as big as a mouse and he'll never be able to catch me." And she ran as fast as she could, out the door and back along the wall the way she had come. . . .

Chapter 15. The Censor Incensed

Alice felt perfectly sure she was coming out the same door she had gone into the Muses' reception room by, but everything had changed in the few minutes she had been inside. She found herself in a queer square hall from which dozens and dozens of passages wound off in all directions. All the passages were dimly lighted, some in one color, some in another. Each began at a neat little arch, set in the gray wall, and each arch was marked with strange letters and numbers.

Looking about her, Alice found the place dreadfully confusing and a little frightening. She decided to go back into the Muses' room and ask directions about getting out, but when she turned back to where the door had been, she found only a blank wall between two passages.

"Oh, dear!" she said aloud. "This is dreadful!"

"Which is?" asked a small, whiney voice from very close by.

Alice jumped. She whirled about to see who had spoken, but there seemed to be no one in sight. She was just beginning to think she had imagined the voice, when it said again:

"*Which* is?"

Alice dropped her eyes to the place the sound came from and saw two small animals with pointed noses. Both wore tall, dull-black hats and had steel-rimmed spectacles on their long noses, and both were dressed in tailcoats, so big that they dragged on the floor, and black baggy trousers and broad black shoes with rubber heels.

"Oh!" she exclaimed, being careful not to laugh at them, "*there* you are!"

"If you will be good enough to say which is dreadful, we will investigate thoroughly," said the larger of the two, "but please don't keep us waiting."

"But who are you?" Alice asked.

"I am a ferret," answered the larger one. "I ferret out the dreadful passages that have to be deleted. And he's an otter," he went on, lifting his little companion up by the ears for Alice to see. "When it comes to reporting the passages, he decides whether or not we otter. Now if you will kindly—"

"But how do you delete a passage?" inquired Alice.

"By due process of law," said the Ferret. "And now—"

"And who do you report to?" interrupted Alice.

"Whom," corrected the Otter.

"To the Censor, of course," said the Ferret. "But you said something was dreadful and—"

"Oh," said Alice. "And does the Censor live on the Censor Ship?"

"Sometimes," replied the Ferret, "and sometimes he lives on the Ship of State. Will you kindly—"

"And then, too," put in the Otter, "he has to look after the morals of the weaker vessels."

"Does he sail them on an ocean?" asked Alice.

"Several notions," answered the Otter. "Mostly the Pedantic and the Specific."

"Really," the Ferret insisted, "I'm afraid we shan't be able to wait any longer—"

"What sort of ships are they?" Alice asked the Otter, who didn't seem to be in such a hurry.

"Clippers," said the Otter. "And some of them are liners—underliners, you know."

The Ferret was looking at his watch impatiently. "*I* think," he said shortly, "that it's high time for you to tell us which is the dreadful passage."

"Yes. That's right," agreed the Otter. "We must note the passage of time."

"But we can't do anything about *that*," said the Ferret, "so it's no use discussing it."

"Our work," explained the Otter, "is to make the country safe for Growing Girls. So the first question is, Are you a Growing Girl?"

"Of *course*, she is!" snorted the Ferret. "I've noticed her growing ever since we first spoke to her. And if she grows much more," he continued, "she will burst out of her clothes, and then she'll be in a pretty mess."

Alice looked down at the floor and saw that it was true. She had grown so that by now she was seven feet tall, at the very least, and her clothes were getting so tight she could scarcely breathe. She was relieved to notice that the ceiling was high and that there was no immediate danger of bumping her head against it.

"If the pretty mess isn't *too* pretty, and if it comes below her knees," said the Otter, "I suppose it will be all right for her to go about in it. Though I've seen *some* pretty messes . . . !"

"I don't like growing so fast," Alice complained. "It's—"

"Growing Girls are growing faster and faster," said the Ferret. "That's why we have to be so careful about them. There are lots of things they mustn't find out, you see."

"It's why we have to delete so many passages," the Otter put in.

"That reminds me!" cried the Ferret. "You were saying that one of the passages was dreadful."

"I wasn't," said Alice. "I was saying that it was dreadful, being here a-mong so many passages and not knowing where any of them might lead to—"

"That's the thing," agreed the Otter. "You can never tell where any of them might lead to."

"This one here," the Ferret explained, "is one of Mr. Cabell's newest ones." He pointed to a passage that was dimly lighted in purple and began at an arch marked "Cabell: s.a.e. pp. 120-125" and asked, "What do you think of it?"

"It looks quite fascinating," Alice replied, "now that you speak of it. I hadn't noticed it before. I think I should like—"

"There!" cried the Otter. "I told you! She never would have seen it, if you hadn't pointed it out. You hadn't otter do that."

"But how am I to know which ones are going to be bad for Growing Girls, unless the Growing Girls look at them?" said the Ferret, bursting into tears. "And how are the Growing Girls to know which ones to look at unless I point them out?"

"All you have to do," retorted the Otter unsympathetically, "is put yourself in her place. And then if it harms you, you know it will harm her."

"That's all very well to *say*," Alice broke in, feeling sorry for the poor Ferret, "but I haven't any place. And if I had, it would be much too big for him. So you needn't think you are so smart!" She leaned over to snap her fingers in the Otter's face, but suddenly she was startled by a loud ripping noise.

"*There!*" shrieked the Otter. "You see!"

"Oh, dear! Oh, dear! Oh, dear!" cried the poor Ferret, walking rapidly up and down, wringing his paws. "What*ever* shall we do now?"

Alice stood still, holding her breath and afraid to look down at herself, for she felt a cold wind and she was sure she had burst quite out of her clothes.

"We might bar her from the mails," said the Otter, "but that wouldn't do any good, because she doesn't want to post herself. Though I must say she isn't very well posted." He looked at the Ferret, who was still showing indications of hysterics. "You're no help," he sniffed. "So there's only one thing to do."

The Otter produced a penny whistle from his pocket and blew three loud blasts on it. Then he shouted, "Censor! Censor! Censor!" and the Ferret took up the cry until the place was deafening with noise.

* * * * * *

As the Otter and the Ferret seemed determined to keep blowing their whistles and shouting until the Censor came, Alice decided that it would be best to see just how far she had burst out of her clothes. She looked and discovered that her dress had split up the side. She caught it and pulled it hastily as close together as it would go, although it failed by two or three inches to meet.

"If only I'd shrink a little," she whimpered, wondering what the Censor would do when he saw her, "or if the dress would grow with me—"

"The modern girl shrinks at nothing," said the Otter, pausing in his shouting.

"And the dress can't grow until it gets instructions from Paris," added the Ferret.

"So—" began the Otter.

"How can she sew without a needle and thread?" asked the Ferret.

"Oh, what shall I do?" cried Alice. "I have no idea—"

"*That's* a mercy," said a voice directly behind her, a deepish voice that quite startled her. "Most Growing Girls are so full of ideas we can't do anything with them."

Alice turned, expecting to see a tall, sad, deaconish-looking man with his hands clasped over his abdomen. She was somewhat surprised, therefore— although she was getting harder to surprise in this astonishing country—to see a large penguin, holding his tall black hat over his white breast and regarding her disapprovingly, with his head tilted a little.

The Ferret nudged Alice—though he was so much smaller than she that all his nudge amounted to was a small poke at her ankle—and placed his finger on his mouth warningly. "Shhh!" he whispered very loudly to make his words carry up to Alice's ears, "it's him."

"*He,*" corrected the Otter.

"Come!" said the Penguin gruffly. "What's the trouble?"

At this the poor Ferret and the Otter began to tremble from head to foot. The Ferret started to mumble something but the Otter shushed him and cleared his own throat to speak. Then the Ferret shushed the Otter and began to mumble again. Alice decided that this was silly and rather a waste of time.

"It's my dress," she said. "I seem to have burst out of it."

"Willfully and with intent to lower the moral standards of the youth of the land," added the Ferret.

"In defiance of the laws of the Delighted States," put in the Otter.

"With malice aforethought," said the Ferret.

"And criminal negligence," the Otter continued, without, Alice thought, any particular sense.

"Hmmmm," rumbled the Penguin. "This is extremely serious. What have you to say for yourself, young lady?"

"May I suggest—" Alice began.

"Good Heavens!" cried the Ferret. "Haven't you been suggestive enough already?"

"But I—" Alice tried again.

"Arrest her!" shouted the Penguin at the Otter, who was so small beside Alice that he looked rather like an insect. The Otter put his paws on both sides of his mouth and shouted up in a small, squeaky voice:

"You are under arrest!"

This seemed so funny that Alice laughed aloud and the Penguin looked shocked.

"This is no laughing matter!" he cried.

"It's a matter of Deportment," screamed the Otter.

"To be taken up by the Deportment Department," howled the Ferret.

"You'll probably be deported," yelled the Penguin, "but first you must be tried."

"Sorely tried," nodded the Ferret.

"Our trials are *very* trying," added the Otter.

"Off to the Court with her!" shouted the Penguin. ("As if," thought Alice, "they could take me anywhere, if I did choose to go!")

"Which Court are the trials being played on today?" asked the Ferret. "The Turf Court?"

"The Turf Court is too slippery, on account of all the Wets they've been trying on it," said the Otter. "Anyway, this is a case for the Dirt Court."

"Nonsense!" yelled the Penguin. "Take her to the Court of Appeals. Part Six. Sex Appeals."

"Very well, sir," said the Ferret.

"Very, *very* well, sir," said the Otter.

"And hurry," ordered the Penguin. "The case may come up year after next. There is no time to lose."

"Come along!" cried the Otter, pulling Alice by a shoe-lace.

"Move on!" shouted the Ferret, pushing at Alice's heels.

"I suppose I may as well go," thought Alice. "It might be very amusing, sitting in the Prisoner's Dock."

"You'll find the Censor Ship moored at it," said the Penguin. "And remember that what you think will be held against you."

"What is the charge?" asked Alice, feeling that she ought to say something that sounded official and legal.

"Oh, that'll be all right," said the Penguin, rubbing his wings. "There is no charge. The People of the Delighted States pay for it, thank you."

"I mean," Alice explained, "what am I accused of?"

"Decent composure," answered the Penguin. "A very serious offense. In fact, it comes under the laws of gravity."

"The exhilaration of falling bodies," put in the Ferret.

"The attraction between messes," said the Otter, not to be outdone.

"You will probably get a very long sentence," the Penguin continued.

"With Subordinate Clauses," added the Ferret.

"And long, long words," the Otter chimed in. "Like 'turpitude' and 'indeterminate' and 'microcosmic.'"

"Several years up the river would not surprise me," said the Penguin.

"Up what river?" Alice inquired.

"The River of Doubt," replied the Penguin. "It is called that because no matter how long you send a prisoner up it for, everybody doubts that he'll stay more than a few weeks. What paper do you expect to confess to?"

"I'm afraid I don't understand," said Alice. "Because, in the first place, of course, I'm not guilty—"

"Oh, *that's* all right," the Penguin reassured her. "Confess that. I hope you've kept a diary?"

"No," Alice replied.

"Too bad," grunted the Penguin, "but it isn't so much trouble to keep one backward. And they're usually better that way. The papers pay more for them."

"What papers?" asked Alice.

The Penguin made a little clucking noise to himself. "Dear, dear," he said. "I'm afraid you have a great deal to learn."

Selected Bibliography
of *Alice* Imitations
and *Alice*-Inspired Works

Adair, Gilbert. *Alice Through the Needle's Eye: The Further Adventures of Lewis Carroll's "Alice."* London: Obelisk, 1988.

"Alice in Numberland." By the author of "Through an Opera-glass," "The Bunting of the Ark," &c., &c. *Fun,* Oct. 9, 1878: 151; Oct. 16, 1878: 157; Oct. 23, 1878: 166-67; Oct. 30, 1878: 174-75.

Allen, Audrey Mayhew. *Gladys in Grammarland.* Westminster: Roxburghe Press, n.d. [c. 1890].

Amadio, Nadine. *The New Adventures of Alice in Rainforest Land.* Surrey Hills, Austral.: Watermark/P.I.C., 1988.

Andrews, Mabel H. *Dorothy's Adventures in Bedroomland.* New York: Century, 1923.

Anstey, F. [Thomas Anstey Guthrie]. *In Brief Authority.* London: Smith, Elder, 1915.

———. *Only Toys.* London: Richards, 1903.

Ashton, S. [E.F. Bosanquet]. *Eve's Adventures: A Submarine Fantasy.* London: Simpkin, Marshall, 1904.

Atkinson, Canon J.C. *Scenes in Fairyland: Or, Miss Mary's Visit to the Court of Fairy Realm.* London: Macmillan, 1892.

Austin, Jane Goodwin. *Moonfolk: A True Account of the Home of the Fairy Tales.* New York: Putnam, 1874.

Bangs, John Kendrick. *Alice in Blunderland: An Iridescent Dream.* New York: Doubleday, Page, 1907.

———, and Charles Raymond Macauley. *Emblemland.* New York: R.H. Russell, 1902.

Barsley, Michael. *Alice in Wunderground, and Other Blits* [*sic*] *and Pieces.* London: John Murray, 1940.

———. *Grabberwocky and Other Flights of Fancy.* London: John Murray, 1939.

Baum, L. Frank. *Dot and Tot of Merryland.* 1901. New York: Emerald City P, 1994.

———. *The Magical Monarch of Mo* [originally titled *A New Wonderland*]. 1900. New York: Dover, 1968.

———. *The Wonderful Wizard of Oz.* 1900. New York: Dover, 1960.

Benet, William Rose. *The Flying King of Kurio: A Story for Children*. New York: Doran, 1926.

Benson, E[dward] F[rederic]. *David Blaize and the Blue Door*. 1919. Garden City, NY: Doubleday, [c. 1938].

Bergengren, Ralph. *David the Dreamer*. Boston: Atlantic Monthly, 1922.

Bernard, Florence Scott. *Through the Cloud Mountain*. Philadelphia: Lippincott, 1922.

Bloch, Robert. "All on a Golden Afternoon." *Fantasy and Science Fiction,* 10.6 (June 1956): 105-26.

Bousfield, Guy. *In Search of Alice: Being the Adventures of William in Underland*. London: C. & J. Temple, n.d. [c. 1950].

Bradford, Clara. *Ethel's Adventures in Doll Country*. London: Shaw, [c. 1880].

Braine, Sheila. *Up the Rainbow Stairs: A Story of Strange Adventures*. London: Blackie, 1889.

Branch, Mary L. *The Kanter Girls*. New York: Scribners, 1895.

Browne, Maggie. *The Book of Betty Barber*. London: Ballantyne, 1914.

————. *The Surprising Adventures of Tuppy and Tue*. London: Cassell, 1904.

————. *Wanted—A King; or How Merle Set the Nursery Rhymes To Right*. London: Cassell, 1890.

Burgess, Anthony. *A Long Trip to Teatime*. London: Dempsey & Squires, 1976.

Burnett, Frances Hodgson. "Behind the White Brick." 1879. *Little Saint Elizabeth and Other Stories*. London: Warne, 1890.

Byron, May, and G.E. Farrow. *Ruff and Ready, The Fairy Guide: Being Dorothy's Adventures in Nurseryland*. London: Alf Cooke, [c. 1905].

Carllew, Loris. *Alice in Plunderland*. London: Eveleigh Nash, 1910.

Carryl, Charles Edward. *The Admiral's Caravan*. New York: Century, 1892.

————. *Davy and the Goblin, or What Followed Reading "Alice's Adventure's in Wonderland."* Boston: Ticknor, 1885.

Chester, Norley. *Olga's Dream: A Nineteenth Century Fairy Tale*. London: Skeffington & Son, 1892.

Corbett, Mrs. E.T. *Karl and the Queen of Queerland* [aka *Karl in Queerland*]. New York: American Book Exchange, 1880.

Corkran, Alice. *Down the Snow Stairs; or, From Good-Night to Good-Morning*. London: Blackie and Son, 1887.

————. *Joan's Adventures, At the North Pole and Elsewhere*. New York: Scribners, 1889.

————. *The Adventures of Mrs. Wishing-to-Be*. London: Blackie and Son, 1883.

Crothers, Samuel McChord. *Miss Muffet's Christmas Party*. Boston: Houghton Mifflin, 1902.

Cuming, Edward D. *Wonders in Monsterland*. New York: Longmans, Green, 1902.

Demijohn, Thom [Thomas M. Disch and John T. Sladek]. *Black Alice*. Garden City, NY: Doubleday, 1968.

Dodge, Mary Mapes. "Alice in Wonderland." *St. Nicholas* 8.2 (1881): 875.

————. "To W.F.C. (With a Copy of 'Alice's Adventures in Wonderland')." *When Life Is Young*. New York: Century, 1894: 150.

Ducornet, Rikki. *The Jade Cabinet.* Normal, IL: Dalkey Archive P, 1993.

Dyrenforth, Jasper, and Max Kester. *Adolph in Blunderland: A Political Parody of Lewis Carroll's Famous Story.* London: Frederick Muller, 1939.

Ellingwood, Lena. *Belda in Blunderland.* Portland, ME: Falmouth Book House, 1937.

Evans, Florence A. *Alice's Adventures in Pictureland.* New York: Dodge, 1900.

Evarts, Richard Conover. *Alice's Adventures in Cambridge.* Cambridge, MA: Harvard Lampoon, 1913.

Ewing, Julianna Horatia. "Amelia and the Dwarfs." *Aunt Judy's Magazine* 8.1 (Feb.-March 1870). Reprinted in *The Brownies and Other Tales.* London: Society for Promoting Christian Knowledge, 1870.

―――. "Benjy in Beastland." *Aunt Judy's Magazine* 8.2 (May-June 1870). Reprinted in *The Brownies and Other Tales,* 1870.

―――. "The Land of Lost Toys." *Aunt Judy's Magazine* 6 (March-April 1869). Reprinted in *The Brownies and Other Tales,* 1870.

Farrow, G[eorge] E[dward]. *The Adventures of Ji.* London: S.W. Partridge, 1906.

―――. *The Little Panjandrum's Dodo.* London: Pearson, 1899.

―――. *The Wallypug in London.* London: Methuen, 1898.

―――. *The Wallypug of Why.* London: Hutchinson, 1895.

Fensch, Thomas. *Alice in Acidland: Lewis Carroll Revisited.* New York: A.S. Barnes, 1970.

Fitzgerald, Shafto Justin Adair. *The Zankiwank and the Bletherwitch: An original Fantastic Fairy Extravaganza.* London: Dent, 1896.

Frankie in Wonderland. With Apologies to Lewis Carroll, the Originator & Pre-Historian of the New Deal. By A. Tory. New York: Dutton, 1934.

Garis, Howard R. *Uncle Wiggily in Wonderland.* New York: R.F. Fenno, 1916.

Gaze, Harold. *The Goblin's Glen.* Boston: Little, Brown, 1924.

Geake, Charles, and F. Carruthers Gould. *John Bull's Adventures in the Fiscal Wonderland.* London: Methuen, 1904.

Gibson, A.L. *Another Alice Book, Please!* London: John Castle, 1924.

Girvin, Brenda. *Round Fairyland with Alice and the White Rabbit.* London: S.W. Partridge, n.d. [1916].

Goldberg, Whoopi. *Alice.* New York: Bantam, 1992.

Habens, Alison. *Dreamhouse.* 1994. New York: Picador, 1996.

Hall, Edith King. *Adventures in Toyland.* London: Blackie, n.d. [c. 1918].

Hartley, George T. *A Few Chapters More of "Alice Through the Looking Glass."* Bournemouth: Sydenham's Library, 1875.

Hawthorne, Hildegarde. *Girls in Bookland.* New York: George H. Doran, 1917.

Hill, William T. *Jackieboy in Rainbowland.* Chicago: Rand McNally, 1911.

Holland, Edward. *Mabel in Rhymeland; or, Little Mabel's Journey to Norwich, and Her Wonderful Adventures with the Man in the Moon and Other Heroes and Heroines of Nursery Rhyme.* London: Griffith, Farran, Okedon & Welsh, 1885.

Hood, Tom. *From Nowhere to the North Pole: A Noah's Ark-Æological Narrative.* London: Chatto and Windus, 1875.

Hope, Edward. *Alice in the Delighted States.* New York: Dial, 1928.

Ingelow, Jean. *Mopsa the Fairy.* 1869. Philadelphia: Lippincott, 1910.

Jambon, Jean [John K.A. MacDonald]. *Our Trip to Blunderland, or Grand Excursion to Blundertown and Back.* London: William Blackwood and Sons, 1877.

Jones, Christine E. *A Story of the Wonderland under the Stainless Flag or A Woman's Reverie.* Kansas City, KS: Press of the Kansas Prohibitionist, 1909.

Kayess, W. "The Land of the Wonderful Co." *Harry Furniss's Christmas Annual for 1905:* 89-126.

Kelly, Maeve. *Alice in Thunderland: A Feminist Fairytale.* Dublin, Attic, 1993.

Kingsbury, Helen Ovington. *All Aboard for Wonderland.* New York: Moffat, Yard, 1917.

Kingsley, Henry. *The Boy in Grey.* 1871. London: Ward, Lock, 1895.

Knatchbull-Hugessen, Edward, Lord Brabourne. "Ernest." *Puss-Cat Mew and Other Stories for My Children.* 1869. New York: Harper, 1871.

———. "Harry's Dream." *Whispers from Fairyland.* London: Longmans, Green, 1875.

Kuttner, Henry. "Mimsy Were the Borogoves." 1943. *The Best of Henry Kuttner.* Ed. Ray Bradbury. Garden City, NY: Doubleday, 1975.

La Prade, Ernest. *Alice in Orchestralia.* 1925. Garden City, NY: Doubleday, 1943.

Leland, Charles Godfrey. *Johnnykin and the Goblins.* New York: MacMillan, 1876.

Lewis, Caroline [Harold Begbie, J. Stafford Ransome, and M.H. Temple]. *Clara in Blunderland.* London: Heinemann, 1902.

———. *Lost in Blunderland.* London: Heinemann, 1903.

Lundwall, Sam. *Alice's World: Terra through the Science Fiction Looking Glass.* New York: Ace, 1971.

Macauley, Charles Raymond. *Fantasma Land.* Indianapolis: Bobbs-Merrill, 1904.

MacDonald, Una. *Alys in Happyland.* Boston: L.C. Page, 1913.

Marshall, Capt. Robert. "Johnny in Thunderland: A Fragment Suggested by 'Alice in Wonderland.'" *Harry Furniss's Christmas Annual for 1905:* 39-52.

Molesworth, Mary Louisa. *The Cuckoo Clock.* London: Macmillan, 1877.

———. *The Tapestry Room.* London: Macmillan, 1879.

Nauman, Mary Dummett. *Eva's Adventures in Shadowland.* Philadelphia: Lippincott, 1872.

Nesbit, E. "The Aunt and Amabel." *The Magic World.* 1912. New York: Penguin, 1988.

———. "The Cockatoucan." *Nine Unlikely Tales.* London: Fisher Unwin, 1901.

———. *The Enchanted Castle.* 1907. London: Ernest Benn, 1956.

———. "Justnowland." *The Magic World.* 1912. New York: Penguin, 1988.

———. *The Magic City.* 1910. London: Ernest Benn, 1958.

Noon, Jeff. *Automated Alice.* New York: Crown, 1996.

Olmstead, Millicent. *The Land of Never Was.* Philadelphia: Jacobs, 1908.

Ostrander, Fannie E. *The Gift of the Magic Staff: Paul's Adventures in Two Wonderlands.* Chicago: Fleming H. Revell, 1902.

Otterbourg, Edwin M. *Alice in Rankbustland.* New York: W.W. Williams, 1923.
———. *Lost in the Bungle.* Garden City, NY: Country Life Press, 1933.
Parry, Edward Abbott. *Butterscotia, or A Cheap Trip to Fairyland.* London: David Nutt, 1896.
———. *The First Book of Krab.* London: David Nutt, 1897.
———. *Katawampus, Its Treatment and Cure.* London: David Nutt, 1895.
Pedley, Ethel. *Dot and the Kangaroo.* London: Barleigh, 1899.
Peedie, Jean Murdoch. *Donald in Numberland.* New York: Rae D. Henkle, 1927.
Pyle, M.C. *Minna in Wonder-Land.* Philadelphia: Porter and Coates, 1871.
Rae, John. *New Adventures of "Alice."* Chicago: P.F. Volland, 1917.
Richards, Anna M. *A New Alice in the Old Wonderland.* Philadelphia: Lippincott, 1895.
Rossetti, Christina. *Speaking Likenesses.* London: Macmillan, 1874.
Saki [Hector Hugh Munro]. *The Westminster Alice.* London: *The Westminster Gazette,* 1902.
Schnittkind, Henry T. *Alice and the Stork: A Fairy Tale for Workingmen's Children.* Boston: Richard G. Badger, 1915.
Sheppard, Nancy. *Alitji in the Dreamtime* [*Alitjinya Ngura Tjukurtjarangka*]. Adelaide: University of Adelaide, Department of Adult Education, 1975.
Sleight, Charles Lee. *The Prince of the Pin Elves.* Boston: L.C. Page, 1897.
Smith, Walter Burges. *Looking For Alice.* Boston: Lothrop Publishing, 1903.
Sontag, Susan. *Alice in Bed.* New York: FSG, 1993.
Stewart, Mary. *The Way to Wonderland.* New York: Dodd, Mead, 1917.
Sweetland, Herbert S. *Tom's Adventures in Search of Shadowland.* Philadelphia: Fisher Unwin, 1888.
Townsend, Ralph M. *A Journey to the Garden Gate.* Boston: Houghton Mifflin, 1919.
Weatherly, Frederick Edward. *Elsie in Dreamland* [aka *Elsie's Expedition*]. London: F. Warne, 1874.
Webb, Marion St. John. *Knock Three Times!* 1917. London: Wordsworth, 1994.
Weis, Margaret, ed. *Fantastic Alice: New Stories from Wonderland.* New York: Ace, 1995.
White, Eliza Orne. *The Enchanted Mountain.* Boston: Houghton Mifflin, 1911.
Wilson, Yates. *More "Alice."* London: Boardman, 1959.
Wojciechowska, Maia. *Through the Broken Mirror with Alice.* New York: Harcourt, 1972.
Wyatt, Horace. *Alice in Motorland.* London: The Car Illustrated, 1904.
———. *Malice in Kulturland.* London: The Car Illustrated, 1915.